Dragon Realms:

Enemies and Allies

James Maxstadt

Dragon Realms: Enemies and Allies
Dragon Realms, Book Two

Printed in the United States of America

First Printing, 2025

ISBN: 979-8-9911712-3-6
James Maxstadt

Visit at jamesmaxstadt.com

Cover art and interior illustrations by Mercedes Meza

Titles by James Maxstadt

Dragon Realms
Book One: Order and Chaos

The Duke Grandfather Saga
Tales of a Nuisance Man

Duke Grandfather Saves the World*
*or at least a small part of it

Duke Grandfather Hears Voices

Duke Grandfather Unleashes Hell

The Lilly the Necromancer Series
Death Lessons

Work-Death Balance

Death, Love, and Happiness

The Fall
Shriven

Bereft

Reborn

The Travels of Solomon
Solomon's Exile

Solomon's Journey

Solomon's Odyssey

Black Friar Quest
How to Trick a Demon

How to Unlock a Magic Door

How to Hike in Haunted Woods

Box Sets
Duke Grandfather: The Whole Story

Life with the Dead, Lilly the Necromancer, the complete story

The Travels of Solomon

The Fall Omnibus

Anthologies
Rejected Worlds: A Short-story Anthology

If the world was attacked by dragons, I'd still want to be with her. To Barb, forever.

Cast of Characters

Viktoria Autumn: Life-taker from Reclium
Lamorak Amberbride: Obristan Honor Guard
Akofi: Free-mage from Lankari Tower, Droy Thus
Nettie Marlow: From Ascana, sailor and third-in-command of the Emerald Kin.
Kori Hordsson: On the run warrior from Usturg

Dragons
Gillbriss: Ruler of Reclium
Haiteng: Ruler of Ascana
Chimbod: Ruler of Droy Thus
Fimbruss: Ruler of Usturg
Tophonoss: Ruler of Obristan
Sillaneth: —

Reclium
Reyson Torneau: Chief Life-Taker of Darkbreath Clan
Dommick Maganti: Only son of Lord Maganti, head of Darkbreath Clan
Lord Mitrik Maganti: head of Darkbreath Clan
Celest Maganit: Only daughter of Lord Maganti
Severina Cloven: Madame

Obristan
Bodwyn Brahan: Honor Guard and friend of Lamorak
Rainaldus Carahad: Honor Guard, young and very competent
Prince Calidor Silvermore: Prince and ruler of Obristan.
Otto: Old man who names his pots and pans
Sebastian: leader of new city watch in Greenfair
Oriana: young girl rescued by Calidor
Vect: Calidor's massive, faithful follower
Cadwent: Honor Guard
Keridoc: Honor Guard
Bolles: Honor Guard with excellent vision

Droy Thus
Kio: Master of Lankari Tower
Bekasi: Free-mage from Lankari Tower, second in scores
Akamah: Free-mage from Onirri Tower, childhood friend of Akofi
Yarah: Free-mage from Orluduna Tower
Sintifi: Free-mage from Orluduna Tower
Oponsi: Master of the True Tower in Orluduna
Korudu: Master of Orluduna Tower

Ascana
Elsdon Drace: Commander of the Ascani Knights
Jarmen Stanford: Captain of the Swift Tide
Wyman: old man in Craydon, Kori's friend
Antonia Bristol: owner of The Inland Trader tavern
Tilford and Radly: Lostin port ship inspectors
Halli Serksson: The Librarian
Ashby: a collector and keeper of the way

Usturg
Estrid Toladottir: Prostitute in Narfasker
Gunnvid: Leader of the Children of Fimbruss
Visgar: Gunnvid's right-hand

Dragonkin
Hersha: Droy Thus, friend to Akofi
Sormat: Reclium, orders Viktoria to break into Darkbreath tower to
steal a book
Shilong: Ascana, welcomes Prince Calidor of Obristan
Lijing: Ascana, ally to Elsdon Drace

Evening Folk
Falaern: Raaleth, Queen of those remaining
Arastug: Helgarlug, advisor to Falaern
Ilvisar: Raaleth
Ryul: Dead king of the Raaleth

Orgoth: Leader of the Yegrub Clan
Shagar: Xarlug spell-caster
The Gerent: Leader of all Xarlug
Glasha: Xarlug spell-caster

The Story Thus Far

Dragon Realms: Order and Chaos

Part One- Order

In *Reclium*, lifetaker Viktoria Autumn is confronted by a dragonkin named Sormat, who charges her with stealing a book from the Darkbreath Clan, the most feared criminal organization in the city of Heldum. While carrying out her mission, she is attacked by Reyson Torneau, chief lifetaker for the clan. Just as Reyson is about to kill her, Dommick Maganti, the son of the head of Darkbreath, hits Reyson from behind, saving Viktoria's life, and then flees the tower with her. Victoria is now in possession of the purloined book but is sure Sormat will kill her upon delivery of it. With that, she turns to her one true friend, Chaol, who sends both her and Dommick away from Heldum, promising to delay Reyson for as long as he can.

Lamorak, senior member of the Honor Guard for the Prince of *Obristan*, is chosen to escort Prince Calidor to Festival, the large gathering in *Ascana*, held just outside the capital city of Manse. Along with him will go the young guardsman Rainaldus, as well as several others. After crossing the border between the two realms, they are met by Shilong, a blue dragonkin, who greets them and accompanies them on their journey. However, the party is disrupted when the caravan is attacked from the forest by two large ballistae bolts, one of which hits the dragonkin, the other killing the leader of the Honor Guard, Lord Campbell. With Lamorak suddenly in charge, the tone of the procession changes, and Calidor enlists Lamorak and Rainaldus to teach him how to fight, using the same methods that the Honor Guard learns by. At first, Lamorak is skeptical, but as the prince takes his training seriously, including the associated welts, he begins to feel a burgeoning respect for Calidor. Once they near Manse, the prince's retinue is met by an Ascani escort sent by the Ministers of Manse, who guide them the rest of the way.

Kio, the master of Lankari Tower in *Droy Thus*, selects Akofi to be one of two mages to be representatives of their town to Festival. Although not chosen as the primary representative, Akofi begrudgingly accompanies Bekasi, who was picked as primary, on the journey north. They stop at a border house where they meet up with mages from other towers, including Akamah, Akofi's long-lost childhood friend. Unfortunately, he also sees some who were never his friends, which results in the other mages playing a cruel prank on him. Akofi allows the joke to pass without answer, but when they are detained on the road by three red dragonkin, it is Akofi who is called aside to hear about the attack on Shilong in Ascana and advised to be watchful, while not revealing the attack to the others. It's only after being confronted and harassed by two blue dragonkin in Ascana itself that he disobeys and tells the other mages what he knows. Any good will with the other mages he had managed to build during their journey disappears, leaving Akofi to finish the remainder of the trip to Festival in the company of Bekasi, Akamah, and Yarah, who is from the distant Orluduna Tower. Upon entering Festival and finding the Droy Thus compound, they discover an intruder, an older, disheveled man, sleeping in one of their rooms. But that discovery is quickly pushed aside as they witness a red dragonkin, unheard of outside of its own realm of Droy Thus, attacking humans, until it's killed by three blue dragonkin.

On board the Emerald Kin, a ship of the Ascani navy, Nettie Marlow survives an assault by the First Mate. Before she can do anything about it, however, she finds herself in an unprecedented battle with not one, but five, Raider ships. The Emerald Kin is doomed, but when Nettie feels all is lost, her prior attacker tosses her overboard, saving her life. Now in the middle of the Elmshome Ocean, Nettie can only watch as the Emerald Kin burns. Her life is saved again when a blue dragonkin surfaces nearby and tells her that he'll take her to safety. In her exhaustion, Nettie falls asleep on the dragonkin's back, only to awaken to find that the dragonkin has begun to submerge. Her cries go unanswered as the dragonkin sinks, leaving her floundering in the water again. When she hears breakers, she swims to them, finally coming to a rocky shore, where she realizes that the darkness around her isn't just nighttime. She is in *Reclium*, with no way to return home. A mute man appears and guides her into a vast cavern complex, where she is attacked by a swarm of beetles, sees wonders of the underground, including what appears to be an ancient temple of some sort, and finally emerges in the mountains overlooking the Reclium port town of Pharax. There, she's saved from a black dragonkin by the intervention of Mrs. Severina Cloven, who is more than she initially appears, and who promises to help Nettie return to Ascana.

Having killed a man who had attacked him, Kori is on the run from Slode, a local gang leader, and his men, when they finally catch up to him in the wilds, far from any *Usturg* town. Just as it appears that Slode will have his revenge on Kori, a snow troll bursts from the snow and kills Slode and his men, while Kori can only play dead, hoping that he won't be the next victim of the snow troll's hunger. His life is spared once more when a white dragonkin arrives, who chases off the snow troll and tells Kori that he should proclaim to everyone about what had happened and how he was saved. Kori returns to Narfaskar to retrieve his belongings, including a book his mother had read to him as a boy. With that, the axe he inherited from his uncle, and not much else, Kori sets forth again, finally arriving in the town of Husnar, where he joins with a caravan heading to Festival to bring beer brewed in Usturg. He also has his first run-in with the Children of Fimbruss, a group of religious fanatics convinced that Fimbruss, the dragon overlord of Usturg, is actually a divine being. Kori leaves Husnar, and finally Usturg itself, behind, convinced that he is done with the north.

Part One- Order ends with the old man found in the Droy Thus compound revealed as Sintifi, a mage from Droy Thus. He was one of those responsible for the magic which caused the dragonkin who had rescued Nettie to swim into Reclium territory, submerge itself too deep, and drown. On his own the next time, Sintifi was the one who had called a red dragonkin to Festival, igniting a wave of attacks that will change the world.

Part 2- Chaos

In the once-realm of *Olequan*, the remainder of the ancient "Evening Folk," as humans call them, feel the effects of Sintifi's spells. Concerned that the humans are using magic not meant for them, Falaern, the last Queen of the Raaleth, instructs her advisor Arastug, to select someone to leave Olequan and find out who had cast the spell and why.

In the meantime, Chaol has helped Viktoria and Dommick slip out of Heldum and sends them to the port city of Pharax, where he assures them that help will be waiting to get them out of Reclium entirely. Shortly after they leave, Reyson arrives and kills Chaol without much effort, then follows after Viktoria and the book she stole.

Lamorak finally guides his party into Manse, leaving most Honor Guard in the compound prepared for them at Festival. He, Rainaldus, and Prince Calidor continue into the city itself, where they are given rooms in the Minister's Building. He notices many dragonkin present in Ascana, while there are none at all in Obristan. That night, he observes several together, all flying in the same direction.

Kori is dejected to learn that his new friends, Authgrim and Asta, are not staying at Festival, but are instead returning immediately to Husnar for another load of beer. He decides that he'll stay near Manse, having no wish to return north, and proceeds to drink too much. But he quickly sobers up when a dead dragonkin falls from the sky, crushing a man to death right in front of him.

Nettie and Viktoria meet at the home and place of business of Mrs. Cloven, whom Chaol had sent Viktoria to. She can help them escape Reclium, but they need to stay hidden for a few days until a suitable ship arrives. During that time, she examines the book Viktoria was sent to steal, telling her that it's written in the language of the Evening Folk and that the cover is made from dragonkin skin.

Akofi and his friends realize that something is horribly wrong and make the decision to leave Festival and return to Droy Thus. However, after some reflection, Akofi realizes they can do more good by staying. All while Sintifi second-guesses his own actions, and hides in fear, waiting for the dragonkin to discover him and what he has done.

In Droy Thus, two blue dragonkin attack and destroy Lankari Tower in retribution for the attack of the red dragonkin at Festival. Kio, the Master of Lankari Tower, is killed in the attack.

At a reception thrown in honor of Prince Calidor at the Ministers' Building in Manse, Lamorak and Calidor first hear of the attacks by dragonkin outside their own realms. They return to their rooms and make the decision to return to Obristan, but as Lamorak looks out a window, he sees Festival burning.

Kori witnesses the red dragonkin's attack on Festival, then several more. He realizes that the world has gone mad and flees, intending to catch up with Authgrim and Asta to return to Usturg. When he does, however, he finds the caravan shattered and burnt, along with everything in it, including his friends.

In Pharax, Mrs. Cloven is finally able to make good on her word and gets Nettie, Viktoria, and Dommick to a ship. There, they're smuggled onboard under the guise of being two of her workers, sent for the crews' amusement. The captain, Jarmen Stanford, tells them he's eager to have them keep his crew happy during the upcoming voyage.

Sintifi flees back toward Droy Thus, only to come across a strange man with powerful magic. After an initially difficult time communicating, he discovers that the stranger is one of the Evening Folk, a Raaleth. Ilvisar introduces himself to Sintifi and insists on accompanying him back to the true Tower of Orluduna.

Festival and parts of Manse are being destroyed by the battle between dragonkin that is growing bigger by the moment as more dragonkin arrive to join the fight. Humans are ignored except where they can't get out of the way. Akofi refuses to leave, thinking he can help save people, while Lamorak and Rainaldus try to get Prince Calidor to safety. They come upon a dragonkin in the street and have no choice but to fight it, a battle they cannot hope to win. But aid comes in the form of Droy Thus wizards, who help them defeat the dragonkin. Akofi and his friends join with Lamorak and his party to flee the area.

In the bowels of the earth, in a secret cavern known only to them, the five dragons meet. The world has gone out of control, and it's the fault of the humans using forbidden magic. They agree to allow Gillbriss, the cruelest of them all, to dictate how they will put down the rebellion of the humans.

Part One

Enemies

Chapter 1- The Five Realms

Brada made ready to close up her shop for the day. It had been horribly busy, with all those who had gone to Festival returning, it seemed, in one unending stream. Fleeing, she supposed would be more accurate.

She "tsked" under her breath as she bent to pick up a crate of carrots. They were old, left over from last fall, really, but they were one of the only things she still had. Most of her produce had been sold already, to individuals and families who'd paid dearly for the privilege. Not that Brada wanted to make money off of other people's tragedy, of course, but business was business, and supply and demand fluctuations were well-established practices.

In some ways, Brada felt she should have gone to Festival. Everance had always told her that she was more like someone from Ascana than Obristan, but he had laughed when he'd said it, so it was never meant to be mean. Besides, her husband had appreciated the money that had come along with her drive, and he never tried to deny it.

She missed him horribly. Some days more than others, even if it had been three years since he'd passed on.

"What is this place?"

The voice sounded strange, even before Brada had turned, with her polite shopkeeper's smile already fixed in place. She'd have to tell whoever this was that she was closed up for the night. Her back ached and her feet were sore. She hadn't eaten since that morning. Although, she supposed if their purse was large enough, she could be convinced to suffer quietly for a few more minutes.

Whoever it was, they were tall, she realized, since the voice came from nearly overhead.

All of that flashed through her mind in the time it took her to turn.

She let out a short, sharp scream when she saw who it was that had addressed her.

Towering over her, its head at least ten feet in the air, was a blue dragon. Dragon*kin*, she supposed. There were only four dragons, and from the little she knew, this one— as big as it seemed to her— wasn't nearly large enough to be one of them.

The dragonkin's scales were such a vibrant blue that they were a color which Brada had never seen before. They shimmered and flashed with every movement, even if it was just the dragonkin breathing. There was a mane of slightly paler blue hair at the end of its long neck, just behind where its head began. Two horns curved gracefully from the crown of its skull, and it stared at her though intense blue eyes, behind an elongated snout.

"A dragonkin!" she breathed. "Oh, my! I've never seen one of you before."

"What is this place?" the dragonkin asked again.

Its voice was deep, reminding her of a much more powerful version of Everance's, so she decided that this dragonkin was a "he."

"It's my shop," she replied easily. She kept her voice calm, even though her insides were churning with excitement. A real dragonkin! There in Obristan!

She would have thought that living and keeping a shop near the border as she did, that she would have seen one before, but she never had. Brada didn't care to travel, even the few short miles it would have taken to get into Ascana. It had always been Everance who'd made any trips when they'd needed something, and now she was established enough that everything she needed came to her.

"What sort of shop?" the dragonkin growled.

Brada almost shivered at the voice. The dragonkin sounded angry, although what it had to be mad about was more than she could tell.

"Food. Produce, mostly. Although sometimes I do have honey or goats milk. Whatever the farmers bring me, if I can afford it, I buy it and pass it on to those travelers who might need it."

"Was this shop approved by Haiteng?"

"Haiteng?" That was the dragon ruling Ascana, wasn't it? "What would Haiteng do with me? Of course he didn't approve it, that I know of. Although I can't imagine that he would disapprove..."

"Shut it down. Now."

"Shut what down? My shop? Well, I am for the night. I'm tired, you know. It's been a long day and—"

"For good. Or until you appeal to the ministers in Manse for a permit to have a shop."

"That's ridiculous," she scoffed. "We're in Obristan, not Ascana."

As she spoke, Brada looked around, trying to see if anyone was watching. Perhaps someone had put the dragonkin up to this as a joke. She didn't know that dragonkin had senses of humor, but, then again, she didn't know that they didn't.

"Are you refusing?" The dragonkin glared at her.

"Of course I'm refusing. This is a joke, right?"

The dragonkin left the ground as if someone had simply picked it up. It had no wings, yet somehow still flew. It made a lazy circle overhead, leaving Brada almost breathless staring at it in awe.

Then it dove straight down, crashing into the roof of her little shop. It was a sturdy building that Everance had built with his own strong hands, but no wooden structure could stand up to a dragonkin.

The blue dragonkin flew back up, then dove again, and again, and again, smashing the building into more and more rubble, until no walls were left standing. The produce inside was pulverized, along with all Brada's possessions and the three small rooms where she had lived in the back of the shop itself.

"Why are you doing that?" she wailed, cowering outside the shop, but the dragonkin ignored her. It lifted skyward again but hovered directly over the ruin.

Brada ran forward, intent on salvaging whatever she could.

Which was when the dragonkin breathed. Steam so hot it drove Brada back with a scream before she had even come close to reaching her destination. Any vegetables that might have survived the attack were now ruined. Brada's clothes, her few books, even the line drawing of her and Everance he'd surprised her with one year were totally destroyed.

Without another word or even a glance at her, the dragonkin flew away, leaving her shaking and staring at what had once been her home.

Gunnvid scowled at the interruption and set down his quill. The feathered pen seemed out of place in his huge, scarred hands. When most looked at him, they would have thought Gunnvid didn't know how to read, much less write. Yet, writing was only one of his many gifts. Given to him by Fimbruss, as were all blessings of those who lived in Usturg. Even those who hadn't come to see the light quite yet.

"What is it?" he growled.

His voice was a harsh rasp that rarely rose above a whisper, the legacy of a wound to his throat some years back. He'd put the man who'd done it into the dirt, so that at least that had given him some satisfaction, but the injury had left him to spread the word more through written rather than verbal means.

"Pardon, brother," a voice said from outside his door. "But I believe there's something you should see."

"Can't you handle it, Visgar?"

The man summoning him was Gunnvid's right hand, the first of those who had listened to Gunnvid when he'd begun his ministry. His smooth voice and commanding presence made him a natural to speak where Gunnvid couldn't.

"It would really be better if you came," Visgar replied.

Gunnvid sighed and rose from his writing table. He smoothed his long, gray beard down over his massive chest and flat stomach, then strode to the door.

"I hope this is worth it," he rasped, but hesitated before saying anything more when he saw his friend.

Visgar's eyes gleamed with... what? Merriment? Excitement?

Gunnvid raised his eyebrows but didn't speak. He knew Visgar well enough to know that it must be something important.

"This way," Visgar motioned as he turned away.

He led Gunnvid back toward the main hall of the temple, his walk sedate, but with a barely restrained impatience that Gunnvid recognized.

Moments later, they entered the hall, and for once, Gunnvid didn't take the time to appreciate the soaring beams arching far overhead, the colored glass of the windows, or the workmanship of the long wooden benches.

Instead, his eye was immediately drawn to their guests. Three of them. White dragonkin, waiting patiently.

"Gunnvid?" One of them asked, in the gentle tone of what he knew to be a female.

"*Brother* Gunnvid," Visgar began, but Gunnvid laid a restraining hand on the other's arm.

"That's me," he rasped. "What can I do for you?"

"We come from Fimbruss," she said. "My name is Lumel."

"It's an honor, Lumel," Gunnvid said. "How can we help you?"

"Well, you have already," she said. "We've come to ask you to do even more, though."

"I am always ready to serve Fimbruss."

"Excellent! And those who follow you?"

"They are as well. With great zeal when need be."

The dragonkin smiled. "That's wonderful news. Fimbruss will be happy. Now, tell me, how do your followers feel about traveling to other realms?"

"To spread the glory of Fimbruss?" Gunnvid smiled back at her. "We would love to."

The dragonkin said. "Then you have a glorious task ahead of you."

Gunnvid glanced at Visgar, who was watching the dragonkin with unconcealed fervor.

He shared his friend's excitement. To be given the mission to bring the holy word to unbeliever? They would come to see the light, whether through the good word or by the sword. One way or the other was all the same to Gunnvid. It was all for the glory of Fimbruss.

Hersha didn't like what he was doing. Not one bit.

It was one thing to be present in the lives of the humans. To help guide them, to teach them, even to become friends with some of them, as he was with Akofi. It was quite another to... supervise them?

He wasn't sure if that was the word he wanted or not. Hersha just knew that now he had to spend several hours a day watching over the classes of new mages, observing and listening to what they were being taught. Any signs of non-human magic needed to be reported to Chimbod immediately.

That meant no dragon magic, which was the basis for the humans' own. But it was easy enough to tell the difference. Humans had to do *things* to cast their magic. Mumble a bunch of words and move their hands around. Dragons and dragonkin just did it, the same as breathing.

The only other magic Hersha knew of was that of the Elder Races, but that was ridiculous, of course. The Elder Races had been gone for centuries, wiped out when they'd attempted to kill Chimbod and her siblings. Their magic had died with them.

But that was the rumor. That *some* humans— and they could only have come from Droy Thus— had somehow used ancient magic of the Raaleth and had caused the actual death of a dragonkin. Hersha didn't believe a word of it and thought it more likely that some of his brethren had simply gotten carried away.

Looking at the ruins of Lankari tower, he would have said that they'd all gotten much too carried away. He supposed, though, that those blue dragonkin who'd committed the crime being executed by the avenging reds was only fair.

So now, classes had to take place outside. The tower was gone, shattered beyond repair, and the humans had been forbidden from rebuilding it. There was even some talk of destroying the other towers, but, so far, Chimbod had held off on that. Hersha supposed that was fine, but he really would have liked it if the humans had been allowed to rebuild Lankari tower. He missed seeing it standing proud, taller than even the mightiest of the jungle trees.

"Is there a problem, Hersha?" a voice said from behind him.

Hersha snaked his head around to see Utain staring at him. She was much larger than he was, and even before the recent trouble she hadn't been one to socialize with humans very much.

"No, not really. I just don't see the point of having to watch them. These are children. They can't use most human magic, let alone anything that would be remotely Raaleth."

"It doesn't matter what you think," Utain snarled. "This is what you're told to do, so you'll do it. Unless you'd like to answer to Chimbod."

"Of course I'll do it," Hersha said. "I just don't understand."

"What's not to understand? Humans— *our* humans— used forbidden magic and killed a dragonkin. They forced others to defy Chimbod's edict and invade Ascana. Do you really think they should just be allowed to continue as they were? Chimbod wants them watched every second, until we know who was responsible. Maybe then…"

"Things can get back to normal," Hersha finished for her. "That would be nice."

He turned back to the class of children learning the basics of magic. They were aware of his presence, as well as that of Utain and the four others who were now in Lankari at all times, day and night. But watching them made Hersha's mind go back to several years before, when a young Akofi was just learning. Even then, he was ahead of most of the others. Hersha had known he was going to be great.

He looked back to Utain.

"Has there been any word on the representatives to Festival?"

"No," she said, but her focus was on the class of older students she was watching. "Why?"

"I just hope they're safe, that's all."

"Oh, right. Your little friend. Whatever his name was."

Hersha didn't like the "was."

"If I were you, Hersha," Utain continued, "I wouldn't get too close to any of these humans again."

And Hersha liked the sound of that even less.

All Farrell could do was scratch his head. He saw *what* needed to be done, he just wasn't sure how to do it.

"I don't know what you're expecting from me," he finally said, turning back to the individual behind him.

"Fix it," the dragonkin said.

Farrell hadn't gotten the dragonkin's name, but then again, the dragonkin hadn't volunteered it, or asked his. He'd merely landed in the center of town and demanded to see any craftsmen, immediately. Word had reached Farrel within minutes, and he, like several others, had walked to the square, wondering what one of Haiteng's children wanted with them.

There, they'd found out that they'd been recruited to help rebuild Manse, which was suffering after the events of two nights ago. Farrel had no idea what events the dragonkin was referring to, but he didn't seem inclined to answer questions. Instead, they'd been marched out of town, where they'd joined a string of others all being herded in the same direction.

Now, after little food and even less sleep, that same dragonkin was behind him as he looked at the ruins of a building. Three streets from the minister's palace, this place had once been someone's home, or so Farrel assumed. Now, it was nothing more than a heap of rubble.

"I can't fix this," Farrel said. "I'm not a builder. I don't know the first thing about putting something like this back together."

"You're a craftsman, aren't you?" the dragonkin growled. "You work with wood, yes? Then… work with it."

Farrel shook his head. "You don't understand—"

The next thing he knew he was lying among the shattered remains of the building with the entire left side of his body feeling as if he'd been hit by a charging bull. The dragonkin was looming over him, his long neck arching so that his head was only inches from Farrel's face. He could feel the hot, wet breath and see the glistening fangs.

For a moment, it all felt like a dream. How was he there? In Manse, rather than his own small town. And why had the dragonkin hit him? He'd done nothing wrong. He was valuable. The furniture he made was shipped to Droy Thus, Obristan, and Usturg. He'd even sent a piece or two to Reclium. The work of his hands brought in significant money for him and his family, as well as Haiteng.

"I understand everything, human." The dragon spoke quietly, but with a hint of steam that turned Farrel's face red. He could feel the perspiration beading on his forehead. "I understand that things have changed. You work for us, now. You will pick up tools and work to put this building back together."

Farrel nodded, anything he might have said in return stuck in his throat. Slowly, he eased back, trying to avoid impaling himself on a sharp shard of wood.

"All right," he whispered. "I'll try."

The dragonkin pulled back, allowing him to get to his feet.

"And hurry up," the blue said as it started away. "I'll be back to check on you." He left the ground effortlessly, but before leaving he looked back at Farrel one last time. "And lest you think of leaving, I know where your family lives. Get to work, or I'll kill them and everyone else in your whole village."

With that, he soared away, leaving Farrel behind.

Farrel had no doubt the dragonkin would do as he said. He looked around. He'd have to find help. Someone who could tell him what to do. He had no experience in building houses, but he knew how to use tools. He could learn, and he would do so quickly.

He didn't know what had changed. Why Haiteng was allowing them to be treated like this.

But he did know he had no choice, and he didn't believe for a moment that he'd be paid for his work.

In Reclium, life went on as it always had.

Chapter 2- The Emsholm Ocean

Nettie felt like crying. She stood at the rail of the "Adventurous Trader" and blinked the tears back, determined not to let them fall.

Next to her, Dommick watched the dark water pass by. Viktoria was below deck, in the small cabin she shared with Nettie.

"Don't look up," Nettie told Dommick. "Or at the water, since it will reflect the light. Maybe keep your eyes closed. This is going to be hard for you."

As for her though, Nettie couldn't wait to see the sun. Captain Stanford had told her that they were almost there. They'd be crossing the border between Reclium and Ascana waters in a few minutes, and, by his reckoning, it would be mid-afternoon when they did. The sun would be incredibly bright, as long as the weather was good, which it should be. There was a sharp line between darkness and light where the realms met, but the clouds moved from one sky to the other without impediment.

Nettie watched the prow as the sunlight hit it and drew in her breath. It almost seemed to glow with a light of its own! The Trader was moving fast, so there wasn't much time.

"Close them," she whispered to Dommick but held her own open.

The sun washed over her like the warmest, most luxurious bath she'd ever had. One moment she was in shadow, the next, she was standing fully in sunlight.

"Oh," she murmured quietly, and this time, there was no stopping the tears that overfilled her eyes and made tracks down her cheeks. She hadn't been in the dark that long. Not really. But it had been long enough; long enough to think she'd never see the sun again, never get home. That her life would never return to normal. But now, here it was, and it felt glorious.

Behind her, though, she heard Dommick hiss in pain. She turned to him, ready to chide him for not listening to what she'd told him. But he had. He not only had his eyes closed, he had his hands pressed to his face.

"Too much," she said.

Dommick nodded. "It's even brighter than the tower."

Nettie wasn't quite sure what that meant, only that Viktoria had claimed the inside of the tower Dommick had called home had been the most brightly lit place she'd ever been. Why she had been there, Nettie wasn't clear about either, anymore than she was about the relationship between her and Dommick.

But no matter how well-lit his home had been, it couldn't compare to the sun itself. Nothing could.

"It's all right," she said and gently took his arm. "Come on. Back below for now. We'll do this in stages."

She guided him across the deck, noting how the sailors of the Trader moved out of their way without complaint or mockery. That spoke mainly to how Dommick had won them over in just a few days. His easy manner, his self-deprecating humor, and— mostly— his honesty, had garnered their approval.

Viktoria, though… not so much. Even after they'd found out that the whole threat that she and Nettie would have to be available for the crew's "entertainment" had been nothing more than a ruse to put the dragonkin on the pier off-guard, the woman had remained off-putting. Even to Nettie, and they'd shared a space for long enough now that they should have at least started to become friends.

She led Dommick to the short stairway that led down from the deck. A tight corridor had three wooden doors on each side. If the Trader had been carrying passengers other than the three of them, those rooms would have been where they stayed. As it was, Dommick had one to himself, while she and Viktoria shared another. The others were being used by junior officers. The arrangement was typical of an Ascani trader, Nettie knew. She also knew that if she'd had enough money, it would have bought her quarters of her own, but considering that she'd been tossed on the shores of Reclium with nothing other than the clothes on her back, she wasn't about to complain.

"There," she told Dommick when they were down the ladder. "You can open your eyes."

He did, reluctantly and warily. The whites of his eyes had now turned red and watery, but still, he had the prettiest eyes Nettie thought she had ever seen on a man. Suddenly, she was very aware of the tightness of the corridor.

"You're okay to get back to your room now?"

"Of course," Dommick replied. "Stupid of me. But I just... I really wanted to see."

Nettie nodded. She understood completely. "I get it." She glanced back toward the opening leading to the deck. "As a matter of fact..."

"Go," Dommick said, a smile creasing his face. "I wouldn't dream of denying you the opportunity." He gave a sort of half-bow, then laughed at himself and started away. She watched him for a moment, then turned to leave, but before she had gone more than a step, he said, "I'm glad you're going home, Nettie."

By the time she looked around, his door was closing.

It was no wonder he'd made friends with the crew so quickly, she thought.

Then, she hurried up the steps, and back into the sun.

Viktoria heard them in the corridor. Nettie and Dommick and their conversation. She could have told the fool that it was idiotic to be up on the deck of a ship when the sun was at its brightest. They came from a land where they didn't know the sun as anything more than a legend, tales told about lands far away that couldn't possibly be real. It didn't matter that they had artificial lights, or that the Magantis were rich enough to light up the inside of their tower so brightly. Their eyes still weren't going to be accustomed to the actual sun.

She could admit secretly, though, that she did want to see it. And, to give her fair credit, Nettie had warned her about how bright it would be. Viktoria had no intention of going up on deck right now. She'd wait until this evening, when the sun was going down, then early the next morning as it came up. They had several more days at sea, according to Captain Stanford, so she'd use that time to get used to the light at a slower pace.

But Dommick? That idiot never listened to anyone. Nettie had given him the same warnings, she was sure, but he'd gotten by on who his family was and his looks for so long that he thought everything was always going to work out for him.

She wondered if he still felt that way, out there in the middle of the ocean, already two days from home and getting further away by the minute. No money, no clothes other than what Mrs. Cloven had given them, and no place to go.

Except that he *could* go home. Lord Maganti would surely take him back into the family.

She couldn't.

And for what?

She looked down at the book, opened in her lap and illuminated by the lantern swinging overheard.

A book she couldn't read in a language that didn't exist anymore. Now, she'd lost her home and might have a vicious killer— far more vicious than she was— tracking her down. Would he leave Reclium to come after her? She believed he would. If Chaol hadn't succeeded in sending Reyson the wrong way, he'd be on her trail until one of them was dead.

She meant to make it him who stopped breathing if they crossed paths again. And that meant training. Their first go-around had shown her how inferior her skills were to his. Even Chaol seemed wary that it was Reyson who was after her. So she needed to train. Every day, in every way she could.

The ship was no place to practice fighting. The cabin was too cramped, but the deck at night moved too much, with too many objects lying underfoot and in the way. Plus, she didn't like the way the crew of the ship stared at her, like she was some exotic animal brought on board for their amusement.

So, she'd made do with what she could do in the cabin. Push-ups and squats until her muscles burned and her arms and legs were quivering. Only once had Nettie come in while she was doing them, but she'd ignored the girl and her foolish questions until she'd gone away again. What Viktoria was doing should have been obvious.

Even now, a thin film of sweat glistened on her skin as she looked down at the book for the hundredth time in an hour. Why she had it out, she didn't know. Mrs. Cloven had told her to keep it safe and keep it hidden. To show no one.

But then, just before the ship was to depart, the old woman had sought Viktoria out.

"There may be someone, dear," she said quietly. "In Ascana. I'm not sure if he'll still be around or not. If so, you'll recognize him. He'll tell you he's asking after the health of your aunt, Mrs. Hatcher. If that happens, he can be trusted. He'll know about the book and— hopefully— who you should bring it to." She'd reached up and touched Viktoria's cheek then, and— to her own surprise— Viktoria had let her. "I hope he finds you. You've been through too much."

Viktoria was about to tell her that she hadn't been through *that* much. Just a rough few days. But then it occurred to her that the old woman was talking about more than just that. She was talking about Viktoria's whole life.

Without waiting for a response, the woman had walked away, back into the arms of Jarmen Stanford, to give everyone who cared to watch something to whisper about with a long kiss goodbye. Viktoria turned away before they broke off.

At the time, she was still believing she'd have to fight the first sailor who thought she owed him something, so it was with some surprise when Captain Stanford summoned all three of them to his cabin. He told them to remain there until they were underway when he would retrieve them. It was only then that she learned of the ruse he and Mrs. Cloven had put on for the dragonkin.

After that, the voyage had lost much of the feeling of doom she'd felt when she'd first boarded. Now, it was the tedium more than anything else that was the danger.

And the book, she thought, looking down again. The damned book.

She sighed and pulled her eyes away. Three more days, the captain had said. Then she'd be off the ship and...

Something. She'd figure out something.

Working the ship felt more than good. It felt right. At first, Captain Stanford had been skeptical, as if he hadn't believed that Nettie had truly served in the navy. Then, as she took to whatever role his first officer assigned her with a willingness and ability that demonstrated her worth, the captain began to accept her.

Now, she pitched in wherever it seemed as if her help was needed.

Dommick had won over the crew by being himself. Nettie did the same, only her being herself involved a lot more work.

As the sun sank below the horizon, most of the day's tasks were done. At night, the helmsman would steer by the stars, but other than him and the lookout far overhead, there wasn't much that needed to be done.

She was just getting set to head back below deck, to join the crew for dinner and maybe some music, when she heard footsteps coming up the ladder. Nettie stayed where she was by the rail as Viktoria emerged. The dour woman had her hand up to shield her eyes against the last rays of the sun. It was already getting dim, but for eyes as sensitive as hers, it must have been painful.

As if to demonstrate the truth of that, Viktoria stumbled over the lip at the top of the stairs, catching herself with a curse.

"Careful," Nettie said cheerfully. "You don't want to fall overboard."

She'd meant it as a joke, but as soon as the words had left her mouth, she wished she could take them back. Going overboard was no laughing matter. She knew that first-hand. And from the scowl Viktoria gave her, she didn't find it amusing either.

Not that the woman found much of anything amusing. Nettie still couldn't figure her out. One minute they were having an actual conversation, the next Viktoria was ignoring her as if she didn't even exist.

"The sun's just about down," Nettie tried again. "But still… it's brighter than it was in Reclium."

Viktoria didn't reply, but she did nod, so that was progress at least.

She made her way to the rail near Nettie, stepping carefully and trying not to let the roll of the ship throw her off-balance. For someone who'd never been on board a ship, Viktoria was doing pretty well. Dommick still staggered around like a drunk, but since he made such a self-deprecating joke about it, no one really seemed to mind.

"I need to train," Viktoria said when she'd gained the rail. Her knuckles were white as she grasped it, and she kept her face turned from Nettie, watching the very last glow of the sun slowly sink out of sight. Nettie didn't know if the tenseness was because of the sky being brighter than she used to, the motion of the ship, or because she actually had to speak to Nettie.

"Train, how?" Nettie asked.

"Fighting. Swords, hopefully. I don't have one though, just one stupid knife." She shook her head. "That won't be enough. I'd prefer my own long knives, but I won't see them again. So a sword it is."

The Trader probably had swords on board somewhere. Most ships did, in case of raiders, especially those who sailed the deep ocean. But taking them out without express orders from the captain was a good way to get set adrift. Too many bad things could happen.

"We can't," she said. "It's not allowed on board a ship."

Viktoria's scowl deepened. "Then what am I supposed to do? He very well could be waiting when we get to… wherever it is we're going."

"Lostin," Nettie supplied. "That's where we're going. And I can't imagine why anyone who didn't have business there would visit. It's just a port city that's a distribution hub. We'll make land, Captain Stanford will have the cargo unloaded, and then he'll take on more to either go back to Reclium, or to a port further down the coast. The cargo he unloads will be sent all over northern Ascana, depending on what it is. The only people who live there are involved in shipping, warehousing, or retired seafarers who like the more northern climate."

"I didn't need the lesson," Viktoria growled. "What I need is a sword. A weapon to practice with."

Nettie had had just about enough of Viktoria's moods. She nodded, then moved away, walking the moving deck with the ease of one who'd spent long hours on it.

"Suit yourself, then," she said over her shoulder. "I'm sure you can find something to swing around up here."

With that, she walked astern, toward the larger hatch that led to the crew areas and cargo hold.

Before she got there, though, Viktoria called to her.

"Wait. I'm... sorry. I know you were trying to help. It's just... it's important that I stay in shape. I don't have a choice."

Nettie froze, unsure now quite what to do. A part of her wanted to ignore the other woman and just continue on. Another part wanted to turn around and walk back with a smile on her face, ready to try again to be friends.

In the end, she did neither. She did turn around, but she didn't rush back. "Why don't you come with me?" she said. "We'll have something to eat. Then, maybe we can talk to the Captain and work something out. He'll probably say no, but it doesn't hurt to ask."

Viktoria hesitated, and Nettie could see why. She hadn't been the friendliest passenger, and now Nettie was asking her to actually mingle with crew. Well, that was too bad. If she wanted to ask a favor, she had to give a little herself. It was high-time the woman learned that.

Finally, Viktoria nodded once and made her much more cautious way across the deck to Nettie's side.

"There we go," Nettie said. "That wasn't so bad, and the rest won't be either."

She led Viktoria to the hatch. Below, the sound of the crew talking and cutlery clinking against metal plates carried clearly to them.

"Oh," Nettie said. "I should get Dommick. He'll want to eat, too—"

Then, laughter broke out. Within it was Dommick's. Nettie thought he must have a particularly singular laugh for her to be able to pick it out of a crowd like that.

"Well?" Viktoria said. "Are we going to go get him or not?"

She hadn't recognized Dommick's laugh.

That was just because she was self-centered, Nettie thought to herself. That was all.

What else could it possibly be?

Chapter 3- Ascana farmland

It was his rumbling stomach that woke Kori. For a few moments, he remained where he was, feeling the straw scratch his neck and the backs of his arms. His mouth tasted like something had rotted in it, and his head was pounding in a way that made the light seem to pulse in time with the throbbing.

And he was cold. Not like at home. But chilly, he guessed he would say.

He looked around for his hooded cloak, but it was nowhere to be seen.

Then, his eyes found the two empty bottles next to him. One standing upright, the other only empty because the remainder of the wine he hadn't drunk had spilled out when it got knocked over. Two bottles that he hadn't paid for with money. No, he'd traded his cloak for them.

And now, he had no way of getting it back, unless he came up with some magical way to return the wine.

He supposed he could stagger back to the farmhouse and demand his cloak back from the farmer. But he seemed to remember that the man had been fairly against the trade in the first place and had kept insisting that Kori was making a bad deal. In other words, the farmer had tried to save him from himself, and he had been the one to insist.

A thought came over him that made his blood suddenly run cold.

He'd found the remains of the caravan two days ago. After burying those he could, he'd wandered on, not even bothering to take the horse he'd bought. He had remembered to take off the bridle and reins, as well as the saddle, so the thing wasn't burdened by all that, at least. Kori figured a horse knew enough to find forage and water on its own.

As for him, he hadn't paid the slightest bit of attention to where he was going. The first tavern he saw got the bulk of his money in exchange for all the bottles he could carry when he'd stumbled out later on.

From there, he wasn't quite sure what he'd been doing.

Which meant...

His hand found what he was seeking, what he had been afraid he'd given away in his drunken stupor. But his axe— his uncle's axe— was still at his side. He hadn't even unstrapped it before passing out in the barn he was now in.

One good thing, anyway.

He raised his hand higher, pressing against his chest, and found that his book was still there, too. He didn't think he would have tried to trade that, but still, it was reassuring to know that he still had it.

And now...now he wasn't sure what to do. His heart still ached, and he didn't quite understand why. Asta had been beautiful, at least to his eyes, and she'd been fiery, smart, and full of life. It wasn't as if they'd had a great love affair, though. They'd shared one kiss, then Kori had allowed himself to fantasize about more. About making a life with her. In reality, they'd been nowhere near doing such a thing.

Yet, somehow, her being dead felt unbearable.

Authgrim, too. The old man had been more than kind to him. Had taken him under his wing, really, and made sure he got out of Usturg.

All of the caravan. In the short time he'd been with them, they'd come to feel like close friends.

Now, they were all gone, and he was lying in the filthy straw of a ramshackle barn, afraid to move because his head hurt too badly. Asta and Authgrim both would shake their heads at his foolishness, and Asta would certainly have some sharp words for him.

It was time for a change. Enough wallowing in self-pity and grief. It was time to figure out where he was going, what he was doing, and how he planned to go about doing it.

The first step, of course, was to get up. He did so— very slowly, very gingerly. Even at that, the motion made his stomach lurch and his headache threaten to split his skull. But he kept on, pushing himself through the pain and nausea.

When he finally gained his feet, he stood there swaying gently, until he reached out for a post to hold onto. That helped steady the world a bit.

When he heard the voices, they didn't even register at first. Then, realized that one of them was the farmer. Kori couldn't really hear what was being said, but whatever was going on, the farmer didn't sound happy about it.

He dragged himself to the wall and pressed his eye against a gap between two of the boards. It was difficult to see, but by shifting back and forth, he was able to get a fairly good view of what was happening. His first thought was that, after all the time that had passed, Slode's men had finally caught up with him, but after he managed to get a better view, he saw that wasn't the case.

Both the farmer and his wife were outside the shack that they called home. His hat was being twisted in his hands, and he appeared to be pleading, while his wife huddled behind him, hands on his shoulders and peering fearfully around him.

When Kori saw who the other speaker was, he couldn't blame them.

A dragonkin was on their farm, its head well above the farmers. They seemed much more scared than a dragonkin should have made them.

Then, it dawned on Kori what the real problem was. As far as he knew, he was still in Ascana. It was chilly at night, yes, but not nearly cold enough to be Usturg, so even in his blackout of the last day and a half, he couldn't have made it that far.

So why then, was there a *white* dragonkin— one of Fimbruss's— speaking to the farmers?

Kori was about to walk out and see if he could figure out what was going on, when he saw the farmer rush forward, hands held out in supplication to the dragonkin.

The dragonkin's claws sent the farmer reeling, his wife's scream reaching Kori clearly.

Kori drew back with a gasp. Whatever was happening was none of his business. The farmer must have done something to—

The sharp squeal of a pig was the next thing Kori heard. Then, the crackle of lightning, laughter that seemed to come from the sky, and then nothing at all except for the wailing of the farmer's wife.

Kori waited a few more moments, then slowly opened the barn door. The farmer was crumpled on his side, his wife kneeling next to him, but at least the old man was moving. His legs were bent oddly, as though the bones had been badly broken.

Near the house, the pen which had held the three pigs the farmer had been raising was a smoking ruin. Two of the swine were dead, that much was obvious from their split hides. The third was gone.

Kori backed away, not wanting to be seen. There was nothing he could do. The farmer was hurt. His pigs were gone. Kori couldn't help that. He put the barn between himself and the tableau of tragedy, turned his back, and walked away.

The last time Kori had approached a town on his own, he'd listened to music playing and wondered how it was that someone had time to do that in the middle of the day. Since then, he'd learned a lot more about the world, so he was half-expecting more of the same as he came upon the one he was now looking at.

Since leaving the farm, he'd angled toward the northeast, the same way the caravan had been heading, only now, he avoided the roads. He had no desire to come upon anyone else at the moment or to meet up with the dragonkin who had attacked his friends.

The town, whatever it was called, was quiet. No wagons rolled in or out of it, and Kori didn't see anyone working in the fields around it.

The section of Ascana he journeyed through was dedicated to farms. Of what type, Kori had no idea, since farming had never been what he was interested in. But he knew enough to know that those who were farmers worked from sunup to sundown. Which made the fact that no one was working close to midday very strange.

Still, he had been walking since that morning and his stomach was telling him that it was time to eat. He had no money left, and the only things he possessed of any value he refused to part with. All of which meant he needed work. And to find work, he'd need to find people.

The town was almost eerily quiet. He walked along the first street he came to, seeing all the normal things he would expect. Peoples' homes. A blacksmith's. A bakery. A tavern and an inn. So on and so forth. None of the buildings seemed to have anyone in them.

Once, he might have seen a curtain twitch to the side as he passed, but when he stopped to look, it didn't repeat and no one returned his gaze from the window.

As he moved on, Kori heard a voice. One lone voice but speaking as if it was addressing a crowd.

When he reached the center of town, he found the people. They were gathered together around a stature of Haiteng, or at least that's who Kori assumed it was supposed to be. He couldn't imagine how a village like this one afforded such a thing, but signs of wealth were more important in Ascana than anywhere else, from what he'd heard.

In front of the statue, moving around it to address the entire crowd that made a large ring, was a blue dragonkin.

And it wasn't alone.

In addition to the blue, two much smaller dragonkin crouched near the base of the fountain. Their scales were so black they appeared to be patches of night come to life. Their eyes, bright yellow, scanned over the crowd, as if they were just waiting for someone to given them an excuse to attack. Each of them had a tail that ended in a fierce looking stinger.

First a white dragonkin from Usturg, now two black ones from Reclium? To say nothing of the red ones Kori had seen during the battle at Festival.

What was going on with the world?

"…expected to do what's for the good of all, not just yourselves. Not anymore!" Kori started listening to what the blue dragonkin was saying. "From now on, all goods will be collected and doled out according to need. If you have skills that would better serve the great realm of Ascana elsewhere, you will be taken there. If your work proves satisfactory, your family may be able to join you at a later date, unless it is determined that they would better serve the greater good in another way."

Kori was having a hard time following what exactly the dragonkin was saying. People would be forced to move? Things wouldn't belong to anyone? What was this?

Whatever it was, he wanted no part of it. He wasn't from Ascana, and now that he'd seen what was happening, he never wanted to be. It was time to go back to Usturg. He could handle the cold and snow. He'd find a way to deal with Slode's men, if he had to. But it was clear that he was going to have to rely on those that lived in the countryside for work. This town, at least, had enough of its own problems.

He edged away, then realized that even that small movement had caught the attention of one the black dragonkin. Its head rose up to better watch him. Kori acted as if he had just been shifting on tired feet and returned his attention to the blue. It took everything he had to not look back at the black, but he managed to hold his gaze on the blue.

After a bit, he felt the tension ease and risked a glance. The dragonkin had gone back to scanning the crowd.

Kori resigned himself to having to listen to the rest of the blue's speech. He just hoped it would be over quickly.

Of course, it wasn't.

By the time it ended, Kori was even more confused. He hadn't paid attention to the whole thing, but enough of it had gotten through. Basically, it was more of the same of what he heard when he first came upon the crowd. In short, it all boiled down to people doing as they were told by the dragonkin, and to not expect any great rewards for doing as they were instructed.

The townspeople didn't seem happy about the new way of things, and Kori couldn't blame them for that.

As for him, he wasn't going to find work in this town, so it was time to move on.

The only problem with that was the dragonkin hadn't gone anywhere. The two black ones had launched into the air before the blue was even done speaking. Now, one of them was sitting on the spire of the small church, the highest point in town. From there, it could see most of the village.

The other one was on the move. It would land on a roof, not seeming to care if its weight or claws sent roof-tiles crashing to the ground, and lean over, studying the lanes below. Then, it would fly off, only to land on another building. As Kori watched, and tried to pretend that he wasn't, he saw that it was concentrating on alleys and streets that the other one couldn't see.

Kori stretched, bending backwards as if trying to ease sore muscles. In truth, he was looking for...

There.

The blue dragonkin hadn't left, either. It was soaring slowly through the sky, making great looping circles over the whole town, ranging out over the fields surrounding it.

There was no possible way for Kori to leave without being noticed. He doubted very much that any protests on his part that he wasn't from Ascana and just wanted to get home to Usturg would matter very much.

A noise from nearby caught his attention. He completed his stretch and turned toward the commotion, trying to act as if he had always meant to go that way.

A cart was tipped over in the street, with an old man trying to right it. For a moment, Kori froze, thinking it was Authgrim, but no... this man was bigger, with thinner hair. He cursed as he looked at the broken wheel.

"Need a hand?" Kori asked.

His offer wasn't entirely altruistic. The man's cart had contained bags of produce, presumably on its way to whatever collection point the blue dragonkin had indicated. Maybe by helping, Kori would be able to get a tomato or two. Anything, really, just so long as he could get something into his belly.

"Thanks," the man grunted. With Kori's help he righted the wagon and shoved a wooden box under it. "Although I should let it all lie here in the street and rot," he said, but Kori couldn't help but notice that he spoke quietly.

"Kori," Kori said, sticking out his hand.

"Wyman," the other man returned.

"Where can you get a new wheel?" Kori asked him, bending to pick up a sack that had spilled out.

"There's a wheelwright a few streets away," Wyman said. "I'm not sure how it works now. But I guess I'll go find out."

"I'll clean up here if you want to get started," Kori offered.

Wyman scowled suspiciously. Not that Kori could blame him. If someone had made him the same offer, he'd have the same thought as Wyman. Thief. When Wyman returned, all the produce, and probably the cart as well, would somehow be long gone.

Then, the man glanced at the rooftops. His eyes jerked away. Kori didn't have to follow his glance to know what was there.

"I'm not interested in stealing," he said quietly, still picking up spilled vegetables. "Even if that thing wasn't watching. I'm just hungry, and yes, if the opportunity presents itself, I'll pocket an ear of corn or a cucumber. Is that a fair trade for my help?"

"More than," Wyman said as quietly. "For all I care, you can have it all now. But ask yourself, friend, is a cucumber worth your life?"

With that, he straightened and nodded. "All right then. If you can finish up, I'll go get this wheel fixed."

Kori nodded also but didn't reply. He just kept working, as if it had been his job for his whole life.

Wyman ambled off, not hurrying one bit. Kori watched him go from lowered lids. He hoped the other man wouldn't get punished by the dragonkin for lingering, but then saw what he was doing. The dragonkin on the nearby roof was watching him go, giving Kori enough time to grab a tomato and some long beans and shove them into his shirt.

The dragonkin's head snaked back around toward Kori, but, by then, he was picking up the last of the spilled items. He put them carefully into the cart, then stood back and wiped his hands on his shirt, making sure his purloined produce was pushed down near the waist where it wouldn't move around too much.

He waited for Wyman to return, then grabbed a handle of the cart and helped him bring it to the "distribution point," where several cart loads had already been unceremoniously dumped.

No one was there sorting it or making any effort to dole it out. In fact, it looked as if it was all being left to rot, just as Wyman had wished for.

Whatever was going on in this new Ascana, it was disturbing.

But for Kori, the real question was how he was going to get out of there.

Chapter 4- South of Manse, Ascana

Akamah wasn't doing well. With help, he could stumble along, but his mind wandered, and if he wasn't held onto he tended to fall. Sometimes, when that happened, he would get up on his own, but most of the time, he needed someone's aid.

Bekasi, and the knight from Obristan, the big one, stayed with him. One or the other always guiding his steps and even helping him to eat. For the knight, it seemed something he just considered to be his duty. But Akofi's heart ached whenever he saw Bekasi.

Usually so strong and outspoken, so sure of herself, her face was now drawn and haggard. Her eyes rarely left Akamah, but when they did, Akofi could see the pain in them. What made him the most sad was that there was nothing he could do about it.

He sighed and set down the stick he'd been poking at the fire with. Across from it sat the other two from Obristan: Lamorak and Prince Calidor. Akofi still couldn't believe he'd happened on the actual ruler of the whole realm. It wasn't anything he had ever imagined when he'd run into Manse, determined to help whoever he could.

His eyes shifted back to Bekasi and the other one, Rainaldus, sitting on either side of Akamah.

If it hadn't been for them... and Yarah... he wouldn't have been able to help anyone. His strength had been at its end, and if another dragonkin had come along, he would have been done for. As it was, Yarah— of all people— had done something. Yet another spell that he'd never seen before. His power hadn't returned all at once, but he could feel it flowing back into him, recovering much more quickly than it normally would have.

At the same time, Yarah had grown weaker. Akofi had seen it happening but had refused to acknowledge it. An act that he felt a bit remorseful about now, but at the time, he'd felt justified. There would have been no reason at all to fight with the dragonkin if it hadn't been for her tower and the secrets they'd kept from the rest of Droy Thus.

But... he had to admit, she'd shown them all what to do to support one another. So when it had come time to try to save that poor, unfortunate man the dragonkin had been torturing, they'd made a good show of it.

It hadn't been enough, but, thankfully, these knights of Obristan— the Honor Guard they'd said they were called— had stepped in to finish the job.

All too late for Akamah, of course, but Akofi was sure his friend would get better. The world simply couldn't be that cruel a place to take such a bright light away.

"Tomorrow we'll need to head back toward Obristan," Lamorak said.

Akofi looked up from where he'd resumed staring at the flames. The knight was looking at him, as if he had some sort of say in what happened to them all.

"All right," he agreed, unsure of what else he should say.

"You could come with us," Lamorak continued. "We could use the help."

Akofi blinked. It had never occurred to him to go anywhere but to Droy Thus. Yarah's admission had compelled him to find those who were the cause of all the trouble. To put an end to it if he could.

"We... well I, anyway... I need to..."

"We have no mages of our own," Prince Calidor spoke. "And what Lamorak is trying to say is that we don't have any dragon of our own. Obristan is open to invasion by the others, so—"

"You do, though." Yarah's voice was quiet.

She'd rarely spoken over the last couple of days. She walked far apart from Akofi, even from the others when she could. Bekasi was distracted, Akamah broken, and Akofi wanted no part of her, so she had stayed isolated from her fellow mages.

"What does that mean?" he spat. "More secrets?"

"Yes." Her voice was barely above a whisper. "More secrets."

Akofi drew himself up to decry her dishonesty, but Prince Calidor spoke first.

"What do you mean 'we do?'" His voice was calm, but his gaze was focused intently on her. "We do *what*?"

"You have a dragon," she said. She drew in a slow deep breath. "Her name is Tophonoss, and she rules Obristan as surely as the others rule their realms. There are five true dragons, not four."

The crackling of the flames were the only thing that could be heard for several seconds.

Then, Lamorak broke that silence. "That can't be true. Prince Calidor rules Obristan, as his father did before him. There are no dragonkin and no dragons. We rule ourselves."

Calidor laid his hand on Lamorak's arm. "How do you know this?" he asked Yarah softly.

"It's part of what we learned in the tower." She nodded miserably toward Akofi. "Ask him. He can tell you."

The men from Obristan turned their attention to him, but Akofi continued to glare at Yarah.

Finally, he looked back to them. "She may be right. Yarah is not what she seems. She lied to us all."

Yarah flinched at his words, then rose slowly and walked away from the fire and into the darkness. Akofi watched her go, half-hoping that she would just continue and never come back.

He ignored the sudden pain in his chest that flared up with that thought. He didn't love her anymore. She had lied and used both him and the others for her own agenda. Whatever that was. She wasn't worthy of his time.

"Apparently there are things the rest of us in Droy Thus were kept ignorant of," he began. He told them of the secret tower and the Raaleth magic that had been used. But even as he spoke, there was a small part of him that was niggling at his thoughts.

Was he really mad at Yarah because she'd lied?

Or was it because she'd revealed how little Akofi really knew about what the world he lived in?

The fire had died down, and, still, Yarah hadn't returned. Akofi lay on his back, staring at the black sky and pretending to rest. Inside, though, his thoughts were churning.

His stomach hurt and acid periodically seemed to crawl up his throat to burn his mouth. His chest ached like there was some sort of heavy band around it, squeezing him tightly. Every time he closed his eyes, all he could see was her face, which changed from laughing to the throes of passion to sneering dismissal in a matter of seconds, then back again.

But most of all, he listened. For the sound of her footsteps, coming back to the fire and the relative safety of where they had camped.

Finally, he couldn't take anymore. He sat up and looked around.

Everyone was asleep, except for the one guardsman— Rainaldus. The large man was sitting against a wall in the dark, his legs stretched out in front of him, staring at the few remaining embers from the fire. In the reddish glow, even his good-looks appeared sinister. Particularly when he looked up at Akofi without saying anything.

But he wasn't an evil man. That was evident, at least to Akofi. He was intense and powerful, which made him frightening enough, but he had also shown remarkable humanity and compassion in his treatment of Akamah.

Akofi rose and made his way to Rainaldus, being careful to tread quietly, so as not to wake the others.

"Has Yarah returned at all?" he whispered.

Rainaldus shook his head. "No. I guess she needed time to be alone."

Akofi nodded, wishing he could find it in himself to not care and to just lie down and go to sleep.

"She shouldn't be out there alone," he said. He was looking off, as if she was suddenly going to reappear by him wishing it so.

They had camped in the ruins of a large building. From the looks of it, Akofi would have said it had been some sort of church or house of worship, but Prince Calidor had told him that the Ascani didn't really have anything like that. It was— instead— a place where people paid money— and quite large sums, at that— to be entertained by actors and singers.

Now, half the building had collapsed, but the roof over the stage was still sturdy, so they'd made camp there, safe from eyes flying overhead.

Tomorrow, they'd be back to it, moving south. Or at least he would be, he supposed. It seemed those from Obristan would be taking their leave. Akofi couldn't blame them. If he'd believed that Droy Thus was unguarded, he'd want to go back there, too. And he wasn't even responsible for the realm the way Prince Calidor was.

None of which was causing Yarah to reappear.

He glanced down at Rainaldus who had returned to watching the embers.

"I think I'll see if I can find her," he said, half-expecting the guard to protest.

"Be careful," Rainaldus said instead.

Akofi nodded and started away from the campsite.

Once he'd left the ring of feeble light, he stood still for a few moments, giving his eyes time to adjust.

The gap in the wall they'd come through earlier in the day was off the stage they'd used as a base and to the right. A lot of the building had been destroyed, but there was an intact doorway to Akofi's left. The door itself was open, although whether it had been when they'd first come there or not, he couldn't remember.

Regardless, it was as good a place as any to look for her.

Through the doorway was a hallway, with several rooms beyond. Some were destroyed, while one or two were more or less intact. But Yarah wasn't in any of them. Beyond that was more of the building, but the way forward was blocked by rubble, and he could see a few stars where a roof had been.

Yarah must have gone outside, after all. He retraced his steps and exited the building.

The night air was colder away from the remains of the fire. Not freezing, but a certain chill in the air made him put his arms across his chest and shiver. He paused to look around, then decided to circle the building, hoping that Yarah had stayed close.

The theater, as Prince Calidor had called it, was in a small city which had been destroyed by dragonkin. Not like Manse, where they'd come mostly to fight each other, the very town here had been the target of the attack. Most buildings had been crushed, with signs of fire everywhere. It had been dragonkin of Droy Thus who had done this, maybe in retaliation for the apparent destruction of Lankari tower.

As for people, they'd seen a few on their way in, but those had fled when they'd seen the mages. Prince Calidor had tried to call to them, but none had listened, and after the first few attempts had ended in failure, he'd stopped trying.

Where the rest of the populace were, Akofi had no idea. Either gone, or dead inside their shattered homes and businesses he would imagine.

He kept one eye on the ground in front of him and the other on the side of the building as he went. It was slow going, but before too long he was at the back. Across the street was another building that had escaped the worst of the carnage, with a large, multi-paned glass window. From the sign that now hung down at an angle and was burnt almost to illegibility, it seemed to have been a tavern.

A feeble light glowed through the window.

Someone who had survived, he thought, and started to walk away. Then, it occurred to him that it could just as easily be Yarah, so he picked his way across the debris-strewn street and walked inside.

It was Yarah. Sitting at a table with a flame burning in the air. He watched her move it, shape it, send it floating away from her and then back. But she did it all with a vacant expression that told him she was paying no attention to what she was actually doing.

Which made him aware— all over again— that she wasn't who she said she was. Akofi had an affinity for fire-magic. He could replicate those things she was doing, but not with nearly the ease. He would've had to concentrate.

But also… she looked so alone sitting there. She was dirty, and her hair was tangled. She had dark smudges under her eyes from being tired. Her clothes were filthy with ash, mud, and blood.

Yet, she was beautiful, and Akofi had never been so glad to see someone.

"Yarah," he said softly.

Her head jerked up with a gasp and the flame wavered but didn't go out.

"Oh, it's you," she said, when she saw him standing in the doorway. "What do you want?"

And there it was. What *did* he want?

Her. He knew that much... but also... not her? The truth was, he didn't know. He *did* know, however, that he wanted her to be safe. And that he wanted her to bring him to Orluduna tower— the real tower— and show him the reasons that made her do what she did.

"You shouldn't be out here by yourself," he said, in lieu of all the things he both did and didn't want to say.

"What do you care?" She returned her gaze to the floating flame.

Akofi looked down to the floor. How was he supposed to answer that?

As usual, he reverted to simple honesty. He pulled out the chair across from her and sat down.

"I was jealous," he said. "And scared. And angry. And hurt. All of them at once and I didn't know how to deal with it."

"You do now? Suddenly?"

He shrugged. "I suppose so. Or a little bit, anyway. It was just... I thought we were..."

"In love?" She scoffed. "I thought so, too."

"But you weren't honest with me."

"Can you really say you were honest with me about everything?"

Akofi took a moment to actually think about that. "Yes," he finally said. "I was. I am."

Yarah opened her mouth to reply but stopped with the words unformed. She shook her head and looked away. "I'm sorry I couldn't live up to that."

The flame flickered in the air between them. Akofi watched it for a moment, then opened his hand, concentrated, and conjured one of his own. He frowned as he pushed it away from him, sending it floating toward hers.

"What are you doing?" she asked.

He didn't answer. He just nudged his flame closer. Yarah scowled and pulled hers out of the way, then moved it off to the side, far more easily and smoothly than he could move his. He narrowed his eyes and sent his flame chasing hers, but she avoided his clumsy movements without effort.

Finally, he let the flame wink out of existence and sat back, a slight bead of sweat on his brow.

"I was the best person I knew of at that. Even Kio couldn't summon and control a flame better than me. Bekasi couldn't either, although there were other spells that she could come close to me in using."

Yarah didn't say anything.

"But you," he continued. "You can do it without even seeming to try. You know things about the world— including an unknown dragon in Obristan— that I have no idea of. And I was top marks for all of Lankari tower. You can use magic I know nothing about."

"What's your point behind all this, Akofi?"

"My point is that everything else I said really all comes down to the same thing. You hurt my pride."

She stared at him for a moment. "And that's supposed to make it all okay?"

"No. Not at all. I don't know that we can get back what we thought we had. But I still love you. I don't want to see you get hurt. And..."

"And what?" when he didn't finish.

"And I want to know what you know. I want to visit Orluduna tower. The real one that you told me about. Seeing all this—" He raised his hand to indicate the ruined city outside the tavern. "It's not right. The dragons have to be stopped. Somehow."

Yarah didn't say anything again, but Akofi was willing to give her what time she needed. He'd just dropped a lot on her, totally changed his tune from a few hours before, and asked her to include him in something so secret the rest of the world knew nothing of it.

"I can't," she said quietly.

"I understand," he said. He did, too. Some wounds were too great, especially when fresh. It was enough, for now, that she knew. Maybe, by the time they'd reached Droy Thus, they could come to a better understanding.

"No," she said. "You don't actually. I can't take you to Orluduna tower, or anywhere else, because I'm not going back."

Akofi smiled. "Of course you are. We all are."

She was shaking her head before he was even done speaking. "Not all. Prince Calidor and Lamorak are going back to Obristan."

"Oh, that," he chuckled. "They don't count. Not with this, anyway. When those three leave—"

"Two," she interrupted. "Rainaldus will go on to Droy Thus. He's been called to Orluduna. I'm going to accompany Calidor and Lamorak."

Akofi stared at her. She might as well have said that she was going to grow another head and howl naked at the moon. What she was saying made no sense.

Yarah rose and came around the table. She put her hand on his shoulder.

"I love you, too, Akofi. And maybe there will be time for us when this is over. But right now, I have to do what's needed. So do you. I go to Obristan. You go back home."

She squeezed his shoulder once, then dropped her hand and walked out, leaving Akofi alone with the flame she'd left behind.

Chapter 5- Pharax, Reclium

From the surrounding mountain slope, he overlooked the squalor of Pharax. Every time he'd been there, it had struck Reyson all over again what a pigsty of a town it really was. Heldum had its good points, he supposed, although they were few and far between, but compared to what lay before him now, it was a veritable paradise.

There was no sense in delaying it any longer, though. He had a job to do, so he'd do it.

The fact that he would actually enjoy this part of his journey had nothing at all to do with how he viewed the town.

When he reached the outskirts, he slowed his pace a bit, keeping an eye out for trouble. Not many in *any* city would care to challenge Reyson. He carried himself the way a natural killer should. Head up, shoulders back, weapon on display. His very walk portrayed a certain arrogance, which he cultivated. Why not? He was far more dangerous than anything that walked on the streets, except a dragonkin, of course, and, truth be told, he wasn't even sure about that. He was convinced it would depend on the kin.

Still, there were always one or two who thought to try him. Either those with an inflated sense of their own abilities, or those too stupid to realize who and what he was.

Although he was keeping his eye out for trouble, that didn't mean he wouldn't welcome it.

It had been a long trip from Heldum to Pharax. He'd requested aid from a dragonkin, but that had gone about as far as such things usually did. No answer; although he should be glad one of them hadn't taken the opportunity to pretend to help, but then deposit him on a forbidden peak somewhere to freeze to death.

In the end, he'd walked and rode the whole way there, leaving a string of broken bodies and stolen mounts behind him.

But the last confrontation had been two days ago, and he was feeling rusty.

He made his way into the city proper— if such a place could be called that— and slowed down even further, giving himself plenty of time to find what he was seeking.

There it was. As he knew it would be. Down a narrow alley, one of many which seemed to be purposely designed into the city as places where mayhem might occur without being disturbed.

Only three men, which was too bad, but they would be enough to get his blood flowing. Three men and one woman, who was fighting them off quite admirably. Reyson took a moment to watch. She was a fighter, he saw, but the outcome was inevitable. Those attacking her were no strangers to violence, either, and the only reason the woman was still fighting is because they wanted her alive.

Whether a robbery or something much more distasteful, Reyson didn't know nor did he care. The woman's fate really didn't concern him. She was simply an excuse.

"That's enough, gentlemen," he said, stepping into the alley. He kept his hand away from his sword belt.

The three men glanced at him, but kept the woman surrounded. The one farthest from him, on the other side of their intended victim, stretched his neck to peer at Reyson.

"Keep moving, old man," he snarled.

"No, I don't think I'll do that. Now, let the woman go."

"Or what?" One of them asked, not even bothering to look at Reyson.

"Or I'll kill you all." He paused, as if considering his words. "Actually, that's not quite true. I'm going to kill you all, anyway."

That got their attention. The one who'd first spoken stopped trying to get at the woman. He dropped his hands and sauntered toward Reyson. The other two glanced at each other, shrugged, and followed along, which gave the woman time to run.

She stopped for a moment and spit. The wad of saliva hit the first man in the back of his neck. He wiped at it with a snarl and curse, and turned to her, but she was already running for the far end of the alley.

Reyson laughed, which stopped the assailant from throwing the knife he'd pulled from his belt.

"Something funny, old man?" he growled.

"You," Reyson said easily. "And the spirit of that girl. Just when I thought this hole of city couldn't bring me any joy, I've run into this little tableau. It appears I was wrong."

"You were wrong all right," another said. This one was younger, barely able to grow the whiskers that sprouted on his cheeks and chin. "Last time for that."

Reyson didn't reply. He just smiled even wider and let them come.

But when the thugs had taken another couple of steps, the first one who'd spoke— probably the brains of the outfit, Reyson decided— stopped them.

"Hold on. Something's wrong here."

Reyson cocked his head, waiting for whatever was coming next.

The man ran his eyes over Reyson, taking in the clothes, the boots, and especially, the sword at his hip. He looked down at the knife in his hand, then glanced at the weapons his friends carried. Weapons Reyson had already taken stock of.

A woodcutter's hatchet, with a handle that had split and was being held together by several wraps of twine. A knife in the hands of the leader, which had a nicked blade and didn't appear any too sharp. And the young one... ah, now he had an interesting weapon. An actual sword, with a hilt that said it wasn't forged anywhere in Reclium. Unless Reyson was wrong, and he never was with such things, that sword had come from Obristan.

"Where did you get that?" he asked, pointing.

The young man stopped and glanced down. None of them, other than the first man, had drawn their weapons.

"I got it from my father," the young man said. "Why?"

"Ridiculous," Reyson scoffed. "A man of your father's station, whoever he was, could never afford such a thing. If it was his, he got it by stabbing some poor soul in the back who'd ended up here for who-knows-what reason."

The youth didn't reply. He just frowned and drew the blade.

Reyson nodded approval. Not at the young man. The way he drew the weapon, the way he held it, the way he stood, were all ludicrous. He'd be dead before he had a chance to swing it. But the blade itself. It reflected the dim light of Pharax so well it almost seemed to shine with its own inner glow. The edge gleamed, and he was willing to bet it was still almost as sharp as when it had been new.

A sword like that belonged with a man who knew how to use it.

He drew his own and looked down at it. Serviceable, as Chaol had found out. But it paled in comparison to that of the young man's.

Reyson looked back to the three men, who were beginning to edge backwards nervously. He smiled at them one more time, then moved forward to claim his new sword.

It didn't take him long to find Mrs. Cloven's house. A few pointed questions asked of those who couldn't be bothered to answer but then suddenly found their tongues.

Now, he stood across the street and watched. Her girls were more than they appeared. Oh, they did the work they advertised, and none of them moved like they knew how to fight. But they were formidable, nevertheless. They kept their eyes moving, taking in everything. They'd already seen him, of course, which suited his purposes just fine. One had gone inside, to report his presence to the old whore.

She'd know who it was and why he was there. What was more, she'd know that *if* he was there, Chaol had failed. And her knowing that was almost better than what was to come.

But the girls continued to ply their trade, disappearing in ones or twos into the house, a man's arm around their waists, then reappearing in varying amounts of time later, only to look for their next paying customer.

The more he stood there, staring at them, not bothering to hide, the more nervous they appeared. Until finally— as Reyson had known would happen— one of them had had enough and marched across the street to confront him.

"What are you doing, you old creep?" she demanded. She was pretty— for Pharax, Reyson supposed. Lord Maganti wouldn't have let her set foot into his tower, though. She wore shockingly few clothes, given the damp cold that seeped into everything in the port town. And her face was so caked in makeup that Reyson wondered how she could move it to talk at all.

"Waiting," he replied calmly.

"Do it somewhere else," she said. "You're making everyone nervous."

"Good."

She seemed taken aback by his reply, then decided that bravado was her best course. "Good, yourself. We don't want you here and none of us are going to take you inside, so go find somewhere else to lurk."

Reyson's backhand caught her on her left cheek. She barely had time to squawk before she hit the ground hard. She lifted her hand to her face and stared up at him in shock.

"Mind your manners, girl," he said, not taking his eyes off the front of Mrs. Cloven's house. "And go tell her that I'm here. I'll be visiting her in… let's say five minutes, shall we? It would be better if she was alone." He stopped to consider, then shrugged. "Actually, I don't care who's with her. The outcome will be the same."

When he was done, he turned his head to look down at her. The girl stared up at him, not daring to move.

"Go on," he said. "I won't stop you. Do as your told."

He returned his gaze to the house and ignored the girl scrambling to her feet and scurrying across the road. The other girls, who had seen him strike her, gathered around and ushered her into the house. One of them turned back and made a rude gesture in his direction, before disappearing herself.

For the first time since he'd arrived, the street in front of her house was empty. Not only were none of the girls standing there, but any potential customers must have sensed trouble and steered clear of the area, as well.

Reyson waited the full five minutes he had promised, then walked across the street, his new sword swinging slightly at his hip. He was looking forward to using it.

The door wasn't locked, which was nice, but it wouldn't have stopped him. He opened it to a comfortable sitting room, lit by a few oil lanterns and the cozy flickering of flames from the fireplace.

On the far side of the room was a curtained doorway, which led, he presumed, to the rooms where business was conducted. He'd half-expected the old woman to be hiding back there, but instead, she sat in a rocking chair, calmly watching him take in his surroundings. When he was sure the room was empty but for the two of them, he turned his gaze to her.

"Hello, Reyson," she said, as if she was greeting someone she had just seen a few hours ago.

"Severina," he replied. There was no cause to be rude. Not yet.

She looked the same as when he'd last seen her, and he hadn't known her age then. All he had known was that she had provided— one time only— entertainment for one of Lord Maganti's parties. She had refused any others. But somehow, during that brief moment when their lives had crossed, she and Chaol had formed a friendship, although Reyson suspected it had been more.

The next time Maganti needed bodies for his amusement, Chaol had contacted someone else. And then promptly quit.

That alone had been a surprise, but Lord Maganti had insisted that the old man be allowed to leave. He had been shaken, making Reyson think that Chaol had some sort of leverage. Reyson suspected Mrs. Cloven had a lot to do with that, as well.

"What can I do for you?" she asked him. "You're scaring away business, so the sooner you move along, the better."

"I couldn't care less about your business," he replied. "You know why I'm here."

"I'm afraid you give me more credit than I deserve."

"Impossible." She was playing a game, but it was one Reyson was very familiar with. Stay calm and focused, until it was time to act. Which meant she had something up her sleeve. The question was what? He narrowed his eyes as he studied her. "What's the game,

Severina? Whatever it is you're thinking, it won't work. Just tell me where the girl went. Chaol didn't and now he can't tell anyone anything ever again."

He'd hoped to rattle her with that, but she took it in stride.

"No games here, boy. I don't know any girl you might be looking for, unless it's one of mine, and I've already given answer to that. Whatever Chaol told you, he beat you in the end. He knew you better than anyone. And if you came this way, it was because he wanted you to." She chuckled. "You never were as smart as you thought you were."

Reyson nodded. It was going about as he had expected. No one could ever say he hadn't tried to be reasonable, though. He sighed and drew his sword.

"Sorry it had to come to this," he lied. "When I'm through with you, I'm going to kill everyone here. Slowly. You'll hear it all, I promise. I'll leave you alive that long. Is the life of one girl worth all that?"

Mrs. Cloven smiled back at him. "Yes. It is." Then, she put her hand to her mouth, and coughed. "Boys," she said quietly.

Reyson should have looked behind that curtain. When the two… whatever they were… came through it, he really wished he had. At least then, he would have been prepared.

Huge, lumbering, taller, broader, and more muscle-bound than any human had the right to be, it was nearly impossible to tell them apart. The first one ducked through the opening, then was followed by his twin. Neither of them wore shirts, which just emphasized the almost deformed torsos.

Their heads were hairless and too small for their bodies. Beady black eyes glared from overhanging brows, and thick lips frowned as they stomped toward Reyson.

Well. He'd fought large men before, although not quite as large as these two. And judging from the expressions on their faces, neither of them were overly intelligent. He was also sure that neither were as fast as he was, and, to cap it off, they were weaponless. Although judging by the sheer size of the fists curled at their sides, they didn't often need to be armed.

But they *were* flesh and blood. Flesh lost to steel every time, and then the blood would flow. The more of it outside of those huge bodies, the better. Then, he'd get to work on the rest.

He didn't wait for them.

Instead, he sprang forward, sword back. He went low, ducking under a punch that would have caved his face to the back of his skull if it had connected. He'd been right, though. They weren't as quick as he was.

As he came back up, he brought the sword around, lacerating the first one across his stomach. The man howled and grabbed at his belly, but, by then, Reyson was already leaping at the second. He led with his right foot, aimed squarely for the next one's crotch. No matter how big they were, a swift kick to the fork of the legs always made them hesitate.

In that brief moment, Reyson realized he'd made two mistakes in as many minutes. Not only hadn't he looked behind that curtain, he'd assumed that both of these monsters were identical. They weren't. At least not in fighting.

The one he leapt at turned in a flash, so that Reyson's kick landed on the side of his meaty thigh. The man growled and lashed out, catching Reyson with a backhand slap much as he had the girl outside. He barely had time to jerk his head back and roll with it, but the force of the blow was still enough to cause him to stagger back, right into the arms of the first one.

That one had ceased wailing over his cut. Reyson felt wetness soak his back as the huge man pulled him in for a bear hug that would cut off his breath and break his ribs if he allowed it to happen.

He reversed his sword and jabbed backward, the point sinking deep into soft flesh.

As the huge arms jerked away from him, he felt a slight sharp pain to the side of his neck. He slapped at it and felt something hard and thin fall away. His fingers came away dotted with blood, but that was all he had time for before the second man was on him.

Reyson spun away from the attack, bringing his blade around in a flat arc, aiming to eviscerate the giant across his abdomen, but the man was too close. He stepped inside the path of the blade and grabbed at Reyson.

Reyson back-pedaled, then realized he was running out of room. He was close to the fireplace. The one he hadn't managed to hurt was blocking his way, and the other had stopped exploring the wound he'd been dealt and was actually growling as he moved toward his brother.

He needed to get out of there. He'd never suspected that Mrs. Cloven would have such bodyguards. He'd never even heard of anything like these two. Out on the street, with room to move, he'd have them easily. But withing these confines, it was too restrictive, too...

The fist smashed into the side of his face, sending him sprawling towards the front of the room. He'd never even seen it coming. He shook his head fiercely and tried to focus, but the punch had knocked him almost senseless.

That and...

Laying on the floor where he'd swatted it away from his neck was a silver pin. It gleamed in the firelight but seemed to waver. As a matter of fact, the whole room was pulsing in and out in time with his breathing. He could even hear it, a roar of air, higher, then lower, until he realized it was his own panting breaths he was hearing.

He was bent down, staring at the floor, drool running from his lips. He was still holding his sword, but his arm felt like lead when he tried to move it.

"What have you done?" His voice came out in a harsh gasp.

"As I said." Mrs. Cloven's voice came like a distant echo. "You always did think too highly of yourself."

Reyson tried to look at her. She'd thrown a pin of some sort at him. Poisoned, surely. The two giants were between him and her, blocking him from getting to her. If he could have, though...

"Goodbye, Reyson," he heard her say. "I hope Chaol is waiting for you."

The floor shook as the two came for him. Reyson used every bit of energy that remained to him and threw the sword. He got lucky and finally managed to hurt the second one. The blade nicked the monster's arm on the way past.

But the distraction was what he needed. He bolted for the door, ripped it open, and stumbled out. His head down, arms windmilling, and steps staggering wildly, he knew he looked like a fool. He didn't care one bit. He just needed to get away, to figure out a way past those two.

Then she would pay. Her and everyone she loved.

He kept moving, pushing off walls, falling into the street before struggling on. Once, someone tried to stop him, but Reyson lashed out almost blindly, and the fellow thought better of it.

There was something driving him on. Something he hadn't felt before.

It wasn't until he crashed to the ground behind a building and was unable to rise that he realized what it was.

"Ah," he thought, as his breathing grew slower and his vision dimmed. He ached all over, his joints felt like they were on fire. He was on his back, which was a recipe for ruin, since he could feel his stomach working to purge whatever poison she'd hit him with. But he lacked the strength to move.

"So this is fear."

He didn't like it. But then, he didn't have long to experience it, either.

Chapter 6- Droy Thus

Ilvisar looked around as he stepped out of the portal, his head turning from side to side surveying the jungle. To Sintifi, he resembled a tourist out for a pleasant stroll.

For his part, Sintifi was much less relaxed. Since being found by the Raaleth, they'd passed through several such magic gates, each one opening further to the south. Now, they'd reached home, or at least Droy Thus. Though they weren't close to Orluduna Tower quite yet, Sintifi took a deep breath, feeling the humid air soak into his lungs and his skin.

If he had his way, he'd never leave the place again.

"This land has changed," Ilvisar said. "It was always warm, as would be expected, but… not like this."

"It's the only way I've ever known it," Sintifi said.

Ilvisar looked at him for a moment, then smiled sadly and shook his head. "All you've known is the dragons' corruption. Heat and humidity, leading to riotous jungles here in your land. Constant cold and snow to the north. Eternal night in the land controlled by Gillbriss. The world was not meant to be this way."

Sintifi frowned. He knew, of course, that the individual realms were reflections of the dragons, but surely that was just the way of things. "How else should it be, then?" he asked.

In answer, Ilvisar gathered up a few fallen branches and stacked them in front of him. He motioned and flames bloomed among them, until a few moments later he had a merry little fire burning.

"Move closer," he said to Sintifi.

Sintifi did so.

"Do you feel it?" Ilvisar asked.

"Feel what? The heat of the fire? Of course I do. Fire is hot."

"Yes. Now, back away. But slowly."

Sintifi didn't get what the Raaleth was trying to show him, and he was beginning to get annoyed. He wasn't stupid. A simple explanation would have done just as well.

Ilvisar motioned, waiting for him to do as instructed.

Sintifi shook his head and eased backward. He really wasn't stupid; not at all. And he recognized his own stung pride. The Raaleth was trying to teach him something. Considering the things he'd seen since joining with the Elder, it might behoove him to pay attention.

So he continued moving backward, feeling the heat from the fire fade from his chest and legs. He took another step, and, of course, the heat lessened, until finally, it was gone all together.

The simple lesson wasn't lost on him.

"Gradual," he said. "You could have just said that the change in climate was meant to be more gradual."

"I could have," Ilvisar replied. "But sometimes, illustration works better. Plus, now we have a fire to cook our dinner on."

Sintifi couldn't tell if he was joking or not. After a moment, he chuckled, and was relieved when Ilvisar did the same. "All right. I get it."

"Perhaps," Ilvisar said. "But I wish for you to truly understand. The power that it takes to cause such a shift in the very earth itself. It defies imagination."

Sintifi set about preparing dinner, which was nothing more than some beans and hard bread. The fire would warm the beans, but it had hardly been necessary. However, as he puttered, he thought about what Ilvisar was telling him.

Magic was easy to use, as long as one was born to it. But born to it or not, people had varying amounts of aptitude and strength. Hard work, training, and study could improve one's skills, but it still required a great deal of fortitude to cast and maintain truly hard spells. The one he'd cast to call the dragonkin to Festival had taken all of his strength. He'd been so exhausted by it that he'd needed to rest after, and had been so out of it that he'd never even heard those young mages enter the tower.

To be able to fundamentally change the nature of a whole realm… then to keep it that way for hundreds of years…

Ilvisar was right. Sintifi couldn't even begin to imagine what sort of power and strength that took.

"So, how do they do it?" he asked, looking up at the Elder. "I think I now see your point. And yes, your little demonstration helped."

"No one knows. The Raaleth could never have done such a thing, and we are the most magically adept of the three Elder races, as you call us."

Sintifi frowned. *Three* Elder races? He knew of one. What were the other two?

"Neither could the dragons," Ilvisar continued. "They may have rivaled the Raaleth in brute force for magic, but not to that scale."

"But they did it, somehow," Sintifi mused. "Those five…"

"When they rose," Ilvisar confirmed. "When they became greater than their kin and swelled in both size and power. It wasn't long after they'd driven the Xarlug away, killed most of the Helgarlug and the Raaleth when they'd created their separate realms."

Sintifi felt like his head was spinning. Ilvisar was speaking of things he'd had no knowledge of at all. He was using words that made no sense. Zaaar-what? What was a Helglug, or whatever he'd said?

Ilvisar must have seen his confusion. "Ancient history, my friend," the Raaleth said. "But important still. Now you see why I go with you to the tower my people built. If those who now occupy it have found a way to hide from powers that could change the very world… then we may have much to say to each other."

"Yeah," Sintifi said slowly. Not for the first time, he was glad he was just a mage. Powerful, at least for his own kind, but still just a mage. He glanced at Ilvisar, squatting across the fire from him.

Let the masters of Orluduna Tower deal with Ilvisar. Once he was there, Sintifi could say his goodbyes. Maybe he'd move to the coast and take up fishing. For sharks. With his bare hands. It was bound to be safer.

Ilvisar watched the human wizard over the fire that burned between them. He'd just given Sintifi plenty to think about, told him things that he doubted any other human had ever known. He wasn't sure how Arastug or Falaern would have felt about it, but the job had been given to him, to do as he saw fit. Plus, Arastug knew very well that Ilvisar longed for the day when he could openly battle the dragons and their dragonkin. When he could start to take back all that had been taken from them.

But there weren't enough Raaleth or Helgarlug left. Not to make any real difference. And if the existence of Olequan was ever to be found out, the five dragons would join together to root it out and destroy them once and for all.

Which was why it was important for him to go to this tower that had once belonged to his people. If humans— mere children, really— could learn to use their magic, and had actually hidden an entire tower from Chimbod... well, then it only made sense that he learned what they knew. It could only benefit Olequan and his people.

Plus, he found that he quite liked Sintifi. The dark-skinned human acted the coward. Always talking about running away, not taking any responsibility. Yet, it had been he who had gone to the human Festival purposely to pull one of Chimbod's children to him. He'd done so at great risk. There was no way he could have been certain that such a spell would work, or that Chimbod, herself, wouldn't have known who had thrown it.

The end result had been more catastrophic than either Sintifi or his masters could ever have hoped for. His one act had initiated others, which led to still more, and then more, until the world was in danger of going up in flames.

The world made by dragons, anyway. Olequan would remain standing in the end.

Ilvisar settled back on his heels and watched Sintifi stir the beans.

The world *hadn't* yet gone up in flames. At every stop they'd made, including now, Ilvisar had taken a moment to search his surroundings. He'd never again caught the sense of one of Tophonoss's children, but there had been plenty of others. Wherever he felt a gathering of humans— whether it be a city or town— he also sensed the dragonkin. Every place had them now, and they were mingling. Haiteng's children with those of Chimbod's, while Gillbriss's and Fimbruss's mixed in as well.

It seemed that rather than cast the realms into war, all Sintifi and his colleagues had accomplished was to draw the dragons together.

Unfortunate, but maybe it was something Ilvisar would be able to take advantage of.

"This tower," he asked the human. "How is it hidden?"

"I don't really know," Sintifi replied, looking up. He handed over a cup of the beans and a hunk of the bread. Ilvisar accepted them, with no plan to actually eat the vile things. "Something to do with the magic of the tower itself, I guess. That really wasn't my area of study."

"No? Then what was?"

"Coercion. Simple as that, really. There were several of us studying the same thing. All with the aim of making a dragonkin do as we'd wanted. With taking control."

Sintifi's eyes almost lit up when he spoke. He was obviously passionate about his work.

"With what end in mind?" Ilvisar asked him.

"What do you think?" the human snorted. "To take over. To make the dragonkin kill each other, maybe even attack the dragons."

A goal Ilvisar could understand and appreciate. But… these *were* humans.

"And then?" he prodded. "What did you foresee happening if it was to work? If the dragons and the dragonkin were gone?"

Sintifi frowned, then shook his head. "I actually don't know. I never got that far. Bigger brains than mine could figure that one out. I just want the rule of the dragons to end."

"They are cruel, then?"

"Cruel?" Sintifi considered. "No, I wouldn't say that. It's more that Chimbod… controls everything. Magic was given to us, so she says, by her, and it's only through *her* grace that we're allowed to use it."

Ilvisar knew that not to be true but let Sintifi continue.

"I know Gillbriss is cruel to the humans in her realm. And I guess I'd want them to be free… but they seem so far away."

He trailed off and watched the flames silently, his brows drawn down.

Ilvisar nodded. "All questions above me, too, my friend. I didn't ask to cause you anguish. It was merely my own curiosity. I have no answers, either. What would my people do if the dragons were to fall? Would we try to rule in their place? Or would it be as it once was, with all races sharing the world?"

"That would be nice," Sintifi said.

"It would," he agreed.

But inside, he had to wonder. There were so many humans. They spread across every land, into every corner. If they succeeded somehow... if they beat the dragons... would the Raaleth be any better off? Was there even room for them in this world anymore?

Things to be settled later on. For now, he would get to the tower, talk to those whom Sintifi deferred to.

Then, he'd make the next decision on what to do. If need be, he could always find a way to let the existence of the tower leak to Chimbod. He only hoped that such a thing wouldn't be necessary.

The final portal deposited Sintifi and Ilvisar far to the south, only an hour by foot along the road from Orluduna tower. Ilvisar had opened his magical gate in the jungle away from the road, however, on the off-chance that they'd encounter someone.

For his part, Sintifi couldn't get out of the jungle fast enough. He loved his homeland and wanted to live in it free from the dragons'— or anyone else's— rule. But he never liked being in the actual untouched jungle. There were too many things that could kill you there. So, as soon as Ilvisar oriented him toward the road, he took off in a careful rush.

Soon, but still longer than he would have liked, they arrived at the road and turned toward Orluduna.

There *was* an actual human mage tower in Orluduna, known to the rest of Droy Thus and run in the same basic manner. Young mages grew up there, advancing as they aged and their magical abilities increased. They graduated, became free-mages, and were able to go where they wished. And, like all other tower villages, menial tasks were performed by the ill-favored.

Most who lived there had no knowledge of the other tower, that one built ages ago by the Raaleth. The only mages who visited *that* tower were invited there, as Sintifi had been when he first left the open tower. Its existence had come as quite a shock to him, to say nothing of what the goals of those already living there were.

The nominal head of the tower was Oponsi. Ancient in appearance, Sintifi had never met anyone who was even close to her in power. And she had a brilliant intellect to match. She stayed in the tower full-time, never leaving it as far as he knew. Instead, she trusted to those others who knew the secret to work outside of it.

What Oponsi did, other than directing their efforts against the dragonkin, was research. There was a vast library in the tower, greater than any other in the world, and all written in the lost languages of the Raaleth and others. Even knowing how to read it, deciphering what the Elder races were talking about was notoriously laborious. There were times when it seemed as if they even thought differently from humans. Oponsi had made it her life's work to bridge that gap.

She was stern and sour. Her wit acerbic and her tongue sharp. She berated as easily as others said good morning.

Yet, Sintifi loved her greatly, like a grandmother, and couldn't wait to see her again.

But as they neared the town itself, a problem arose in his mind. Ilvisar looked nothing like anyone from Droy Thus, or from any of the other human realms. With his bald head, great height, lithe build, and— especially— skin that was almost golden in color and ears that were much too pointed, he was going to attract attention.

"We can't just go in like this," he said to Ilvisar. "Do you have a way to disguise yourself?"

For anyone else, he would have been concerned that magical disguise would be easily sensed, but he thought a Raaleth probably had ways of making sure they weren't seen.

"I do," Ilvisar replied.

He stopped walking, and change came over him. His skin darkened to almost match Sintifi's. Dark hair sprouted from his head and his chin, while his build became shorter and stockier, until he was a little shorter than Sintifi. His ears rounded, and after only a couple of moments, Sintifi would never have guessed that anyone other than a Droy Thus wizard stood before him.

"Shall we?" Ilvisar asked. Even his voice had changed, becoming more like a human's than the almost liquid sound of his own.

Sintifi nodded, but before they went, he cast a quick spell, trying to detect the magic the Raaleth was using to disguise himself.

Ilvisar smiled. "Did you find anything?"

"No." The thought that Ilvisar knew what he was doing brought a strange comfort to Sintifi. It was just another reminder of how far ahead of him the Raaleth was.

When they reached the town, Sintifi was even more glad of that fact.

The first thing he saw was a dragonkin. Not the red scales he would have expected, but the white belonging to one of Fimbruss's. The sight made him stop in his tracks, feeling suddenly disoriented, as if he wasn't really awake but was walking through a dream.

The dragonkin barely took notice of him. Instead, it was watching a group of students, all outside Orluduna tower. Nearby was another group, being watched by a red dragonkin.

"I don't get—" he started to say, but a hiss interrupted his thoughts.

He turned, only to find a smaller, jet-black dragonkin crouching on the path behind him.

"Where are you coming from?" she demanded.

"From… there…" Sintifi pointed dumbly, knowing that he wasn't answering what the thing really wanted to know, but unable to formulate a better answer.

The dragonkin growled, then spit. A wad of acid splattered to the ground next to Sintifi's right boot, sizzling madly as it burned into the earth.

"Once more, human." The dragonkin's voice was sly, as if it couldn't wait to spit its acid right into his face.

"Festival!" he cried, the words coming to him now. "We were at Festival! It took us a while to get home, because—"

"We?" the dragonkin interrupted.

"Yes, we—"

But when Sintifi looked around, no one was with him. Ilvisar, no matter what form he was wearing, had disappeared, leaving Sintifi alone to face the dragonkin.

Chapter 7- Great Trade Highway, Ascana

Everywhere was either devastation or control, Lamorak thought. The fields that marked the farming districts of well-laid out Ascana were mostly untouched by dragonkin fire or steam, but there were more of the creatures than he'd ever thought he would see. All around, the harvested crops were being piled into huge wagons, pulled by horses, oxen, or even teams of men, and taken away. He noticed many a thin, hungry face miserably watch them go, but no one dared to object.

The villages were a different story. Some seemed mostly intact, with dragonkin patrolling the air above, keeping everyone in line. Others were little more than ruins, some of which still smoked and wavered with heat, indicating that that they had only recently been burned.

Yarah, the female wizard from Droy Thus, was proving to be a valuable traveling companion, although Lamorak still mourned the loss of Rainaldus. He'd always known there was something different about the young man. Finding out that he was probably a member of some secret cabal trying to overthrow the dragons rule didn't really surprise him all that much.

But for all his great abilities, the guardsman wouldn't have been able to do what Yarah did.

The three had found clothes that mostly fit them in an abandoned house. Rough spun and poorer quality than their own, they were an effective disguise for the Prince of Obristan. Add to that several days' worth of road grime and no bath, and no one would suspect the bedraggled, miserable soul making his way across Ascana was Prince Calidor.

But what they hadn't counted on was that movement throughout Ascana was now monitored and controlled. Gone were the days of a villager leaving his home to visit a distant cousin. Everyone had their jobs to do, and do it they would, unto pain of death.

They'd seen evidence of that, as well.

But Yarah had hidden them. Well, not hidden them so much as made them beneath notice, according to her. Lamorak didn't understand it. What he did know however, was that when a dragonkin would come in sight, Yarah would murmur under her breath, her hands would move slightly, and she'd slow their pace. If the dragonkin even looked toward them, its gaze would pass right over, as if they weren't there.

"How are you doing that?" Calidor asked her one evening, as they huddled in the ruins of a house, on the outskirts of a village that must have offended the dragonkin.

"It's my strength," she said. "Adapted from Raaleth magic, but I'm one of the best at it. Oponsi herself said so."

"So, you can make us invisible?" Lamorak asked, not for the first time.

She smiled a little. "No." She glanced at him, seemingly aware that he was jesting. "They just don't think we're important or out of place. It's like us seeing an ant cross our path. We don't even think about it."

"Unless we step on it," Calidor frowned.

"We aren't ants, though," she replied. "We can watch for the dragonkin and take steps ourselves to avoid any accidental contact."

So far, it had worked. For the last five days they'd been working their way back toward the border. Lamorak could feel the impatience and anticipation radiating from the prince. Of course, even when they reached Obristan, it was still several days walk to Greenfair.

But they hoped that Obristan was still free. Now that they knew there was— in fact— a dragon-overlord of their own realm, they'd hoped that the edict keeping dragonkin out still stood. Then, they could abandon their disguises, commandeer a few horses, and be home in two days, rather than a week.

From what he'd seen crossing Ascana, though, Lamorak didn't really think there was much chance of that.

"I don't suppose you have any way of moving us faster," he asked Yarah. The thought had occurred to him earlier today when they'd slowed down yet again due to another dragonkin nearby.

Yarah shook her head. "No. No one can do that. There are rumors that the Elder races could, but if so, no one has figured it out yet. Even when or if they do, it can sometimes take years to understand what they're talking about and *then* try to adapt it to be used by us."

Prince Calidor nodded. "It's fascinating," he said. "The things you can do. I would love to see the towers someday. I've always meant to…" He stopped and shrugged. "But finding the time is hard."

"You'd be welcome," Yarah said. "Especially now. Since it would mean we were free once more."

They settled into talk of what had happened to bring humans under dragon rule. There was debate over whether humans had ever been truly self-governing. And what would happen if the dragons were gone.

All of it was a bit much for Lamorak. Honestly, until the disaster of Festival, he'd never really thought the world was that bad a place. Oh, he supposed he wouldn't have wanted to live in Reclium. But even there, he felt quite sure that those born to it knew no better.

He watched Calidor and Yarah discuss these things, only half-listening. He had to smile, though. Yarah was an attractive woman. Very attractive. And Lamorak didn't think for one second that fact was lost on the prince.

Well, they were all adults. He just hoped that whatever happened between them, if anything, Yarah kept making the dragonkin pay no attention to them. He didn't like his odds of fighting one without Rainaldus nearby.

Lamorak let out a huge sigh of relief when he saw the same border house that they'd stayed in when they'd first crossed from Obristan to Ascana. It was still standing, apparently unscathed.

After everything they had been through in Manse, the terror of trying to escape the city, and then the constant fear and apprehension about being discovered as they'd made their way toward home, he had been sure that they would have found their way blocked. But he couldn't even see any sign of the stupid barrier the Ascani soldiers had put across the road to demand a toll.

The one thing that was missing— and that gave him reason to be cautious— is that there didn't appear to be any other travelers, either. Which meant that their presence was going to attract notice.

"Yarah," he said. "How long can you make us unremarkable for?"

"I don't have to try hard with you," she said.

He glanced at her in surprise, but her barb had been half-hearted. She was standing beside him, peering at the seemingly empty way-house like he was.

"I suppose the road wardens are holed up in there," Prince Calidor said.

Lamorak nodded. "At least. But that wouldn't really bother me. From what I saw of them, we could handle ourselves if need be."

"Are you forgetting that you don't have your armor?"

"Never."

And he hadn't. Nor could he. For Lamorak, not wearing his armor felt like he was walking around naked. At least in times of trouble. he had to admit, though, it had turned out for the better that he and Rainaldus had left theirs in Manse. It would have been harder, if not impossible, for Yarah to do as she had if he was wearing it. Plus, it would have slowed them down a great deal.

He was still Honor Guard, however. He had still dedicated most of his life to making sure the prince was safe at all times. He trained every day.

Border guards would have no chance against him. With or without his armor.

"No," Prince Calidor smiled. "I don't suppose you did forget. Still, if we can get past without conflict, all the better."

"Of course," Lamorak said.

He felt a brief surge of disappointment. After the last several days, he felt like he could use a little pressure relief. But, the prince was right, of course. Why look for trouble they didn't need, especially not knowing what awaited them on the other side of the border?

"Let's just go slow," Yarah said. "I'll cast the magic, but something doesn't feel right here."

They continued toward the way-house that was tucked under the eaves of the forest behind it. The same forest where the bolt that had killed Lord Campbell had come out of. This time, Lamorak very much doubted there were any hidden assassins. If any still remained alive, they were keeping their heads down for the moment.

As they neared, the door to the way-house opened and a man stepped out. He wore the same uniform they'd seen before, but he didn't appear to be looking for them. Instead, he squinted up at the sky, yawned, and stretched his arms as far overhead as he could get them. He sniffed and walked into the road, looked up and down it, with his gaze passing right over the three of them, then walked toward the back of the building and the small privy.

"Maybe it's just him," Lamorak said quietly.

Of course, they knew it wasn't, but since there wasn't much traffic, they hoped any others would be asleep or occupied. Probably only one at a time actually bothered to watch the road, and the man whose turn it was had just wandered off to answer the call of nature.

All they needed to do was get past the way-house at the border and a few hundred feet down the road. They'd be well into Obristan by then, plus the road took a turn, so they'd be out of sight.

As they drew near the house, they saw a dragonkin lying on the far side of it. They hadn't even noticed it before because it was on the shady side of the building and its black scales blended in with the shadows.

Only one, though, Lamorak thought. Yarah can keep us safe from that one...

As soon as that thought went through his mind, the dragonkin's eyes opened, and it stared directly at them. It was almost as if some unseen informant had whispered in its ear.

The dragonkin sat up and spoke.

"Who are you and where are you going?"

Lamorak and Yarah both froze, unsure of how to answer. If the dragonkin had sensed Yarah's magic, he wasn't acting letting on. Still, how to answer?

It was Prince Calidor who took the lead.

"Begging your pardon, your lordship," he sniveled. He'd put on an accent that made him sound the most uneducated lout to ever grace the earth. "We've come a long ways, you see. From Festival. Bad doings, there, your lordship. Bad doings. Now we just want to get home to the farm." He shook his head sadly and allowed a hitch to enter it. "We never should have left it. My poor Linelle. She… she…" Calidor sniffed loudly and wiped his nose on his sleeve, before breaking off into a mumble.

The dragonkin studied them intently.

"From Obristan? All of you?"

He was staring directly at Yarah as he said it. Her dark skin clearly marked her as being from Droy Thus.

She bent her head quickly. "My parents were ill-favored, sir. They escaped Droy Thus and made it to Obristan. Started a little farm of their own. My beau here," she snaked an arm through Lamorak's, "thought to take me to Festival."

The dragonkin snorted, obviously believing he had nothing worthwhile in front of him.

"Who told you that you could wander the land freely?"

They looked at each other, then back to the dragonkin. "Why, no one, your lordship," Calidor whined. "We haven't seen nary a soul since being on the road."

An outrageous lie, and one unlikely to be believed. The dragonkin narrowed its eyes.

"And how did that happen?"

"We traveled at night," Lamorak put in, trying to keep his voice as humble as he could. "We were afraid of robbers and thugs. So we hid during the day and only traveled in the dark."

The dragonkin studied Lamorak and took in the sword hanging from his hip. "Farmer, huh? Then why do you carry the weapon?"

"This?" Lamorak tried to act as if he was surprised to find the thing hanging there. "Oh. I don't really know how to use it." He drew it clumsily but noted that the dragonkin readied itself even with that. He took an awkward swing and half-dropped it. "I found it... on a man who... well, they didn't seem to need it anymore. I thought maybe it would deter someone who was looking for trouble."

The dragonkin didn't reply. Then, "No one is supposed to be on the road. Certainly not here. Turn back."

"But my farm—" Calidor began.

The dragonkin reared back and spit. A wad of some thick liquid flew past Calidor's face. The prince cried out, almost in his own voice, and grabbed at his cheek with his hand.

"Run, human—" the dragonkin snarled, but before it could continue, it was cut off as easily as it had just stopped Calidor's words.

"Prince Calidor? Is that you?"

They spun to see yet another dragonkin land in the road behind them. This one was much larger, with no wings and brilliant blue scales that shone brightly in the sunlight.

Lamorak cursed under his breath. It was Shilong, the same dragonkin who'd greeted them when they'd first entered Ascana. The same one whose wing had been shot through by the assassins.

"Prince Calidor?" the prince laughed wetly. "No, your lordship. Not me."

Shilong tilted her head to study the prince more closely.

Next to Lamorak, Yarah had stiffened. Her lips were moving very slightly, and Lamorak knew she was trying to help Calidor fool the dragonkin. He only hoped her efforts would still go unnoticed.

"They're heading back the way they came, Shilong," the black dragonkin snarled.

Shilong glanced at the other, then returned her gaze to the prince. She studied him, then looked to Lamorak. He felt sure she recognized him as well, even without his armor. Then, she glanced at Yarah, and Lamorak knew for a certainty that the dragonkin knew what she was doing.

"My mistake," she said suddenly, pulling away. "Where are you all going?"

"Home, your ladyship," Calidor said. "Or least-ways, we were. But now... I don't know."

"Go on, then," she said. "And hurry along. I have better things to do than watch the likes of you."

"I said they were to run back the way they came," the other dragonkin growled. "They should count themselves lucky I let them do that."

Shilong stiffened, left the ground in a rush, then crashed to it again in front of her smaller cousin. "I say they leave," she growled. She towered over the other dragonkin and steam rose from her nostrils. "I don't want their filth in Ascana. What we have to put up with now is bad enough."

The black bristled at her implied insult and reared back. Shilong stood her ground, though, and after a moment, the black dragonkin snorted and dropped back to all fours. Its next words made Lamorak's heart freeze over.

"Nothing stops me from following them. Maybe I'll just kill them all when you turn away."

Shilong stepped even closer. "I couldn't care less about them," she snarled. "But now… they're under my protection. Just to make you angry. If any harms comes to them, I'll kill you."

The black seemed to want to fight, but also seemed to know it had no chance against the much larger blue. "And what if it wasn't me?"

"I'll kill you anyway," she said. "If you don't like it, go back to the dark where you belong."

She continued to stare at the black until he looked away from her. Only then did she turn back to the travelers.

"Go now, before I regret letting you live. Don't come back here. Obristan can keep you."

They hurried past, keeping their heads low and their eyes averted.

When Lamorak saw the prince glance up, however, he took the chance himself.

It might have been his imagination, but he didn't think so. As Calidor passed Shilong, the dragonkin inclined her head ever so slightly. Then, she turned and flew off, leaving them free to escape Ascana and enter Obristan.

Chapter 8- Somewhere

The mood in the immense cavern was no better than it had been for many days now. Ever since the first attacks on Haiteng's children, the dragons had snarled at each other, threatened combat, and finally agreed to hand over control of the situation to Gillbriss.

Already, Haiteng was beginning to regret that decision. He'd always known her to be cruel, but the methods she was using now bordered on sadistic. And the worst of it was, his realm was bearing the brunt of it.

He'd almost lost track of the towns and villages in Ascana that had been burnt to the ground by Chimbod's dragonkin or smashed flat by those of Fimbruss and their lightning. To say nothing of the terror Gillbriss's children were inspiring. Even Haiteng found them disturbing, with their almost unnatural ability to lie in wait unseen, until they were suddenly there. For humans, it must have been beyond terrifying. It was no wonder she had such tight control over Reclium.

And, yes, there was a part of him that envied his sister and what she'd done with her realm. But it was a very small part. He was finding that he missed the days of his people being happy and prosperous. Working toward the greater good, even as they enriched themselves in the process.

Now, though. Now his people were suffering. Crops were gathered and taken away without compensation to those who grew them. Families were separated and everyone forced to work, whether the task at hand was their chosen profession or not.

"I think it's time to stop," he began, starting off the meeting he'd called for.

Three of the others were there, at least as far as he could tell. No response had come from Tophonoss. He'd privately asked Chimbod to check for her presence, but his red sister had seemed preoccupied, and if she did, it was a very cursory check. If Tophonoss was there and actively hiding, it would take more than that to find her. And Chimbod was the only one with even a chance of discovering her.

Haiteng found that even more unnerving than Gillbriss's children. Their methods were creepy, yes, but at least they didn't have the ability to cause him harm. Tophonoss, though… well, who really knew what she could do.

But three of them were enough to resolve how to move forward now.

"And why is that?" Gillbriss kept her voice calm, but her yellow eyes were focused steadily on him.

"Because it's enough," he said simply. "They've been punished. The world can go back to how it was."

"This isn't about punishment," she said. "It's about making sure it never happens again."

"Do you think it will?" he argued. "After all this? Who would dare?"

Gillbriss snorted and turned her attention to Chimbod.

"And you, sister? Have you found those responsible?"

Chimbod looked up from where she had been staring at the stone floor. "What? I wasn't listening."

"That's obvious," Fimbruss laughed. "What's got you so engrossed?"

"The whole thing," Chimbod said. She settled back. "We say that the magic must have come from my wizards. I'm not disputing that, but I've found no evidence of it. None at all. The classes are monitored, watched over by my children and all of yours. I've forbidden the rebuilding of the tower that was destroyed. All new magic must be reported to my children. And yet we've seen no signs that anyone has re-discovered Raaleth magic. Or developed such magic on their own."

"Then you're not looking hard enough," Gillbriss snarled. "Watching and listening isn't enough. You need to put one or two of the masters, those who control the rest, to the question. Use fire, teeth, and claw. Whatever is necessary but get them to talk."

Haiteng could see that Chimbod had no desire to do such things. He couldn't blame her. He wouldn't have wanted to either.

"So what are you saying?" Fimbruss asked her. "That you don't think your humans are responsible after all?"

Chimbod took in a deep breath. "No. I'm not saying that. Yet. But it does make me wonder if our other sister may be right after all."

"Tophonoss?" Haiteng said. "What about her?"

"For centuries she's been claiming that some Raaleth still live, and for centuries we've been mocking her for it. What if she's right. What if we're looking in the wrong place?"

"Tophonoss is a fool to think that!" Gillbriss spat. "The Raaleth and their ilk are long dead. And if any do still remain, they're a pitiful last gasp of their race. They wouldn't dare draw our attention. Stop stalling, Chimbod. The attacks came from your realm, so it's time to increase the pressure and find them out!"

"If that's the case," Haiteng said, "then why are we destroying my realm?"

"Destroying?" Gillbriss laughed. "Hardly destroying. Changing… for the better. To make it more secure. We were wrong about one thing. We were wrong to impose the edict of separation. Look how well our children are cooperating. At the things they're accomplishing."

"Yes, but at the expense of my realm," Haiteng said. "Whether you like the way I ran it or not, it is mine!"

"Not just yours," Chimbod said. "My realm is suffering change, as well. And so is Tophonoss's."

"Neither of you have had villages and towns razed to the ground. At least, not to the extent I have. And you!" He spun to Fimbruss. "What are you doing? Your children are in our realms, yet nothing seems to be happening in yours!"

"Oh, it is," Fimbruss said easily. "I just don't need to waste my children's energies on it. They can help where it's needed most, which apparently is your realm, for the most part. At least that's what Gillbriss tells me."

He smiled at Gillbriss, who merely stared back at him.

Haiteng snorted. "Always the opportunist, are you?"

"Me? No. If anything I've been more careful than any of you realize. You keep fighting your humans. Make them hate you the same way Gillbriss's do her. I've taken a different route, and now— now that things are bad— that route is about to pay off."

Haiteng shook his head, unsure of what his brother was talking about, but giving up trying to figure it out. Fimbruss never had been the brightest of them. Let him do what he would. In the grand scheme of things, he was really almost irrelevant.

"I want it to stop," he said again. "The burnings. The killings. All of it."

"It's too late," Gillbriss said. "We can't stop what's in motion now."

"Lies," he said. "We can do whatever we wish."

Now, finally, Gillbriss did smile. "We can. And I don't wish to stop it. But we can be fair. I wish to continue our strategy, making the realms safe, until Chimbod has uncovered who was responsible for the attacks, or until Tophonoss's ridiculous fantasy comes true and she finds hidden Raaleth. You do not. You wish to open us back up to our children being impudently attacked." She looked at the other two. "Who else would like to side with Haiteng?"

"Not I," Fimbruss said. "Not yet, anyway."

Haiteng had expected nothing more. But there was a flaw in Gillbriss's little plan.

"What happens now? We're tied at two and two, so—"

"We're not," Chimbod said quietly.

Haiteng's jaw snapped shut and he gawked at his sister. He had just taken it for granted that she would back him as he would have done for her. They had always stood at each other's side.

"But how could you—?"

"Gillbriss is right," she interrupted. "There is something more. Something still hidden." She stared at each of them. "I will find it, and if that means I must use my sister's methods, then so be it." She snorted and shook her head sadly. "It won't be only your realm that feels the effects now, Haiteng. My realm will suffer as well. And when it's over, no one will ever dare oppose us again."

Chapter 9- Craydon, Ascana

There seemed to be no way out of Craydon, now that Kori was there. Somehow, in his travels across Ascana, trying to get back to Usturg, he had missed being spotted by any dragonkin. Had he been, he learned, he would have either been gathered up and deposited where they felt he would be the most use or simply killed. Either way, it wouldn't have been a kind fate.

Now, he was beginning to wish that had happened.

For three days he'd been staying with and working alongside Wyman. The older man had been generous in allowing Kori a place to stay, as well as a cover story as to why he was there in the first place. Wyman and Kori's mothers were sisters, and Kori had been visiting his cousin on his way to Festival, which explained how someone from Usturg ended up in that small town.

It wasn't much, as far as deceits went, but the dragonkin seemed to buy it, or at least not care enough to really question it. As long as they worked.

And work they did. From sunup to sundown. In the fields outside of town, harvesting crops or readying the soil for the next round. Moving the vegetables to a central distribution point, where huge piles of the same were already rotting. Guarded over by a black dragonkin, Kori had already witnessed one man torn to pieces for daring to pocket a half-rotted pepper.

If the farm work was done, there was cleaning to do. The statue of Haiteng needed to be kept pristine, with no bird offal to mar its splendor. Streets needed repair— holes filled in and missing cobbles replaced— although where they were supposed to get the new stones, no one seemed to know.

At midday, and then again at sunset, everyone in town lined up for the meal. It was usually a thin, watery gruel with a few scraps of vegetable in it, and maybe— if they were very lucky— a small hunk of grayish, tough meat. Kori ate every morsel and licked every drop of broth from the bowl, no matter how disgusting it tasted. Better that than to have an empty stomach.

To make matters even worse, there was no beer, no wine, no mead, no anything. Water drawn from the central well was the only thing they were allowed to drink, and the dragonkin hadn't put a limit on that. Not yet, anyway.

"I have to get out of here," Kori said, not for the first time.

As had become their custom, Wyman just nodded, then said, "All right. How?"

"Yeah, well, that's the problem, isn't it? Those things are always flying overhead. If not the blue, then one of the blacks."

Craydon appeared to be under the supervision of one blue dragonkin, native to Ascana, and two black ones, who should have been lurking in the ever-night of Reclium. Since they all cooperated, Kori supposed that meant the fights he'd witnessed at Festival were over and done with.

Too bad, really. The blue was much larger than the blacks. He thought that maybe, if they did fight, they just might kill each other.

Wyman nodded. "And those not flying are always lurking somewhere. Who would have ever figured something that large could move so quietly?"

Kori sighed and looked into the cold hearth. That was another thing collected to be "shared" and then parsed out sparingly. Firewood, they were told, was too precious to allow it to be used when not needed.

"I have to get out of here," he said.

Wyman nodded. "Yep. How?"

Kori scowled at him. "You don't really have to answer every time, you know."

"You don't have to keep saying it," Wyman returned. He glanced out the window at the darkening sky. "Anyway, it's time for sleep. Early day tomorrow."

Which was another routine they'd fallen into in a few short days. But saying it again and again didn't mean it wasn't true. It *was* going to be an early day. They all were.

"'Night," Wyman grunted and pushed himself to his feet.

He shuffled into the small room that passed as his bedroom and shut the door, leaving Kori alone to sleep on the floor. Rough bedding, but Kori didn't really mind. There was a roof over his head to keep the rain off and the wind away. That was enough.

So it wasn't the floor or lack of a pillow that kept him awake. It was the visions when he shut his eyes. Authgrim's charred body, still upright on his wagon, almost baked into place. Asta, sprawled on the road and barely recognizable.

Those sights had been with him every time he closed his eyes since he'd first come upon them. Most nights, they stayed dead, not moving from where he stared at them as he approached, over and over again, each time hoping to see something different. Other nights, they moved and pointed at him accusingly, or cried out to him in dry, husky voices, telling him that he had abandoned them and that if he was there he could have saved them.

But now, they weren't the only ones. He'd close his eyes and tell himself that tonight was the night he would truly sleep. Tonight, he wouldn't wake up with sweat beading on his face and arms, his breath too quick, and a stifled scream caught in his throat.

Yet every time, they'd be there. Authgrim, Asta, and now… the farmer and his wife. The ones he'd walked away from. Maybe he could have done something there. Maybe he could have stopped the farmer from getting hurt, or maybe even convinced the dragonkin to just leave them in peace.

Probably not. During the light of day, he knew that. But at night? When he saw them again? It was much easier than to feel that he'd been nothing more than a coward, just as he had been for fleeing Usturg in the first place.

Maybe he should have just stayed put and faced Slode's men. Maybe he shouldn't have run.

It was fully dark when he sat up, resigned to the fact that he wasn't going to get any sleep tonight. At least, not yet. He climbed to his feet and crept to the window, trying to muffle his footsteps so as not to wake Wyman.

Outside, nothing moved. No lights glowed in windows, and the tavern he could see down the street was as dark as everywhere else. No one even went there, now, since they weren't allowed to drink.

He sighed heavily and continued to look up and down the street, even overhead, trying to spot a flying dragonkin. But his gaze kept returning to the tavern.

They weren't allowed to drink alcohol. Yet, he'd never seen anyone bring it all out of the tavern. It might still be in there.

Which meant someone— a careful man, perhaps— could get in there.

For the first time since coming to Craydon, Kori felt a slight smile cross his features.

He opened the door slowly, inch by inch, so that any creak might be lessened. Not that he expected Wyman would get up if he did hear it. He would just assume that Kori had gone out to use the privy. Even before the dragonkin came, Craydon was apparently a town with very little crime. Now, no one would dare.

Except me, he thought, as he crept out. Assuming that breaking into the tavern for a purloined beer was actually a crime.

It was, of course, but... there were crimes and then there were crimes. At least that's how he was going to justify it to himself.

As soon as he was outside, he shrank against the side of the building, trying to look everywhere at once. He wasn't too concerned about other people. Most would be sleeping by now, and those who weren't would be huddled inside, hoping that they'd done nothing to attract any attention.

But the dragonkin were still there, and even if he could be sure he'd spot the brilliant blue of the one in time to hide— which was no sure thing, at all— the black ones blended into the night very well. Now that he'd had a taste of it, he couldn't even begin to imagine what constant life was like living under their rule in Reclium. At least in Craydon, they got some relief when the sun came out.

No one appeared and he didn't see the dragonkin. Taking a deep breath, he crossed the street as quickly and quietly as he could. The axe at his side gave him some comfort, even though it would be small help against the dragonkin. During the day, he left it hidden under a couple of loose floorboards Wyman had shown him. It was also where the old man had hidden a well-wrapped hunk of bread, a clay bottle of spirits, and a few coins. So far, they hadn't needed to dip into any of it.

But as soon as the day's work was done, Kori would take out his axe and rehang it from his belt. Wyman had asked him why, and all Kori could do was shrug and say that it made him feel better to have it on him, which was nothing more than the truth.

He kept his hand on it to stop it from swinging too much as he loped across the street. He took a moment to try the front door, but as he suspected, the tavern was locked tight.

So, it was on to plan B. He slipped down the narrow alley between the tavern and the building next to it, glad that the windows of that place were dark as well. It was the home of an older man and woman, who should have been spared from the work due to their age, but the dragonkin didn't seem to care. Kori had done what he could to ease their labors, but it wasn't enough. Both of them looked near death by the end of every day, a little worse each one. He didn't think they had much longer.

Around the back of the building was the door used to accept deliveries. Kori imagined more than one drunk had probably been tossed out that door at one time or another, but then reflected that this was a pleasant little town in Ascana, not Usturg. Maybe these folks didn't drink like those of the north.

Not that it mattered. This door was also locked, but there was some give to it. He put his hand on the latch and pushed with his shoulder, grunting softly with the effort. It moved slightly, then stopped. He pulled the door tight to the stop, then lifted the handle, pulling upward as hard as he could. He felt something catch, then he shoved hard.

There was a sharp snap and the ring of metal hitting the floor. It was loud in the otherwise silent night, but Kori stepped inside quickly and shut the door quietly behind him. With the latch now broken, it wouldn't stay closed, so he moved a wooden crate over in front of it.

Now, anyone who passed would see only a closed door. Plus, if someone did come in, he'd hear the box slide across the floor.

Kori grinned in the darkness. He was in! Now all he needed to do was find his way to the front, where the kegs of ale were stacked on their sides in great wooden "x's" behind the bar. There should be plenty of mugs, and he'd be in business.

Across the room was the brighter patch of darkness of a doorway. He made his careful way toward it, moving slowly so that if he did bump into something, he wouldn't knock it over.

But he'd only gone halfway when a light appeared in the front room and moved to the doorway.

"You could have just knocked," a voice said. A figure appeared holding a lantern. "You didn't have to break my door."

Kori froze, then realized how stupid that was. Not only did the person already know he was there, but they could clearly see him. The voice was that of a woman, but there was no trace of fear in it, which made him think she already had a plan in place should he turn out to be the violent type.

"I was thirsty," he said. "Thought maybe I'd grab a beer."

"We're closed," she replied.

"Everything is closed." He was hoping that she'd offer to pour him one anyway, but she didn't. Instead, they just stood there, she looking at him and he looking at a shadow behind the lantern.

"I'll go," he finally said. "I really didn't think anyone was in here anymore, so—"

"So you thought it was okay to steal from me?" The words were harsh, but not the tone. She sounded more curious than anything.

"I suppose I did," he said. "Not from you, specifically. But from the place, I guess."

She didn't say anything else for a minute, then she lowered the lantern a bit, giving Kori his first glimpse of her.

She wasn't much older than him, if that. Certainly not more than thirty. Dirty blond hair that was in need of a comb, and pretty-enough features, with a pug nose that he thought looked good on her. She wasn't a thin woman, but she carried herself with a certain confidence.

For some reason, she reminded him of Asta. Not so much physically, but— attitude-wise, maybe?

"You're not from here," she said.

"You caught me. I'm from Usturg. I've been trying to get back there."

"And now you really are caught," she said. "Where are you coming from?"

"Festival. I was part of a caravan that brought beer down from the north. Decided to stay and see the sights a bit. Then... well, you've seen it. The world went crazy."

She nodded. "You were at Festival?"

"I was."

She seemed to hesitate for a moment, then said, "You must have stories of things you've seen."

"I do." Not that he wanted to remember them all. "But telling tales is thirsty work."

"I suppose so." She turned away, but over her shoulder said, "My name is Antonia. You can call me Toni. Everyone else does."

He hesitated, then followed her into the front room. He was about to ask her if it was wise to have the lantern, when he noticed that she'd blocked the inside of the windows with fabric, pulling it tight so that no light leaked out.

Toni was already behind the bar, pouring beer into a mug which she then set on the bar top before pouring another. Kori left his untouched until she turned around and indicated that he should take it.

He took a long, slow sip, letting the beer wash over his tongue and holding it in his mouth for a few seconds before swallowing. He looked back at her and sighed.

"Best thing I've tasted in what feels like forever. My name is Kori Hordsson. It's nice to meet you."

"Nice to meet you, too, Kori-Who-Broke-My-Door."

"Sorry about that," he said, and he really was. "I can try to fix it."

"Don't bother. No one comes out now, anyway. You might as well drink up. It'll all go bad soon enough."

In answer, he took another long pull, then lowered his mug and wiped his mouth with his sleeve as he looked around.

"Nice place."

"Thanks," she replied. "My father built it. He used to be a sailor. Worked for a trader until he'd saved enough to move inland. Swore he'd never want to see the ocean again. But, considering what he named the place, I guess it was harder to let it go than he'd thought."

Kori hadn't even noticed the sign hanging, if it still was. Some people grew awfully attached to the sign advertising their business, or at least to the amount of money it had cost to have it made. Toni might well have brought hers inside for safe-keeping when the trouble had started.

"I missed it," he said. "What's the name?"

"The Inland Trader." She took a sip of her beer and shrugged. "He wasn't very imaginative."

Maybe not, but Kori thought it was a fine name for a tavern. He would have liked to have been there when it was full of people, all laughing, singing, and having a good time. Sometimes, lately, it felt like those times were gone for good, no matter where you were in the world.

"Stories," Toni said abruptly. She pointed her mug toward his. "That's the price for the beer. Keep me entertained and you can have another. Entertain me enough and we can talk about you coming back tomorrow night."

"All right," Kori agreed. "What do you want to know about?"

"Everything." Toni moved from behind the bar and took a seat at a table. "What else is there to do?" She tilted her head toward him. "You can start with that axe. It looks way too nice to be—"

"Mine?" he finished for her. Then he laughed at the look on her face, well aware of how his appearance had suffered ever since leaving Festival. Long days, longer nights, and no place to clean up. Not much had changed on that front since reaching Craydon, either. "No, you're right. It is. It was my uncles, who was the most worthy man I've ever met. I wish I could live up to him…"

Chapter 10- Lostin, Ascana

Nettie hadn't slept a wink. She'd lain awake all night, thinking of the next morning.

Home. She was going to be home. Not home as in where she grew up, but close enough. Home in Ascana. Out of Reclium forever. Away from its darkness, its horrible people, and, especially, its cruel dragonkin.

Captain Stanford had told her it would be mid-morning when they'd make the port at Lostin. He'd laughed at her obvious eagerness and told her that they could be the first ones off the ship, as long as she didn't hold up traffic at the end of the gangplank by taking the time to kiss the earth. Nettie had promised she wouldn't, but now she wasn't so sure she could live up to that.

Home. She was almost home! She shifted on her back, trying to get comfortable and still be able to see the light change through the small porthole of their cabin.

"Would you please either lie still or just get up already?" Viktoria muttered.

The other woman was lying on the inside of the bed, closest to the ship's hull. She'd fallen into the day/night routine of Ascana— having an actual delineation between the two— remarkably easily. Even if she still squinted when up on deck and preferred the evening hours.

Nettie had never known anyone to adjust to such a radical change in as short a time. With the little that she'd gotten to know Viktoria— the little Viktoria had allowed, really— Nettie had discovered that she was a woman of singular drive and focus.

She didn't train with her anymore, either. None of the crew did.

To Nettie's surprise, Captain Stanford had allowed Viktoria to take two short swords from the armory. Nettie had taken another, and the two of them— again with his blessing— had sparred up on the deck. Nettie knew she was outmatched in the first few moments. She lasted a few seconds more only because of the pitching and rolling of the deck beneath her feet, something which she was far more used to than Viktoria.

But, just as it had been with trying to see in the daylight, Viktoria adapted. She began to use the motion of the ship to her advantage, attacking when it tilted her way, retreating and evading when it didn't.

Nettie had the thought that the attack which had destroyed the Emerald Kin would have been much different if they'd all been able to fight like her.

Of course, the crew believed it was because Nettie was soft or that she'd felt sorry for Viktoria. But when three of them who had stepped up next were nursing bruises and a few nicks, they'd quickly changed their tune.

As a matter of fact, the only one who showed any sort of chance against Viktoria was Dommick. He laughed as he blocked her thrusts, grinned when he snuck in a swat with the flat side of the blade to her hip and laughed again at her disbelieving expression. None of it was mean-spirited, though. When he saw Viktoria's face darken with anger, he stopped taking it lightly.

Nettie noticed that his footwork slowed, as did all his movements. Several seconds passed before Viktoria thumped him squarely in the nose, and he went down with a squawk. The crew grumbled at that, since they cared much more for Dommick than they did Viktoria, but he defused the situation with a sudden outburst of pure merriment, before jumping up, bowing deeply to Viktoria, and thanking her for the lesson. Then, he called for wine and off he went, followed by several of his new friends.

Nettie had stayed on deck with Viktoria, both watching Dommick walk away.

"Can't stand that guy," Viktoria had murmured, just loud enough for Nettie to hear it. But she wasn't so sure she believed her. Not the way her eyes tracked him, anyway.

She shifted again, turning on her side, even though that brought her nearly face to face with an irate Viktoria.

"Just get up," she growled again. "You haven't been sleeping. You're as anxious as an orphan being watched by a kin. And worse, you're keeping me awake."

"Sorry," Nettie sighed. "I'm just excited."

She did roll out of the bed, though, making sure to leave the blanket over Viktoria.

"No kidding," Viktoria muttered. "I never would have guessed."

Nettie grinned. Not even Viktoria's sour mood was going to spoil today. And she was right, anyway. Nettie wasn't sleeping. She hadn't been most of the night and she wasn't going to fall off now. So, she sat and drew her boots on, eliciting another groan from Viktoria, and left the cabin.

The sun was coming up when she reached the deck. She climbed up next to the wheel, nodded hello to the helmsman on duty, and stared out at the sea.

There was a dark line across the horizon that hadn't been there the day before. Through the morning haze, it was indistinct, but Nettie didn't need to see it clearly. It was calling to her like a long-lost love. She knew exactly what she was looking at. Home.

A sudden misgiving came over her, and she slowly spun in place, scanning not just the steadily-nearing land, but the surrounding ocean. They weren't much farther out than this when the raiders had caught the Emerald Kin, but there was no sign of any other ships.

"Relax," the helmsman told her. "Jarl is in the nest. He's got the eyes of a dragonkin. If anyone could spot trouble, he would. We're in the clear. Even if he sees something now, there ain't a ship on the water that could catch us in time."

Nettie tilted her head back to look up. Near the top of the main mast was a wooden-barrel like construct. And in that was a man who didn't return her gaze. He was busy looking everywhere else. A man who knew his duty and took it seriously.

Nettie respected that, and it brought her a great deal of comfort.

She smiled at the helmsman, who returned it, then nodded toward the line on the horizon.

"Welcome home," he said. "I'm sure you've missed it."

"You have no idea," she breathed.

The line moved closer, grew larger with every passing minute. Somehow, though, they still seemed to be hardly moving at all.

Viktoria lay in bed, stubbornly squeezing her eyes shut, determined to get more sleep. She'd growled at Nettie, but, in truth, she hadn't slept much either. Unlike Nettie however, it wasn't because of excitement. It was because of something that she wasn't much used to.

Fear.

She didn't know where she was going or what she was supposed to do when she got there. Mrs. Cloven had told her that someone would probably meet her, but who? What did they look like and how would she know them? And what did they want with her?

Not her. Whoever they were, it wasn't her they were concerned with. It was the book.

She couldn't have counted the number of times she'd considered throwing the thing overboard during the voyage. It had brought her nothing but woe and trouble since she'd heard of it. Since Sormat had forced her to climb that tower.

Which brought her mind around to Dommick. What was *he* going to do? Not that he seemed too worried about it. He was the type that made friends wherever he went, with his good-looks and his outgoing personality. He'd probably have three women offering to share their homes and everything else with him as soon as he stepped off the boat.

With a curse, she threw the cover off and rolled out of bed. She pulled her boots on, ran a hand through her hair, and opened the cabin door. She didn't follow Nettie up to the deck, however.

Instead, she simply stepped across the narrow hallway and shoved open that door. It hit the wall with a bang, making Dommick spring up. He looked around blearily, his eyes wide open.

"What…! What's going on?"

"Nothing. Everything." Viktoria stepped close to the bed and glared down at him.

He didn't sleep with a shirt on, she noticed, and hoped that his immodesty ended there. It was hard to tell with the blanket covering his lower half.

"How did you do it?" she demanded.

"Do what? What time is it?" He glanced out the small porthole. "The sun isn't even up all the way yet. Why are you waking me?"

"I want to know how you did it," she repeated.

"And I still want to know what you're talking about," he returned.

Now that he was awake, he was becoming more aware. He turned away from the porthole and peered up at her.

"Should I read into this?" he asked, just as she was opening her mouth.

She shut it with a snap, then muttered, "Read into what?"

"This." Dommick indicated it all. The now-open door, the cover over his legs, the bed itself. "You barging in here. Are we going to finally figure it out?"

Her mouth opened, then snapped shut again. Then opened again. She was aware that she was gaping like a fish out of water but seemed unable to either formulate an answer or move.

"Oh, relax," he laughed. "I'm just kidding. Mind your legs."

He tossed his blanket away, revealing— to Viktoria's relief— that he did indeed sleep with his pants on, and rose. His shirt was tossed at the end of the bed, so he grabbed that and slid it over his head. Then, he sat back down and reached for his boots under the bed.

"So, what is it that you want to know how it was I did it?" He paused and looked up thoughtfully. "I think."

"The other night. When we sparred. How did you do that?" The words rushed out of her.

It had bothered her ever since it had happened. Viktoria wasn't stupid, especially when it came to fighting. Chaol had taught her well, and she'd learned plenty more on her own. She knew that Dommick could have beaten her whenever he wanted. He could have taken both swords from her in seconds, had her helpless in as many more. But he hadn't. She'd caught that he'd slowed down, given her openings, even the one she finally took to bash him in the nose.

It had infuriated her. How did this... this *fop*... manage to be so good at swordplay?

Dommick, as was typical of him, laughed. "That? That's what's bothering you and made you storm over here?" He shook his head. "Did you think that the son of Lord Maganti was left defenseless? I was taught by every life-taker Darkbreath Clan had at its disposal. And yes, that included Reyson. I hated it all, but that didn't mean I didn't learn. And Father brought in others to teach me as well. I can read several languages, including those not even spoken anymore. I know the proper form of address in the unlikely event I should run into the prince of Obristan or even one of the dragons. I can do sums in my head and know the value of all sorts of commodities. In short, my dear Viktoria, I was groomed to be heir to the throne. The next head of Darkbreath Clan."

"And yet you spent all your time being a drunken lout," she said when he wound down.

"Well, not *all* my time. Just a significant part of it. I found that I much preferred the company of a bottle of wine to that of a fighting master who reveled in leaving bruises. Who wouldn't?"

"Anyone who had to fight every day to survive," she told him.

His answer made sense, but it didn't bring her any comfort. Instead, it just made her feel worse.

Her, and people like her, did fight every day, in one way or the other. Just to survive the streets of Heldum. To keep one step ahead of those who wanted what little she had. To avoid the dragonkins' notice, to not be made into a plaything for their amusement.

And here *he* was. Raised rich and with every advantage, and he'd shown her just what a difference that made. He took the one thing that she thought set her apart, the one thing that made her somewhat special, and made a mockery of it.

But his face had fallen at her words. "I never thought of that," he said. "I suppose... well, I'm sorry that you—"

"Forget it," she said and spun away from him. "I'm going up. When we've landed, good luck to you."

She stepped back into the hallway and turned for the ladder leading to the deck. Behind her, Dommick might have started to say something, but if so, it was drowned out by the cry from overhead.

"Land in one bell! Land in one bell!"

"A bell is an hour of time," Nettie told Viktoria.

The woman's sour mood hadn't improved any once she had arisen, too, but Nettie wasn't going to let that bother her. Instead, when Viktoria had stomped up to her, demanding to know what the fool up in the mast was shouting about, Nettie simply told her.

"Why doesn't he just say that, then?" Viktoria scowled.

"Noise. Sometimes, when the wind is up and the waves are crashing, it's easier to hear a bell than it is to hear a voice. So, one bell means one o'clock. Two, two o'clock, and so on."

"So we're landing at one o'clock?"

"Not in this case," Nettie smiled. "The way he said it just meant it would be one hour before we were there. If he'd said two bells, it'd be two hours and—"

"I get it," Viktoria cut in. "Seems pretty dumb to me."

Nettie just shook her head and turned away. Let her think what she wanted. In an hour, a few minutes less now, they'd have docked and Viktoria could go her own way. Nettie wouldn't have to see her again. Plus, she doubted Viktoria would ever be on a ship again, so her opinion of maritime traditions didn't really mean all that much.

"I'm going forward," Nettie said. "You can join me or not."

With that, she made her way along the length of the ship until she stood in the prow. It wasn't going to get her home any faster, but it felt like it was. She was now on the end closest to land.

And when she got there? Then what? That was a question that had been gnawing at her ever since Captain Stanford had taken them on board. Nettie loved the sea. She loved the work that came with being a sailor. But… she'd almost died, several times now. She wasn't sure she wanted to take the risk anymore. Maybe it was time for her to truly go home. Back inland, to where her parents still had a small farm, as far as she knew. She didn't really want to be a farmer, but maybe could make something out of herself in the nearby village, open a business of some kind.

Maybe. But as she felt the spray of the ocean on her skin and smelled the brine, she wasn't so sure she could give up the ocean. Maybe she'd just take a short rest, somewhere near the shore, and then go back to sea when the waves called for her.

"What's it like?" Viktoria asked from behind her.

Nettie glanced back, but Viktoria was looking at the shoreline, not her.

"What's what like?"

"Living free. To not have to worry about dragonkin tracking your every move or who's trying to take everything you have and leave you for dead."

Life in Reclium, Nettie knew. She couldn't claim to have a large amount of experience with it, but what she had seen had been enough.

"It's... wonderful," she said. "If you had asked me a few weeks ago, I wouldn't have said that. I would have said that it's just life. It's just how things are. Now I know that's not the same everywhere."

"How do you decide what to do, then?"

Now Nettie did turn around. An unusual tone of— self-doubt?— had crept into Viktoria's voice. It occurred to Nettie for the first time that this woman was heading into a complete unknown. No friends, no family, no... anything. It must be terrifying.

"The same as the rest of us," she said kindly. "You just make the best choice you can."

Viktoria nodded, but seemed unconvinced, and Nettie knew how inadequate such advice was. Viktoria was looking for guidance, not platitudes.

"Tell you what," she said brightly. "When we land, you stick with me. I know you can't wait to get away, but we'll find the Minister's office. He won't be like the ones in Manse. They control everything in Ascana for Haiteng. But this one will be able to point us in the right direction, maybe help you find a job or give you contacts to move on to somewhere else if you choose."

Viktoria was silent for a moment, her eyes fixed on the horizon. "Why would you do that?"

Nettie thought back to a tongueless man who had walked through great danger to help her. "Because I can. Because it's the right choice to make."

Viktoria snorted, glanced at Nettie and said, "It's a wonder you made it out of Reclium."

"No kidding," Nettie agreed. "And I'm never going back."

They stayed at the rail watching the shore draw ever closer. The minutes ticked by, although not fast enough for Nettie. She couldn't wait to land. As much as she loved the sea, landing meant her long nightmare was truly over.

She could see the workers on the docks now, and even a little further into Lostin itself. Horses pulling carts, people walking and talking.

Next to her, Viktoria stiffened.

"What's wrong?" Nettie asked, but the other woman didn't answer.

Until finally, through gritted teeth, she said. "It can't be. It's not possible."

"What's not?" Nettie tried to see whatever it was that had Viktoria almost paralyzed by fear.

Then, she saw it. At the far end of the dock, creeping along with its head down.

A black dragonkin of Reclium. In Ascana.

Chapter 11- The Wilds, Usturg

The tent was much more opulent than his quarters in the temple, and Gunnvid wasn't sure he approved. Heavy furs across the camp bed, rugs laid out over the frozen ground, a sturdy wooden chair with a thick cushion and a large table that could serve as both an altar and as a surface for maps were arranged in the space, according to his specific instructions.

"Nice place," Visgar said, as he entered through the flap.

"You didn't knock," Gunnvid rasped, but his friend only smiled.

"Of course I did. You just didn't hear me because canvas doesn't make much noise when you rap on it."

Gunnvid grunted his amusement and turned his attention back to the tent.

"It's all a bit... much. Isn't it?" he asked.

Visgar shrugged. "Maybe. More than you've ever needed before, but nothing less than what you've earned. You're the head of the Children of Fimbruss. You need to portray yourself as such."

"It will slow down the march."

"It won't," Visgar reassured him. "We have plenty of good, strong men who are only too happy to load everything into a few carts and then set it up again that night. Trust me. All you have to do is get on your horse, lead the army, and off we go, ready to do Fimbruss's work."

Visgar could tell that Gunnvid was still uncomfortable with it all. But ever since being almost killed in a raid, then waking to see the brilliant white dragonkin standing over him and the wound of his throat closing by some miracle, he'd known that Fimbruss, and by extension his children, had been watching over them all. The fact that they'd allowed others to be killed just meant that they had a special fate in store for Gunnvid. The fate to spread the word of his glory, to bring others to his light.

By word or by sword, the choice was theirs. But one way or the other, the glory of Fimbruss was going to spread to everyone. Usturg first, or at least some parts of it for now. The dragonkin had come to their temple in Hofsfell, a smaller city about halfway up Usturg, going south to north. Their mandate now, according to Gunnvid who'd met with the dragonkin alone, was to march for Obristan. It was time to bring Fimbruss's mercy to those who had none of their own. On the way, they were to recruit more acolytes, bring the towns they came to into the fold, by whatever means necessary. And as their flock grew, they would spread Fimbruss's glory across the rest of Usturg, then into Obristan and beyond.

Gunnvid sighed and picked up the hammered silver chalice that rested on the table. He took a long swig of what Visgar knew was nothing more than pure, clean water. One of the many vices Gunnvid warned against was strong drink. Such things clouded the mind, took attention from Fimbruss, and left one open to falling deeper into depravity.

Visgar didn't know about all that. He was partial to a little beer or mead at times. Wine, when he couldn't get those. And having a little to help ease the transition of a young woman into the lifestyle that awaited her as a sister in the temple… well, that never hurt, either. Sometimes, he wondered if Gunnvid knew and just chose not to say anything to his second about it.

"How far are we?" Gunnvid rasped.

"A day. No farther. We should reach Narfasker by mid-afternoon, maybe early evening."

Gunnvid nodded thoughtfully. "Do we have a foothold there, yet?"

"A small one. Some true believers, a small temple that's really a converted store."

"It's a good place to stop, then." The older man shook his head sadly. "A town like that… it's begging for guidance."

"It is," Visgar agreed. "Tomorrow night, you can sleep in a real bed. We'll find a place in town to use as a headquarters while we bring Fimbruss's peace to the place."

Gunnvid nodded and groaned as he sat in the wooden chair. He hadn't wanted to bring it, but Visgar had insisted. His friend wasn't as young as he used to be, and riding all day took it out of the best of them.

Still, he thought, looking at his leader, he wouldn't have wanted to try Gunnvid in a fair fight. The man *was* getting older, but he was still all hard muscle. From his head to his feet, there wasn't a soft spot to be found. Not physically nor emotionally. It was actually one of the things that made him so effective. He projected a picture of strength and fortitude, even if his wounded voice wouldn't carry to a crowd.

Visgar's voice spoke for him. Most of the time, he even believed what he was relaying for Gunnvid.

"Have my tent set up outside of the town," Gunnvid said. "As well as those of the men. We'll go in when we arrive, give them a chance to come willingly into Fimbruss's glory."

"If not, we may need to spend a few—" But Visgar stopped talking when Gunnvid shook his head.

"No. There will be no delays. Those who see or are willing to keep open minds and come to us… those will be spared."

"And the rest?"

Visgar thought he knew. He was even a bit eager. Not so much for the bloodshed, but it would get the men fired up. They'd been promised glory and acclaim, but so far both had been in short supply. A little action, in the name of the cause, would go a long way.

"The rest," Gunnvid said, looking directly into Visgar's eyes. "The rest we burn."

Visgar entered Narfasker first, leaving the main body of their army to set up camp outside. The tents they raised, including Gunnvid's that was far larger than the rest, were easily visible from the town. He was sure their arrival had been noted, but he'd taken his horse out of the way before then, looping around town to the south, so that he could arrive when eyes were turned to the north.

All in order to give himself a chance to see what the town's capabilities were. Did they have a good, organized defense? Not many did, since it wasn't that common for armies to attack. Not when either side could be obliterated by dragonkin or Fimbruss himself. Skirmishes were accepted, and personal duels common enough to be almost beneath notice, but full scale attacks? Hardly ever and swiftly put down.

Which is what the Children of Fimbruss were counting on. The fine people of Narfasker would think it was a hoard of fools camped on their doorsteps, destined to be wiped away. Little did they know that they were about to meet those that spoke *for* Fimbruss, who were chosen to spread his glory.

Or something like that, anyway.

He left his horse tied up outside an inn, confident that it would be there when he returned, since he paid the innkeeper good money to ensure it was so. Walking along the streets, he could see why the place would need the Word brought to them. Dirty, run-down, and dangerous. Those were the first words that sprang to mind when he gazed around him.

He kept his eyes open for the "temple" that he'd told Gunnvid was there but was unable to find it. Maybe he'd been told wrong, or maybe it had already been abandoned, the Word dying out in this dung-heap of a town before it could take root.

That would be too bad. Such things didn't bode well for their acceptance when it was going to become necessary. Which was going to happen very soon now.

Still, people seemed amiable enough. The innkeeper had been friendly and only too glad to take his coin. Visgar greeted those he passed and most returned it with a smile or at least less of a frown. There were a few, to be certain, that had the appearance of those up to no good, but that was only to be expected. There were always a few.

Now, take this girl, for example. She was a pretty one, especially for a town like this. For any town, really, he saw as he drew closer. Blond hair, a nice figure, and fine features all helped, but it was really the way she held herself. Like someone who was proud, almost dignified.

"Hello," he said as he stepped near and held out a hand. "Visgar. I'm new in town."

She looked at his hand for a moment, then took it briefly. "My name is Estrid. It's nice to meet you."

"You, too. Estrid. Now that's a pretty name for a pretty woman."

She didn't blush at the compliment, which began to tell Visgar the type of woman he was dealing with. Either self-confident enough to accept the compliment, or someone who'd heard it enough to not take it seriously. He was finding himself intrigued to discover which it was.

"Thank you," she answered. "What brings you to Narfasker?"

"Business," he answered.

"Not much here for business."

"Well, we bring our own with us," he smiled.

"We?" She made of show of looking around and behind him. "Do you have a rat in your pocket? Or are you royalty?"

He laughed, caught off-guard by her sudden wit. "Neither," he finally said. "My... friends... are setting up outside of town. They'll be coming along soon."

"That sounds ominous," she said, and her voice was only half-teasing.

A smart one, he thought to himself, but to her, "It shouldn't be. Not with Fimbruss's blessings."

He watched her face at that. Her expression didn't change, but she did drop her eyes and say, "With his blessings."

"Ah, so you're a true believer, then? That's good."

"I am," she answered. "Through Fimbruss and his children, all things are possible."

She meant the dragonkin, he knew, not the army camping outside of town. Still, she was a believer. Visgar didn't want anything bad to happen to her, like being cut down before she could profess her faith. He would much rather get to know her better.

"Listen," he said, "why don't we—"

But her eyes suddenly flashed over his shoulder, and her already pale face grew even paler.

"That's enough talk, mister," a voice said behind Visgar. "If you want more of her time, let's see your coin."

Visgar turned slowly. The man approaching him was huge and one obviously well-used to meals. He was taller than Visgar with thick arms and legs, but with a prodigious stomach that hung over his waist. His beard and hair were almost jet-black, and he sneered at Visgar with the casual arrogance of a man used to being obeyed.

"Ah. I'm sorry, I don't think we've met," Visgar said. "You are...?"

"The one who's either going to take your money or have the cost of her time you've already spent taken out of your hide. Your choice, but make it quick. I've got things to do."

"Meals to eat, more like" Visgar said easily. "And I owe nothing. The young lady and I were merely passing the time, which is hers to do with as she wishes, no matter what you may say."

The man's eyes narrowed, but Estrid said quickly, "He's not from here, Hogni. He doesn't know who's in charge, okay? We can just let it be, right?"

"Shut it, girl," Hogni snarled, still staring at Visgar. "If I say he owes for your time, then he owes. So, mister, you can either pay now and walk away intact, or you can take more time with her, doing whatever you feel like, and pay more for the privilege. Or I suppose you can try to talk your way out of it, and then we can all have a good time."

As if his words summoned them, and some secret sign surely had, three other men materialized, all with weapons at their belts.

"Just pay him," Estrid said in a hiss. "Please, mister, I don't want to see—"

Visgar turned to her with a pleasant smile. "Please don't concern yourself, my dear. We'll resume our conversation in just a moment."

He turned back to Hogni. "I suppose appealing to your love of Fimbruss is out of the question?"

"Love of— what?" Hogni's eyes grew wide before he burst into laughter, his gut shaking. "Did you hear that. This guy asked—"

His voice cut off with a squawk as Visgar stepped closer, smoothly drew a long dagger, and slid it across Hogni's stomach. He stepped back before the man's innards could soil his boots.

Visgar took good care of his weapons, and the knife was no exception. It was wickedly sharp and sliced through the leather vest and linen shirt Hogni wore, as well as skin and the muscle underneath it. It would take a few minutes to happen, but Hogni was as good as dead before he sank to his knees.

Behind him, Estrid let out a squeal, but Visgar kept his attention on the other three men. They stared at Hogni, who was just beginning to topple forward, then at Visgar.

"I'd really rather not have to kill you all," he said calmly. 'But Fimbruss will forgive me if I do."

The men glanced at each other. One of them set his face into what he must have thought passed for hardness. "You can't get away with this," he snarled. "Hogni was Slode's brother. He controlled the—"

"*Was*," Visgar emphasized with a smile. "Not is. *Was*. By your own admission. I have no idea who this other— Slode, did you say?— was, but he's gone, too, presumably. So, I believe that makes them a horrifically stupid family, unable to determine whom they should bother and whom they should leave alone. How about you men? Can you tell the difference?"

He made no threatening moves. He didn't even hold the knife like he was ready for an attack. Instead, he held it loosely at his side, in his left hand. But his right was at his belt, where he'd hidden a smaller throwing blade. He could have it out and buried in an eye before the men could take two steps, leaving only two to deal with. Visgar liked his chances with those odds very much.

"Let's go," one of them said quietly. That one's eyes hadn't stopped darting between the now-still Hogni and Visgar, becoming wider and wider until Visgar thought they might pop out of his head. He, at least, recognized when he was outmatched. His fear just might make him an excellent addition to the Children. Fearful men became much braver and dedicated to a cause when surrounded by those who thought the same.

The one who spoke first continued to glare at Visgar. He thought he'd probably have to kill that one, at least. But then the man's gaze shifted and settled on Estrid.

"You keep track, girl. Every minute, you understand? You still work for us."

"She doesn't, though," Visgar said easily. He reached out a foot and nudged Hogni's body with his toe. "He and I came to an agreement. He got my blade and I got the girl." He smiled at the frowns his jest provoked. "What? Not funny?" He glanced down, then back up at them, almost daring them to move toward him. "No, I suppose it wasn't. The fact remains, though. Sweet Estrid no longer works for you." He looked over his shoulder at her. "Unless, of course, you still wish to."

"No," she said, her voice little more than a whisper. "No. I don't want to."

"It's settled then." He held out his hand behind him, and she took it. "This way."

With a nod to the three men, he led Estrid down the street. He didn't bother, but she kept glancing back, her disbelieving expression slowly registering belief.

"They're not coming after us," she said.

"I didn't expect they would," he told her.

"Who are you?"

"I told you; my name is Visgar."

"Yeah, I got that. But... *who* are you."

He looked over at her and smiled. "A child of Fimbruss, of course. As are we all."

She nodded but continued to stare at him. Visgar found that he quite liked the way she looked at him. He was suddenly very glad that— while not nearly as grand as Gunnvid's— he had his own tent to return to.

"Where are we going?" she said as they approached the tavern where he'd left his horse.

"To safety." He mounted, then lowered a hand to help her up behind him.

"Safety?"

In the distance, from the north side of town, a noise was arising. Not much at the moment, but it wouldn't be long before the screams were more clear.

"Yes," he said. "The safety of your new home. Welcome to the Children of Fimbruss."

Her arms felt nice around his waist as he rode out of town. Visgar was very glad he'd decided to visit first.

Chapter 12- Southern Ascana

It was harder going without Yarah turning the dragonkins' attentions away. Instead, they had to rely on simple stealth, and for that, as it turned out, the young man from Obristan who had chosen to stay with them was proving invaluable.

Akofi couldn't count the number of times Rainaldus said to hide, only to see a dragonkin pass by a few moments later. Most of the time, the dragonkin seemed to be on a mission, heading resolutely toward some unknown destination. Only a few times had one appeared to be actively searching for anyone who might be around.

For the most part, the dragonkin were gathered in the towns and villages that were still mostly intact. Akofi, Bekasi, and Rainaldus avoided those, keeping Akamah moving along with them. The other mage was slowly beginning to come around, although he was still a shadow of his former self. He had difficulty speaking and, at times, didn't seem to know where he was, who they were, or even remember that there was any danger. Akofi had begun to despair of him ever truly healing.

There were free mages who could have helped him. But any Akofi or Bekasi knew of were still far away, in Droy Thus, and they couldn't imagine any of them willing to travel to Ascana, with things the way they were. They would just have to hold on, hope that Akamah stayed strong enough, and get home as quickly as they could.

It wouldn't be too long now, Akofi thought. Surely no more than another day or two, then they'd be in Droy Thus. Hopefully, a mage skilled in healing would be at the border house. If not, at least they should be able to obtain gulari there. Then they would make much better time getting back to Lankari.

Another day or two, he thought as he hunched over and wrapped his arms around his legs, until they could be warm again.

Even though it was summer in Ascana, the nights were still chilly, at least to those used to the heat and humidity of the jungle. Rainaldus didn't seem particularly bothered by the chill, but then, he didn't think the young man was bothered by much. Beyond his hatred of the dragonkin, that was.

He studied the guardsman. Rainaldus sat with his back against the wall of the abandoned house they'd found. They hadn't dared build a fire, but at least they were inside. Even sitting, he seemed to be on guard, ready to explode into action at a moment's notice. It was a strange sort of comfort. Not that the wizards needed him to protect them, but his calm demeanor reassured Akofi.

"Why do you hate them so much?" he asked suddenly. Then, he stopped and laughed softly. He hadn't even been aware that he was going to ask. The question had just sort of popped out. "Well, I guess I should ask why you hated them before all of this. It's easy to tell why now."

Rainaldus turned his gaze to Akofi. He didn't laugh along with him, but neither did he scowl or frown, so Akofi didn't think that he'd annoyed the man.

"The world was never meant to be ruled by them," he said. "I just don't like the idea of humans being under their control. I never have."

Akofi frowned at that. He'd never really thought of them as being under Chimbod's control. Granted, she was the one who allowed them to use magic. And the dragonkin always seemed to be around for further instruction or guidance. But... control?

He shifted uncomfortably. What he had just been thinking actually *did* sound a lot like control.

"It wasn't so bad." Bekasi spoke up. "Droy Thus has flourished under Chimbod's guidance. Ascana has done very well under Haiteng. I don't know much about Usturg, but I've never heard of anything horrible from there. Besides, isn't it kind of hypocritical that a man from the one realm no one knew even had a dragon is the one complaining about it?"

Rainaldus's answering smile was tight. "You forgot one realm," he said quietly. "And before you make the argument that Reclium isn't controlled by those others, ask yourself this. Why do they allow it?

There are three others. Well, four others, really, I guess. Couldn't they ensure that those poor people weren't so tortured?"

Bekasi shrugged, but Akofi could tell by her body-language that she was warming up to the topic. He sat back and prepared to watch the debate, suddenly glad that he had brought it up.

"Maybe they have their reasons," Bekasi said. "Maybe any sort of conflict between them would be worse than letting her do what she wants. Look how bad even a minor skirmish turned out."

"That sounds like an excuse," Rainaldus said. "As if you're saying that your life is good, so it doesn't matter about anyone else's. Which, even if I agreed with that, the current— well, recent— situation wouldn't last. Eventually, they'd come for us, the same as they did in the past."

"Why?" Bekasi asked. "What would we have done to cause that? I'm assuming you're referring to the Evening Folk. But they went to war against the dragons and dragonkin. They were the losers, that's all."

"They were nearly wiped from existence. That's not war. That's annihilation."

"Maybe they deserved it."

Rainaldus didn't answer that, and it was even too much for Akofi.

"You don't mean that, Bekasi," he said quietly.

She glared at him, then glanced back at Rainaldus. Then, her eyes found Akamah, who was curled up asleep, as he was soon after every stop they'd made.

"No," she sighed. "I don't mean it. I was just… arguing. I don't like what's happening. I want the world back the way it was, and— right now— I don't care about Reclium."

"Understandable," Rainaldus said. "I don't like what's happening now, either. Which is why we're going to try to make them better."

"All we need to do is get home, right?" Akofi said to Bekasi.

He glanced at Rainaldus, but the young man was looking at the ground between them and wouldn't meet his eyes.

"Do you know something?" Akofi asked him.

"No. Why would I?"

Akofi considered the guardsman for a moment. He wondered if, like so many others had, Rainaldus was underestimating him. Akofi's nature had often given others the impression that he was arrogant, which led them to believe he was not nearly as smart as he pretended to be. He knew that about himself, but it was hard to pretend to be something he wasn't.

"You know more than you're letting on," he finally said. Why would Rainaldus hide anything now? "I think you knew Yarah before we had ever even met each other."

Rainaldus drew back a bit. "I didn't. I'm not sure why you would—"

"Okay, then. You didn't. But you knew *of* her. Or at least something like that. The revelation of this hidden tower of hers didn't seem to surprise you. And even if you knew nothing of Droy Thus— which I don't believe, by the way— for some reason, she says you've been called to that tower."

"No, it wasn't that... I..."

For the first time since running into the men from Obristan, Rainaldus appeared rattled. Bekasi had been watching the two of them, her brows drawn down.

"What are you talking about?" she said. "I don't understand."

"There's a whole... diverse... group. Spread throughout the realms." Rainaldus said, still answering Akofi.

"A group?" Akofi asked. "For... what? An anti-dragon thing?"

"Yes." Rainaldus looked up at him. "Like-minded people, I guess you could say. Even in Obristan, where we don't have dragons. There aren't as many of us there. But there are a few. Most of them come from your realm. Or at least, most of those I know about."

Akofi supposed he shouldn't have been surprised by Rainaldus's revelation. After all, he'd just learned of the existence of a whole secret tower, with its own Master that no one seemed to know about. And, that the woman he loved was a part of it and had never told him. So, finding out that there was some far-spread coalition wasn't... well, yes, actually it did still surprise him.

"Were you in on it?" Bekasi asked the guardsman. "Did you know what was going to happen?"

"No, not at all." Rainaldus shifted. "I'm not sure what happened. As far as I knew, there were no plans to attack any dragonkin. When the white one was attacked... when we lost Lord Campbell... I was as surprised as anyone. But I also knew what would happen if those men had been caught. They would have revealed everything they knew, which probably wasn't much, but might have been enough. So, I..."

"Killed them," she said flatly. "Right?"

"Yes. And I had to make it look like I had done it in a blind rage." Rainaldus took a deep breath. "It wasn't something I enjoyed. To be honest, it made me second guess what I was involved in, but then. . . Well, you know. Things really fell apart."

"What I don't understand," Akofi said slowly, "is how you became involved in the first place. Or any of you, really. You say this group is spread across the realms, but how does someone in... Reclium, for example, know about it? Are there free mages from Droy Thus going around recruiting people?"

"I don't know," Rainaldus said. "None of us were told everything. I didn't even know that we had a dragon. All I can speak for is myself."

"Then do that," Bekasi said harshly. "Tell us how that happened. Because I'm not sure I believe you. I think maybe you *did* know it was going to happen, and that you let it." She stopped and looked over at the still sleeping Akamah. "How many people have been hurt or killed because of what your group did?"

Rainaldus seemed to wilt under her anger. He shrank back against the wall as if recoiling from a physical blow.

"I didn't know," he half-whispered. "I swear. I had been told the time was going to come when we took action, but I had no idea it was going to be like this."

"You knew something, though," she said. "So give. How did your part in this come about?"

Rainaldus heaved a deep sigh. "My mother. She was the one who told me about the dragons and what had happened in the deep past. With the Evening Folk. She told me stories of them and how grand they had been. How the dragons had wiped them out, trying to kill every man, woman, and child. When she told me these things, it wasn't like a story to her. It was with anger in her voice, as if she were telling me of a great injustice that had happened only yesterday."

Akofi frowned. His own parents had been loving, doting people. He'd heard his share of bedtime stories, but they'd been delivered with funny voices and exaggerated gestures. He had loved them and understood at times that there was a lesson to be learned, but he had never been scared of them, never felt his parent's anger at an unjust world come through them.

"Anyway," Rainaldus continued. "As I got older, she encouraged me in a lot of things. Reading. Writing. She had a lot of books, more than anyone else I knew. But she also encouraged me to learn the martial arts. She put a wooden sword in my hand as soon as I could walk. And she trained me before I ever went to the Honor Guard."

"*She* did all this," Bekasi echoed, leaning forward. "Your mother. Where was your father in all this?"

Rainaldus shrugged. "I never knew him. My mother didn't speak of him, but... after some time, I had my suspicions."

"And they were?" Akofi asked.

"My father wasn't human, I think," Rainaldus told him. "Or at least not wholly."

Akofi looked at Bekasi, who was staring at Rainaldus. She snorted and sat back again. "So, you're still going to sit here and tell us lies. Try to make us believe in fairy stories. To what end, exactly? Just so we won't blame you and your group?"

"Hold on," Akofi said. "Even if it's not true, that doesn't mean he's lying."

Bekasi merely huffed in reply.

"He said he had his suspicions. That doesn't mean he was right. Unless he found proof of his father's... otherness... somewhere."

"No," Rainaldus said. "Nothing like that. I just believe it because of the things I'm able to do. Even when my mother dropped me off in Greenfair, at the Honor Guard, and walked away, I was already faster, stronger, and better than just about anyone else." He stopped and rolled up his sleeve. Across his forearm was one faint scar, almost invisible in the dim light. "Scars are like a badge of honor for the

Honor Guard. They show that we're working hard, we're training for all we're worth. They prove that we can take pain, that we won't be distracted when it comes to battle." He grimaced at his own arm. "I don't have many. This one and a couple of others. Two of them from Lamorak, as a matter of fact. The thing is, we can't just *let* ourselves get cut. That would defeat the whole purpose. The scars have to be fairly earned. When I try, even if I do hold back a bit, there isn't anyone in the Honor Guard who can touch me."

"Why not?" Akofi really did wonder. He'd watched both Rainaldus and Lamorak as they'd attacked the dragonkin. Both had seemed excellent swordsmen as far as he could tell, but he also wasn't an expert. Maybe there were subtle differences that told them apart.

"When we fight, it almost feels like time slows down for me. Everyone else is so slow. I can see their blows coming and feel like I have plenty of time to block or get out of the way. When I come for them, their parries seem clumsy."

"And that makes you more than human?" Bekasi asked.

"No, no more than having the ability to use magic makes you more." Rainaldus stopped and sighed. "But then again... yes. Not because I can use a sword well or fight better than most. It's because of the blood that flows through my veins."

"Right," she said. "Back to that. Your 'not-human' blood."

"Yes." Rainaldus looked at her, clearly seeking her understanding. "My father, I believe, had to be one of the Evening Folk."

Bekasi stared at him, then burst out laughing. Akofi, however, didn't. Instead, he quietly studied the earnest young man. If Rainaldus was making it up, he was a remarkably gifted story-teller.

"Of course he was," Bekasi snickered. "I knew you were going to say that, too. I just can't believe you actually did."

Rainaldus's face darkened with anger. "It's fine that you don't believe me. I didn't really expect you, or anyone else, to. Let's just sleep. Then we can try to get you back to your town. From there, I'll continue on, and you won't have to suffer my company any longer."

With that, he laid down with his back to them, facing the wall he'd been sitting against.

Akofi frowned at Bekasi. Even if she didn't believe him, there was no reason to mock the young man. He'd done nothing but help them ever since they'd met. Bekasi glanced at him, her expression neutral, as if she didn't care one bit what he was thinking. Then, without another word, she shifted over to be close to Akamah and laid down next to him.

Akofi remained sitting up with his back against the wall, thinking. What Rainaldus was saying had to be impossible. The Evening Folk were long gone, so how could his father be one of them? Unless his mother was as long-lived, which was impossible, of course.

He thought it more likely that the guardsman was just an incredibly skilled fighter, a prodigy with abilities beyond those he trained with. He suspected that in the wide world, Rainaldus would find others equal to his own capabilities. Humans could do amazing things.

The alternative, that he really was somehow different, that his father really was from a long-dead race, was... well, not impossible. Akofi had learned after the last several days that few things apparently were.

He sighed and stretched out, trying to find a comfortable spot to rest. Tomorrow, if all went well, they'd be back in Droy Thus.

It was then that it occurred to him that Rainaldus had deflected his initial question. If he really did know something of what they were going to find there, he hadn't said. Akofi didn't like the thought of that. But they had no choice. He needed to get back to Lankari and regroup. Find help for Akamah and let Kio know what was going on.

After that...

He turned his head so he could see the motionless Rainaldus. After that, he might just accompany the guardsman. He really thought he'd like to have words with the mysterious master of the true Orluduna Tower. That one, whoever it was, had a lot of explaining to do.

Chapter 13- Outside Pharax, Reclium

Everything was pain, on the rare occasion he was aware of it. For most of the time, though, he was just gone. Not even asleep, since there were no dreams. Only brief moments of awakening, followed almost instantly by gut-wrenching agony. His entire body seemed to be on fire, especially his right shoulder.

He was dead. Reyson was as sure of that as he'd ever been about anything, and one thing he had never lacked was self-assurance.

Why then, did he keep waking?

When it came again, through the agony, he caught something new. Cold. Cold like he'd never known. It cut through him, set him to shivering worse than the pain did. It was enough to bring him around a bit more, to the point that he saw dark sky overhead, the air clear enough to see stars. Something moved near him and the fire in his shoulder bloomed anew. So much so that it made him cry out.

Whatever that was near him laughed. A low, sibilant hiss-like laugh. Reyson knew the sound from somewhere, but he couldn't place it.

Then, more pain and, blissfully, the world went away again.

"Get up, human."

The words sank though the agony-filled fog in his mind. Reyson slowly became more aware, conscious of the fact that he had been awake again for some time now. Seconds? Minutes? Hours? That he didn't know, but the words weren't the first thing he'd noticed.

Instead, it was— as had become his life— the pain.

Only now, it didn't seem to be so much worse in his shoulder. That area still throbbed, for sure, but not much more than the rest of his body, both inside and out. Not enough that he would have noticed it had it not been so terrible before.

"Get up," the voice said again.

Get up? It was all he could do to open his eyes, and even with that, he wasn't very successful. His lids fluttered open and he saw that he was still somewhere outside, and it was still night. Bitterly cold again, too, this time with wind that seemed to suck the heat from his body and fling it away.

"Pick him up," the voice said.

Reyson screamed as whatever had caused the pain in his shoulder before returned, only this time on his left side, every bit as bad.

It made his eyes come all the way open, and he saw the world seem to tumble by, turning from one direction to another. It took him a moment to realize that it wasn't the world that was moving, it was him. He was being lifted, dragged by that shoulder, across stony ground, then up, until he was dangling from one arm like a broken puppet.

He managed to turn his head and look down at his shoulder, then immediately wished he hadn't.

Something black and wickedly sharp stuck out of his chest, directly beneath his left shoulder. Blearily, he looked away from it, and found himself staring at a dragonkin, lying on the ground only a few paces away. Even in the mental state he was in, Reyson realized that the kin was red, not black.

Black like the thing piercing his body…

He had a difficult time controlling his head as he tried to twist to look behind him. He didn't get very far before the pain held him rigid, but it was enough to set-off the kin behind him into another spate of hateful laughter.

A black dragonkin was holding him up. It had its stinger driven through his shoulder and was dangling him like a worm on a hook in front of the other kin.

So, he was bait. To catch what, he had no idea.

"Are you awake now, human?" the red kin asked.

Reyson nodded dumbly. Sure, he was awake and fit as a fiddle. Anything they needed, just so they would put him down and let him curl-up into to sleep, or death, or wherever it was he had been dragged out of.

"Drop him, Sormat," the red said. "Let's watch him crawl."

Before the black let him down, her head came around to face Reyson. Yes, he saw, without much surprise. It *was* Sormat. Oh, good. They were old friends. He chuckled at his own foolishness and felt a warm, sticky trail down his chin. He wondered if he had bit his tongue or if the blood was from somewhere inside of him.

"Hello, Reyson," Sormat hissed. "Do you have it?"

"Haaa'waaa?" Reyson tried to ask, but his numb lips wouldn't move.

"An idiot, like all humans," the red snorted. "I don't know why you insisted that we needed this one."

"He's useful. Or at least he has been in the past." Sormat turned her head toward the red. "Maybe we can make him that way again."

"I doubt he's worth the trouble."

Sormat looked back at Reyson. "What do you think, Reyson? Are you worth the trouble?"

He didn't know what they were talking about. But one thing was becoming clear, even through the pain. He *was* alive. The old woman had failed. Her poison hadn't killed him after all, which meant he could still go back for her. He could still make her rue the day she'd ever met Chaol.

He forced himself to nod. "Live… to… serve…" he gasped out.

Disgusting, really, and not at all what he meant. But it would play to the egos and vanities of the dragonkin, just as his obedience had to Lord Maganti for all those years. A small price to pay for the comfortable life he'd led. Up until now, at least.

"Of course you do," Sormat growled, and Reyson didn't think he had fooled her. "Well, let's just make sure."

She jerked her stinger back out of his body in one swift motion but angled it up so that the point tore more tissue on the way out. Reyson hit the ground hard and collapsed. He rolled onto his left, then back again when the pain lanced through him.

Then, he stopped rolling and laid still. He closed his eyes and breathed, pushing the pain down and away. It wasn't gone. He wasn't sure it would ever really be gone, but it was distant enough in his mind that he was able to slowly— very slowly— stand.

There. He may be wavering, and he doubted he'd stay there for more than a few moments, but at least he was on his feet.

Now, he opened his eyes again and stared directly at Sormat and the red dragonkin.

"What do you want of me?" he managed to ask.

Sormat had moved around to stand next to the much larger red dragonkin. For a second, Reyson hoped the red would crush her, but he knew better. Not as long as they had some mutual interest in him, anyway.

The red started to say something, but Sormat stopped her. "Wait. Let him find out."

Reyson wasn't sure what it was he was supposed...

His blood began to heat, almost like it was on fire. Within seconds it was flaring through his body so intensely that he thought his limbs would burst into flame. He cried out, fell to his knees, then pitched forward, slamming his face on the cold, hard stone of the mountain they'd brought him to. He never even felt his nose crush.

Reyson couldn't move. Whatever was happening to him was locking his muscles, freezing his joints. Even his chest didn't want to expand, and he couldn't draw a single breath.

A sharp stab in the center of the back, like he'd been pierced by a knife, and more pain, which he didn't think was even possible. But... he was now able to move. The fire slowly receded. To his shame, the sounds he slowly became aware of were his own sobbing, hitching breaths, and the dampness he felt between his legs was from his bladder releasing.

"The poison that's in you won't ever go away," Sormat said, her words coming to him as if she were announcing that he had just won a fabulous reward of some kind. "Never. It will kill you, unless held in check by my own."

So that was what the stab in his back was. By his count, Sormat had stabbed him now three times in... well, he didn't know exactly how much time had passed, but he thought it wasn't long. The old woman's poison had been fast working. Or Sormat had jabbed him many more times than he'd realized.

Slowly, he drew himself up. He could barely hold his head straight.

"What do you want?" he asked again.

"You belong to me now," Sormat said. "Not to Lord Maganti. Not to yourself. To me."

Reyson dropped his head. "Of course," he said. "Whatever you want."

This time, he meant it. Anything to keep that horrible pain at bay.

"Your job isn't done, yet," the dragonkin told him. "I need that book back. You're going to get it."

If it was that important, Reyson didn't understand why she didn't just send another dragonkin for it. But he wasn't going to ask.

"Oh," the red dragonkin said. "I just thought of something. How can this poor human go on with that poison in him, when you're the only one who can stop it from killing him?"

"Hmm. I hadn't thought of that." Sormat growled the answer, but she stared directly at Reyson, letting him know that this was all a show for their amusement. Whatever came next, it had already been decided.

"Well, the only thing I can think of is to make it so that the poison *can't* kill him." The red grinned, revealing long, sharp teeth.

"There's only one way to do that," Sormat replied, still staring at him.

"Please," Reyson said, using a word he had rarely uttered in his entire life. "Just do whatever it is you're going to do. Then I'll go get your damned book."

"So, you agree to our terms?" the red asked.

No terms had been spoken of. Not that it would have made a difference. Reyson had no way of stopping or avoiding whatever was coming next. Not only that, but his blood was beginning to heat up again. Now that he knew what to look for, it wasn't going to be long before he was on fire once more.

"Yes," he said. "Anything. Please, hurry."

He was begging. If he hadn't been in such pain, he would have laughed. He'd never once, in his entire life, begged for anything. He'd made plenty of others grovel, that was true, but he'd never been forced to himself.

"Remember, Reyson," Sormat said, moving closer, until her snout was directly in front of his face, filling his vision. "Retrieve the book. At all costs. Retrieve the book."

Beneath his line of vision, her tail snaked around and she stabbed him again, this time directly in the stomach. Even more intense than the stings that had pierced his shoulders, this one felt like it had ripped him open.

He screamed and would have fallen, but he couldn't. His body was again locked in place, arms thrown out to the side.

Sormat moved back to where the red dragonkin was speaking, fast and low, in a language Reyson had never heard before. He could see and hear clearly, he could feel the bitterly cold wind biting at him, but he couldn't move.

Sormat smiled again and began echoing the red, until their voices blended together. Then, the red stopped, letting Sormat carry on the intonations. She opened her mouth...

"No," Reyson tried to moan, but his jaw was as frozen as the rest of him.

The dragonkin's fire bathed him from head to foot. He could feel every second of it as his hair burned off, his skin crisped. He stopped being able to see when his eyes burst, and the heat was so intense he couldn't breathe.

Yet, he remained aware, until the flame had burned all the way through him, then there was nothing but black.

He woke, lying on his back, while the wind whistled around him.

The pain was gone. He felt like he might be able to move, so he tried, and managed to sit up much more smoothly than he would have thought he'd be able to. When he looked around, he was alone.

He could see more clearly— into the shadows of rocks and further down the mountain, as if the dark was no longer able to hide things from him. His hearing was better, too. He heard the cry of a mountain goat from another peak, as whatever had stalked it finally caught up to it.

What had they done to him? He looked down at himself and discovered that he was naked, but the cold wind didn't seem to have any effect on him. His skin was completely hairless and the puncture wounds from Sormat's stinger were gone, healed over completely.

The book. It was an imperative. As soon as he rose to his feet, he began walking, until he reached the edge of the small plateau he was on, then he began climbing down, ignoring the sharp rocks cutting into his hands and feet.

The book. It was somewhere out there, and he would find it. Before anything or anyone else. Above all, he would find the book.

Then he would...

The book.

Nothing else mattered. Not his desire for...

Nothing. Only the book.

Chapter 14- Orluduna, Droy Thus

The only thing that Sintifi could come up with was to drop his head and start weeping. Maybe— hopefully— that would confuse the black dragonkin long enough for him to think of something else.

"I forgot," he moaned. "She was with me for so long... then... in that town when the white dragonkin came and..." He broke off, redoubling his sobs.

He heard the dragonkin snort and felt a shove as she pushed past him, heading into the town. Sintifi took a chance and glanced up, but she had ceased paying any attention to him. Apparently, the grief of a human was enough of a spectacle to drive her away. Still, he remained where he was, hands raised to his face, prepared to continue his ruse if she turned back to look.

When the dragonkin had moved far enough away, Sintifi stepped off the path and back into the riotous growth of the jungle.

"Ilvisar!" he hissed. "Where are you?"

The Raaleth didn't answer. Sintifi looked around carefully, trying to spot a tree that didn't quite look like a tree, or boot prints that appeared from nowhere, or some spot of thin air that didn't seem quite thin enough. He honestly didn't know what he was looking for, though, so he just tried to keep his eyes and mind open to anything at all that could tell him where Ilvisar had gone.

All for naught, though. Try as he might, his search came up empty.

Finally, he peered toward the road again, then stepped back out onto it when he was sure it was empty.

There was nothing else for it. He'd have to go on to the tower by himself. Oponsi must be told— warned, he supposed— that a Raaleth was nearby. She'd need to know, and Sintifi was very curious to see how she would implement that knowledge into her plans. He could easily see her arranging some sort of delegation to journey to wherever it was Ilvisar had said the others yet lived.

That was something he wanted to be a part of. Not only was the chance to meet more Raaleth and see where they lived intriguing, but it was probably also the safest place in the world right now. If more Raaleth were indeed still alive, they had hidden from the dragons for centuries. The chances of them being found in Sintifi's lifetime seemed very small.

But first... he wasn't sure how to get to the true tower.

All of the villages of Droy Thus were sinkholes of magic. Concentrations of wizards, both those tied to the towers as teachers and other free mages who stayed nearby, made such places rife with spells. Chimbod and her children not only allowed it, they'd actually encouraged it. Advances had been celebrated and the study and refinement of already-known magic was a thing to be lauded.

Which made it easy to cast a few relatively minor spells allowing one who was in-the-know to travel undetected to the true Orluduna Tower.

Now, however, he could already feel the difference. Magic was still present, but there was a lot less of it. Less of the human type, anyway, and much, much more of that of the dragonkin.

Oponsi was nothing if not cautious. Sintifi was certain she must have taken steps to ensure the true Tower wasn't discovered. And, while he was a powerful mage in his own right, he was a novice compared to her. So, if she didn't want anyone finding her, no one was going to. Sintifi doubted that even Ilvisar would find the way without a guide.

He frowned as he studied the town. The red dragonkin had by now disbanded his class, but the white was still watching over his. The black had disappeared, and Sintifi guessed she was probably skulking around the town, watching for anything she deemed a danger to them, or at least an excuse in order to hurt someone. Sintifi had heard enough of what went on in Reclium to have no doubt as to the disposition of that one.

He would carry on his ruse of coming back from Festival, he decided. He would gain access to the tower that everyone knew about, and, from there, he'd be able to journey to the real one.

And if Ilvisar found him in the meantime, that was fine. If not, the Raaleth was on his own, and Sintifi hoped his disguise held out. Even Ilvisar would be hard pressed to defeat three dragonkin at one time. If, he reflected, that was even all that there were. Conceivably, another black could be lurking in the jungle right now, watching him dither about on the road.

With a shudder and a quick glance around, he made his way into Orluduna.

Ilvisar supposed he should have felt some remorse for abandoning the human, Sintifi, when the black dragonkin had shown up. Yet, as much as he liked the human, he was just that… a human. Cursed with unbearably short lives, did it matter that much if the dragonkin did kill him?

He supposed it mattered to Sintifi a great deal, but that wasn't why Arastug had sent him. He'd been sent to find out where the magic that compelled the dragonkin had come from. The magic of the Raaleth which some humans had apparently learned how to use. The life of one human wasn't worth betraying that mission. Not when the lives of so many more— to say nothing of his own people— hung in the balance.

The humans didn't know what they had unleashed. They seemed not to realize the savage extent the dragons would go to in order to remain in power. They would kill them all, down to the youngest babe, if they felt it necessary. And the humans weren't Raaleth. They didn't have the power, the knowledge, or the skill to hide like the remaining Raaleth and Helgarlug did.

Besides, Sintifi had shown himself to be resourceful. Ilvisar was sure he'd find a way to avoid any sort of true confrontation with the dragonkin.

And while he was doing that, it made it easier for Ilvisar to slip away.

Now, he needed to find that tower.

The human wizards had hidden it well, there was no doubt of that. He believed what Sintifi had told him. The last Raaleth who had lived there had hidden it, then a human had stumbled upon it and had added to the tower's magic, making it even more difficult to discover. But a home to Raaleth couldn't remain unseen to Ilvisar, and human magic was no obstacle to him. So, it should be fairly easy to find.

Except that it wasn't. He walked through the jungle, wrapped in shadows, unseen and unheard as he crossed in front of fearsome predators and skittish prey alike.

He saw nothing but jungle. There was no path, no magic gate that would lead to a far distant land, no anything.

Ilvisar stopped and considered. Perhaps he was going about it wrong, after all. If he had stayed with Sintifi, trusted his own magic to fool an unsuspecting dragonkin, then he might very well be at the tower already. Sintifi obviously knew the way.

He turned back, at once annoyed with and yet admiring the human wizards who had done such a masterful job. He'd have to make sure to compliment them.

But when he returned to the path where Sintifi and he had encountered the dragonkin, there was no one there. There was no sign of violence, either, which was a good thing, but Ilvisar needed to find the human wizard. It was either that, or continue searching on his own until he either stumbled on the tower itself or some faint sign of magic which would lead him to it.

His disguise still intact, he walked down the path and into the town of Orluduna.

Most of the buildings were simple huts, made of sticks and thatch. At first, Ilvisar wrinkled his nose at the primitiveness of it, but then began to see the village for what it really was. It was actually a masterpiece of humans working with what was available, rather than trying to force their presence into a hostile environment that would resist their efforts. Far easier to replace local logs than to import other materials from far away.

But the tower at the center of town? Ah, now *that* was a different story.

Made of some yellow stone, it soared into the sky high enough that Ilvisar had to tilt his head back to see to the top. The joints of the stone were so fine and fit so perfectly that they could have been the work of the long-gone Xarlug, but Ilvisar was sure the humans themselves had done the construction. Yet another example of what they could do when they set their minds to it.

Arastug had been right to send him out. In the years the Raaleth had stayed hidden, the humans had grown in all ways. Ability, power, knowledge, and— especially— numbers. It was no wonder the dragonkin were so concerned about them.

"New in town?"

The voice was friendly enough, so Ilvisar lowered his head from where he'd been gazing at the top of the tower.

"I am," he said. "I just arrived."

The person speaking to him was a female human, with hair that hung halfway down her back, dark brown skin, and a sturdy build. Ilvisar wondered how she'd react to his own golden-hued skin and pointed ears. But he kept the smile off his face as she addressed him.

"We're not getting too many visitors these days." She set down the bucket she had been carrying. Ilvisar saw a rag floating in the water that halfway filled the pail. "The dragonkin don't want anyone moving around."

"I must have been mid-journey when that was decided," he told her.

"Where are you from?" she asked.

Ilvisar smiled at her. "Far. It's a small village, really, up near the border."

"Oh." He thought she might question that, but she didn't. It did, however, make him aware that he needed to come up with a better story. "Well, I'm glad you made it here safely."

"Thank you. I am, too."

"Are you going into the tower?" she asked. "Or are you ill-favored, like me?"

"Ill-favored?" Ilvisar felt his brows draw down. "I'm afraid I don't know what that is. Although... I've never felt particularly ill-favored. Am I that hideous to look upon?"

She laughed, a harsh noise compared to the musical merriment of his own people, but still... from her, it was pleasant.

"No. Not like that. Don't you have ill-favored in your little town? It means those who can't use magic. Like me."

Ilvisar was confused. "I don't understand. Surely there are more people in the world who can't use magic than those who can."

The woman shrugged. "Maybe. Maybe in the other realms. But in Droy Thus, it's all about magic and who can do it. Since I can't, I get to do other jobs." She glanced down at the bucket.

"I see. And what sort of jobs are those?"

Before the woman could answer however, another voice cut in. This one belonged to an older woman, who strode to the pair of them as if she had something important to say.

"Why are you bothering this man?" she demanded of the girl, ignoring Ilvisar for the moment. "You know better than that. Resume your duties at once."

The first woman— the ill-favored— bowed deeply without another word, picked up her water bucket, and scurried away. It was only after she was out of sight that the new woman turned to Ilvisar.

"Who are you?" Her tone didn't change, just the person it was directed at.

"My name is Yeboah," Ilvisar said. "And you are?"

"Yeboah," she repeated, ignoring his question. "Are you expected here, Yeboah? Does anyone know you've arrived? Why are you here?"

She fired off the questions one after the other, making it impossible for him to answer even if he'd wanted to. The thought to shut her up with a simple spell tempted him, but he pushed it off, knowing that doing so would expose him. Simple or not, any magic he used would be different from that of the humans, and they'd know it immediately.

"I am not expected," he said pleasantly. "I'm a simple traveler. My family had a very successful mercantile in Ascana. I've been using some of that money to roam the world. My goal is to see all five realms before I die."

"Keep it up and that will happen sooner than you think," the woman scoffed. "Aren't you aware of what's been happening? The dragonkin are killing anyone they find who isn't where they're supposed to be."

Ilvisar let himself look concerned. "Surely not. This isn't Reclium after all."

He said it as a jest, but in a case of perfect timing, the same black dragonkin that had accosted him and Sintifi came around the corner. It was peering side to side and hadn't seen them yet.

The woman followed his gaze and her face paled. Without hesitation, she grabbed Ilvisar's arm. "Come with me. Now," she hissed.

Ilvisar allowed himself to be led away, feeling the woman slip her arm through his as they went, so that it didn't look like she was pulling him away. Instead, they were simply two friends out for a stroll.

"I don't buy it," she said quietly. "Your story of traveling. But I won't stand by and see what one of them will do to you. Keep quiet and do what I tell you."

She led him down the street, around a corner, and into her house. This was a nicer version of the structures he'd noted before, with several rooms that led off the main one.

As soon as they were inside and out of sight, she let go of his arm and whirled on him.

"Talk," she demanded. "Don't try that ridiculous story again. You're obviously not from Ascana. You're as much from Droy Thus as I am."

Ilvisar didn't know how she could be so sure, until he caught sight of his own hands. Of course. He'd darkened his skin to match Sintifi's. Humans were ridiculously aware of such things and most of them having pigments like he'd adopted came from the realm he was in now.

"You've found me out," he tried. "I'm a free mage, just trying to find where I might fit in."

"Try again," she said.

Ilvisar smiled, then took in a breath and sighed. "All right. Here I am."

He let his disguise go, revealing his taller form, golden skin, bald head, and pointed ears to her. The woman gasped and reeled back toward a chair, into which she sank, shaking badly.

"What... what are you?"

"Isn't it obvious?" He was already preparing the spell. Before he threw it, though, he walked swiftly to her, lifted one of her hands, and pressed his lips to it. "I thank you for the timely diversion. Now, it's time to sleep."

His spell hit her before she even had a chance to be aware of it. Not that it would have mattered if she had been. Her head dropped to her chest, and her breathing became deep and regular. Ilvisar took a moment to walk through the house, until he located her bedchamber. She was almost weightless in his arms as he carried her to the bed and laid her down.

She'd wake the next morning, hungry and thirsty, but none the worse for wear. And she'd have no memory of him, at all. Perhaps a slight headache when she tried to remember what the curious hole in her memory was, but even that wouldn't affect her much.

Ilvisar had been sincere when he'd thanked her. He could have escaped the black dragonkin easily enough, but she had thought she was doing something for a stranger. Such things should be rewarded. He muttered another spell and placed his fingers on her forehead.

There. Now the dreams she'd have would make her happy.

With that, he walked out of her house and resumed his search for Sintifi.

Chapter 15- Western Obristan

If Lamorak was prone to poetry, he would have said his heart broke anew each time he looked at Prince Calidor. Even not being much for literature or the arts, he might have said it anyway.

Their entire hope, ever since escaping the destruction of Manse, had been to get back to Obristan. Back to where there were no dragons or dragonkin and, therefore, back to safety. But Rainaldus had tried to warn Lamorak. What would happen, the young man had said, if the dragons decided to attack their realm? Without one of their own, they'd be defenseless.

Lamorak had thought Rainaldus full of hot air, to be honest. Griping about just another "what-if" to justify his hatred.

Now, he wished he could have looked him in the eye and told the younger guardsman he was right.

After crossing the border, they found that the red dragonkin from Droy Thus had burned farms and inns. The whites had devastated whole tracks of land with what could only have been lightning strike after lightning strike, while blue dragonkin had taken over towns to run in the name of Haiteng.

As for the black ones they saw, and what they had done to their victims, Lamorak didn't even want to think.

It was as if each of them had taken out their fury on the one realm that had no protector. Its people helpless, its leader away— or maybe even dead— Obristan was ripe for destruction.

"Why?" Calidor said, not for the first time. "We had no part in what happened. Why would they do this?"

"Because they can," Yarah told him gently.

"But…" He turned an anguished face toward her. "You said that Obristan does have a dragon ruler, even though we never knew it. Why would he—"

"She," Yarah interrupted. "And no one knows much about her, other than that her name is Tophonoss. But no one has seen her, so no one knows what color she is, or how big, or... well, anything beyond her name really. No one can even agree on whether or not she even has dragonkin of her own."

"She, then." Calidor took the correction meekly enough. His voice sounded to be that of a man about to break into a million pieces. "Why would she allow this?"

"Because she's as evil as the rest of them," Lamorak said. "Rainaldus was right the whole time. Whatever happened, it didn't take them long to turn on us." He looked around and sighed.

They stood in the ruins of what had once been a pleasant little town. Lamorak had never been there before, but it was like so many that dotted the countryside of Obristan. Not everyone wanted to live in a major city like Greenfair. Some liked to know their neighbors, be "bigger fish" in smaller ponds, or simply avoid the near-constant turmoil of such a place. To Lamorak, it seemed like a boring existence, but to each his own.

He couldn't imagine what had happened to make the dragonkin raze the place the way they had.

Very few buildings were standing. Most were shattered as if heavy weights had been dropped on them. Anything wooden was nothing more than charred scraps. And bodies were everywhere. Some simply left lying where they had died, no one left to bury them. But some had been... toyed with, he guessed he would say.

He didn't like to look at those. They had come upon them suddenly, as they came around one of the few still-standing walls. They'd been affixed somehow to large "X's" made of wood. Arms stretched overhead, legs apart. Their faces had a strange quality to them, almost as if they'd been melted. But the disfigurement wasn't enough to disguise the fact that they'd died in agony.

Calidor had turned his back with a sob as soon as he'd seen them. It wasn't the first such sight in the last few days, but they were getting more difficult to accept, not easier.

"We can't stay here," Lamorak told him.

"Why not?" the prince asked. His eyes were wide and slightly wild, as if he was about to lose control of himself. "Do you think they'll be back to knock down these few walls? Or to torture those poor souls some more?"

"Because we're out in the open. And even Yarah's magic is only going to go so far."

"He's right," she agreed. "I'm hiding us now. Turning any attention away, but if a dragonkin comes along, especially a red, they very well might sense the magic, even if they don't see us right away."

"We have to bury them," Calidor said weakly.

Lamorak scanned the area. The prince was right in that it *was* the proper thing to do. But even if he could find an intact shovel among the debris, it would take the three of them weeks to dig all the graves that were needed.

"No, Your Highness," he said softly. "We can't. Maybe someday we can come back and do… something. But today, we just have to go. We need to get back to Greenfair."

At that, Calidor's head snapped up. "Do you think they've been there as well?"

Lamorak shrugged, although his heart said that almost certainly they had been. "We'll just have to see. One thing at a time. First is to get you there safely. After that, we'll figure it out."

Prince Calidor closed his eyes for a moment, took a deep breath, and held it. Lamorak wondered how he could do it with the stench of decay that lay over the place. But when he opened his eyes, Calidor's momentary weakness seemed to have fled, or at least retreated for the moment.

"You're right," he said. "Let's move on. But hold this place in your memory, Lamorak. Tell your fellow Honor Guard about it. If it comes time to fight them, use it."

"I will, Your Highness," he promised, wondering if that's what he had been doing with the deep breath. Trying to draw it in so that he would always remember it.

Calidor nodded and began walking, turning back the way they'd come so they wouldn't have to pass by those poor people who had been toyed with.

But he'd only gone a few steps when he froze. Lamorak started to ask him what was wrong, but the prince's hand snapped up, telling him to be silent.

Then he heard it, too. The soft sound that had caught Prince Calidor's attention.

The sound of weeping.

Someone was still alive. In the midst of all this devastation, the near total destruction of the town, someone still had enough life in them to cry.

"Find them," Calidor said, using that tone that Lamorak had grown to know. The one that said he expected to be obeyed.

Not that he needed the order. Before the prince had even spoken, Lamorak was on the move, trying to pinpoint the sound.

"Over here," Yarah said, her voice subdued.

Lamorak hurried to where she stood, looking down. A small leg stuck out from beneath a slab of brick, still held together by its mortar.

"Get them out of there," Calidor said from behind him.

Lamorak bent and worked his hands under the slab of brick. He could feel how fragile it was and knew that if he lifted too quickly it would crumble in his hands. So he straightened slowly, pulling it up just a bit. It was enough, though. Yarah darted forward, grabbed the child, and dragged her out.

She couldn't have been more than ten, maybe twelve, years old. Lamorak was no judge of children, not having had any of his own or even siblings that he could recall. He had been sent to Honor Guard when he was about the age of this girl. He supposed his mother and father might have had other children, but, if so, he'd never met them.

The girl lay where Yarah had pulled her, her eyes still squeezed shut. Her face was bloody, but Lamorak thought most of it came from her nose and a cut on her scalp. Her one arm was bent at a weird angle, though, which didn't look good. Other than that, she was thin and filthy, but appeared to be in remarkably good shape, considering what she would have gone through.

Her sobs had quieted, but she didn't open her eyes. Yarah touched her gently on the shoulder and the girl flinched and shuddered but made no other movement.

Lamorak stood by, not sure of what to do. He wasn't good with children, and what could he possibly say to this one? "Sorry, kid. I'm pretty sure your whole family is dead, but at least you're still here?"

It turned out that he didn't need to worry.

Prince Calidor knelt next to her, while Yarah moved out of his way. From the look on her face, she wasn't any more comfortable with children than Lamorak was.

"Hello," the prince said softly. "We haven't met. I'm Prince Calidor. Who are you?"

Nonsense. That was the first word that came to Lamorak's mind as the prince spoke. "Hello?" This wasn't a casual greeting in the street.

The girl didn't reply.

"I understand if you don't want to talk," Calidor continued. "I wouldn't want to, either. Whatever happened here... I'm sorry I wasn't around to stop it."

The girl still didn't open her eyes, but the tears had stopped, leaving pale tracks in her dirt-covered face.

"They're gone now," the prince said gently. "The ones who did this. It's just me and my friends. There's Yarah. She's a beautiful woman all the way from Droy Thus. Can you imagine? That's a very long way from here. Say hello, Yarah."

"Hello," Yarah whispered, staring at the girl.

Her eyes twitched, just once and rapidly. The lids fluttered, up, then back down to squeeze tightly shut again. But she had seen Calidor and Yarah in that brief glance. Enough to know that it wasn't a dragonkin trying to trick her, anyway.

"There's one more, too," Calidor continued. "His name is Lamorak. Now, if you take a quick peek at him, you might be tempted to be scared. He's very big, and he's pretty ugly, too. But he's a good man. He's Honor Guard, if you know what that is. If not, I'll just say that he's a hero."

Lamorak felt both insulted and pleased by the prince's words. The insult faded, however, when he realized that his presence— his size and the scars he carried— might scare the girl if she wasn't warned.

The girl opened her eyes and left them open this time. But she didn't spare Lamorak more than a fleeting glance, and he didn't think she would ever be scared of a mere human again, anyway. She did, however, keep her full attention on Prince Calidor.

"Are you really a prince?" she whispered.

"I am. Although…" He sat back on his heels and looked around. "I don't think I'm doing a very good job of it right now."

The girl didn't respond to that. She blinked rapidly and asked. "What about my mother and father? What about Georgie?"

Calidor shook his head. "I'm sorry, dear. If they were here, I don't think they made it. But we'll look and see if—"

The girl sat up with a cry and threw her arms around his neck. She buried her dirty face into his shoulder and cried. She sobbed as if the world had ended and she was the only one left in it.

Lamorak supposed that, for her, it had.

They risked a small fire that night. Tucked away into the forest, far back from the road, they hoped it wouldn't be seen by anyone passing. Even a human could be dangerous at this point. Some who might try to curry favor with the dragonkin by reporting anyone attempting to hide in the woods.

But after the sights they'd seen that day, they needed it. Lamorak had caught a wild hare which was slowly roasting above the fire, the juice dripping into the flames and making his stomach growl. Across from him sat Prince Calidor and the girl. She was sitting with her left side molded tightly to his right.

Her right arm was in a sling and splint that held it steady. Lamorak knew some basic first aid from his time in the Honor Guard, and Yarah had taken the girl's mind away from any pain while he'd set the break. Even now, she wasn't showing as much discomfort as Lamorak would have expected. Yarah's spell had either been exceptionally good, or she was still blocking some of the pain.

Speaking of… he looked up as Yarah came back into the small circle of light. She'd gone off a short way, to feel— as she'd put it—

for any danger. Lamorak didn't know what that looked like, really, but he'd been around her enough by now to realize that magic was something beyond him. He understood nothing about it, so anything she said she needed to do, he believed.

It was a bit strange to trust someone so completely that he barely knew, but Calidor seemed to, and Lamorak had learned over the last few weeks just what an astute man the prince was. Far from the foppish, vain exterior he put on, there was a sharp mind there as well.

At the moment, that "sharp mind" was engaged in coming up with the most outrageous story Lamorak had ever heard. Three-headed talking dogs, a princess who could turn into a frog, and the moon watching over it all seemed to be the gist of it. He was mildly amused as he half listened, but the girl was thoroughly enchanted, which was the purpose, after all.

Finally, as her yawns grew bigger and more frequent, the story wound down. Calidor gently laid her down, wrapped in his own cloak, near the fire and motioned for Lamorak and Yarah to be quiet. Not that they had been saying anything.

It wasn't until the girl's breathing had deepened that he moved away from her and joined them on the opposite side of the fire.

For a few moments, they all stared into the flickering flames, before Lamorak asked the obvious question.

"What are we going to do with her?"

"Keep her," he thought the answer would be. But that wasn't what came.

Instead, Calidor didn't answer. He just kept staring into the fire, until, finally, he said, "I don't know. We can't leave her here. But she's not safe with us, either."

He was right, of course. They were still making their way across a land occupied by a cruel, hostile force. One that would think nothing of killing them all, if they were lucky. But…

"Is she safe anywhere?" he asked. "She was home in her village when everyone was killed around her. If that wasn't safe… what is?"

Prince Calidor nodded, as if the same thought had already occurred to him.

"They're in Greenfair already, aren't they?"

It wasn't the question Lamorak would have expected, but it had never been far from his mind, either.

"I would think so," he answered. "They can fly. They don't have to hide. We've already skirted small towns the blues have taken over. Why would they spare the capital city?"

"My thoughts exactly. Even though I haven't wanted to say it aloud. Saying it makes it feel more real, somehow."

Lamorak nodded. "It does. But saying it or not, I think we have to be prepared for what we find there."

"And you think that will be. . .?"

Lamorak thought about it. "Death, most likely. Maybe the Honor Guard and the Palace Guard, and the City Watch are all gone. Or maybe they answer to Haiteng now." He considered a bit more. "Actually, I think that's more likely. Why would they leave some towns intact, but destroy Greenfair? Especially since—"

Calidor glanced up at his sudden stop, his face set in a wry expression. "Especially because I wasn't there, you mean. No, it's fine. You're right. Of course, none of us knew this was coming, but still… maybe I should never have gone to Festival."

"Right or wrong," Lamorak replied, "it's done. And, for the record, I don't think it *was* wrong. Like you said, there was no way to know. But now, we have to get back there, right? See what we can do to fix things? Right the wrongs?"

Again, Calidor didn't reply. Only this time, he wasn't staring at the fire. He was looking beyond it, his eyes resting on the sleeping little girl.

"There are going to be more," he said.

"More what? Kids? I'm sure there will be, but—"

"Not just kids. Parents. Men, women. Old people. Everyone. Those who escaped somehow. Those who were driven out."

"I suppose there will be, Your Highness. I don't see how—"

"They're my people, Lamorak," Calidor said, cutting him off again. "I can't abandon them."

"I'm not quite sure what you're saying."

"Neither am I. It just… it feels like things are changing, again."

Silence fell, while Lamorak tried to puzzle out what exactly Prince Calidor was saying.

Chapter 16- Tophonoss

She was uneasy, and Tophonoss didn't like being uneasy. It wasn't a feeling that came naturally to her, or that she had to suffer with very often.

The worst of it was, she couldn't explain why she was.

It wasn't from watching what Gillbriss was doing. If anything, Tophonoss was enjoying watching her sister spread her own special kind of rule to the other realms. Even to her own. Tophonoss had never cared about her humans or what they were doing. As long as they didn't grow too powerful, and their silly weapons and armor were no danger in that regard. Let them play at their tournaments and their "preparations" for danger. They had no idea what real danger was.

So Gillbriss sending in her children to cause misery wasn't a concern. Neither was Haiteng extending his rule to some of the cities, including Greenfair, the human capital. And Chimbod's children could only help if it turned out that Tophonoss was right and the Raaleth yet lived.

As a matter of fact, it brought her great amusement to see the discomfort of her sister and brother. Neither Chimbod nor Haiteng seemed to care for Gillbriss's methods, which just made their smaller sister employ them all the more. If she wasn't careful, though, there'd be no more humans to serve them.

And Fimbruss?

Tophonoss had to admit to a certain regard for her brother. Another feeling she wasn't used to. For many years now, centuries even, she'd considered him to be the most vain of them all. She had also thought of him as the least intelligent, more concerned with his own self-image than anything else.

Now, she saw that neither of those things were true. Fimbruss had put plans into motion long ago. He'd let them develop at their own speed, bringing the humans into his "fold," as it were, and letting them think it was all their own ideas. Now, his realm was at war with itself, but only one side had any power or authority behind it. The side that Fimbruss chose, of course. From there, those humans who believed him to be some sort of divine being would spread into the other realms, converting more and more to their cause.

She should have backed Fimbruss to lead the way, she realized, rather than Gillbriss.

But, no matter, really. Gillbriss's methods work just as well.

So, why then, she mused, was she feeling as she did? Why did she have a sense of doom stalking her?

She flew low over the Great Forest, deep to the east in Obristan. Vast, unexplored tracts of virgin woodland. If the Raaleth were anywhere, it would be there.

But she saw no sign of them. Not a single indication of a person. Not a spark of magic. Nothing.

The others thought she was wrong. They always had, but Tophonoss knew better. The Raaleth, and maybe some of the others, those Helgarlug, were still alive. Hiding, but... possibly pulling the strings?

The magic that had sent one of Chimbod's children north and out of her territory had been Raaleth. Tophonoss was as sure of that as she was anything. So when had the humans been given such a thing? Chimbod could foolishly say they had stumbled on it themselves all she wanted. Tophonoss knew better. The Raaleth had come out of hiding long enough to share their magic with the humans.

There was no other answer.

Below her, she caught the fleeting sense of one of her own children. Fewer in number than any others, they were abroad in the world. They kept an eye on what was happening and reported to Tophonoss, keeping her aware of all that transpired. Yet, she still spared several of them to comb the Deep Forest.

The Raaleth would be found. They'd be destroyed utterly this time, along with any humans who had been in contact with them, but only after revealing what they'd been taught, of course.

Then… maybe then Tophonoss would try to convince the others that it was over. That Gillbriss could pull her children and her rule back into Reclium. Chimbod and Haiteng would approve, of that there was no question. Fimbruss, as well.

The world could go back to how it should be. The humans serving the dragonkin, the dragonkin serving the dragons. And the only ones left roaming the world at large would be hers.

But still… Tophonoss was uneasy.

Chapter 17- Craydon, Ascana

It was three days later when Wyman confronted Kori.

"Where are you going at night?" the old man asked him as they worked at picking up the broken cobbles from one street to bring to another. The street had been torn up by a white dragonkin, for reasons no one seemed to know. The prevailing feeling was that it provided busy work for the humans trapped in Craydon.

Kori turned his head slowly to peer at his friend. "I'm not going anywhere."

Wyman looked around, including overhead and at the tops of the structures on either side of the street.

"No one around but us," he said. He picked up another stone and dumped it into the wagon. "Even the other crew is off dumping their load."

Kori took his own look around. Not that he didn't trust him, but his eyesight was better than the old man's.

"Maybe so," he agreed. "But that doesn't mean I'm going anywhere."

Wyman chuckled and bent to retrieve another stone. "One thing about being old, Kori. You rarely make it through the night without having to heed the call of nature. Now, I don't know if you've noticed, but you're a large man. Tall, broad, and you snore like a herd of cows. You make a huge lump on the couch when you're sprawled on it at night. And an even bigger hole in the air when you aren't."

Kori scowled. Of course, Wyman got up at night. He was such a deep sleeper himself that he'd never heard him, so, up until that moment, it had never occurred to him. He had to laugh.

"All right, you caught me. I've been meeting a friend. Just to talk."

"Just to talk, huh?" Wyman gave a sly smile. "Well, if that's true, it seems like a damn waste. Look, I'm not telling you not to do it. If I was a younger man, and a braver one, perhaps I'd go find a 'friend', too. Just… be careful. All right?"

Kori nodded. "I have been. I always check to make sure I'm not being watched. Along the street, in the air. Everywhere, really."

"Good. And you bring your axe?"

"I do." Kori's hand stole to his belt where it usually hung. There was nothing there now to meet it. "To be honest, I feel naked without it. I haven't had call to use it that much, but I've been carrying it for so long it feels like a part of me."

"Understandable." Wyman put his hands to the small of his back and stretched. "That's enough for now. We don't want to make this cart too heavy." The sound of an empty cart rumbling into the street a bit down from where they stood signaled the return of the other crew.

Kori grabbed the handles, hefted, and began pulling the heavy load across the now rough ground. He grunted and didn't say much until they had reached the next street, which was still intact. There, the cart was still heavy, but at least it rolled more easily.

"Do me one favor, though, will you?" Wyman asked.

"Sure," Kori grunted. "Name it."

"Since you keep going to the Inland Trader, the least you could do is bring me back a beer."

Kori's laugh was more genuine than anything he'd let go in a long time. There was no moss on Wyman, that was for sure.

"I'll see what I can do," he said.

Toni opened the door to his soft knock that night. Kori had fixed the broken latch the next time he'd come back and had made it stronger. Now, even he'd have a hard time kicking it open, especially after a long, hard day of labor and not much food.

"We're going to have to stop meeting like this," she said, her eyes twinkling in the light of the lantern she held.

"Why do that?" he returned. "Seems to me, we've got a good thing going."

She didn't answer, but she did step aside to let him enter. Without waiting, she led the way to the darkened front room, where she already had two mugs of beer drawn.

"And what is this thing we have?" she asked him, as she picked hers up.

Kori followed suit and took a drink before answering. "Friends, right? Two people who have something in common and are helping each other through a rough time."

"And that's all, huh?"

Kori wasn't sure what she was asking. "Should there be more?"

"No," she said, with a little laugh. "No, what we have is fine. Why complicate it?"

He was reminded of what Wyman had said earlier. He hadn't really allowed himself to see Antonia as more than a friend. For one, Asta still ate at his conscience. He'd loved her, even if he hadn't known her all that well, and even if she hadn't returned the feeling. It felt... wrong, somehow... to consider being with another woman so soon after Asta had been so brutally murdered.

Plus, he liked Toni. He liked talking to her, laughing with her, even just sitting in the semi-darkness and nursing a mug of beer with her. She was... comfortable.

Romance could lead to all sorts of trouble.

"It's not that I don't want—" he began, but she held up her hand to stop him.

"It's really good, Kori. I'm just lonely tonight, that's all. Sometimes what's been going on gets to me, you know? And someone I knew disappeared today. I was supposed to meet her at the well. We were to bring water to the crew working the south field, but she never showed. I asked one of the dragonkin there, and it just stared at me. But I swear it was laughing when I'd turned away."

"Who was it?" he asked.

"The girl or the dragonkin? It doesn't matter, either way. It's no one you know. You would have liked her, though. She was pretty. Not like me."

Kori felt his brows draw down. "What are you talking about?" He was genuinely confused. Antonia *was* a pretty woman.

"That's why you haven't tried anything, right?" she looked at him over the rim of her mug, and Kori hoped the brightness he saw there was just mischief gleaming in her eyes.

"No! I mean, yes! Wait. Yes, you're pretty. Very pretty. I haven't tried anything because I didn't think you'd want me to. It'd be like… I don't know. Forcing myself in here to— to— well, you know."

"Rather than just forcing your way in here to drink all my beer?"

She laughed at the look on his face, then set her mug down on the table and walked toward him. She stopped directly in front of him, put her arms around his neck, and leaned in close.

"For the record, this isn't forcing," she said quietly, "This is just—"

Then she was kissing him. Deep and long, and after the initial surprise, Kori was kissing her back. She felt good in his arms, and her lips were warm on his. She broke the kiss and pulled back a bit, eyebrows up, as if waiting for whatever he had to say.

"—nice," he finished for her.

The budding romance, whether he had sought it out or not, made the days even longer. He and Wyman finished their task on the shattered street, then Wyman was called away to help rebuild a house which had "mysteriously" burst into flame, while Kori was put to work moving the cobblestones back to repair the exact same street he'd just moved them from.

That was life under the dragonkin now, apparently. Senseless busy work, designed to exhaust bodies and break spirits.

Better that, than what he'd heard lately, though.

Wyman had heard it from one of the other workers on that house and relayed it to Kori later on. *That* fellow had supposedly seen it with his own two eyes.

Two men had been forced to fight to the death. Craydon had one white, one red, and two black dragonkin in residence, although where they all actually stayed was something no one seemed to know.

The blacks had apparently decided to rebirth a favorite activity of theirs from Reclium. They'd taken two men, had them strip to the waist, and told them to fight. They weren't to stop until they were ordered to do so. There had been a clear victor after a few minutes, but— according to what Wyman had been told— when he'd stopped hitting the other man, one of the dragonkin had spit acid at him and told him to continue. They hadn't let him stop until he had shattered the other man's skull, and his own hands in the process.

Kori hadn't wanted to believe it, but Wyman seemed pretty sure it had actually happened.

"You didn't see his face," he told Kori, meaning the man who'd told the story. "I've never seen such misery and anguish in the face of a man."

"What's the point, though?" Kori asked. "Why would they do that?"

"Why ask why about anything they're doing? They just are because they can. And there's not a damn thing we can do about it."

The story was still on Kori's mind as he made his way to The Inland Trader that night. It was a beautiful night, or at least it would have been if he was somewhere else. Still, it was a relief to be off the street and safely inside.

Where he wasn't very good company. He'd only half-heartedly returned Toni's affections, saying that he was tired after a long day, that was all. She might have been a little hurt, but she tried to hide it.

At least until he didn't reply to whatever she'd just said one too many times.

"What's with you?" she exploded. "If you don't want to be here, you don't have to come. I won't die if I don't see you one night, you know."

"It's not that!" Her anger snapped him out of his glum mood. "Not at all. This is the best part of... it's the only good part!... of my whole day. I think about you all the time."

"Not right now, though, huh?" Her tone had calmed a bit, became a bit more teasing.

"No, I guess not." He took a drink and heaved a heavy sigh. "Things are getting bad. Really bad."

He told her what Wyman had told him, holding nothing back. If Antonia really wanted to know what had him so bothered, she needed to know it all.

"That's horrible!" she said when he'd finished. "It's…"

"Life now," he said. "At least here in Craydon. And apparently it's common in Reclium. Who knows? Maybe everywhere is like that now?"

"But where were the other two dragonkin while that was going on? Surely they would have put a stop to it, right? They're not like the black ones."

"You really think so?" Kori snorted. "They don't care about us. To them, we're just things to be used. I'm surprised they've left any of us alive."

Toni didn't say anything. Instead, she took a long drink of her beer. "You're just a barrel of laughs tonight, Kori," she said when she lowered the mug. "Maybe we really should—"

But if she was going to say they should go up to her bedroom or call it a night or even just get wildly drunk, Kori never found out.

The front door made a loud groaning noise, causing both of them to turn toward it. Before they had even made it all the way, though, the door exploded, the wood flying through the air in shards. Kori flinched when he felt a sharp pain in his cheek as a chunk caught him, and he heard Toni cry out, as well.

But a small cut in his face wasn't anything. Not when he saw what had caused the destruction. One of the two black dragonkin was in the doorway. Its head was inside the tavern, but its body seemed too big to fit through the remains of the opening. Yet, even as he watched, the dragonkin moved forward, the rest of it squeezing through the doorway.

Toni had been thrown from her feet when the door blew in, but now she scrambled up, holding onto her left arm, which was bleeding from a shard of wood driven into her bicep. Her face was pale, but Kori thought it more likely because of the dragonkin than the wound.

"Well, well, well," the dragonkin purred, enjoying the fear he must have seen on their faces. "What do we have here? Two humans, awake well after they should be asleep. And together in a place that should be empty." He cocked his head and looked past them, toward the bar. "And drinking alcohol. You both must know that's been forbidden. Humans get stupid ideas when they drink."

The dragonkin shook his head, as if he were confronting two young children who had disappointed him. Then, he drew in a quick breath, jerked his head back, then forward, and spit. A huge wad of something flew past Kori's face and hit the beer barrel in the upright "X" behind the bar. The force of it cracked the end, and immediately the acid began to eat through the wood. Within moments, beer was leaking out in an increasingly fast stream.

Kori kept his eye on the dragonkin, though, even while Antonia watched the end of her beer run onto the floor.

"This hovel will need to be burned, now," the dragonkin said. "I could summon Eillu and let her have the fun of setting it alight herself. Or… I suppose I could be merciful and let you do it yourself."

Neither Kori nor Toni said anything. This was the black dragonkin being cruel, as they were known to be. There was no real choice. If he hadn't already called for the red, he would at any moment. The question of whether the Inland Trader was going to burn or not wasn't real. It *was*. The real question was whether he and Antonia would be inside when it did.

"You don't have to do that," Toni finally said. "This place was my father's and I—"

The dragonkin spit again, this time hitting the bar front close to her. Some of the acid splashed on her leg, and she yelped and tried to wipe it away. Kori moved to help her, but the dragonkin's tail lashed around, catching him around the ankles and causing him to crash to the floor with a bone-jarring thud.

"Not so fast, hero," the dragonkin said. The amusement in his voice made Kori start to see red.

He turned his head far enough to see the dragonkin without getting to his feet. He was being watched in return. When Kori stayed down, the dragonkin withdrew a bit, then turned its gaze back to Toni.

"You were saying, human? Something you thought I should care about?"

"No," she said quietly.

She was being stoic, but Kori could see by the way she was standing that the burns on her leg were causing her great pain. That and the wound in her arm were going to add up soon, if he didn't come up with some way to get her out of there.

But how? This was a dragonkin. The same as the one who had destroyed the snow troll so casually. Who he'd seen crush a man so completely there was nothing left.

Who had threatened and almost killed a farmer and his wife who had truly done nothing wrong.

Just like Toni. And him! He hadn't done anything, either. It wasn't them who had made the world go to hell. It was... someone else, anyway.

He turned his head and looked at Toni. She was standing awkwardly, one foot half off the ground, one arm holding the other, blinking back tears of pain and fear as she regarded the black dragonkin.

And suddenly, it wasn't just that she was in pain. Her face was melting, the skin running off the bone beneath. Smoke rose from her body, and then she was burnt to a cinder. A human shaped statue of a cinder, still staring at the dragonkin. Just like Asta had been.

Kori shook his head and blinked. No. That wasn't going to happen. Not again.

He rose swiftly, and the dragonkin's head whipped toward him. But not in fear. Never that for a dragonkin. Instead, he was smiling.

"Hero," he said. "Will you save this building? Even at the cost of your own life?"

Kori's hand dropped to his axe, a move that wasn't lost on the dragonkin.

"You compound your crimes," he snarled. "First ignoring the rules, then drinking strong drink. And now... a weapon?" The dragonkin smiled bigger. "Thank you for giving me reason. Not that I needed one."

By the time he even finished speaking, he had spit again, but Kori was moving as well. The gob of acid flashed past him, splatting somewhere behind. His axe was in his hand, although how it had gotten there he wasn't quite sure. All he knew... all he felt... was rage. A white-hot fire that burned behind his eyes and made it hard to see anything other than the smiling face of the dragonkin.

That face grew rapidly, until it filled his whole vision. Kori heard a roar and wasn't sure what it was, until he realized it was coming from his own throat.

Even through his rage, though, he knew it wasn't going to be enough. He was just one man, with an axe, and this was a dragonkin. Those who had ruled the world for centuries.

Time slowed down to a crawl.

Why then, he had a quick moment to wonder, was it drawing back? Why did the gleam in its dark eyes suddenly seem to be filled with fear rather than amusement?

The eyes which weren't actually watching him. They were focused entirely on Kori's axe.

He was in the air, taking a giant step onto a tabletop and leaping toward the dragonkin. His axe came around so that he grabbed it in both hands, raised it high over his head.

When it came down, it was a small, pitiful thing compared to the size of the dragonkin's head, which was as big around as Kori's body. Surely such a blow would only cause a scratch, a minor inconvenience to such a creature. By the time he struck, Kori was starting to wish he'd sold his life a little more dearly.

Only the blow, when it came, was true.

Time sped back up.

The axe hit the dragonkin squarely between the eyes. There was a flash of light, bright enough to illuminate every corner of the Inland Trader. The blade bit deep and kept going, until the axe was buried in the dragonkin's head up to where Kori's hands had ahold of it.

The dragonkin tried to retreat but couldn't seem to get his legs to work. They scrabbled at the floor, smashing tables and chairs and sending others flying. His tail hammered a fast beat against the floor and there was a vile smell as he lost control of his body. The dragonkin coughed, and Kori grimaced, expecting the acid to hit him, but it wasn't spitting. It was choking.

The whole ordeal lasted only seconds. Then, the dragonkin was dead, and Kori was standing in front of it, dumbly wondering how he was going to get his axe back out of its skull.

"What did you do?" Toni breathed from behind him.

Kori could only stare down at the dead dragonkin. "I don't know." His voice sounded leaden. He swallowed hard. "I don't think we can stay here anymore, though."

Chapter 18- Lostin, Ascana

Even as they stared at the unbelievable sight of a black dragonkin in Ascani territory, Nettie felt a scream rising within her.

Why was it there? It couldn't be after her. No one had even been aware that she was in Reclium. And it had happened by accident, unless you counted the dragonkin of her own land trying to drown her as purposely putting her there. She groaned and moved back from the rail. None of it made sense at all.

Then her eyes fell on Viktoria and Dommick, both still standing at the rail, their eyes fixed on the same thing hers had been.

"You!" she spat. "It's here because of you, isn't it?"

Dommick turned to her with his mouth open, but she wasn't glaring at him. She was staring at Viktoria, who had tensed at Nettie's words but hadn't faced her.

"Look at me!" Nettie demanded. "Why else would it be here? You did something to bring it here, didn't you? Something horrible."

"I don't think…" Dommick started to say, his gaze shifting from one woman to the other.

Finally, though, Viktoria did turn to look at her. Her face was even paler than usual, and her eyes were wet with unshed tears.

"And if it is? What of it? Do you think I'll turn you over to the dragonkin to save my own hide?"

"Yes!" Nettie exclaimed. "Of course, you would! Have you ever once cared about anyone other than yourself?"

Viktoria drew back as if stung. Instead of answering, though, she only stared at Nettie, then finally said. "It may or may not be here for me. But I don't think so. Why would your Haiteng allow one of Gillbriss's children here? Why wouldn't he just turn me over to them himself?"

That was… well, that was a good point, Nettie had to concede.

Without the dragonkin actually in sight, now her sudden panic was beginning to fade. In its place was a vague sense of shame. Shame that she had allowed herself to succumb to it in the first place, and even more so that she had instantly blamed Viktoria. It didn't escape her that she had not for a moment thought to blame Dommick.

"Ladies," Captain Stanford said as he approached the rail. He kept his eyes toward shore and didn't look at them. "A boat has cast off and is heading this way. I have no idea why there's a black dragonkin in Lostin, but I suspect neither of you wants to be found. Nor you, boy," he said to Dommick. "They've seen me already, but I don't think they have you. Go to my cabin and wait for me there."

"But I—" Nettie started, but Stanford had already turned his back on her.

"Come on, Nettie," Dommick said quietly. He took her arm and gently led her to the rear of the ship and the door to the captain's quarters, with Viktoria following behind.

Once they were all inside, Nettie shook off Dommick's hand and cracked the door open, so that she could press one eye against the opening and hopefully see some of what was happening.

She could just make out Captain Stanford, standing at the rail near where they had been only moments ago. He was scanning the shoreline, but then something lower down, in the water, perhaps, caught his attention.

He spoke, although Nettie couldn't make out what he was saying.

Then a head rose up over the side. Nettie gasped. It was a blue dragonkin! One of their own! And bigger than any Nettie had ever seen. If the dragons were bigger yet, she couldn't imagine ever seeing Haiteng for herself. She didn't think her mind would be able to grasp it.

The dragonkin's head hovered over Captain Stanford, who had needed to step back in order to peer up at it. Water sluiced from the brilliant blue scales, but the dragonkin didn't seem to care that it was dripping on the captain. That made Nettie frown. In her few dealings with them, or at least those she'd heard of, the dragonkin were always respectful of their human allies. This one, however, wasn't proving that to be true at all.

Captain Stanford nodded toward shore, and the dragonkin responded. The captain was difficult to hear from where Nettie was hidden, his voice little more than a mutter, but the dragonkin was very clear.

"You will draw in closer, Captain, and drop anchor. No one will disembark until the dock agents have thoroughly searched your ship."

Captain Stanford muttered something else, but the dragonkin cut him off.

"They're here by the invitation of Lord Haiteng himself. Would you question that?"

"No, of course not." Nettie heard that easily enough. She also heard the "they." Was there more than one black dragonkin in Ascana?

"Then do as you're instructed, Captain," the dragonkin continued. "O else I'll need to consider this ship as suspect. It would be easier to inspect in pieces, wouldn't it? Nowhere for you to hide contraband from Reclium then."

Nettie felt like she was witnessing something that simply wasn't possible. First the black dragonkin, now a blue actually threatening a law-abiding trader? And what contraband? She couldn't think of a single thing Reclium had that anyone in Ascana needed.

The dragonkin finished giving its orders to Captain Stanford and sank back down out of sight. It could easily come up again, on any side of the ship it chose, but Nettie hoped it wouldn't. For the first time in her life that she could remember, she didn't want to see a blue dragonkin any closer.

When she stepped back and shut the door, she noticed how dark the cabin was. While she had been watching, Dommick and Viktoria had drawn the drapes to cover the two large windows at the rear of the room.

"Did you hear that?" she asked them.

"I did," Viktoria said. "I guess that black kin isn't here for me after all, huh?"

Nettie couldn't reply to the venom in Viktoria's voice. The woman was right, after all. She'd had nothing to do with the dragonkin's presence, yet Nettie had instantly jumped to that conclusion. She didn't want to feel the guilt welling up in her, but it was there anyway.

"No, I guess it isn't," she said, hanging her head. "Sorry about that. I was just... thrown."

"Understandable," Dommick said. He was looking over the sideboard where the captain kept a few bottles stored in deep holes in the top. He lifted one out, uncorked it, and sniffed at the contents. "You don't think he'll mind, do you?" Without waiting for an answer, he poured himself a healthy drink into a nearby mug. He held the bottle out to the two women. "Anyone else?"

"Put it back," Viktoria growled. "Before you get us kicked off the ship and given right to that thing out there."

Dommick snorted and drank half of what he had poured in one swallow. "We won't be. If we were, the Captain would have done it already."

Any reply was cut short by the door opening and Captain Stanford stamping in. He was sweating badly and his eyes had a wild cast to them. He spotted Dommick drinking and said, "Good idea, boy. Pour me one."

Dommick took the opportunity to refill his own mug while he was at it. He smirked at Viktoria over the rim before taking another swig.

"Never heard of anything like this before," Stanford muttered. "It doesn't make any sense." He downed his drink and held the mug back out to Dommick. "It's damn strange. Disturbing." He took the next drink slower, but looked over the three of them while he did. "I can't help but think it has something to do with you three. Then again, it might not. Maybe it's bigger. We've been away for too long to get much news. Either way, though, I don't think you two want to be found here."

"I don't either," Nettie said. "I don't know why, really, but I just don't want to be seen now."

"We certainly don't," Viktoria said. "But I don't know if we have much choice."

"We might," Captain Stanford said.

He crossed the room to the large desk that took up much of the floor space. It was made of dark wood and looked to weigh several hundred pounds. It was attached directly to the floor so that it wouldn't become a hazard in high seas.

He opened the top drawer and reached inside. There was an audible click. Captain Stanford stood, put his hands against the desktop, and pushed.

The whole thing moved, exposing a hole underneath.

"It will be a tight squeeze," he said. "But if you don't know the trick, there's not a force short of a dragonkin that can move the desk. Get in, stay quiet, and I'll put it back over you. When it's safe to come out, I'll get you. Until then, try not to worry."

He smiled wryly and tossed off the rest of his drink.

Dommick was the first one to the hole. He looked down at it, then hopped in. The floorboards came up to just above his knees, so Stanford hadn't been exaggerating when he'd said it would be a tight fit.

"Well, good thing we all know each other so well, isn't it," Dommick said. He squatted down and wormed his way under the floorboards.

Nettie and Viktoria looked at each other. Whoever went next was going to be pressed into Dommick for who knew how long.

"Well, go ahead," Viktoria said. "We both know you want to."

Nettie opened her mouth to protest, then thought better of it. Instead, she stepped into the hole and repeated what Dommick had done. Viktoria crawled in after her. There was barely enough space for the three of them. Nettie hoped the inspection wouldn't take long.

"All right," Captain Stanford said. From outside came the sound of the anchor chain being let out. Voices called from a distance, indicating that the rowboat was drawing near. "We'll try to be quick, but we can't make it look suspicious. I'll be back as soon as possible."

With that, he walked to the other side of the desk and pushed. The same click they'd heard before, only much louder and more ominous in the enclosed space, came again. The light was gone. Now there was nothing to do but wait.

With nothing to distract her from her thoughts, Viktoria's mind was racing. She couldn't get too upset with Nettie thinking that the kin was there for her. When she'd seen it, she'd thought the same thing. Only, it didn't really make sense.

Even from as far away as she was, she had been able to tell that the kin on the dock wasn't Sormat. Had it been, her panic would have been real enough to maybe make her leap off the ship on the other side in an attempt to hide.

But it wasn't. And Viktoria had begun to believe that Sormat was playing some game of her own. Something that had nothing to do with Gillbriss. So the dragonkin wouldn't have risked sending another here to retrieve her and the book. She would have come herself.

Then, the blue dragonkin Nettie who had spoken to the captain had confirmed her suspicions. The blacks were here by Haiteng's invitation?

That was unprecedented as far as Viktoria knew. There was something bigger going on than a couple of fugitives from Reclium. What that might be, she had no idea, but hopefully, it meant those coming to search the ship wouldn't be focused on finding them.

It was hot under the floor and getting worse with every passing second. Nettie's body heat radiated from her like the girl was on fire, and she really hoped that had nothing to do with her being pressed so tightly against Dommick. As soon as she had the thought, she wished she hadn't. Things were bad enough without having ideas like that running through her mind.

So, instead, she concentrated on listening. Viktoria had no experience whatsoever when it came to ships, but she had plenty when it came to hiding. When she'd just started out as a life-taker, before Chaol had even taken her under his wing, she'd often had to hide when a job had gone bad. That had happened more often than she liked to admit, so there had been plenty of time scurrying around a corner to bury herself in a heap of stinking refuse, or crawling between things into a crack that should have been too small.

This was the first time she'd ever had to share such a space, though.

"Do you think they're done yet?" Dommick hissed.

"Shut up, fool," Viktoria growled, keeping her voice as low as possible.

She knew he wouldn't. Dommick seemed incapable of understanding when danger was real. But if he had been about to say anything else, the cabin door banging open and Captain Stanford's voice stopped him short.

"This is only my own cabin," he was saying. "You're welcome to look about, but surely you can't expect to find anything in here."

"We'll determine that, Captain," another voice said.

It was the type of voice that made Viktoria want to punch the speaker. Nasally, with a tone to it that indicated the speaker clearly thought they were superior to those they were speaking to.

"Yes, just stand aside, and we'll be done as quickly as we can be."

The second voice was better. Normal, sounding almost apologetic, as if the speaker knew what they were doing was a waste of time but needed to do it anyway.

Footsteps sounded above them as the men moved about the room.

"Tell me again," Captain Stanford said. "How does a black dragonkin end up in Lostin?"

"Two of them, actually," the second voice replied. "And don't ask me. But I know something big happened at Festival a little while ago. Dragonkin from all over. Supposedly, Manse has been nearly destroyed."

"Enough gossip, Radley," the first voice said. "Keep your eyes open."

"Oh, relax," Radley said. "Captain Stanford has been doing this for years. His reputation is spotless. You'd know that if you had actually worked the docks, rather than just pushing paper in the local minister's office."

There was silence for a moment as both men stopped moving.

"Careful," the first man hissed. "I've been appointed dock commissioner by the dragonkin themselves. You wouldn't want me to report you, would you?"

A heavy sigh escaped Radley. "No, Tilford. I wouldn't."

The footsteps resumed. A moment later, the drawers were pulled from the desk directly over their heads. One was taken completely out and crashed to the floor, sending a painful well of noise through their hiding place.

"Whoops," Tilford said. But there was no sound of him picking it up or putting the drawer back into place.

It seemed like they searched everywhere. It took forever before they finally left the captain's cabin.

Tilford must have gone first, because Viktoria heard the other, Radley, mutter quietly to Captain Stanford.

"Sorry about this, Jarmen. He's in a mood, so we might be at this for a while."

"I've got nothing to hide," Stanford told him. "Take all the time you need."

Viktoria felt like screaming.

Chapter 19- Droy Thus Jungle

"They've been here, too," Akofi said.

He didn't know why he had expected anything to be different. He knew that red dragonkin had been in Ascana and had been responsible for most of the trouble. So why had he been so sure his own homeland would have been safe?

The Kanega Border House was in ruins.

Akofi hadn't exactly been looking forward to seeing the room with the hole he'd blown in the wall again, assuming it hadn't been fixed. It was a reminder of him losing control and the beginning of a rivalry and hatred between him and Edoo that had led to the others refusing to listen back at Festival. He still had no idea what had happened to the other tower representatives. They could all be dead, making their way across war-torn Ascana, or be back in their respective villages, safe and sound. Even with his dislike for Edoo, Akofi sincerely hoped it was the latter.

"This is... horrible," Bekasi said, her voice little more than a whisper.

The Border House had been almost totally destroyed. The main building was razed and the rooms where they had stayed were collapsed in on themselves. Off to the side, the corral where Gulari had been kept was shattered, the stout rails looking like so many twigs that had been snapped by a petulant child.

Rainaldus walked to the corral, his head down, eyes scanning the ground.

Akofi supposed he should go with him. He should be trying to aid the guardsman in figuring out exactly what had happened, even though they already knew.

But the smell was bad enough from where he stood. He had no real desire to go closer to the corral than was necessary.

There had been several of the giant birds contained there. How many, it was impossible to tell, since pieces of them were scattered about. They had been there for a few days now, judging by the sour stench which permeated the whole area.

"How are they still there?" Bekasi asked. "Something should have come out of the jungle and taken them. There are plenty of scavengers living in there."

"Because whoever did this keeps coming back." Rainaldus had heard Bekasi and answered her question. "There are plenty of dragonkin prints here. Some are fresher than others. Fresh enough that they could have been made right before we got here. Come take a look."

Neither Bekasi nor Akofi moved an inch closer to where the dead Gulari were. Akamah waited behind them, his expression still vacant. They'd gotten so used to it that Akofi didn't even look around to see if the other mage was going to answer Rainaldus's summons.

"I trust you," Bekasi called to him. "Is there anything else?"

Rainaldus shook his head. "No. Just dragonkin prints and torn up birds." He stopped and sighed. "I would have liked to see them alive. I've heard of your Gulari but have never seen them."

"They're wonderful," Akofi agreed, although, really, he didn't see anything so special about them. Beasts of burden with feathers and beaks, rather than hooves and manes. "I think we should move on. If those tracks are fresh, like you say, then the dragonkin might not be—"

He might as well have opened his mouth and shouted an invitation. There was a cracking, rustling sound from behind them. Akofi whirled in time to see a dragonkin, long, sinuous, and with flashing blue scales, emerge from the jungle on the far side of the road. Its eyes were already focused on them, and— most horribly— it was grinning. Its teeth were stained crimson from the blood of the gulari it had apparently eaten, and there was an almost manic gleam in its eyes.

"Rainaldus!" Bekasi yelled.

She needn't have bothered. Rainaldus already had his sword out and was racing toward them. Without his armor, the young man was incredibly fast, and before the dragonkin had emerged all the way from the bush, Rainaldus was at their side.

The dragonkin snarled, a sound more bestial than any Akofi had ever heard a dragonkin from Droy Thus make.

"We haven't done anything wrong," Bekasi tried to tell it. "We were merely returning from Festival and hoped to get some Gulari to ride the rest of the way to our village. That's all."

The dragonkin turned its gaze on her but didn't reply.

"We'll leave," Akofi added in. "This is your home, now. We can see that. And we have an injured friend, so we'll try to get help somewhere else."

As he spoke, he began backing slowly away, putting a hand behind him to make sure Akamah was moving as well.

But Akamah didn't move. Nor, for that matter, did Rainaldus.

Akofi looked over his shoulder. Akamah was staring at the dragonkin with wide eyes. His chin trembled and his mouth worked soundlessly. A thin sliver of drool ran over his lip and down his chin. He looked like he was a fit of some sort, or having a waking nightmare, maybe. Whichever it was, it held him immobile, even when Bekasi took his hand to try to lead him away.

As for Rainaldus, Akofi liked the look on his face even less.

The guardsman was staring at the dragonkin with undisguised hatred. His eyes flashed and his lips curled back in a sneer. Then, that sneer became almost— but not quite— a smile.

"He's looking forward to this," Akofi realized. "He wants to fight it! He and Lamorak killed that other one, with our help, and now he thinks he can do it again."

"Come on, Rainaldus," Bekasi said, but her voice shook. She must have reached the same conclusion Akofi had. "Let's just go."

"You go ahead," Rainaldus answered her, but his eyes never once left the dragonkin.

The blue noticed also. It returned Rainaldus's smile, its own much more wicked and brimming with death than the human's.

And then, it sprang forward.

Jaws agape, front legs raised, the dragonkin came off the ground and lunged at Rainaldus. With no wings to lift it, its flight had to be magical, but Akofi couldn't sense any sort of spell. Some innate ability, he had time to think, before the blue was on the guardsman.

Only, Rainaldus hadn't remained still, either. With a grace unlike any Akofi had ever seen in a human, Rainaldus side-stepped the dragonkin's attack. His sword swung in a flat arc, cutting across the blue scales right below its left eye. The dragonkin's head jerked away, and Rainaldus followed, stepping closer and striking, point-first, aiming for that same eye.

The dragonkin moved faster, causing Rainaldus to miss, the point of his sword sliding along the scales and doing little harm. But Rainaldus didn't stop there. He slid forward, keeping the distance between the two close, not letting the dragonkin pull back enough to bring its front claws into play nor allow its head to come around and use its teeth.

But that strategy was only going to go so far. The dragonkin was long, but it was supple. It could almost tie itself in a knot like a snake, and as soon as it brought its tail around, it would have Rainaldus trapped.

Akofi raised his hands and summoned a ball of fire, rolling his hands to compress it, pushing it tighter. The globe grew smaller, but hotter with every passing second, until the heat was intense enough that Akofi could feel it in his hands and his face, despite the protection that came from it being his own spell.

He grunted and threw his hands out, sending the ball of fire speeding toward the opposite side of the dragonkin's head from where Rainaldus fought.

The fireball exploded against the scales, and the dragonkin screamed and reared up on its hind legs. Rainaldus took advantage, stepped forward and sliced his sword through the dragonkin's stomach. Hot, red blood spurted from the wound, along with a cloud of steam, and the dragonkin raged even louder.

It crashed down, moving so fast that Rainaldus didn't have time to get fully out of the way. The weight of the thing clipped his shoulder, sending him sprawling and his sword spinning from his hand. He rolled and jumped to his feet, only to come up facing the dragonkin.

It was too late. As fast as he was, the dragonkin was faster. Only now, it had learned. It knew not to let Rainaldus close in again. Akofi shuddered as one eye sought *him* out, and he saw nothing but his own promised death in that glance.

Dragonkin were large, fast, very strong, and had magic at their command.

And yet, they still had one other weapon that was even greater.

The dragonkin growled, then took in a deep breath, an act which took only a moment.

Rainaldus began to move, dashing to the side, but he might as well have been crawling. The steaming hot breath of the dragonkin was going to catch him and cook him in his own skin.

And Akofi had no way of stopping it. He was already summoning up a sheet of flame, to drop it in front of the dragonkin and maybe distract him, but he didn't have much hope that it would work.

Then, a cry, almost inhuman in its tone and volume, came from behind him. Akofi's head whipped around.

Akamah was still staring at the dragonkin, only now he was no longer twiting and muttering to himself. Tears were running down his face, and he stepped forward, raised both hands above his head, then brought them slashing down with a cry of rage.

It was as if something huge had plummeted onto the dragonkin's head. One moment it was raised up, its lungs full of the steam that would kill Rainaldus. The next, its chin slammed into the ground hard enough to partially bury it. The dragonkin gave a loud grunt, as if it had tried to bellow but couldn't open its mouth.

Akamah cried out again and repeated his motion. The dragonkin's head bounced, hit again from overhead by some vast and implacable force.

Rainaldus stood stunned for a moment, his eyes flicking from Akamah to the dragonkin. Then, he ran so that he was behind the dragonkin's front leg. He picked up his sword, grabbed the hilt with both hands, put the point against the dragonkin's side, and pushed.

The dragonkin flinched, its body writhed, but every time it started to raise its head, Akamah hit it again.

Akofi didn't know how he was doing it. A spell like that, using that much force, was draining. To do it once would tire a mage. Twice would exhaust him. More than that... Akofi didn't know. But Akamah had hit the dragonkin three, four, five times, now. His voice was growing ragged and sweat was mixing with his tears, but he didn't stop. He either didn't hear or ignored Bekasi's pleas.

"He's killing himself," Akofi thought.

Rainaldus continued to push his sword deeper, seeking the dragonkin's heart.

Finally, something inside the blue gave way, and his sword slid in all the way to the hilt. Blood welled over it, covering Rainaldus's hands. Akofi could hear the sizzle and see the stream from where it touched the guardsman, but Rainaldus didn't relent. No more than Akamah did.

The dragonkin spasmed, ripping the sword out of Rainaldus's hands and sending him flying when its body slammed into his far smaller human one.

But it was a death throe, nothing more. The dragonkin coiled into knots, its tail thrashing and curling around and over its body. It let out one final, gurgling roar, which died as quickly as it had come and then crashed to the dirt, its blood continuing to pump out through the wound Rainaldus had dealt it.

Akofi stood shocked. Besides the hilt of Rainaldus's sword, the dragonkin's head was an almost shapeless mass. Even if Rainaldus hadn't killed it, Akamah might have done it himself.

So he wasn't overly surprised when he turned around to see his oldest friend sprawled on the ground, with Bekasi leaning over him and weeping bitterly.

Akofi hurried to her side, but even before he got there, he could see that it was too late. Akamah wasn't breathing. His face was an ashen gray, his eyes staring sightlessly at the sky. He knelt next to Bekasi and put his arm around her shoulders, half-expecting her to throw him off. To his surprise, she didn't. She leaned against him and cried even harder.

A movement caught his attention, and Akofi looked up through his own tear-blurred vision to see Rainaldus kneel on the other side of Akamah's body. The man was badly injured, worse than Akofi had thought. His hands were scalded a bright red color and already huge blisters were forming. His fingers were crooked into claws, yet— somehow— he had gotten his sword back into its sheath.

Rainaldus didn't say a word. He only bent over Akamah and touched his chest softly with the back of one his injured hands. He stayed that way for several seconds, then pulled back and stood in one fluid motion.

Akofi didn't watch him walk away. He could only see Akamah, lying motionless in the dirt, after an effort that few could have matched and which had cost him his life.

"Akofi."

Akofi ignored the voice. Whoever it was, whatever they wanted, it could wait.

"Akofi," the voice said again.

He looked up in annoyance, but it was only Rainaldus. He was staring down at the dead dragonkin.

"What is it?" Akofi asked quietly. Even through his grief, he recognized that whatever Rainaldus had to say, it was likely important.

"We have to move on," the guardsman said. He turned from his study of the blue to look at Akofi. "This one wasn't alone."

"How do you know that?" Bekasi's voice was bitter, but Akofi didn't think her bile was really directed at the guardsman.

"It's feet. Claws. Whatever you want to call them. Some of those tracks over there," he nodded toward the corral. "They're not the same size. This one was bigger."

The implications of what Rainaldus had said seeped slowly into Akofi's mind. They seemed to do the same to Bekasi, since she slowly sat up and pulled away from him.

"We can't leave him here like this," she said.

"No, we can't." Akofi agreed with her, but then... what could they do? If another dragonkin came now, which was something that seemed likely to happen at any moment, they would be dead. The new one would see its dead cousin and attack immediately, probably before they even knew it was there.

"We can take him a short way," Rainaldus said.

He strode over, put his arms under the still body of Akamah, and lifted. Akofi winced at the thought of the pain the young man must be feeling from his hands. Yet he made no complaint.

"Not for long," he agreed. "Just enough that they don't..." He couldn't finish what he was going to say, but they all knew it anyway.

"We can't stay on the road, either," Rainaldus said. "We're too exposed."

Akofi nodded, until he realized what was being suggested. He should have known at once, but his mind felt foggy. There was too much happening. He needed to pull himself together.

"Through the jungle, you mean?" he gasped. "We can't! It's much too dangerous! There are things in there that—"

"That are worse than an enraged dragonkin?" Rainaldus interrupted. "One that wants revenge?"

"Well... no. I don't think so, anyway. But plenty dangerous on their own."

"I have no doubt that's true. It might mean our deaths if we try to travel there. But I know it's certain death to stay on the road."

He was right, of course. They wouldn't get very far, especially carrying Akamah's body, if they stayed where they could be found.

"Enough debate," Bekasi said. Her voice was still angry. "Rainaldus is right. We go through the jungle."

She didn't wait. Instead, she headed for the same spot the dragonkin had come out of.

Which was smart, Akofi thought. The dragonkin had already crashed through the plants. Any sign of their own passage would blend right in.

Rainaldus followed, still carrying Akamah, and Akofi brought up the rear.

He paused before going into the darkened interior, though. Every muscle in his body cried out against it. Every bit of common sense told him it was a bad idea.

Then, he looked back at the shattered Border House and the massacred Gulari. All behind the great body of the dead dragonkin.

Bekasi and Rainaldus were right. Death in the jungle was only a near certainty. Death if they stayed on the road was assured.

With no choice left to him, Akofi followed the others.

Chapter 20- Orluduna, Droy Thus

The tower— the human-built one that everyone knew existed in Orluduna— beckoned. Sintifi was, of course, allowed free access to it. He'd spent his childhood there as a student, then returned to teach on occasion, as was his right since he had scored top marks for his year.

As a matter of fact, Sintifi had scored top marks every year that he had attended classes in the tower. No one had even come close to him. Not in spell-casting, not in spell-design, not even in simple brute strength. His magic was cleaner, more effective, lasted longer, and was cast with less effort than any of his classmates, and most of those in the years above him as well.

Which made it only natural when someone had approached him a few years after he'd left the tower to tell him the greatest secret he'd ever heard. It was then that he learned of the existence of the *true* tower of Orluduna, the one that few knew about.

Of course, he'd gone along immediately. His first trip there had been under the effects of a confusion spell that even he had never experienced before. A spell so subtle and powerful that he wasn't even aware it had been cast on him, until he stood blinking at the new— well, ancient, really— tower, with no memory of how he had gotten there, where it was located, or who had told him about it.

Normally, such a thing would have sent panic racing through him. Even as a young boy, Sintifi had not liked his mind to be played with. He supposed no one did, really. But this…

This was something different. This time, the beauty of the magic had fired his imagination and rather than make him angry, it had only made him curious— hungry to learn how it was done and how he could do it himself.

The tower door had opened, seemingly on its own, and Sintifi had entered. He'd met Oponsi, found out just how much he had yet to learn, and his life had never been the same.

Now, though, he was anxious just to get inside the tower in front of him. Oponsi wouldn't be there, she never left the true tower, but it would be safe, nevertheless. No dragonkin could fit inside the building.

Except if they changed shape, of course. Sintifi didn't know if all of them could do such a thing or if that was magic only the reds possessed, but it was better not to think on that. Inside was safety. It had to be.

He dashed across the few remaining feet and passed through the open doors.

Inside, he was struck by the silence. Normally the tower was alive with sights and sounds. Students rushing from class to class, some using the stairs that wound around the walls until they vanished into the gloom above, some through doors that led to other rooms or less-common passages. Ill-favored were always around, cleaning and tending to whatever it was they did, while visitors, some guided by older students, gawked at the height or the precious works of art dotted around the huge space.

Now, there was no one. The classes had all been moved outside, where dragonkin of various colors could watch over them. There were no more visitors, and any Ill-favored must have been put to work elsewhere.

In the short time that he'd been in Orluduna, Sintifi had seen dragonkin from all four realms. At least, he'd assumed that's all that was there. He hadn't taken the time to search carefully for any sign of Tophonoss's children. Such searching could just as easily alert them that someone was looking.

It seemed that dragonkin were everywhere, though, but at least they had ignored his movements once he was in the village.

Life *did* go on. On his way to the tower, traders haggled in the market, bringing goods from Ascana, Usturg, and Obristan. Not as many, and with not nearly the variety of wares as he'd seen in the past, but some intrepid souls were still trying to live as if everything was normal.

The blacksmith he'd passed was busy making arrowheads and spear points. The baker had been setting out fresh loaves.

And the students listened to their teachers, practiced magic, and tried to ignore the looming dragonkin.

It was all too much, but given the things he'd seen in Ascana, Sintifi had breathed a sigh of relief when he'd realized that Orluduna, although occupied, had been largely untouched by violence.

Now, he needed to go up, to speak with Korudu, the master of this tower. He needed information, and Korudu knew almost everything there was to know. Besides, the silence of the place was beginning to get to him. It was too cavernous, too vast, to be so quiet. It made him shiver.

Sintifi walked quickly to the stairs, ascended thirteen of them, turned to the wall, muttered a few words and moved his fingers, then stepped forward. Darkness, complete and absolute, blinded him for a brief moment, then he stepped from the wall at the top of the stairs, already facing the interior of the tower. Large windows, set far above the jungle trees, let in bright light. Across a short hallway was a massive set of hardwood doors, carved with the likenesses of fearsome beasts, some of which roamed that very jungle below.

Before he'd even taken a step, however, the doors opened soundlessly on their own.

In spite of the light, it was impossible to see who was inside.

"Come in, Sintifi," a voice floated out. "I've been waiting for your return."

Sintifi took a slow, measured step, complying with the invitation, but taking his time.

The voice that had greeted him hadn't been that of Korudu. It had sounded like Oponsi. Which was impossible, of course.

He took another step, chiding himself at his foolishness. The voice must have been Korudu's. He just hadn't heard it in a while.

But, why then, were his hands clenched into sweaty fists?

He stepped across the threshold and was in a large, well-appointed office, fully illuminated by sunlight streaming through the same type of windows in the antechamber outside. On the floor was a large, finely-woven carpet, with designs in dark blue and deep purple picked out against a black background. An impressive wooden desk, carved at the bottom to resemble dragonkin claws was at the far end, while in-between the windows there were large shelves, lined with books and other artifacts of Korudu's life and work.

There were other chairs, with deep cushions, two in front of the desk, and another four set in a semi-circle near a large unlit fireplace. Nearby was a model of the world, a globe, that Sintifi knew opened to reveal crystal decanters full of the best honey-wine and other spirits brought in from afar.

He'd spent many a pleasant afternoon and evening in that room, discussing magic, life, and love with the tower master. Korudu had become a friend since Sintifi had graduated to become a free-mage.

But none of that could prepare him for what met his eyes. He'd expected to find his friend there. He was master of this tower, after all.

He had never even dreamed of finding him in the company of Oponsi, however.

Sintifi supposed that in his mind, he would have put Oponsi over Korudu, in terms of importance. But the two acted now as if they were equals. Instead of sitting behind his desk, as he would have if his visitor had been a student or supplicant of some kind, Korudu and Oponsi both sat in the chairs on the other side of the desk, glasses in hand and returning his stare, although neither of their mouths were hanging open as he knew his was.

"It's about time you've returned," Oponsi said, her voice sharp. "You were expected days ago."

Sintifi shook himself to gather his wits. Oponsi was never the most cordial person he'd ever met, always ready with criticism and slow to praise, but even for her, this was too much. The obvious unfairness of her statement snapped him out of his daze.

"Maybe you haven't noticed," he replied angrily, "but our little plan has set off much more than we ever thought it would!"

She snorted and took a sip of the drink in her hand. "It's got them stirred up, hasn't it? That's what we wanted, wasn't it?"

"Are you mad?" He almost whispered it. "Do you have any idea how many people have died?"

"Several, I would imagine. So have several dragonkin. A fair trade, I would say."

Sintifi could only stare at her, then he turned his gaze to Korudu. "Do you believe this?"

To his credit, his friend did look uncomfortable. Then, he sighed and said, "I don't know that I can really take a side in this. After all, I just found out about a whole other tower here in Orluduna." He paused and looked significantly at Sintifi. "Something *you*, however, already knew."

"I couldn't tell you," Sintifi said. "I couldn't tell anyone. It's part of being accepted there. I'm sorry."

"Don't be." Korudu took a drink. "I would have done the same."

"If you two are done with the dramatics," Oponsi interrupted, "it's time to discuss what's next."

Sintifi didn't want to. He really didn't. What he had wanted was to talk to Korudu, be reassured that the world was going to return to normal and that everything was going to be okay. To have a drink, or two, or maybe six, and to fall asleep. To forget about dragons and dragonkin, to leave Evening Folk— or Raaleth, or whatever they were called— behind, and to pass into oblivion.

Now, Oponsi's presence made that impossible.

The woman was a force even sitting in a chair at her "ease." Stick-straight, her back didn't even touch the back of the chair. Her knees together, her hands circling her glass, she looked like a predator waiting for her prey to make the wrong move. Her face, gaunt and angular, was smooth yet somehow carried the impression of age and wisdom, an appearance accentuated by her shaved head.

As a matter of fact, now that he'd met him, Oponsi reminded Sintifi very much of Ilvisar, just a different shaded skin and ears that weren't as pointed.

Beyond that, the arrogance was almost equally matched.

"What's next?" he finally said. "What are you talking about? What's next is hiding! Making sure they never know that we were the ones responsible."

Oponsi shook her head once, forcefully. "Ridiculous. Now is the time to press our advantage. To hurt them even more, drive them into blind rages so they will attack one another again."

Sintifi couldn't believe what he was hearing. A woman who never— at least until now— had left her tower was demanding more sacrifice. Again, his mind flashed back to those young mages he'd met briefly at Festival. Those same mages who were probably dead by any one of a hundred horrible methods by now.

"What advantage?" he cried. "We have none! We had hoped to cause a war between them, but all we've done is pull the dragonkin more tightly together. Now they openly visit each other's realms! Which means the dragons themselves have agreed to it. Our 'grand plan' has backfired! We need to stay hidden!"

Oponsi opened her mouth, but Korudu held up his hand. "If I may. I don't entirely understand. All that's happening is due to... what? Some plan that the two of you cooked up together?"

Sintifi could hear the bewilderment and hurt in his friend's voice. He was looking from Oponsi to him and back again, disbelief writ large on his features.

"No," Sintifi sighed. "Not just us. There were several of us who——"

"A council," Oponsi cut in. "Made up of those who work from the true tower. Those who know the truth of the world and our place in it. Those who know what the dragons have taken from us!"

"Taken from us," Korudu repeated slowly. "You mean more than the lives of those in Lankari killed when their tower fell? Those who were caught between fighting dragonkin in Festival? Not to mention all those since then, who they've killed for nothing more than sport, from what I can tell."

"Yes," Oponsi spat. "All that and more!"

"I don't understand," Korudu said.

"Nor do you need to." Oponsi glared at him from her dark eyes. "I have come as a courtesy and because I needed to collect this one." She jabbed a bony finger in Sintifi's direction. "Beyond that, your involvement has ended."

Korudu sat back in his chair, apparently humbled. Sintifi didn't like to see it, but there weren't many— none that he actually knew of— who could stand up to Oponsi's ire.

Then, Korudu sighed. "I'm afraid my involvement hasn't ended. Not at all. You're going to sit here for as long as it takes and tell me everything. About this other tower. About this council who has taken it upon themselves to speak for the world. About this secret history of the dragons you hint at. All of it."

"I haven't the time to—" Oponsi started.

"Make the time," Korudu interrupted. "Or I will go down to the nearest dragonkin I can find once you've left and ask the the same questions. Would that be better?"

Oponsi's eyes flashed dangerously. Sintifi swallowed hard. She was a horribly powerful mage. If she decided that it was better to eliminate Korudu rather than appease him…

But he wasn't going to let that happen. Instead, he walked over to stand next to his friend's chair.

Oponsi was strong. The strongest mage Sintifi had ever met, by far. But Korudu had power to spare as well. And Sintifi himself… he was second only to Oponsi. Between the two of them, her power wouldn't be enough.

She glared at him, which made his heart skip a beat, then— unbelievably— she seemed to wilt.

"Fine," she rasped. "But I'll have another drink first."

She thrust her glass forward. Sintifi took it without a word, refilled it from a bottle in the globe, and poured himself one while he was at it.

By the time Oponsi had finished, the light was beginning to wane.

Korudu sat quietly the whole time, asking few questions, which impressed Sintifi to no end. When he'd first heard all that Oponsi had just related— less, even— he had been full of questions. But that had been a different time, of course. One without dragonkin destroying whatever they felt like on a whim.

"So now," Korudu began slowly, "you've started something that you really don't know how to end."

"Bah," Oponsi spat. "You're as bad as he is." She cast a withering glance in Sintifi's direction. "There is no end. Don't you understand? This is only the beginning. We will continue to fight, to strike from the shadows, until the dragonkin are so few that we can destroy them completely."

"I can see that," Korudu said, surprising Sintifi since he didn't think what Oponsi was saying was even remotely possible. "But you're forgetting something. Destroying dragonkin is one thing. What do you have in mind for the Five? The dragons, themselves?"

For the first time since he'd arrived at the tower, Sintifi saw Oponsi squirm. As much as she ever did, at least. She glared at Korudu, finished off her drink, then shook her head. "We don't know yet. We suspect that the dragons draw much of their power from the dragonkin. That when the dragonkin are depleted, they'll be weaker. At that point, we hope to—"

"Don't know," Korudu held up one finger. "Suspect." Two fingers. "Hope" The third and final finger. "That's a lot of supposition to base the fate of humans on."

"It wasn't supposed to go like this," Sintifi told him. There was a part that Oponsi had left out. "We had been able to influence a couple of dragonkin from a distance, but only when there were several of us working together. We caused one of Haiteng's to swim deeper than it would be able to recover from. Even that took a lot of effort. I was then supposed to attempt to draw one to me, causing the dragonkin to defy the edict of crossing into another realm." He stopped and grimaced. "It went too well. It was far easier to pull one to me, than it had been to force some random action from far away. After that... they just kind of went crazy and everything started to fall apart."

"And now the dragons are aware of the magic," Korudu said. "Or at least that something has changed. And we are alone. The other realms don't have magic. Not like ours. We will have to fight the dragons ourselves if it comes to it."

"Actually..." Sintifi said.

In his confusion at finding Oponsi present there, then the subsequent arguments, he'd almost forgotten.

"Wait!" Oponsi sat up even straighter, if such a thing was possible. Her eyes went wide, then her lips curled in a sneer. "There is something in the tower. Something that doesn't belong."

"Which tower," Korudu asked. "Mine or yours?"

"This one!" she hissed. "It's not human... or dragonkin..."

"Oh," Sintifi said, sitting back and sipping from his glass. "That must be Ilvisar."

Chapter 21-Obristan Forest

Every time Lamorak woke, Prince Calidor was also awake, staring into the embers of their fire. Every time, it took Lamorak longer and longer to go back to sleep again, until, finally, with the sky just beginning to brighten in the east, he groaned and rolled from his meager bedroll.

"You haven't slept at all," he said to Calidor.

"No," the prince replied quietly. He glanced at the girl, still wrapped in the prince's cloak and sleeping soundly. Lamorak wasn't sure how she was able to but figured that exhaustion had finally taken its toll on her.

"We should move on," Lamorak said. "Back on the road to Greenfair."

"I've been thinking," Calidor said in way of reply.

"Okay." Lamorak stretched, then sat down next to Calidor. "Anything you want to share?"

"Maybe." Calidor looked around at their surroundings. "This is a good place, yes? Hidden, for the most part?"

"For the most part," Lamorak agreed. "Nothing is perfect, though."

"No, of course not. But still... we felt safe enough to build a fire for the first time in several nights."

"Because of her." Lamorak nodded at the sleeping girl.

"Because of her." Calidor nodded in agreement. "Still. We did it."

"Don't forget. We also have Yarah with us. She's been keeping us from being the focus of any dragonkin's attention. But she can't do it forever, so we need to get to safety."

"That's just it, Lamorak. There is no safety. That's what I've been thinking about."

Lamorak remembered his first real conversations with the prince. When he'd been surprised to find him to be more than just a drunken, lecherous spoiled brat. When he'd realized there was a sharp mind and a willingness to learn. What Calidor had just said might have sounded like pure despondency in anyone else.

From Calidor, though, Lamorak had the feeling he was leading up to something, so he remained quiet and waited for the prince to come to it on his own.

"Greenfair has surely fallen to the dragonkin," Calidor finally said. "I've been thinking and thinking, and there's no reason to suspect anything else. Not even with what Yarah has told us about Obristan actually having a dragon overlord. She's never shown interest in us up until now, so I can't imagine she'll suddenly protect us from her own kind."

The same thoughts had been occupying Lamorak for some time, but he hadn't wanted to bring them up to the prince.

"So, it's pointless to head there," Calidor continued. "If I suddenly show up, I'm sure to be taken prisoner, killed, or worse."

"Maybe not," Lamorak said. "Maybe they'll..." He fell short, unsure of what he was thinking. What *would* the dragonkin do with the prince?

Use him as a figurehead, in the best case. Make him tell his people to do what they were told, accept the world as it was now, and obey the dragonkin above all others.

Lamorak wouldn't have wanted to be used in such a way, either.

"I see your point," he conceded. "So, what's better?"

"I began to see it last night," the prince said. "Even before you and Yarah fell asleep. I began to see the idea of what I needed to do."

Lamorak glanced at the sleeping girl. He had heard Calidor the night before, but it hadn't really sunk in.

"You're going to gather up those you can," he guessed.

Calidor nodded. "I need to. They are my responsibility. I need to see to their safety."

"But... then what? So you gather together a bunch of people and... what? Live in the woods?"

"Yes. Here. Or somewhere like it. Hidden, with resources."

Lamorak looked around them. Everywhere was growth. The trees rose high on every side. Undergrowth was rampant in some spots, making it nearly impossible to pass through. Moss covered rocks and ferns grew in shady spots.

And he didn't have the first idea what to do with any of that abundance of life.

Neither, he suspected, did Calidor.

The prince noticed him gazing about and must have seen his dubiousness. He gave a soft laugh. "No. I don't know how to survive here, either. But I expect I'll find those who do. Those who have made their homes in the more wild areas, hunting, fishing, growing… things."

Now it was Lamorak's turn to laugh. "Growing 'things'? You mean like gardens? We might as well move into a town then."

"No, not gardens. Believe it or not, I actually know what those are. No, I just mean they'll know which plants are safe to eat or cook with and which ones aren't."

Living in the woods hadn't been something Lamorak ever would have guessed he'd be doing. Certainly not at his age.

Then again, he had been about to leave the Honor Guard. He was going to travel the world and see everything he could. He supposed this could be just one stop on that journey. A rest until the world went back to normal.

"Do we build huts? Or houses? Or find caves? Or…?"

"None of those." Calidor turned to look at him. "At least not for you."

"What's that supposed to mean?"

"It means you're not staying. You're continuing on. To Greenfair."

"No, I'm not." Lamorak kept his voice firm, but even with everything that had happened, he found it hard to defy the prince.

"You are." Calidor's voice was just as firm. "I could be wrong. Greenfair may still be safe. If so, I can bring my people there. If not… find out what happened to the rest of the Honor Guard. To the Palace Guard and the City Watch. All of it."

"And then? Bring them back here? You'll have a much more difficult time hiding, then."

"No. You're not to bring them here. You're to use them. Strike where and you're able. Take control and use them to fight in whatever manner you can."

"But I'm not—"

"You are, Lamorak," the prince said. "You will go with my seal, my blessing, and my authority. If there is any resistance left in Obristan, *you* will lead it."

By the time the others woke up, Lamorak was ready to go. He still didn't like the idea of leaving the prince there on his own. His whole life, ever since he'd been dropped at the Honor Guard as a child, he'd been trained to protect the prince's life at all costs. Going away now went against everything he'd ever been taught.

Then again, he had also been taught to obey the prince. For a long time, he'd thought that meant turning a blind eye to the prince's behavior. The same sort of pretending that he'd done on the road as they'd made their way to Festival. Now, he saw it as much more than that. Now, he knew the man better and found that he liked and respected Calidor a great deal.

Which made obeying even harder.

"You're sure about this?" he asked for what had to be the tenth time.

"Very," Calidor replied. He showed no sign of impatience.

"You'll stay with him?" Lamorak regarded Yarah.

She nodded, slowly. Lamorak wasn't sure if she was indicating reluctance or not.

"I will," she finally said. "I'm not entirely sure why. It's not what I should be doing, but…" She shrugged. "Something tells me this is the place where I can be of the most help."

If Calidor really did gather a large number of his people together, then Yarah's help would be irreplaceable. Not only would they need to remain in hiding, but Lamorak thought many of those they might find would be like the girl or worse. Wounded, to various degrees, either inside or out.

He nodded, then enfolded her in a brief, awkward hug. It felt strange, somehow, to leave this woman he barely knew, yet feel as if he was leaving someone dear to him. She patted his back and stepped away, giving him a moment with the prince.

Lamorak didn't know what to say, and he found his gaze wandering to the little girl. "I'm not sure how many you'll find like her," he said. "I would think most are either dead or caught in the towns the dragonkin are ruling over."

Prince Calidor glanced at the girl, then back to Lamorak. "If I hadn't found her, she'd be dead now. So it was worth it. It will be worth it no matter how many we find."

"All right, then." Lamorak sighed and held out his hand. "It's truly been an honor, Your Highness. I mean that sincerely."

Calidor smiled. "More so than you thought it would be, I'm sure." He laughed at Lamorak's expression. "Don't be ashamed. I would have thought the same. We'll meet again, Lamorak. At least I hope so."

"As do I," Lamorak said.

Then he dropped the prince's hand, turned away, and walked off through the forest, heading back toward the road.

For a while, he'd follow that. See what there was to see. If need be, he'd walk in the woods again, but since he was alone and had no need for a fire, he'd take his chances for the sake of speed.

He took several steps before he looked back, but already, the trees hid the sight of the prince and Yarah.

Lamorak turned back around and kept going.

Night was creeping in when he next stopped or was forced to stop, really.

The road continued through forest, with the trees growing heavily on both sides. Woodsmen and hunters made up the bulk of the population of the area, Lamorak knew, with the occasional way-house or pub dotted here and there to accommodate any trade traffic on its way to or from Ascana.

He'd passed two of those during the day. One was shut up tightly, boards nailed across the door and the windows. The other was nothing more than a pile of long-cold ashes. And throughout the entire day, he'd never come across a single other traveler.

If Prince Calidor was going to find refugees to take in, he was going to have to look hard for them. But Lamorak didn't doubt the man's drive to do so. He just hoped it all wasn't a horrible mistake.

At the same time, he was afraid the prince had made an even bigger one. He'd told Lamorak to take over the Honor Guard, the Palace Guard and whatever else was left. To organize a resistance to the dragonkin. Lamorak couldn't imagine too many others more ill-suited to that task than he was.

He could fight, there was no doubt about that. Other than Rainaldus— and he briefly wondered where that young man might be— there wasn't anyone in the Honor Guard who could defeat him consistently. He was schooled in the "art of warfare," if you wanted to call it that, even though Obristan had never been in an actual war as far as he knew.

But to lead others? To be responsible for what they did, how they proceeded, and to keep them alive? Or worse, to decide how best to spend those lives?

That wasn't something he was comfortable with. Not in the least.

All of it, of course, might come to nothing. Maybe Greenfair was still untouched by the dragonkin— although he doubted that very much. More likely, the Honor Guard and everyone else had already been disbanded or killed outright. By the time he arrived, there'd be nothing left for him to lead.

Then what? Maybe to Droy Thus to find Rainaldus? Or back to Calidor, more likely. Or…

The man stepped from the side of the road several paces in front of Lamorak, a sword held loosely in his hand. Even from there, Lamorak could see the poor condition of the thing, and the man didn't have the stance of a ready fighter, either. But he was wearing clothing that allowed him to blend in with the woods. And he looked at Lamorak with that sneer some men get when they assumed they'd have the upper hand.

"Stop right there," he said. His voice was higher-pitched than Lamorak had expected, more of a whine than a threatening demand.

"And if I don't?" Lamorak slowed a bit, but he kept moving.

"Then you'll be stopped." The man shrugged, which surprised Lamorak a bit. He wasn't a very big fellow, but he also didn't seem to be bothered by Lamorak not doing what he was told.

"I see," Lamorak said, his face breaking into a smile. "You and what—"

He really needed to learn to stop saying such things. Before the words were even out of his mouth, two others stepped from the opposite side of the road. Dressed in similar fashion to the first man, one held an axe which seemed to be in much better condition than the sword of the first. The other, though, was even more disconcerting.

That one, the oldest of the three, held a bow, an arrow already knocked and half-drawn. Lamorak had seen his like before. It was in his face, which was steady, with no sign of fear or anxiety, but no notion of being bothered by what he was doing, either. And in his eyes, which watched Lamorak closely, ready for any sudden movement.

Even if he had his armor, Lamorak would have hesitated. A bow like that could punch an arrow through his plate-mail. Now, without any protection, he'd be a sitting duck.

So that was the one who needed to go first.

Then, a noise made him turn his head. Two more men, two more swords, stepped into the road behind him.

"Guess you found your army after all, huh?" he said to the first man, who wrinkled his brow like he hadn't a clue as to what Lamorak was saying.

"I've stopped," Lamorak continued. "Now, what do you want?"

"Everything you've got," the first said. "Money. Food. Water. That sword."

Lamorak looked down at his hip. His armor was gone, so much slag back in Manse, he assumed, but his sword...

"I can't do that, friend. You wouldn't want it anyway. It brings too much trouble."

The first man scowled, before one of those behind him, called. "Look at it, Sledge. He's Honor Guard."

"How do you know, that?" Sledge yelled. "Not like we see them around here."

"I been to Greenfair when I was a boy! My Dad took me. I remember seeing swords just like that. My Dad said they all had them and they were the only ones who could—"

"Maybe this guy stole it! Ever think of that?"

"I didn't," Lamorak said. "Listen to your friend. I am Honor Guard. As a matter of fact, I now lead the Honor Guard. Now, I know times are hard and you men are desperate. I understand. I'm just trying to get home to Greenfair, so if you just step aside, I'll be on my way and no one gets hurt."

Mostly him, he thought to himself. But his little speech was having the desired effect. He'd turned sideways, so he could keep everyone in sight. They were glancing at each other, shifting nervously. Waylaying some random person walking the road was one thing. Honor Guard had a reputation, though, and Lamorak towered over these men, outweighing their heaviest with several pounds of muscle. They hadn't counted on that and were now trying to work out what to do.

Except for the man with the bow. He watched Lamorak with every bit as much steadiness as he had before learning who he was. Honor Guard made no impression on him, whatsoever.

"If you're Honor Guard, what are you doing here?" Sledge said. "Shouldn't you be with that prince— what's his name?"

"I should be," Lamorak agreed. "But he sent me ahead to do something for him…"

As soon as he'd said it, he realized his mistake. It was something he should have guessed already. Sledge may have been the first one out on the road. He might have been doing most of the talking. But he wasn't the leader. He wasn't the brains. Any more than Lamorak felt he was going to be.

The man with the bow raised it slightly. "Sent you on ahead, did he? So where did Calidor end up?"

"He's back in Ascana," Lamorak lied. "Stayed with the ministers in Manse to try to figure out what's gone wrong."

Bow nodded. "The same Manse I saw burning? That one?"

Lamorak hadn't counted on him being there. "Not all of it. I got out. So did a lot of others." He decided to try a different tack. "Hey, do you know if Greenfair is still safe? That's where I'm headed and—"

The man shot him.

Lamorak had been right about him. He *was* experienced. No change of expression came over that flat, cold face as he lifted the bow, pulled it taut, and released in one smooth movement.

Lamorak's only saving grace was that he had been watching the bowman as carefully as the bowman had been watching him. As soon as the bow rose, he spun and leapt for the woods.

It felt like he got punched by a giant's fist in his left shoulder. The impact spun him and sent him crashing into the dead leaves and sticks that littered the forest floor. Then, the sharp pain set in.

But he was who he was. He closed his eyes for one quick second, then forced the pain away, back, deep into his brain to be dealt with later. He grabbed his sword hilt, glad that he was right-handed, and drew it.

The men were coming for him, while the bowman stayed on the road.

They weren't counting on him recovering as quickly as he did. He sprang up, charged at the men, and ran past them, fending off two clumsy blows as he went by. The bowman saw him coming, knocked another arrow, and fired again, but Lamorak timed it well. He dodged as the bowman fired, letting the arrow whistle by his right ear. He hoped to hear a scream from behind but was disappointed in that.

He'd never realized how fast he could be without all that armor weighing him down. With fear pumping through him; fear of these men finding Calidor and Yarah and the little girl. Fear of getting shot by another arrow.

The bowman's eyes widened as he realized he had no chance of getting another shot off. As a matter of fact, he barely had time to raise his bow in a futile attempt to block Lamorak.

Even one handed, Lamorak's sword sliced through the ash of the bow like it was nothing. The bowman's head didn't fare much better.

He could feel the hot, stickiness flowing down his back. Already his breathing was becoming labored and his muscles were starting to quiver.

It didn't matter now, though. One man was already running. Sledge from the look of it. The other three, one axe, two swords, were staring open-mouthed at their companion, sprawled in the road, his face barely recognizable as such.

Lamorak wanted to kill them, too. To take away their threat from anyone else traveling the road.

But more than that, he needed the battle finished quickly. It was going to be hard enough to treat his wound on his own.

One of the two swordsmen swore and rushed at him. Lamorak could have laughed if he wasn't keeping the pain in his shoulder at bay.

These men weren't warriors. Not even bandits, except for maybe the one already dead at his feet.

The blow, when it came, was as if it was from a child. An attack he could have countered by the end of his first-year training. Lamorak wondered briefly if the man had ever even held a sword before he took it, and the man's hand, off with one swipe.

The man howled and fell to his knees, holding up the squirting stump like he couldn't believe it had happened.

"Come get him," Lamorak said, backing away. "Get him help and get out of here. Go back to whatever you were doing before this one—" He kicked the body of the bowman "—put this idea into your heads."

He kept moving slowly backward, afraid that any faster would put him down. He needed this to end. Pushing pain away was one thing. Blood leaving his body in such a flow was something else.

Slowly, the other two came forward. The one with the axe was smart enough to put in into the loop on his belt. After a moment, the other did the same with his sword, which didn't even have a sheath.

They gathered up their sobbing friend and hurried down the road, away from Lamorak, following Sledge and not giving the dead bowman a glance.

Lamorak did. If he could have worked up the strength, he would have spit on him, but now that the fight— such as it was— was over, the pain was coming in waves.

He needed to take care of it. Get the arrowhead out, treat it so that it didn't get infected, stop the bleeding, and...

He shook his head, unsure of what he'd just been thinking.

He looked down, wondering how the front of his shirt had gotten so wet, then remembered the arrow. He reached up gingerly and felt the arrowhead protruding from the front of his shoulder.

"Oh, good," he thought. "I can break it off..."

Then the road rushed up at him and any pain he was feeling was gone.

Chapter 22- Narfasker, Usturg

Visgar supposed the room he woke up in *was* an improvement over his tent. It would have been for sure, if it wasn't for the smells.

Old smoke and ash were the first things to hit his nostrils, but that was closely followed by other, even less pleasant smells.

One of Gunnvid's decrees had been that the fallen— the unfaithful— had been made examples of. That had meant heads stuck on poles, bodies left swinging in cages, and others left unburied where they'd been hewn down.

It might have had an effect on those still left alive in Narfasker. They certainly weren't putting up much resistance to the Children of Fimbruss anymore. Not that they had fought all that hard to begin with. Most never even had the chance.

Visgar wasn't sure what they were still doing there. To his understanding, they had been mandated to spread the word of Fimbruss's glory across the south of Usturg, then down into northern Ascana and Obristan. He'd thought that meant they would "visit" a town, gain some recruits, and move on.

But Gunnvid had read it differently.

"We haven't shown them the light," he rasped to all his commanders, after the initial day of terror had ended. "We've shown them Fimbruss's strength. We've made them see what happens to those who refuse to believe. Now, we need to show them mercy. We need to show them that Fimbruss's glory includes salvation for those who come into the fold."

That was more than Visgar had ever heard his friend and leader speak at one time. Even before the injury that took most of his voice, Gunnvid was never the most verbose fellow Visgar had met. That little speech had left his voice barely above a hoarse whisper, and Visgar had needed to step in to finish the meeting for him.

But at the first sign of burying the dead, Gunnvid had ordered it stopped, saying that neither mercy nor salvation extended to those who had dared to take up arms against them. He hadn't seemed to make a distinction between those who had actually done that and those who had merely been in the way.

"It stinks here," Estrid muttered.

She was lying next to Visgar, one arm held over her nose, her eyes still closed.

"It does," he agreed.

Not enough to distract him, however. It had been a good day when he'd found her. She'd made the stay in Narfasker much more pleasant.

And not just in bed, he reflected. She was smart as well as pretty. She had opinions that she wasn't afraid to voice, although he made sure she knew not to do so in front of anyone but him. She was a true believer in Fimbruss, much more than he was. And, most amazingly to Visgar, she had dreams.

"I didn't always want to be what Slode made me," she'd told him just the night before, when they had finished with what he wanted and had been lying in the bed together. "I wanted to leave here. I wanted to see Festival and the ocean. I wanted to see the jungles and wizards." She gave a little laugh. "When I was a girl, I thought I could *be* one of those wizards! Silly, I know, but my Dad had a book about them. I didn't understand it all, but I loved looking at the drawings."

Visgar hadn't laughed. He didn't have dreams as a boy. He didn't have books to look at, or a Dad who wanted to show them to him. What he did have was a childhood that made him tough, able to take a punch or a kick. A childhood that was as full of violence as the rest of his life had become.

Which made spending a few precious hours with Estrid even more enjoyable.

He wondered how long it would last.

"Smell or not," he said, swinging his legs out of the bed, "I need to get going. Gunnvid wants us in his tent before the sun is fully up."

"Why doesn't he just move into town, here?"

Visgar shrugged. "He doesn't like being comfortable. He thinks it's an indulgence and a sign of weakness."

"Oh." She looked thoughtful. "I suppose it could be. But if that was so, why would Fimbruss give us the opportunity to be comfortable."

He snorted. "Good question. Maybe someday you can ask him."

She sat up at that. "Really? Do you think maybe today? I'd love to meet him and—"

"No." His voice came out harsher than he'd intended. So he bent down and kissed her softly on the top of her head. "No." More gentle this time. "Gunnvid is… busy. Maybe another day."

He finished dressing and moved to the door. "Don't go too far," he said before he left. "I'm not sure when we're leaving, and I want to be able to find you."

She nodded and blinked back the tears that stood in her eyes. What for, Visgar wasn't sure. After everything she'd seen, he couldn't imagine it was because he told her no about meeting Gunnvid. He grimaced, left the room, shutting the door behind him, and went down the stairs to the street below.

He had only been trying to be nice to her when he'd said that she should ask Gunnvid her question. Their leader had no time, or patience, for questions. And he had little to no use for women. If he found out what Visgar had been up to… well, he wouldn't do much, not to him anyway, but Visgar had no doubt that Estrid would be taken away. What would happen to her then wasn't worth thinking about.

And he didn't want her wandering far from the room he'd taken as his own, because the fact was that the army of the Children of Fimbruss was growing. They weren't particular in who they took on. As long as they swore allegiance and praised the name of Fimbruss, they were part of it. All men, no women allowed in the army itself. Useful as seamstresses, cooks, nurses, and cleaners, sure, but not part of the army.

Visgar didn't want Estrid finding herself among some of those men who didn't know who she was. Didn't know that she was with him. For that matter, a lot of them probably had no idea who Visgar was, even. Not yet.

They would, but until that time, he didn't trust a single one of them.

His horse was in the stable behind the building. He brushed it for a moment, enjoying the good, clean scent of the beast, which blocked the other odors for a moment, before he saddled it. Then, he was up and on his way, thundering down the main street toward the sea of tents that still surrounded the mostly ruined town.

Estrid lay back again after Visgar had shut the door. She tried to keep her breathing shallow and not think too much about those she had known who might now be contributing to the stench that hung over the city. There hadn't been many in Narfasker who had truly been kind to her, but there had been a few. She was just glad that her parents weren't among them. They had died when she was young, which was how she'd ended up alone and easy enough prey for someone like Slode.

For all of her adult life, Estrid had "belonged" to one strong man or another. Before Slode, there had been Hoskuld, who she'd grown up with. They were only little more than teenagers when Estrid's parents had been killed by the ice troll. He had just gotten his first real job, his first place to live on his own, and he'd taken her in.

She supposed she had loved Hoskuld, in her way. She hadn't minded the things he wanted to do. Then came the drink and the fighting. He'd lost his job, lost any friends he'd had, and moved to Narfasker, where he'd run afoul of Slode.

From then on, she'd belonged to him. At first, it hadn't been bad, but he'd soon tired of her and passed her along to friends, then to whoever had money. She went without complaint, because it was better than the alternative.

And then… Kori.

Kori had been young, handsome, new to town, and had no idea who or what she was. He'd treated her like a real lady and expected nothing more from her. Even when they'd returned to the room he'd taken, he hadn't known, and she found— for the first time— that she didn't have it in her to ask for money. She couldn't bear to think about the way his face would change when he looked at her.

She wiped away a random tear, now, laughing at herself. Outside the window there were piles of dead bodies. The Children of Fimbruss had done horrible things, and she was crying because one man had looked at her with kind eyes?

What was worse, was that when Slode found out, he went after Kori for the money she hadn't taken from him. It had ended bad enough for Slode, but Kori was gone for good now. She wondered if he'd ever made it to Festival, and— given the rumors that had even reached that far north— wondered even more if he'd gotten away.

Now…

Well, now she was where she was. At the moment, lying in a large, comfortable bed. Naked, but when she chose to dress it would be in one of several dresses Visgar had made his men round up for her. They'd brought heaps of the things to her, and she had enjoyed herself going through them, picking out not only which ones fit her, but which ones she truly liked as well.

She supposed, all things considered, that her life hadn't taken a bad turn.

She believed in Fimbruss. Not just that he existed, that was easy enough. If dragonkin walked the earth, why was it hard to believe in a dragon? That only made sense.

No, she believed in his divinity, she guessed she would call it. She believed that if she remained faithful to him, he could grant her wishes. He could make her life better than it had ever been, at least since her parents had gone.

To that end, she really couldn't have fallen in with anyone better. Visgar was a believer, too. Although there had been a time or two when she thought she saw something— amusement? Surely not outright mockery— in his eyes when she'd talked of Fimbruss and what she'd hoped for. And he had been kind to her, like Kori had been.

When the Children moved on, she hoped Visgar would take her with them. She wasn't sure if he would, and he hadn't said. The thought of staying there, though, in what little remained of Narfasker, almost paralyzed her with fear.

Stay close, he had told her, right after he'd yelled at her. Not really yelled, she knew, but spoken harshly. Not that that mattered. Harsh words were nothing, really. Not when things could have been so much worse.

"Stop being so stupid," she said to herself, whispering the words out loud.

There were things to do.

She would see what she could find to eat. Food was scarce, she was sure of it, but she'd find something nice, even if she needed to use Visgar's name to get one or two of the Children to help her. She'd make him something to take away any hunger he'd have after a long day.

When that was done… she'd do whatever else she could to make him happy.

As long as he took her with him when he left.

Visgar was the last one to arrive, which wasn't lost on Gunnvid. He could see in their leader's face as soon as he pushed the flap aside and entered the tent. But Gunnvid didn't say anything. He wouldn't in front of everyone else, but later on, when it was just the two of them, he'd make his displeasure known.

"Now that we're all here," Gunnvid rasped as soon as Visgar was inside. "We can begin. The conversion of Narfasker is going well. Report."

Visgar settled into one of the chairs to listen. Half-listen, really. He didn't care all that much about the number of young men who had signed on or the amount of bread and meat they'd gathered from the shops and homes. That wasn't his area of expertise.

All things considered, he supposed he wasn't sure exactly what his area of expertise was.

Then, as he listened to the occasional question from Gunnvid, he remembered. He was there to make the speeches, to talk when his friend couldn't.

Visgar was an exceptionally good speech-maker. He had a smooth voice that projected well, and people told him he was likable. When he spoke, he did his best to sound sincere, even when he thought the words were nonsense.

Not that he would ever tell Gunnvid such a thing. Gunnvid believed every word of what he said, and he trusted Visgar to relay those words for him. That was a trust that Visgar would never betray, whether he really believed the same things or not. Gunnvid had saved his life, just as Visgar had saved his. They came from the far north, where the air was so cold it felt like it would freeze his lungs if he breathed too deeply.

There, it wasn't at all like the south. The villages, if they could even be called that, were much smaller. More open to raid and attack. It happened with such frequency that Visgar often marveled that anyone was left alive at all.

But he and Gunnvid? Together they were unstoppable. Which made it only natural that others wanted to join with them.

Not long after the first of those, Gunnvid had found Fimbruss. An old man, whose last words had been to forgive Gunnvid in the name of the great dragon, had at first intrigued Gunnvid. Even as Visgar had laughed at what he believed to be the ravings of a dying, old lunatic.

But the words kept at Gunnvid, who decided to find out more. Before Visgar even knew what was happening, Gunnvid was telling him about Fimbruss and all that he'd done for Usturg. How they were the most blessed people in the world, living in a veritable paradise, the envy of the other realms.

Visgar had looked at the ice and snow, thought about the constant fighting and death, and had his doubts, but Gunnvid was convinced. Since then, they'd joined the Children of Fimbruss, and now, they were the mighty arm of the holy order, bringing the word to unbelievers with fire and sword.

At least, they had been. Until they'd taken their first town. Now, Gunnvid seemed to be settling in, reluctant to move on.

Visgar was just getting set to put this very idea forth, although couched in much more diplomatic terms, when there was a commotion outside.

The tent flap was torn open and a man rushed in, his cheeks red from exertion.

Visgar grunted. Whatever it was, it must be important. No one would disturb Gunnvid and his commanders without reason. Not if they valued their head being attached to their shoulders.

"Lord Gunnvid!" the man was out of breath and shouting was only making it worse.

"Calm down, son," Visgar told him. "Take a breath, then tell us what you have to say."

"Outside...the sky...." The man was panting, his eyes wild in his head. If Visgar's words had any calming effect, it was minimal at best.

Shaking his head, Visgar stepped out to see what was going on.

Everywhere, men stood with their heads tilted back and their jaws open. Several were on their knees, hands pressed together, as they peered into the sky and muttered prayers.

Visgar looked up as well and almost fell onto his backside.

Something was up there, but… it couldn't be. Whatever it was, it was simply too big to be in the air. It was as if the whole town of Narfasker had suddenly risen into the air.

Whatever it was, it was moving, crossing from north to south above them, gliding slowly.

Visgar shook his head, denying what he was seeing. He knew exactly what it was, although he'd never heard of anyone actually seeing him.

Fimbruss flew overhead, his great wings hardly moving, surely not enough to keep that massive body alight. His neck was so long that Visgar thought he could have run along it for ten minutes without stopping.

It couldn't be, though. Fimbruss was never seen.

Someone grabbed his hand and yanked hard, pulling him to his knees. He was so caught up in watching the dragon that he sank down without a fight, until he shook the hand off and realized it was Gunnvid. Their leader was praying as hard as any other man. When others saw him, they copied, until everywhere Visgar turned, men were kneeling, praying, even weeping.

Visgar did none of that, other than stay on his knees.

Fimbruss didn't even appear to look down at them. If he had come to visit, he was making short work of it. Even as Visgar watched, the dragon slowly glided away, until finally he was little more than a speck, then he was gone.

But still, no one rose. Everyone waited to take their cue from Gunnvid, who stayed knelt, his eyes screwed tightly shut, lips moving furiously in prayer.

Finally, after what felt like far too long to Visgar, he opened his eyes.

Gunnvid looked directly at him and said, "Gather the men. We leave at once."

Chapter 23- Lostin, Ascana

Dommick had been snoring softly, but he came awake at Nettie's furious nudge when she heard the voices approaching. Fortunately, he had the rare, good sense to not say anything. He froze in place, not moving a muscle.

She supposed she should have been glad— for him, anyway— that he had been able to fall asleep. She wished she could have. It felt like they had been hidden in that tiny hole for hours.

At first, it hadn't been so bad. It was dark and tight. She had been pressed into Dommick, her back to his front, and— although she would never admit this to Viktoria or anyone else— it had felt kind of nice. Viktoria pushing her back into Nettie's front wasn't so nice, however, which sort of ruined the whole effect, but she'd tried not to think about that too much.

Then the heat had begun to build. She became aware of a rapidly spreading slickness over her entire body. Sweat dripped down her head, falling into her eyes and stinging, but they were too tightly packed for her to move her arms to wipe it away. Dommick no longer felt nice, now he felt like a sticky, smelly *thing* pressed into her. The same went for Viktoria.

She was sure she was no more pleasant to be next to than either of them, but at least they only had her body on one side of them.

So when she heard Captain Stanford approach the cabin, it was with the hope that he'd slide the desk away and let them climb out of their stinking prison. Those hopes were quickly dashed when she heard more than one voice.

"Sorry about this, Jarmen." That was the voice of the one called Radley, the one who had seemed more reasonable.

"It's no problem," Stanford replied. "He can take his time. I have nothing to hide."

What he really had to hide wanted to scream from directly beneath his feet, but Nettie bit her lip, closed her eyes, and tried to not think about how badly her arms and legs were cramping up.

"Drink?" she heard Stanford ask.

Behind her, Dommick shifted the tiniest bit. Usually, she would have scoffed at that, but at the moment, the thought of something to drink was almost more than she could bear. She didn't want anything from one of those bottles the captain kept in his cabin, though. Nettie wanted nothing more than cool water and a lot of it.

"I shouldn't," Radley replied. "On duty and all." He paused, then, "But why not? I did my part, right?"

"Right you are," Captain Stanford said jovially. "Besides, what else are we going to do while we're stuck here? Should we take them out on deck?"

Before Radley could answer, however, another set of footsteps approached, walking rapidly. The door to Captain Stanford's cabin slammed open and the steps carried into the room.

"Hello, Tilford," Radley said easily. "Finally done? Are we good to let Captain Stanford go about his business?"

"Hardly," Tilford sneered. "Not when I've found *this!*"

Of course, she couldn't see, but Nettie could picture the man— even though she'd never seen him, either— holding something up triumphantly. Some artifact of some sort that would prove to the world that Captain Jarmen Stanford was a thief and a smuggler.

But no one said anything for a moment, before Radley snorted.

"A book? You found a book? And that's bad because…"

"It's not just a book, you dolt," Tilford spit. "Look at it! What does it say? What language is it written in?"

"May I see that?" Stanford asked.

His boots approached where Tilford had stopped directly over where Nettie was hiding. She heard motion that sounded as if he had simply taken the book out of Tilford's hand, rather than waiting for it to be handed over.

She heard pages being turned before Stanford said. "Where did you find this?"

"In one of the cabins," Tilford said. "Hidden under the mattress."

Nettie felt Viktoria stiffen. She'd seen that book in Viktoria's hands and had wondered about it. Now, she knew it must be something important.

"Huh," Stanford said. "Must have been that kid's. I bet he's not happy he left it here."

"What kid? There are no children on this ship." Tilford sounded as if he'd caught Stanford in the lie of the century.

"Not this trip. The last one. We headed for Droy Thus. A family had booked passage, well-to-do, obviously, or they wouldn't have been able to pay the fare. Their kid was weird. He was white as snow and obviously from Ascana. But he wanted to be a wizard from Droy Thus. Wore a red robe, tried to speak in a spooky voice, as if he was privy to arcane secrets." Jarmen chuckled. "I saw him reading that thing a lot. I guess he really wasn't reading it, though. I don't know. Looks to me like some sort of prop the kid made to appear mysterious."

Radley laughed. "Kids, huh? My oldest boy thought he'd go to Usturg. He was filled with tales of fighting and heroism. Then we got a cold snap and a few inches of snow, and he was suddenly much more interested in numbers. Now, he's finishing up his school to apprentice in a dock master's office." Radley sounded proud of his boy. Then his voice changed a bit. "A real dock-master, you know? Someone who comes from a real seafaring background."

Someone— and it had to be Tilford— huffed. Nettie heard something slam down on the desk overhead.

"Bring your ship in when you're given the signal, Captain Stanford. Stay on course. If you don't obey, if you try to come in too early, or you deviate from course, I'll have you sunk."

With that, he stamped from the room.

"He's an ass," Radley sighed. "Don't worry. He can't do anything. He can ask one of the dragonkin, but it's up to them really, and they don't seem too concerned by what we're doing. At least not the blue ones. Those black, though... well, I guess it would be better to stay on Tilford's good side, after all."

"Does he have one?" Jarmen asked. "I hadn't noticed."

Radley laughed, and Nettie heard a glass being set down.

"It was good seeing you, Jarmen. If you have a few days in port, look me up and we'll share a mug or two."

"Sounds like an excellent plan," Captain Stanford returned.

Radley's footsteps walked over their hiding place and out the door. Captain Stanford muttered, "Stay put. Almost done." Then he followed Radley from the cabin.

The book! That cursed book was going to be the death of her one way or the other. Viktoria could just feel it.

First, the disastrous foray into Darkbreath to try to steal it for Sormat in the first place. Not only had that exposed her to Reyson and caused him to come after her, but it had saddled her with Dommick, as well.

Then, it had brought her to the special attention of Mrs. Cloven, and— sure— the woman had tried to help, but what was next? She had said someone would meet her to show her where to go, but how was that even going to be possible?

And now, the book had brought suspicion down on Captain Stanford, who had been nothing but courteous and well-meaning toward her. One of the few people that she'd ever met who seemed to truly be what he seemed, with no ulterior motive.

"I'm throwing it overboard," she thought to herself. "As soon as I'm out of this hole, I'm taking that book and tossing it into the ocean. Sormat can swim for it, if she wants it so badly." And if Reyson showed up, she'd tell him the same, whether he killed her or not.

But she knew she wouldn't do any such thing. That book was important, somehow. Exactly how or to whom, she had no idea, but it *was* important.

"Stop squirming!" Nettie hissed in her ear.

Viktoria hadn't even realized that she was. Now that Nettie had said so, though, she realized that her left leg, the one she was lying on, was in horrible pain. She was trying to shift a bit, just to get some of her weight off of it.

"You stop squirming," she shot back, even though she hadn't felt Nettie move at all.

The woman must have nerves of steel. Yes, Viktoria had spent years learning how to hide, but that didn't make it pleasant. Being crammed into that dark, stinking hole, with the ship rocking back and forth, back and forth, underneath her was almost more than she could bear. She tried to swallow, but her throat felt as swollen as her lips and tongue did.

But Nettie seemed to be taking it in stride. Well, why wouldn't she? When they got of there, she could pass as one of the crew and disembark with the rest of them. How would she— and Dommick, for that matter— do the same? Their pale, pale skin showed clearly that they weren't Ascani. At least not sailors, used to being in the sun and the wind for hours on end.

For a moment, she envisioned her new life as being completely on this ship. A rat, caught in the hold and never again to go ashore.

If that was the case, she decided, she'd follow the book overboard.

After what felt like hours more, but must have been only minutes, Captain Stanford came back into the cabin. Viktoria heard a drawer open above her, a loud click, then daylight flooded into the hole as he pushed the desk away.

She blinked rapidly and must have pulled back sharply, because she heard a sudden squawk from Nettie behind her.

"Sorry," she muttered, but she was already letting Stanford help her up and out.

She staggered across the cabin, her legs barely supporting her, and felt the roll of the ship more than ever. For a moment, she thought she was going to get sick, but then she collapsed to the floor, legs stretched out in front of her.

Nettie came next, looking weak and bedraggled, but not nearly in as bad a shape as Viktoria felt. The other woman glared at her, then shuffled to the other wall to sit the same way she was.

Dommick was last. He grinned at Captain Stanford, who chuckled and shook his head. Then Dommick promptly doubled over and threw up, right back into the hole they'd just come out of.

"You're cleaning that up," Stanford told him, but took him by the arm to guide him to a chair. "And you better hope you don't need to go back in there before you do."

A brief knock sounded at the door, and Viktoria tensed, but it was only the cabin boy. He had a skin of water that he wordlessly handed to Stanford before retreating without even looking at Viktoria or the others. As if they weren't even there.

"As far as the crew is concerned," Stanford said, handing the skin to Nettie first, "you three are gone already. You weren't even here, as a matter of fact. Not that anyone is asking, mind you, but if you try to speak to one of them and get the 'you're a ghost' treatment, you'll know why."

He took the skin from Nettie and handed it to Viktoria.

Water. Only slightly warm and with a faint musty taste, like maybe the skin wasn't all that clean, it was still the sweetest drink she'd ever had. She took a slow sip, aware that too much at once was going to have her heaving like Dommick had. Then a deeper one, then another, before she held it out for Dommick.

"I don't suppose there's anything a little less... watery?" Dommick asked.

"There is," the captain said. "But right now, it's that or nothing for you."

Dommick nodded sadly, took the skin, and drank deeply. When he lowered it, he didn't seem disappointed.

"Now we have to talk about how we're really going to get you off the ship," Captain Stanford said. "We have a little time. If I know anything, and I do, it will be some hours before that preening little popinjay calls us in. Punishment for not having any contraband on board."

He walked to the desk and picked up the book. "Except, of course, for this." He looked directly at Viktoria. "Anything you want to say?"

"A dragonkin named Sormat wants it." What was the sense at this point of trying to be evasive or making up some lie. "She ordered me to break into Darkbreath Tower. They're a clan... like... I don't know, really, if you have an equivalent. A family that controls things."

She jutted her chin toward Dommick. "It's where I picked him up. He's one of them."

"Guilty as charged," Dommick said. His voice was muffled. After drinking, he now had his head cradled in his folded arms on the desktop.

"You didn't give it to this dragonkin, though," Stanford said. It wasn't a question.

"No. She would have killed me anyway. And if she wanted it, I didn't want her to have it. Then... well, Mrs. Cloven told me it was important. Said it was written in the language of the Evening Folk."

"And what?" Nettie asked. She looked angry, as if she was just now hearing about things that might have greatly affected her own life. Which, of course, she was. "*You* were going to read it? Are you an expert in ancient languages, now?"

"No," Viktoria replied tiredly. She was getting tired of constantly clashing with Nettie. "But she asked me to bring it here. She said there were those who were working on... something. She didn't say what. And that the book might be important."

"Someone in Lostin?" Stanford sounded dubious. "There isn't much here, beyond the port. I mean, I guess goods go out from here to all over Ascana, but... here?"

Viktoria shrugged. "He's supposed to find me here."

She fell silent and wouldn't meet Nettie's eyes. She could feel them boring into her, blaming her for everything.

Nettie wanted to get up and slap Viktoria. She didn't for a few reasons.

One, she was quite sure Captain Stanford— and maybe Dommick— would have stopped her. Two, she wasn't sure she even had the strength to get up right then, let alone start a fight.

Three, she knew her anger was misplaced.

Withholding information about that book hadn't brought Nettie to Reclium. It hadn't sent her through those dark tunnels or into Pharax. It hadn't forced her to hide in the hold of a ship. None of it had been Viktoria's fault, and all of it would have happened whether she'd had the book or not.

She was angry because she was home. Ascana was right there! A five-minute walk if she could tread across the waves. All she needed to do was get off the ship, then she'd be able to get hired on as a wagon guard or something to get further inland. It might take time, but she could work her way all the way back to her parents.

Maybe, someday, she'd go back to sea. But, at the moment, she felt that she never wanted to see it again.

However, she couldn't do any of that. Because for some unearthly reason she had yet to understand, vile, horrible, cruel black dragonkin were in Lostin! In Ascana, where they had no right to be.

They were what was stopping her from getting home. Not Dommick, not Viktoria, and certainly not some stupid book.

She dropped her eyes, not wanting to glare at Viktoria anymore. She was tired of blaming her for everything, tired of feeling like she had to live up to the other woman.

"You're not really a problem," Captain Stanford said, and with a jolt, Nettie realized he was talking to her. "You're a sailor and no one here knows the crew. Just me and the other officers. But you two…"

He turned to Viktoria and Dommick.

"You're a different story." He scratched at his beard. "I'm not sure what to do with—"

"I do," Nettie said.

The others all looked at her. She had been thinking of it while they baked beneath the floorboards. A plan had formed, and now all she needed to do was put it into place.

It shouldn't be hard. Not at all, really. The trick was going to be staying alive after she'd pulled it off.

Chapter 24- Fimbruss

Fimbruss couldn't say that he really understood Gillbriss's methods. The way she'd always run her own realm had been a mystery to him. Why even bother having humans if all you were going to do was isolate and torture them?

Fine, throw the mountains up. Make movement throughout the territory difficult, if not impossible. Why not? They'd each done as they'd pleased with their realms when they'd changed the world. Except for Tophonoss, who had merely inherited hers and seemed fine with that.

But why make yourself hated?

Now, Haiteng and Chimbod... they had it nearly right. They'd nurtured their humans to do things which pleased them. Chimbod with her fascination of magic and encouraging her humans to learn it. Showing them how, even, until they'd begun to evolve into having the innate ability at a rate almost rivaling the dragonkin. In hindsight, maybe that hadn't been so smart, but Fimbruss understood why she'd done it.

And Haiteng? Fimbruss didn't necessarily understand his fascination with money and commerce, but he suspected it was a sort of mental exercise his brother enjoyed. Whether that was true or not, Haiteng's humans revered and respected him. All to the good.

But neither of them had gone far enough. The current situation was proof of that.

Both Haiteng and Chimbod had been forced to radically change their relationships with their humans. Instead of remaining benevolent overlords, watching out for their charges' best interest, they were now terrifying enforcers of arbitrary rules, their children wreaking havoc whenever they chose to. Their realms were on fire, sometimes literally.

Usturg, however...

Usturg was under control, and he'd needed to do almost nothing to make it happen. Dispatch a couple of his children to speak to a select group of humans. Now, they marched, in his name, to do his bidding.

Neither Haiteng nor Tophonoss had agreed to his army— his Children of Fimbruss, as they so pathetically called themselves— coming into their realms. But once they'd done away with the edict and allowed dragonkin to go where they pleased, or where they were sent by the dragons, what difference did it make?

When all was said and done, if a few villages in the northern reaches of those two realms now spoke Fimbruss's name in worship, what of it? The land would turn cold and white, that was all. Then it would become Usturg, and soon enough, no one would even remember it had ever been anything else.

He knew they all thought him obtuse, which was fine with him. It was an image he'd cultivated, a game he'd played for long, long years. Let them believe it. They weren't watching him nearly as much as they did each other.

He rolled and let his great body fall through the air. As usual, he flew higher than even the largest of his children could go. He loved the solitude and the way the stars glittered in the frigid air. Now, though...

He dropped through the clouds and leveled out, rolling again so that his belly faced toward the ground. He slowed down, so there was no chance he wouldn't be seen.

Beneath him, a herd of deer scattered. He thought about taking one but decided to let them all live. He was in a generous mood.

Soon, he saw his destination and slowed even further. His wings flapped majestically, propelling him through the air with little effort.

The humans cried out and fell to their knees. The city— Narfasker, he believed it was called— was smoldering in some places, ruined in yet others, and strangely intact in sections. Which made him frown. The Children weren't supposed to be destroying his cities, only bringing those who didn't yet fully believe in line.

But perhaps, he thought, that was the only way to do it.

He didn't look down as he flew over. Let them wonder if he had deigned to notice them.

As he drifted off, he rose again, climbing even higher than before.

Far below, through the clouds, the world spread out. When all was said and done, a little bit more of it was going to belong to him.

Chapter 25- Craydon, Ascana

"Wake up!" Kori shook Wyman again.

The old man was sleeping the sleep of the exhausted, and no wonder. The dragonkin had worked his crew hard that day. When Wyman had come home, before Kori went to see Toni, he had told him so in as few words as possible. He'd eaten a small amount of the food Kori had given him, stumbled to his bedroom and was asleep by the time Kori had looked in a few minutes later.

Now, it was the middle of the night, and Kori might have thought Wyman was dead if he hadn't been snoring so loudly.

"Come on…wake up!"

"Wha? Who? Kori? What are you doing?"

That was more coherent than Kori would have been able to manage being awakened from such a deep sleep.

"We need help, Wyman. We're in trouble."

"We? Who's we?"

The old man sat up, peering past Kori to the outer room where Toni was silhouetted against the light of one lantern they'd lit.

"Oh." Wyman looked at Kori and shook his head. "Got her in the family way, did you? That's not something you need my help for. It will come to you—"

"No!" Kori said quickly, cutting off whatever Wyman had been about to say.

He raised his hands, noticing that they were trembling and unable to make them stop, and ran them through his hair.

"It's not that. It's… worse."

Wyman had seen Kori's hands, too. "All right, then. Tell me what it is. It can't be that bad."

Kori took a deep breath. "It is, though. I… killed a dragonkin."

Saying it out loud, even daring to speak of it, made it seem even more unreal than it already did. He'd killed a dragonkin? That was ridiculous. No human could do such a thing, especially not one man, single-handedly *and* with too much beer in him. It simply wasn't possible.

"Hmph," Wyman snorted, then chuckled. "You almost got me, there, Kori. For just a minute, I thought... but... you couldn't have..."

He was watching Kori's face and whatever he saw there must have told him that Kori was serious.

"Kori," he breathed. "You can't have. It's just not—"

"I know. Believe me, I know. But it was going to kill us. I didn't have a choice, and now we have to—"

"Get out," Wyman said, cutting Kori off in turn.

"Yes, we have to get out, but I don't know how."

But Wyman was shaking his head. "That's not what I mean. I mean you need to get out of my house. Right now."

He was scrambling out of bed, pushing Kori to move. Kori stood, blinking stupidly in the half-light of the bedroom.

"I will. I just need to know where to go. How to—"

"No!" Wyman said again, louder this time. "*You* did this! Not me! I'm not getting killed as the accomplice of someone who killed a dragonkin. Do you know what they would do to me?"

"There's no way they can know," Kori protested. "At least not yet. Just let us hide here tonight, maybe tomorrow, until we figure out—"

"Get out!" Wyman yelled. There were tears streaming down his weathered cheeks now. "I took you in! I gave you a safe place to stay! And this is what you bring me?"

Kori's mouth opened, but Antonia stepped close to him and closed her hand on his arm.

"It's okay," she said quietly. "We understand. Come on, Kori. We need to go."

"But—"

Wyman pushed past him and rushed to the couch where Kori had slept. He gathered up the few possessions Kori owned, including his book, and threw them on the blanket he'd given him. He bundled it all together, hurried back, and shoved it into Kori's arms.

"There. That's your stuff and my blanket, which you're welcome to. Now go."

Kori backed away from the old man. There was a part of him that wondered where that rage, the same rage that had flared up in him so instantly at the dragonkin was. But there was no anger toward Wyman. There wasn't much of anything, really, other than a great sadness.

Numbly, he let Toni guide him out the door.

He turned to say that he was sorry, but Wyman had already closed it behind him. Kori heard the *snick* of the lock being turned, then the bolt being thrown.

"Now what?" he asked Toni.

After leaving Wyman's they'd stayed to the shadows as much as they could, always making their way toward the edge of town. Now, they were huddled against the side of a building, a barn from what Kori could make out, looking out over the fields.

On all sides of Craydon were fields. At one time, the town had grown several crops, depending on the season. They had been harvested, processed in one manner or another, and sent out across Ascana, either to other towns and cities who grew none of their own, or to be sold to other realms.

Inward traffic had consisted of meat and other materials. Craydon was just one cog in the vast machine that was Ascana. A machine that hadn't so much broken down, as it had been deliberately smashed.

None of which made getting across the vast expanse of open farmland without being seen any easier.

"We go," Toni said. "What choice do we have?"

Kori wasn't so sure. For one, Toni still had a chunk of wood embedded in her upper arm. And her leg was badly burned in a couple of spots from the dragonkin's acid. Even if they had enough speed to reach cover before sunup, when the townspeople would start coming to "work," and the dragonkin would be watching, he doubted she'd have the strength to manage it.

"No," he sighed. "Not now. We have to go when it's just gotten dark. We'll never make it now." He looked at the barn and said, "Wait here."

Moving around to the front, he tried the door, but it was locked, as he had feared it would be. So he made his way around the side. A couple of water barrels and crates were dumped there, so he stacked one on top of the other, until he could clamber up them and get to a high window. It wasn't much. It was there to provide ventilation, not a view. But it was just enough.

He prayed— not to Fimbruss, just in general— then worked the blade of his axe under the bottom of the sash and pried.

He almost cried when the window swung open from the top.

There was no way he was fitting through with his axe in his belt, so— stomach in his throat— he passed it through and let go. There was no clatter of it hitting the floor, so he hoped it had fallen on something soft.

Then he pushed himself up, wriggled his head and shoulders through, and balanced there on his stomach, trying to see.

It was dark inside, of course. Too dark to make out much of anything. There was nothing for it but to finish the job, so he wiggled some more, scraping his stomach on the sill, until he overbalanced and fell all the way in.

Like his axe, he landed on something that was soft and yielding.

Kori tumbled down to the floor, then felt his way toward the front of the building while his eyes adjusted. The door was easy enough to open from the inside, and when he did, he found Toni already there, slumped against the wall next to it.

"About time," she said, her voice having already grown weak.

"I decided to stop for a little sit-down first," he answered, but he was already helping her though the door. He pulled it shut behind him and relocked it, then tried to figure out where they were.

He could see bales of hay and sacks filled with. . . something or other. Since Kori had never been a farmer, he wasn't sure what it was, but what he could determine was that the barn was far from full. He assumed that, come daylight, the doors would be opened and more of whatever they were now looking at would be brought in.

The trick was going to be to hide throughout the day. Afterwards, they could leave as soon as darkness fell again, moving slowly and hoping to stay unobserved. He was sure dragonkin could see in the dark, but at least then, those would be the only eyes they'd have to worry about.

He guided Toni toward the back of the barn, trying to note how the bags and bales were stacked. Maybe he could move some of them and create a space where they could conceal themselves.

Toni stumbled as they went.

"You doing okay?" he asked her.

"Dandy," she said, but it came out slurred.

It was just exhaustion, Kori kept telling himself. At the same time knowing it was more. Her arm was oozing blood where the chunk of wood was still embedded. Not a lot, but, over time, the amount she'd lost was adding up. He needed to get it out of her and bind the wound, soon. Otherwise, all sorts of bad things were going to happen.

He led her to a bale and told her to sit. His eyes had adjusted to the light enough so that he could see what it was he was doing.

Okay, pulling the wood out was straightforward. It was going to hurt, but there was no helping that. But what to use for...?

Of course.

"Hold on," he said to her. "I'll be right back."

Toni hadn't been thinking clearly, and in his worry over her, he'd forgotten as well.

He hurried back to the door, unlocked and cracked it open. No one was about, so he rushed around to the side of the building.

There, right where he'd left it, was the bundle Wyman had pushed into his arms. Including the blanket. Kori grabbed it, ran back, and was with Toni again in just a couple of minutes.

He untied the knot he'd made in the blanket. There was nothing in the bundle he needed to keep other than his book, which he shoved back inside his shirt where it had stayed for so long. He then located his axe and, holding it between his knees, used the blade to make a cut in the blanket.

Moments later, he had several long strips of cloth. Enough to wrap Toni's arm and have some left over to change it when needed.

"Give me your arm," he said.

Toni was slumped against the stack of bales behind her, but she roused a bit at that.

"You mean my hand?" She giggled tiredly. "Strange time to ask me to marry you."

"Your arm," he said again. "We need to get that wood out of it."

"Oh." She looked down at the hunk of wood sticking out of her bicep. "Hey? Is that part of one of my tables?"

"Might be," Kori said. He took her arm and raised it to be level, tucking her hand under his armpit. "This might hurt."

"Then don't— owww!"

Kori was proud of her. What he was doing must have caused excruciating pain, but she gritted her teeth, hissed, and let the tears flow, while making very little noise.

It wasn't as straightforward as he'd thought it would be. The wood was slick with her blood, which, combined with the smooth finish on one side of it, made it difficult to grab. When he tried, no matter how careful he was being, he couldn't seem to help jarring it, so that it rocked back and forth. When he managed to get a handle on it, the wood would begin to come out, but then his fingers would slide off of it, and it would sink back in.

"I can't get a grip," he muttered, blinking sweat from his eyes.

"Do it, would you? Or else let it be!"

No matter how hard he squeezed, though, he just couldn't hang on to it.

Finally, he took her arm in both of his large hands, one near her elbow, the other up near her shoulder. He bent over it, like a man about to tear into a turkey leg, and took the wood in his teeth. He bit down hard, almost gagging at the foul taste of the fluid that came from the fibers.

He jerked his head straight back, trying to make it as smooth as he could.

The hunk of wood slid free. Toni stifled a scream, then a sob.

Kori spat the wood out, grabbed a strip of the blanket, which he folded over and pressed to her arm.

"Ouch! What are you doing?" she groaned.

"It's going to bleed now. Best that we let if for a few, but not enough for you to get weaker. I'll bind it in a minute, then go see if I can find some water. Both to wash this and to drink."

"Never would have pegged you as a nursemaid," she said, but her voice had grown quieter again. The rush of the pain was wearing off and the rest was catching up with her.

"Hold this tight," he told her, placing her other hand over the bandage. He waited to make sure she would grab it, and when she did he moved to the back of the barn. He shifted a few things around to create a hole among the stacked bags, then went back for her.

When he got her settled in and the pad he'd made tied securely to her arm, she fell asleep almost immediately.

Then, he hurried back to the front and snuck out the door again. Water wasn't going to be hard. There were rain barrels aplenty in Craydon. Water was the one thing the dragonkin weren't restricting. Slaves couldn't work for long without water.

When the morning came, Kori felt like he'd hardly slept at all. He'd lain there, cramped in the little nest he'd made them, and listened to Toni's breathing. At first, the sound had kept him awake. She was having a hard time of it, her breath growing ragged at times or sounding phlegmy. Then, it was when it went too quiet. When her breathing evened out and became almost silent; he'd jerk awake, sure that she had died.

So he was awake before she was, but he remained still, and just watched her. Her color was a little better, and she didn't seem quite so fragile. All to the good, since he'd been sure at time last night that she would die, just as Asta had.

He'd awakened her to drink some water, which she'd taken readily, before falling back asleep. Unfortunately, they didn't have any food with them. He hadn't thought to bring any, since he'd assumed they'd be hiding in Wyman's house for the day. Now, they were about to head back into the wilderness with nothing.

Of course, they were still in Ascana. The wilderness may go on for a bit, but it was nothing like the wilds of Usturg. He was sure they'd be able to hunt or forage something or come across a farm where they could beg food.

Something, anyway.

While he had been thinking, Toni had woken up again. She sat up with a soft groan and looked around.

"Are we in a barn?"

"We are," Kori shrugged. "It was open. Open enough, anyway. I figure we can stay here today, then try to sneak the rest of the way out tonight."

Toni looked down at her arm. "You took it out. Good. That was really starting to bother me."

"How's it feel now?"

"Horrible. Hurts like someone cut my arm off, but at least I'm not hitting that chunk of wood on everything now."

"That was the idea," Kori said. "I thought, for a little while there, that… you know…"

"I wasn't going to make it?" She gave a brief laugh. "That would figure, wouldn't it? We make it through a dragonkin attack, and then I die because a piece of tabletop gets lodged in my arm."

Kori grinned, too, but it faded quickly. The attack was still too fresh, the ramification for what they were going to do now too real.

"What was it?" she finally asked.

"What was what?"

Toni's eyes dropped to the axe, once again at Kori's hip. "You killed that dragonkin. With one blow. And there was a flash of some kind when you hit it."

He grimaced and put his hand down, almost as if he were trying to hide the axe. "I don't know. I'd never used it on a dragonkin before. Obviously. I mean… who would have thought I would have to?"

"But you *have* used it, right? And not just to chop wood?"

"I have," he nodded. It wasn't something he liked to think about, really. "I never wanted to, though."

"I'm glad to hear *that*," she replied. "But that's not really the point. Did it do the same thing, then?"

"No. It's just a normal axe."

"But it's not. That's obvious. Whatever it did— magic or something— must only work on dragonkin."

His grimace spoke for him, but still he said, "We don't know that—"

"Of course we do," she interrupted. "You killed a dragonkin. A *dragonkin*! With one blow. I like you a lot, and I think you're strong and all, but... I mean, come on."

Kori didn't say anything. He pulled the axe loose and looked down at it.

"Where did you get it?" Toni asked him.

"It was my uncle's." Kori shrugged. "He was more of a father to me than my own was."

"You told me about him. You just never mentioned that he happened to have a magic, dragonkin-killing axe."

"I guess he did? He never told me that or where the axe came from."

Toni considered. "Keep it hidden," she said. "As best you can, anyway. I have a feeling that any dragonkin who happened to see it would be *very* interested in it."

Before Kori could answer, the sound of a key in the lock to the door caught their attention.

Kori had been right. The barn was going to be open and used during the day. His axe wasn't the only thing that needed to stay hidden.

Chapter 26- Reyson

The thought of "the book" burned in his brain. Brighter and hotter than the fire which had consumed his body and then put him back together. Which was a memory that was very fresh in his mind. No matter how much time passed, he could still feel it: his skin crisping and peeling away, his muscles literally falling off, then his bones turning to powder.

And then...? He was "there" again. Whole. Looking much the same as he ever had. If he didn't know better, he would have said it was all a nightmare, that he'd never even met Sormat and been taken to that peak, abandoned there to make his way down, naked and without food.

But the pain— that constant, never-fading pain— told a different story. That said that it *had* happened.

That, and the fact that his clothing had disappeared.

Reyson had returned to himself, at least mostly, half-way down a steep incline. He'd been sliding along, moving faster than he should have been, when he suddenly remembered who he was.

He'd looked around in confusion, unsure of where he was or how he'd gotten there. Wondering what he was doing on the side of a mountain with no clothes and the wind whipping past him so hard it was a wonder he stayed on his feet.

Which was all that was needed for him to miss a step and overbalance. Before he could even think to stop himself, he was sliding, tumbling, end over end, down the slope. There was nothing to grab onto, no ledges, just hard rocks that jutted out of the snow and did more damage when he hit them.

By the time he stopped, where the slope evened out a bit and a tree strong enough to stop his plummet grew, Reyson had a broken leg, several broken ribs, a gash across his forehead that bled into his eyes, and his left hand was shattered.

He felt every bit of it, even though the blood that ran over his face was almost as cold as the snow he was lying in.

The bones knitting almost made him scream. His lower leg was bent in a sharp angle, between his knee and ankle, right where a leg shouldn't bend. But even as he looked down, it began to straighten. He wasn't doing it, but whatever was didn't care whether or not it felt good. The bone cut into his skin as it slid back into place, his foot moved on its own, until his leg was straight again, and the skin closed back up.

His hand made audible cracking noises as his bent and twisted fingers pulled straight, and sharp, agonizing pains flared through his chest as his ribs mended.

He screamed. Not caring who heard him or if it set off an avalanche. He actually hoped for the latter. Maybe several tons of snow, ice, and rock would do what Sormat hadn't.

But none of it happened. The "healing"— if that's what it could be called— went on and on. Days? Probably not, but surely hours. Several hours, at least. It surely couldn't only be minutes.

When it was done, and that pain ebbed away only to reveal that the agony of immolation was still very much with him, Reyson stayed where he was, breathing softly and cursing Sormat and every other dragonkin.

With that, the pain got worse. Not just the pain across his body, but within his head.

The Book. The Book. The Book.

It was a refrain that got louder and more insistent, until it was screaming inside his own mind, loud enough that he felt like his head was going to explode.

"All right!" he screamed again. "I'll go!"

He scrambled to his feet gingerly, testing his leg before putting his full weight on it. He needn't have worried. It supported him as easily as the other.

The Book.

He continued downhill again. One good thing had happened. His fall down the mountainside had taken him far along. The terrain was still harsh. He *was* still in Reclium, after all, but it wasn't the almost sheer-cliffs of the higher peaks.

The screaming insistence in his mind began to fade as he walked. It never left, any more than the burning did, but it did allow him to think.

That girl he'd been after— what was her name? Viktoria... something. She had the book that Sormat wanted. So he needed to find her. Which was all to the good, since Lord Maganti had given him the same task.

The problem was, Reyson had no idea where she'd gone. He knew she'd been with the whore, but after that? Mrs. Cloven had gotten the better of him, and where Viktoria had gone from there, he had no idea and no way of finding out. Short of going back to Pharax and trying to get the information from her.

But the old woman was smart. Reyson had underestimated her once, he wasn't going to again. He also had the feeling that if he failed again, Sormat would take revenge. Somehow. Somehow that would make what she'd already done seem like a picnic.

So, the answer was to find out what the book was. Where Viktoria might be taking it.

For the first time since Sormat had found him near-dead from Mrs. Cloven's poison, Reyson smiled.

Heldum and Darkbreath Tower. That was the place to go. Lord Maganti obviously knew what the book was. So he might know where it was going.

And if not, Reyson was looking forward to getting the answer from him, anyway. The man had a tower full of life-takers at his disposal. Even before his "change," Reyson would have looked forward to the challenge. Now? Now it wasn't a challenge at all. And no one in the world was going to shed a tear for Lord Maganti.

The book, the inner voice insisted.

"Yes," Reyson answered it. "The book."

The voice quieted down. The burning, however, remained, hurrying Reyson along.

Chapter 27- Obristan Forest

It was hard to see through the leaves, but he was pretty sure there were people still alive. At least, there was *something* moving in the ruins of the building.

"What do you think?" Calidor whispered.

Yarah was at his shoulder, both of them peering toward the heap of rubble. "I don't know. Could just be a cat or something."

"Could be," he agreed. "But it might not be."

"It might not be," she agreed.

Neither of them made a move, however. The building had once been an inn, with an attached stable and what looked like a blacksmith's forge across the yard. Calidor didn't know, but it seemed that it had been a nice place, once. He could imagine the innkeeper and his wife, smiling as they greeted guests. Maybe it was their son who had taken up blacksmithing as a trade— a noble profession and much needed. Their younger son, or maybe daughter, had been responsible for stabling travelers' horses, rubbing them down and giving them oats and clean water.

He knew none of that, of course, but in his mind, that was how inns worked. At least those in Obristan. The roads were safe, thanks to the Honor Guard, which sent its members out on long patrols, to hone their skills and enforce the Prince's Peace.

Now, *nothing* was safe and the Honor Guard might be a thing of the past. Lamorak and Rainaldus the last of them, and both gone away.

He sank down with a sigh, then looked back a few steps to where the young girl waited. After her initial questions when he had pulled her from the rubble of her own house, she hadn't cried again. Neither had she spoken, but there was something in her eyes… something hard.

Which was no good. She was a kid. She should be doing kid things. He didn't know what those were anymore than he knew who had owned the inn they were hidden near, but he knew she shouldn't be there!

"I'm going to look," he said quietly. "You stay here."

Yarah put her hand on his arm before he could rise, however. "I should go. You stay."

He shook his head. "No. They're my people. I appreciate it." He patted her hand, then removed it from his arm. Strange, though. For a moment, he could have sworn he still felt it there. "Watch out for her, okay? Don't let her follow. She's seen too much."

To add to the ever-growing list of things he didn't know, Calidor had no idea what he'd find that she shouldn't see. But the possibility that he was going to come across bodies, broken and torn to pieces, was very real. If he did, he would spare her the sight, if he could.

Yarah scowled but didn't protest.

Calidor nodded at her, turned back toward the once-inn, and slowly moved forward, cautiously pushing the low branches aside and being careful to ease them back into place. He stepped as lightly as he could, putting one foot down and moving it slightly back and forth, trying to find any twigs or dead leaves before he put his full weight on them.

He'd never make a bandit, he thought, as a branch he hadn't felt cracked anyway.

He froze, but nothing moved other than him.

The woods ended here. The inn had stood at the edge of them, the road crossing in front of it as it ran from the low hills to the east toward where he'd crept forward. Once it entered the woods, it ran uninterrupted to the Ascana border, so it was— or had been— a fairly busy thoroughfare. Now, no one was on it.

Once he left the cover of the forest, he froze.

If he was being honest, he wasn't sure what to do now, what the best course of action should be. Should he stride brazenly forward, as if he had every right to be there? Or should he drop down and crawl, ready to sprawl into the dirt at the first sign of movement?

In the end, he did neither of those things. He approached slowly, but upright, half-turned, as if he could run back into the safety of the woods at a moment's notice.

It was funny, really, how much easier it had been to approach a town, ruined or otherwise, with two Honor Guard and a few Droy Thus wizards at his side. He was suddenly regretting telling Lamorak to go on to Greenfair. Maybe he would have been better served to stay with him.

When he was still several feet away, the movement he thought he'd seen from the woods came again.

The main building had collapsed, but it had once been two stories, so the pile of debris was fairly large. Not large enough to hide a dragonkin from view— or at least that's what Calidor hoped— but large enough.

Unless it was a smaller dragonkin, like some of the black ones he'd seen.

Calidor clamped down on that thought. It wasn't a dragonkin that was moving, and most definitely not a black one.

Something flew out from behind the pile, but not at Calidor. Whatever it was went to the side, in a lazy arc, almost as if whatever or whomever had tossed it had done so casually.

And it hadn't been big.

It was followed by another, this one identifiable as a metal plate of some kind. It clattered against the hard ground.

Calidor heard muttering.

"No good. Not much left, really. Not much at all. Can't rebuild. With what? Use what for tools? This? Ha!"

Something else… what might have been the ruined handle of a tool of some sort, joined the plate.

Whoever was talking, it certainly wasn't a dragonkin. Calidor froze and listened, but the voice had dropped to a low mutter, and he couldn't make out what was being said.

He cleared his throat. "Hello?"

The muttering instantly stopped. There was no sound of anyone moving, either. Whoever it was, they had frozen the same way he had.

It was going to be hard to hear anything, Calidor realized, over the beating of his own heart. It pounded in his head, and when he swallowed, it was loud enough that a whole gang of dragonkin could have landed behind him and he wouldn't have heard them.

"Hello!" he tried again, trying to put more princely authority into his voice.

A head stuck out from behind the rubble and stared at him. A fringe of gray hair circling an otherwise bald pate stuck up in every direction. The face beneath it was lined with age, and the wide-open eyes and mouth set in an "O" of surprise gave the man an almost comical appearance.

At least, it would have, if anything at all was funny these days.

From the little Calidor could see, the man wore a gray shirt, with a brown vest over it. The same thing he would have envisioned an innkeeper wearing.

The man didn't move. His watery eyes blinked once, like an owl caught in the daylight.

Calidor cleared his throat. "Erm. Hello. Are you… hurt?"

The man blinked again, then suddenly drew back, now reminding Calidor more of a frightened turtle than an owl.

"Too much time in the forest," he thought to himself. "I must have animals on my mind."

Behind the pile, he heard the muttering again. "Wants to know if we're hurt. Not hurt, but… scared? Yes. Scared. Then again… he might not be real."

Calidor took a step forward but froze halfway through it when the man peeked around the pile once more, then disappeared again just as suddenly.

"Yes, real. I think. Must be real. He's talking. And walking. Not at the same time, though, which is strange."

"I am real," Calidor called. He tried not to yell too loudly, having no wish to attract anyone— or anything— else that might be in the area. "My name is Calidor. I'm the Prince of Obristan, if the name doesn't mean anything to you. I'm here to help."

At his words, the muttering stopped. Calidor strained his ears but didn't hear anything that he thought might be the man running away.

He kept moving forward, tensed and ready to dodge should the man decide to throw something at him.

When he came around the pile, he found the man still there. In addition to the shirt and vest, he had on brown pants and sturdy boots, one of which had ripped along the side and been tied back together with a bit of twine. He was sitting on a clump of stones, hunched over and turned away from Calidor.

"Hello," Calidor said again, even though he felt it was an inadequate introduction.

The man blinked again, then rapidly rose to his feet. He turned quickly, almost tripping in the tangle of rubble he was amid.

"Real." He reached out a trembling hand. "You're real."

"I am," Calidor assured him. "You are, too. What's your name, friend?"

"Name? My name. My name was… Otto. Yes. Otto, was me."

"It still is you, Otto," Calidor smiled. "Was this your inn?"

Otto looked down, then around at the piles of rubbish that had once been his home and business. "Yes. It was mine. Mine and Ophelia's. It fell down. Two nights ago."

Fell down, Calidor thought. Either the man didn't even realize he'd been attacked, or he'd blocked it out.

"Ophelia is your wife?" he asked.

The man nodded and wrung his hands.

"Where is she now?" Calidor asked him.

Otto nodded toward the big pile. "There. She's sleeping under there, now. I hope she's comfortable."

He didn't want to look at the pile, and Calidor couldn't blame him. Whether he'd truly been driven mad by what had happened, or if he was just in the throes of grief, Calidor didn't know. What he did know was that he couldn't just leave him there.

"Do you want to come with me? Join our little group?"

"I couldn't," Otto replied. His eyes flickered to the rubble. "I can't leave her like that," he whispered.

"Then we won't," Calidor decided. "Come on. We'll find her and give her a proper rest."

He knew what Lamorak would say if he was there. There wasn't time. The dragonkin who had done this could be back. There were dead everywhere; it didn't make sense to bury the one.

But it made sense to Otto. Maybe they had been together since they were children, or maybe only a year. Calidor had no way of knowing, but he knew pain when he saw it.

Without waiting for Otto, he grabbed a board and pulled, shifting it from the pile. It was heavy, but he dragged it free and dropped it. Then he went back for another, and another after that.

Soon, Otto joined in, grabbing hold of the other end of a beam, one that must have supported the roof or maybe one of the floors. It was long and heavy, and the two of them barely managed to get it free and moved away.

When they had, Calidor leaned back and stretched. He wiped his brow, and his hand came away slick with sweat.

It was some time later that he noticed another set of hands, darker and thinner than his own, move a stone. He hadn't even noticed Yarah pitching in, or the girl, who took smaller pieces of rubble.

"She shouldn't be—" he began, but the girl scowled at him and kept moving.

All right, then. He'd tried to shield her, but maybe the world had become that type of place. The type where children aren't allowed to be children for long.

They found her arm first, encased in the sleeve of a blue dress. Otto gave a cry and knelt next to her, bending over her hand and weeping.

For a moment, Calidor wondered why. Surely he had to know that she was already gone? But then, it occurred to him that until he actually saw her body, Otto had allowed some sort of hope to live in him. Now, that hope was gone.

He and Yarah carefully uncovered the rest of her.

Like her husband, Ophelia was not young. Calidor thought she must have been a great beauty, though, and not even death could take that from her. Somehow, the way the inn had collapsed around her left her relatively unscathed. Her neck was bent at an angle that it shouldn't be, however, which told Calidor how she had died. He didn't think Otto had noticed, which was probably just fine.

"We need to bury her," he said softly.

"With what?" Yarah asked him, bending to speak into his ear. "We don't have anything to dig with, unless you want to start sifting through the other piles for a shovel."

Calidor looked around. He didn't want to do that. Not at all.

But...

The inn had had a fireplace made of stone, which had tumbled down like the rest of it. Those stones were scattered across the ground and in with the debris. It had been more than two stories high, a large structure.

"We'll build a cairn," he said, "and lay her to rest in that."

To his surprise, the girl gathered the first stone. It was too big for her, really, but she struggled with it to a clear place in the yard and laid it down. Then she went back for another.

It took some time, but they finally had enough to surround her body. Calidor helped Otto gently lift her and lay her within. Otto closed his eyes, said a few words, then folded her hands on top of her chest, and under his direction, since Calidor had no idea how to go about it, they used more stone to cover her over.

When it was done, they stayed by the side of the cairn for a few moments, giving the old man a chance to say goodbye.

Finally, he looked at them.

"Thank you," he said simply, and Calidor thought maybe a bit of the madness had left him. Maybe just finding her and being able to say goodbye had helped.

"Come with us," Calidor said. "There's nothing here now."

"Is there with you?" Otto asked. He *was* sounding much more coherent, even able to ask such an astute question.

"No," Calidor replied honestly. "Not at the moment. We have nothing but each other. But... we're going to. We're going to gather up all those we can. We're going to save whoever needs it and—"

"Okay," Otto said.

"Okay?" Now that he's started, Calidor had thought he'd have to sell his idea harder.

"Okay," Otto repeated. "I don't have much to bring to the table. Except that I can cook. Been doing it my whole life. Maybe I can…"

He went back to the pile his inn had once been and rooted around. Calidor heard him muttering again, but it didn't have the same lost, almost deranged, tone of earlier.

"Ah." Otto straightened, holding a dented pot. "Potunia," he said proudly, then bent again and came up with a spoon. "Spoony. Here. Hold them," he told Yarah, thrusting them forward.

By the time he was done, each of them were juggling several items. Pots, pans, knives, spoons. All of them with different names. Maybe Otto's mind wasn't quite as sound as Calidor thought it had become.

"All right," Otto said. "That should do it."

"I hope so," Calidor said.

They left the inn, with Otto taking one last lingering look at the stone cairn where his wife lay and reentered the forest.

Calidor really hoped no dragonkin were around. The racket they were making now was impossible to hide, and he didn't think even Yarah's magic would make them inconspicuous.

Then again, he thought, if Otto really could cook, it would be worth it. As long as they could find something to put in all those pots.

Chapter 28- The Eastern Road, Obristan

Lamorak felt as if he was drowning in water that was too thick. Like he was floating in the midst of a great, heavy sea, but unable to draw any of it into his lungs. At first, it was almost peaceful, but then his chest began to burn. He needed air, but he couldn't move his arms or legs to swim to the surface. He couldn't even thrash around. He strained every muscle, which only made his need for air that much stronger.

With a final, desperate heave, he shot up—

And found himself lying with his back on the ground.

What had happened? He remembered confronting the would-be bandits. Fighting them. Chasing them away. Most of them had been cowards and not even real bandits. Except for one. That one had been more ruthless and smarter... and he'd had a bow.

He'd shot Lamorak. Now he remembered. The sudden shock of the arrow punching through his shoulder, then the pain, then pushing it away to deal with later. He remembered feeling his back and front both wet and sticky with his own blood, thinking it was probably a lot of it... then, nothing.

Although his nose hurt, which made him think he had fallen on it.

He closed his eyes again, just for a moment, to try to concentrate.

He'd fallen on the road, but... he wasn't there anymore. The ground he was lying on wasn't hard-packed dirt. Plants and weeds grew around and underneath him. The road had run through trees, and now, as he opened his eyes again and looked up, there was nothing obstructing his view of the sky.

So, either he had managed to get off the road and find a place to collapse, or someone had moved him.

He raised his right hand and touched his left shoulder, where the arrow had gone through. He already knew the shaft couldn't be behind him anymore or else he'd be lying on it. But the point was missing as well. In its place was what felt like a bandage.

"You're going to be fine," a voice said. "You just lost a lot of blood."

It was a voice that Lamorak recognized, although he couldn't place where he knew it from. A female voice, but somehow different. It came from somewhere behind his head, so there was no way to see who it was without moving.

Although, moving was something he had to do anyway, right? He couldn't just continue to lie there.

Lamorak had never been one to back down from a challenge or something that needed to be done. He wasn't about to start now, either. So he pushed himself up, bracing for the pain from his shoulder.

To his surprise, he felt a twinge, but not much more. Gingerly, he raised his left arm and worked it in a small circle. It was sore, but not nearly as bad as he would have expected, and he could use it.

"What's funny," the voice continued, "is that until all this madness happened, I wouldn't have even been here to help you. Of course, you might not have needed it, then."

It came to Lamorak whose voice it was. He turned slowly, unprepared to believe he was going to see what he knew must be there.

Shilong. The blue dragonkin who had greeted them when they'd first entered Ascana on the way to Festival, then had helped them back across the border when they were fleeing.

"What are you doing here?" he asked.

His voice came out in a harsh rasp, and he suddenly realized how thirsty he was. His mouth was as dry as if he'd drunk too much beer and slept with it gaping open all night long.

"Rescuing you, it seems. Again." But Shilong's voice sounded amused, which Lamorak supposed he should have been grateful for. He was in no condition to fight a dragonkin or even flee from one.

"Thank you." He suddenly remembered his manners. He looked around at where he was. There wasn't much to see, only a clearing in the woods. A sort of glen, hidden by the trees on all sides, although of course it would have been clear as day for something that could fly. Like a wingless dragonkin.

"Is there water?" he asked.

"There's a stream right over there," Shilong answered, nodding her head off to the right. "Can you make it, or should I help you?"

"No, I'm okay, thanks." He rose slowly, then tried to stand still as the world wavered around him. "I think," he said, then shook his head quickly and walked the way she'd indicated.

He felt like a newborn baby. Or at least what he assumed a baby felt like, since he didn't remember being one and had had scarce contact with any since. But his legs felt wobbly, his balance unsteady, and he was already thinking he could lie back down and sleep again.

He made it to the stream, though, pushing through a thin curtain of undergrowth. A short, but steep, bank led down to a swiftly moving brook, bubbling merrily... as if the world hadn't gone mad.

It wasn't easy to get down to it. Lamorak actually sat and inched his way down the slope, then turned so that he could lie down with his face toward the water. He only needed to stretch a bit, then he'd be able to reach the surface.

The water was amazing. Clear, cold, and the most wonderfully refreshing drink ever devised. Whoever had come up with water deserved to be applauded, he thought, as he drank deeply.

Once his thirst began to ebb, it opened up room in his thoughts for other questions.

For instance, how had Shilong found him? And why had she helped? And... how did she make a bandage to put on his shoulder and out of what? He knew dragonkin were magic and all, but that seemed... weird?

"Are you okay?" Shilong's voice came to him.

"I'm good," he called back. Normally, he would have been much more careful about making noise, but if Shilong wanted him dead, he already would be. Or she would have just left him in the road. And if there were other dragonkin around, he'd have to trust her to deal with them.

Humans? What human would be stupid enough to intrude on a dragonkin?

He took a final deep drink and pushed himself to his knees. That was better, now. The world was steadier, and he didn't feel so unbalanced. He thought he might even be able to ascend the short slope standing up.

When he got back to the clearing, Shilong was lying on her stomach, blinking lazily in the sun.

"The climate here is cooler than Ascana," she said. "I knew it was, of course, but to actually feel it! I never thought I'd be able to, but now…"

She left it unsaid. With the dragons canceling their edict— their ban on visiting each other's territories— the dragonkin had spread out. Mostly to attack human towns, but apparently there were some, like Shilong, who were just there to visit. Just because they could.

"Where are we?" Lamorak asked her.

Shilong looked around. "The woods? I don't know what you call them. Not too far from where I found you. A man and his wife helped me get you cleaned up and bandaged. They seemed very scared of me, which was unfortunate, but, on the other hand, they did what I asked right away."

"I bet," Lamorak thought.

"Where is Prince Calidor?" Shilong asked. "Is he safe? I'd like to see him again."

"He's… around," Lamorak said. "He's trying to help his people."

"And you abandoned him?" Shilong's voice took on a tone of disapproval.

"No! I would never. He sent me away. I'm supposed to go to Greenfair, to…" No. Even though Shilong appeared to be on their side, telling her he meant to try to organize an armed resistance to the dragons' rule might be too much. "It's just home," he finished, hoping she would buy it.

"I understand," Shilong responded. "Or at least I think I do. Dragonkin don't really have a 'home.' Not if you mean like a building where they live all the time. But I know you humans do and that you get attached to them."

"We do," Lamorak agreed. He sat down with his back against a rock and looked at Shilong. "A lot of peoples' homes have been destroyed lately, though."

He was no expert in reading the expressions of dragonkin or what they might mean, but Shilong's seemed to say that she was at least disturbed by what was happening.

"I don't like it," she said, confirming what he'd thought. "I like even less that my brothers and sisters are participating so eagerly in hurting humans."

"Why are they doing it, then?" Lamorak asked.

Shilong turned from where she'd had her head up to feel the breeze to really look at him. Her eyes were the most brilliant blue, even more so than her scales. And if Lamorak had any misconception that he was talking to an animal, it was put to rest at that moment. Those eyes were old. Older than Lamorak, by far. Maybe even older than Greenfair itself. There was a deep intelligence there that made him feel like he was a child, asking questions of his elders.

"Because they can, I suppose," she finally said. "It's not something that I want to admit, but I think that might be the reason. They're having fun, like human children I've seen who build a tower out of blocks then knock it down." She stopped and considered. "No, that's not right. The blocks don't feel anything, do they? I think its more like when a child kicks over an anthill, just to see them scurry, and then stomps on any they can."

Lamorak wasn't sure ants could feel much either, but he got the analogy.

"And you?" he asked her. "You helped us. Back there at the border. And you're helping me again, now. Aren't we ants to you, too?"

"No. But… I'm older than most of my siblings. Almost as old as Haiteng, himself, if you want to know the truth. I'm old enough to remember—"

"Remember what?" Lamorak prodded at her sudden stop.

"The others. Those you call the Evening Folk."

"Really?" He sat up at that. "I have a friend who would love to hear about them." As long as it wasn't *you* telling the story, he thought, but kept that to himself. "He's fascinated by them."

"They were fascinating people. Small, though. Not much larger than you humans. Some were taller, of course, but not as broad, while others were quite short compared to you. Then, the others, about your same size, but... different still. I'm not sure what they called themselves, but they were considered friends of the dragons."

"That's what our old stories say, too," Lamorak told her. "The Evening Folk were friends to the dragonkin until there was a war. They attacked the dragonkin. I'd guess out of jealousy? The stories aren't really clear on the why. It didn't end well for them, though."

"The stories change through the years, I would think," Shilong said. "For instance, you use the term 'dragonkin.' There was no such thing, then. Not at first. We were all dragons."

Lamorak frowned. He didn't quite understand. The dragonkin were smaller, less powerful, versions of their parents. He didn't know if that was meant literally, like every dragonkin had sprung from a dragon's loins, or if it was meant to be figurative, the way some referred to Prince Calidor as being the father of Obristan. The dragons were immense creatures, capable of destroying whole cities in a moment or, conversely, of granting great boons to those deemed worthy.

He'd never actually known of a city that a dragon had destroyed— until now, of course— or of anyone who had received such a boon, but that was the lore.

"So... I don't get it. How were you all *dragons*? Surely the world isn't big enough for so many of you. I can hardly believe it can support the four."

Shilong laughed quietly. "Five," she said, but didn't elaborate. "No, Lamorak. The five dragons came from within. They were just as the rest of us, until... they found a way. A way I don't understand. I don't know anyone else who does, either. They became... more... and then *they* were the 'dragons' and the rest of us were merely 'dragon*kin*.'"

If he didn't know better, Lamorak would have said that Shilong was bitter. But he didn't see how she could be.

Then, another thought occurred to him.

"How long ago was this?" She was referring to a time *before* the war between the dragons and the Evening Folk. That had to be… well. . . longer than he could even contemplate.

"Long, long ago," Shilong answered. "Even for me, it was long ago."

"Yet, you don't sound like you you've forgotten."

"Dragons— dragonkin or not— do not forget." She stretched and sighed. "But I see you are better now. Your shoulder will heal. That man and his wife were very thorough. Plus, I helped some where I could."

Lamorak assumed that meant with magic.

Shilong rose to her feet, then stopped and looked at him again.

"Did Prince Calidor really send you away from him?"

"He did." He considered carefully what he was going to say next. "He's hiding. He wants to help those he can who have been harmed by what's going on. We don't understand why so many people are being hurt. Why they're being terrorized."

"Gillbriss." Shilong growled the name. "It wasn't enough for her to harm her own people; she would spread her madness to the world."

All Lamorak knew of Gillbriss was that she was the overlord of Reclium, a place he'd been considering visiting at one time, but had always heard bad things about.

"Why are they listening to Gillbriss?" he asked. "Why isn't Haiteng protecting his people?"

"The world has indeed gone mad, Lamorak. I can't give you any more answer than that."

He nodded. "I understand." He didn't, though. Not really. What he did understand was that she wasn't going to tell him anything else. "Calidor— Prince Calidor— has sent me on a mission. I'm not just going to Greenfair to go home. I'm going to see what's left of it. To find who's still alive."

Shilong cocked her head. "Why doesn't he go?"

"He's afraid of what will happen to him if he's found. You helped us at the border, so you must know that nothing good will come of him being discovered alive."

Whether Shilong had instructions from Gillbriss to watch out for Calidor or not, Lamorak would never know. But she didn't argue his point.

"He will wait to hear back from you, then?"

"He will. Assuming I make it back before something happens to him."

"It's a long way to Greenfair for a human on foot," she said.

"It is. Especially when I have to hide." He wasn't sure what he was thinking. Asking for help of some sort? Did he want Shilong to accompany him? He'd never be able to hide with her by his side, and if they came across any other dragonkin...

"All right," she said suddenly. "I'll take you."

"Pardon me?" That wasn't what he had been after.

"I'll carry you. We can get there much faster, you can see what you need to, and return to the Prince's side."

"Um. No. Thanks, but..." He could picture himself, dangling by his shirt color from Shilong's claws.

"Yes," Shilong said, as if her word was the final say on the matter. He supposed, even though he could argue, it was.

Then, to his surprise, she stretched out on the ground. "Behind my front legs would be best, I think. I've never done this before, but it should work."

"What am I supposed to hang onto?" There was no way he was climbing onto Shilong's back to go soaring through the sky. If man had been meant to fly, they'd have wings or at least the magic of a dragonkin to allow them to.

"You won't fall," she said. "I'll make sure of it."

"How?" His voice squeaked out in a higher register, as it dawned on him that this was going to happen.

"Magic." And she winked at him. As if she was joking. But was she?

He *wasn't* doing it. He was *not* climbing up onto her back and trying to cling to her smooth scales.

And that definitely was *not* him screaming as the ground shot away from him, taking his stomach with it.

Chapter 29- Droy Thus Jungles

Akofi had been in the jungle for any length of time on only a few occasions. Mostly when he was younger and more adventurous. Only, that wasn't entirely true. He had never been all that adventurous. He had gone in with other kids a couple of times, not wanting to appear afraid or too stand-offish. Those times had been horrible, even though they hadn't gone in very far or stayed very long. Each time he'd emerged, he'd breathed a sigh of relief and swore never again.

By the time he'd hit his teen years, he had stopped caring about what others thought enough that the "never again" had become real. He hadn't even stepped foot out of the tower villages or off the paths in years, and never wanted to.

Now, here he was, bringing up the rear as Bekasi angrily shoved branches and plants to the side, taking out her fury over the death of Akamah on anything that came to hand. Rainaldus walked behind her, carrying their friend's body. His hands and arms were red and blistered, and the burns must have been causing him immense pain, but he never uttered a word of complaint.

Given that, it was the least Akofi could do to not make a big deal out of being someplace he hated.

He slapped at his neck again as something bit him. It wasn't the first time, nor would it be the last.

And again, he looked to Rainaldus, who didn't even have a free hand to do that much. Even as Akofi watched, a bloated blood-sucking fly launched itself from behind Rainaldus's left ear, leaving an angry welt behind.

"That's enough," he called. "We can't keep going on like this."

Bekasi stopped and whirled to face him. "What do you mean? We can't go back there!"

"No." Akofi gestured toward Rainaldus. "But he can't keep doing this. Look at him. His arms are a mess, and if we keep going, he won't have a drop of blood left in him. The flies will have gotten it all."

Bekasi glanced at Rainaldus, but only briefly. Her eyes more fell on Akamah's body, before flickering away. Then, she grimaced and forced herself to actually *see* the young guardsman. Akofi heard her sharp in-drawn breath from where he stood.

"I'm fine," Rainaldus told him. He made no move to put Akamah down. "I can go on for a while longer and—"

"To what end?" Akofi asked. "Even if we make it to Lankari, that wasn't Akamah's home. And it's probably been taken over by dragonkin, if it even still stands. So what will we do? Leave him in the jungle then?"

Bekasi frowned. He knew what she was thinking. One way or the other, Akamah needed to have a better end than just being left to rot or his body ravaged by some wild animal.

But that wasn't what he was proposing. He should have thought of it earlier.

"Lay him down," he told Rainaldus.

Rainaldus looked around, but there wasn't a suitable place to do such a thing.

"What are you doing, Akofi?" Bekasi asked, her voice low and dangerous. "I won't leave him—"

"*We* won't," he corrected her. "He was my friend, too. One of my few. I'll take care of him. In some lands, this is an accepted way of saying goodbye."

She stared at him, then nodded slowly. "Hold on."

She gestured and muttered some words and the plants began to wilt in a circle around her. The effect spread, causing Rainaldus to take a step backward, but Akofi held his ground. He was impressed. This was a spell he knew, but not one he was good at. He knew it wouldn't affect him, though, only the vegetation. It was how large sections of jungle were cleared to expand the villages when they grew too big, or to push roads through the heavy growth.

In a few minutes, she had created a clearing where nothing grew. Even a large tree— an old, jungle giant— had turned to dust, whispering as it fell like rain.

"Now," she said. "Lay him here."

Rainaldus stepped into the small clearing and slowly, carefully, set Akamah onto the ground. He grimaced once as the mage's body slid, pulling some of his burnt skin loose, but he remained silent.

"Would anyone like to say anything?" Akofi asked.

Rainaldus shook his head. To Akofi's surprise, so did Bekasi.

He felt like he should. He should say something about this man who had been his friend as a child, then moved away. Who had reappeared and stood by him, even while others had mocked him.

He found that he couldn't. There was either too much or too little. And either way, his thoughts were his own.

Instead, he stood silently, letting the others do the same with their own thoughts.

After a few more moments, he raised his brows at Bekasi. She nodded slowly, and Akofi used his own magic.

He made the flame hotter than he could ever remember doing. Even with that, he kept a careful control on it. The fire sprang up in and on Akamah but didn't spread beyond his body.

Akofi loved fire magic. The purity of it. The power and— yes— the danger of it. Right now, however, he just wanted it to be over. Hotter, still. Burning faster. Burning fast enough that Akamah would be gone before they could see anything horrible... more horrible than they already had, anyway.

Two minutes, maybe three, and he was gone. Even his bones had been reduced to nothing. There was nothing left of their friend but a burned patch of ground in the shape of his body, and soon, even that would be gone.

Akofi was tired. Tired like he had rarely been, even when he'd helped kill the dragonkin in Manse.

"Thank you," Bekasi whispered. "For making it quick."

Akofi just nodded, then drew in a breath.

"It was well done," Rainaldus said, his voice rough. "I am sorry. For both of you."

"Us, too," Akofi sighed. "But now we have to go. If there are any dragonkin nearby, that magic we just used might draw them."

"Only if they were looking for it," Bekasi said.

"If that other one came back and found its friend dead, it *will* be looking for it," he said. "Let's move."

With one last, lingering glance at Akamah's resting place, they plunged back into the thick of the jungle.

They were lucky— so far— in that they'd encountered none of the bigger threats. The huge cats with sharp teeth, or the large apes, too intelligent to be mere animals. That didn't mean they didn't encounter danger, though.

Once, Bekasi put her hand out for support when she stumbled over a protruding root. She drew back with a cry, her hand covered with tiny mites which swarmed up her arm. She used magic to wipe them away, but not before her arm had been covered by tiny bites that itched furiously.

A snake lashed down from overhead, narrowly missing Rainaldus's head. It was only his quick reflexes that saved him. Akofi watched in disbelief as the guardsman struck back, grabbing the reptile behind its head and snapping its neck in one quick movement. He held the body aloft, showing that it was longer than he was tall, but thin. "Good to eat?" he asked.

"No!" Bekasi shuddered. "Those things are poison through and through. Get rid of it."

Rainaldus flicked it away into the brush, while Akofi wondered how Bekasi had known that. He had never given much time to studying the jungle and what might be in it. He'd never cared that much, since he'd never had any intention of visiting it again. She must have felt differently or at least been interested enough to learn something about it.

The trip from the Border House to Lankari should have taken two days. That was by Gulari, however, not on foot. And they were making much slower progress through the jungle.

And that was assuming they were going the right way, of course.

When night fell, they huddled together, and Akofi used his magic to light a small fire. He also lit several more in a circle around them, to try to give them warning should anything attempt to approach. It wasn't difficult magic, but he'd have to stay awake to keep an eye on them. Not that Rainaldus or Bekasi seemed overly worried.

"How much farther do you think it is?" he asked Bekasi.

She had been twisting a twig back and forth, breaking it into smaller and smaller pieces that she fed to the fire. Her gaze wasn't even focused on the flames but was far away. At his words, she stopped, then looked at him.

"What do you mean?"

"How much farther? To get to Lankari Tower?"

"Why are you asking me?"

"Because you're guiding us."

"I'm not guiding anyone! I'm just walking!"

Akofi stared at her. "You're in front. You're walking, and Rainaldus and I are following you. Aren't we?" he asked the guardsman.

"I'm not from here," he said, a strange half-smile on his face. "I'm obviously not leading."

"Well, neither am I," Bekasi said.

"Wait. Just wait a minute." Akofi put his head in his hands. "If you're not sure of where you're going... why did you just keep walking?"

Her mouth moved silently for a few seconds as she worked through what he was asking her. "I guess I assumed you would tell me if we were going the wrong way," she finally spat out.

"How would I know?"

"How would I?" she shot back.

It was grief. That was the only possible explanation. Now that he'd thought about it, they had never once stopped to talk about how they were going to find their way through the jungle or keep track of what direction they were going in. They'd simply plunged in, eager to be off the road and away from any dragonkin's notice.

Now...

"Do you have any idea where we are?" he asked her now, afraid he already knew the answer.

She shook her head. "Don't you?"

To his surprise, Rainaldus burst out laughing. It was the first time since meeting him that Akofi had heard such a noise coming from him. Or from anyone in all that time, really. There had been scant reason to laugh.

"What's so funny?" Bekasi asked him.

"Nothing. It's just... both of you live here. And now..." He spread his hands, still burnt, and gestured around him.

His laughter seemed to jolt her from her funk. "It's not funny! We're probably going to die out here!" But her mouth quivered a bit, until she, too, broke into a smile, then began laughing.

"You're both insane," Akofi muttered. He had to chuckle himself, though. It was rather ridiculous when he thought about it. Besides, they'd find their way out. They had to.

"Your arms and hands need help," Bekasi said, as her laughter died down. "I'm not a healer, but I know a little bit."

She moved over next to Rainaldus. He lifted his right and looked at it. "I'll have scars," he said. "Not the kind we usually get, but I suppose these were honorably come by."

"I'd say so," she said. "If not for you. You and Akamah, anyway..."

She trailed off but took his right arm gently in her hands. She muttered under her breath. Akofi watched, fascinated. He was struck again, as to why Kio had chosen her as the Tower Representative. Akofi was stronger, by far, than she was. But Bekasi was more diverse. She knew pieces of magic that he had never bothered to think about.

The fact that he had never attempted to learn any healing magic was something he was going to have to look at. What did it say about him that he hadn't?

Probably the same thing most people said about him.

A few minutes later, Bekasi did the same to Rainaldus's left arm. The bright red was still there, but the blisters had gone down, and Rainaldus could move his hands without grimacing.

"Better?" she asked.

"Much," he told her.

Which he probably would have said even if he'd felt no change, Akofi thought. Rainaldus took being stoic to levels he never would have guessed possible. Whether that was a good thing or bad, he really couldn't say.

"Let's get some sleep," he said. "You two go first. I'll wake Rainaldus in a couple of hours. If the fires die down too much, you can wake me back up."

"Or I can just feed them with wood," Rainaldus said. "It'd be good to move around anyway."

"Either way," he agreed.

Rainaldus and Bekasi lay down on the ground, and Akofi settled against a tree to keep watch.

Night in the jungle was dark. Darkness that he had never experienced in the villages. Without the fires, he wouldn't have been able to see a thing. Even with them, beyond the ring of light, he was blind. Anything could be out there, watching them. Or anyone, he supposed.

That didn't bear thinking about, though. One thing at a time, and that meant staying awake for a couple more hours.

He reached out and felt the fires, coaxing them just a bit higher. No, he wasn't afraid. He was prepared. Anything that came near any of his little blazes was going to be in for a very big surprise.

"Akofi! Wake up!"

Bekasi's hissing voice woke him from a dream that he barely remembered having. In it, he was running from something. That was all he knew, but it was enough to leave him gasping, even as it faded away completely.

It was still dark, even more so now than when he had woken Rainaldus a few hours before.

"What is it?" he said, sitting up.

But he saw it right away, before she could even say anything.

All of the fires, except for the one right beside him, were out. Completely. Not even the feeble glow of dying embers showed in the near total darkness that surrounded them.

"What happened?" he asked. Rainaldus would have fed the fires wood. If Bekasi hadn't done the same, she knew enough fire magic to keep them burning. It wasn't a hard spell to perform.

"I don't know," she whispered. "They just went out. A few minutes ago and all at once."

Akofi slowly climbed to his feet, trying to see if anything was moving in the jungle. If it was, it was beyond his ability to make out.

In the meantime, Bekasi had moved to Rainaldus and woke him. The guardsman came fully awake in an instant, coming to his feet and his hand going to his sword hilt in one smooth movement.

He noticed the fires as quickly as Akofi had. "Has anything approached?" he asked.

"No." Bekasi shook her head. "But something put out the fires."

"Dragonkin," Rainaldus guessed.

"Maybe," Akofi said. "I don't think so, though."

He wasn't sure *why* he thought it wasn't a dragonkin, but something about this felt off. If it had been one, especially if it had tracked them from where they'd killed the other, it wouldn't be toying with them. It would be on them, killing them one after the other while they slept. Why would it take a chance on facing those who had already proven they could kill one of its kind?

"I think maybe it was—"

He had been about to say that it was probably some... weird fluctuation in his magic or something. Maybe whatever he'd been dreaming about had been enough for him to reach out in his sleep and extinguish the flames.

Before he could finish that thought, though, they heard a rustling noise.

It sounded like footsteps, walking through the jungle. Not four legs, but two. The same sorts of sounds they had made during the day when they were pushing through the brush.

A moment later, a voice spoke, but in a strange, guttural language Akofi had never heard before. Another answered it, then a third.

Rainaldus drew his sword and Bekasi began a spell.

"Wait," Akofi said quietly. "Let's see who they are first."

He reached out to the fires with his magic, to see if there were any remnants of his earlier spells. There weren't, but he didn't necessarily need them. He moved his hands, said a few words, and a column of fire appeared near where he thought the voices had come from. It was bright enough to see... nothing?

No, that wasn't true.

There was a surprised exclamation of some sort, then a shuffling of a body— at least one— moving out of sight. Before he could identify more than a wavering of a branch, though, his fire-column simply went out. It was as if someone had snipped his spell short, cutting him off from it completely. He tried to bring it back, but it was futile. Repeatedly, before the fire would even begin to come to life, it was cut off again.

The voices resumed, sounding angry now, as if they were arguing with each other.

The three of them stood silent, peering into the dark and listening hard. But the only things that they now heard were the night insects.

"I think they might be gone," Bekasi said.

The voices came again. A little further off, perhaps. Then another answered, much closer and off to their right side.

They spun but couldn't see anything. No one approached close enough to be seen in the light of their one remaining fire.

"I don't think we're getting much more sleep tonight," Rainaldus said.

Akofi attempted his magic again, to no avail. Bekasi spread her hands helplessly. "Whoever they are, they keep shutting down my magic."

"Mine, too," he admitted.

They stayed alert, refusing to sit, even though nothing more happened. For the next couple of hours, until the sun finally began to lighten the sky, they heard the voices, every now and then, sometimes closer, sometimes further away.

It wasn't until daybreak that they first caught sight of one of their visitors.

He was as tall as Rainaldus and heavily muscled. He wore a loincloth and not much else, which highlighted his light gray skin. Black hair was tied in a topknot, and his lower jaw thrust out past his upper, allowing two tusks to stick up from it. Around his waist was a rope, with a loop from which hung a large axe. It was much more modern than anything else about him. He glanced at them, apparently unfazed at being seen, then melted back into the jungle.

"What was that?" Bekasi asked.

"No idea," Akofi replied.

Whatever he was, there were more of them. That warrior hadn't been talking to himself.

"They aren't all dead," Rainaldus breathed.

"What? Who aren't?" Akofi had no idea what the young man was talking about.

"Evening Folk," he said. "That was one of them."

Akofi frowned. "That didn't look like any Evening Folk I've ever heard of."

"Me, neither," Rainaldus agreed. "But what else could he be?"

"Who knows? Cannibal, maybe? Psychotic jungle hermit?"

Rainaldus smiled. "Then why didn't they kill us? Come on. Let's find him."

He moved off before Akofi could protest. He looked to Bekasi, who returned his gaze with wide eyes.

"I don't want to go on without him, do you?" she asked.

Akofi remembered the snake. To say nothing of the dragonkin, of course, or how Rainaldus had been the one to know that it hadn't been alone.

"No," he said. "I definitely don't."

With that, he shook his head, and muttering about what a bad idea it was, he and Bekasi hurried after Rainaldus.

Chapter 30- Orluduna Tower, Droy Thus

"What," Oponsi said, her voice low and dangerous, "is an 'Ilvisar?'"

"An Evening Folk," Sintifi said calmly. "Or Raaleth, as they apparently like to be called."

He had to admit, he was quite enjoying the looks of consternation on both hers and Korudu's faces. It was nice to know something that they didn't, for once.

"Impossible," Korudu said. "The Evening Folk are long gone. Exterminated when they went to war against the dragonkin."

"You'd think that, wouldn't you?" Sintifi took another drink. "Yet, there's one here in your tower right now. I don't think any wards of ours are going to keep him out or stop him from coming up here, either." He held up his finger. "And he's not alone."

"There are more of them here?" Oponsi asked.

Sintifi shook his head. "Not here. In their city. Or their land. To be honest, I'm not sure what it is, but it's called Olequan, and I think it's somewhere in Obristan."

"And you didn't think it was important to tell us this?" she demanded.

"To be honest, I was so surprised to find *you* here that it slipped my mind."

She scowled at that, but, really, what could she say? If she wanted to spend every waking moment for years locked inside one tower, she could hardly blame him for being shocked when he found her somewhere else.

"What does he want?" Korudu asked.

"I would imagine to talk to both of you. Mostly Oponsi. He's very interested in the true tower, of course."

"You *told* him about that?" Oponsi's voice had risen a register.

"He was coming this way, anyway. I don't think we could have hidden it from him."

"Probably not for long, anyway." Ilvisar's voice came from the doorway. "Hello, again, Sintifi."

"Hello, yourself," Sintifi snorted. "Nice of you to leave me at the mercy of that dragonkin."

He hadn't been expecting abject apologies, but neither did he appreciate Ilvisar's grin. "You got away from it. I was certain you would."

"Good joke, Sintifi," Korudu said.

Sintifi spun to him, eyebrows raised nearly to his hairline. Korudu was shaking his head, and Oponsi was glowering like a thunderstorm.

"What are you—? Oh. I see. He's in disguise, of course."

Ilvisar still retained the appearance he'd adopted when they'd first come to Orluduna. He looked no different than any other mage in Droy Thus.

"I would think it would be easy to tell what I am," Ilvisar said, a slight frown creasing his features. "Perhaps my hope that you will prove to be valuable allies is misplaced."

"Just show them," Sintifi muttered. He rose to his feet and went to get more wine.

He didn't even bother to turn around at the involuntary gasp he heard. From Korudu or Oponsi, he didn't know, but it didn't matter, either. Both were now staring at the Raaleth revealed.

"It's true," Oponsi said quietly. "But… we had no way of knowing…"

"I would hope not," Ilvisar replied. He began walking about the room, examining the books and items on Korudu's shelves. "If we can successfully hide from Tophonoss and her children for this long, I would hope that we could hide from mere humans."

Sintifi scowled at the "mere human" remark but decided to let the other two deal with it. In truth, as much as he wanted to see Olequan— to be selected to go there— he was getting a bit tired of Ilvisar and his air of superiority.

The fact that the Raaleth *was* superior in every way that he could see didn't really help matters.

"What—" Korudu started to ask a question but stuttered to a stop.

"What am I doing here?" Ilvisar stopped his perusal of the chamber and turned to him. "I came to ask you the same question. What are you *doing* here? How did you use Raaleth magic? Although, I think I know at least part of the answer to that last one."

He crossed to where Sintifi stood and took the wine glass from his hand. He took a sip, grimaced, and handed it back. Sintifi peered into the contents but couldn't see anything wrong with it, so he took another drink.

"We didn't mean to—" Korudu began, but Oponsi cut him off this time.

"No. No answers. Not until we have some of our own."

Sintifi almost spat out his wine. Oponsi was a tough character, everyone who knew her knew that. She had almost challenged Korudu and Sintifi together just a few minutes ago, and she must have known that wasn't a fight she would win. Now, she was faced with a legend come to life and was already taking the offensive. If there was one thing Oponsi valued, it was being in control.

Ilvisar looked at her calmly, before grinning. "What would you ask me?"

"Where have you been, to start," challenged Oponsi. "Especially now, these last few weeks. Why haven't your people done something to—?"

"Save you from yourselves?" This time, it was Ilvisar doing the interrupting. "We didn't tell you to use magic against the dragonkin, to get them to fight. That was your doing. Why should we put ourselves, put Olequan itself, at risk to help you?"

"Why? Why *shouldn't* you? Or are you just scared?" Oponsi raised her chin and looked down her nose at him. "Or is that what your people do now? Cower in the shadows and leave the living to us?"

Sintifi stopped with his drink halfway to his mouth. There was a part of him that was really enjoying this. Oponsi was acting as she was because she was off-balance and desperate to regain control. He didn't think she realized that she was up against something much bigger, much older, and much more powerful than she was.

Then again, he reflected, out of everybody, Oponsi had studied the Evening Folk the most. Maybe she knew something about how to treat them that he didn't.

Either way, he was planning on getting good and drunk while the attention was off him.

Ilvisar found that he quite liked the old, human female. Although little more than a baby in years lived by his standards, she was fiery. For her kind, she had lived long and obviously felt she didn't need to bow to anyone.

The other one— Korudu, he believed was the name— was interesting, as well. He didn't say nearly as much, and he had let Ilvisar's sudden appearance bother him more than the female, Oponsi. Yet, there was a kind of quiet power about him. A roiling, just beneath the surface, of magic potential that had yet to be tapped.

It wasn't the first time he'd felt such a thing. Sintifi had it as well. If anything, his was even greater. It was just that he was a mess of fear and insecurities. If he could find someone to mix Sintifi's power with Oponsi's nerve and self-esteem… *then* he might have something.

But humans were as they were made. And these particular humans came from long, long years of being shaped by Chimbod. The mere fact that they had done the things they had was astounding in its own right.

There may be something, after all. Something that would benefit Olequan, and maybe the humans, as well.

"We lost," he said simply, in answer to Oponsi's question.

His answer seemed to throw her for a moment.

"Lost? Well, yes. Even we know that."

"I'm sure. You hardly know the full story, though. Or do you think you do?"

"Of course not," she snorted. "Only a fool would think they know everything."

"Then allow me to enlighten you." Ilvisar took a seat and looked at each of them. Even Sintifi, who probably had guessed at some of this by now, seemed to be listening closely.

"The world changed, long, long ago. Before even I was born. I was one of the first to come into the changed world, after Olequan was hidden. But what had happened to my people is told to all. The dragons betrayed us. I've told Sintifi this already. They found a way to rise, to become greater than they had ever been— than anyone ever would have thought they could be. They took dominion over their own kind, then tried to do the same with the other races."

"Races?" Korudu leaned forward. "Implying more than one."

"Three, actually," Ilvisar said. "The Raaleth— my people. The Helgarlug. Almost as ancient as the Raaleth and valiant warriors. And the Xarlug. Quick to anger, fierce in combat, but loyal to a fault."

"I've never heard of them," Oponsi said quietly. "The other two, I've come across, but not these... Xarlug."

"I don't know much about them myself," Ilvisar told her. "Only that they refused to run from the dragons. They kept up the fight, until they were no more."

"But the rest?" she asked.

"Our king and queen hid fair Olequan. They moved it, in its entirety, from where it had been, to where it is now. They cast great and powerful magic, making it unseeable. Anyone who doesn't know the way can't find it, not even by accident."

"Yet, you can come and go," she said.

"*We* can. Anyone that I choose to bring there would be able to find the way as well."

He noticed Sintifi perk up a bit at that. So, despite his anger at Ilvisar leaving him with the dragonkin, he still wished to go. That was good. Ilvisar was coming to believe he would be the most useful.

"We hid from the dragonkin for many years," he continued. "When the dragons rose, they attacked so suddenly, and with such force, that my people were decimated. Our numbers were diminished to the point that outright conflict would be impossible. Instead, they struck back 'from the shadows,' as you put it."

"To what end?" Sintifi finally put his glass down long enough to ask a question. "What good did it do?"

Ilvisar smiled again. "More than you can imagine. Our king is gone. All that is now left is Falaern, our queen. To her, all the remaining Raaleth and Helgarlug owe their allegiance. But we do so partly in the name of Ryul, our king who gave all."

"What's that supposed to mean?" Oponsi asked.

"He had given much of his strength to hide Olequan. He and Falaern both. He maintained the shroud they threw over it for years while others worked to take up the burden, to make the spell permanent. But for all that, we were discovered."

"Tophonoss," Sintifi guessed, glancing at Oponsi and Korudu.

"No. By Sillaneth, the one who came before her. Ryul fought her on his own. A feat that should not have been possible. He held her off, then died from his effort, but took her life as well. The death of the dragon and the Raaleth king at the same time released vast amounts of magic. Enough so, that before Falaern could stop it, another rose to take Sillaneth's place. That one remembered, as if Sillaneth had somehow given her memories to this new dragon, who took the name Tophonoss. But it was incomplete, as she appears to be herself. Tophonoss seems more a shadow of a dragon than an actual one. For all that, though, she is still dangerous. Maybe even more so."

"But she doesn't know where Olequan is," Korudu said.

"She does not," Ilvisar replied. "Although she has a suspicion. And she knows, somehow without ever seeing one of us, that the Raaleth yet live. It is her obsession, and the reason why we must devote so much of our energy to staying hidden from her." He turned to Oponsi. "You asked where we were? If we only stayed hidden? This is your answer."

"But now *you're* here." Oponsi sounded much calmer. A fact that wasn't lost on Ilvisar. She might, indeed, be a worthwhile ally to have. Not in Olequan, though. Her temperament wouldn't do well there, and, besides, her talents would be better used elsewhere.

"I *am* here. To find those who used ancient magic. To understand how the impossible was done. And to determine if, at long last, there was hope for Olequan to emerge from hiding."

Pretty words, thought Sintifi. Except that he remembered some of their other conversations. What if Olequan did reemerge? What did that mean for humans? Would they simply be trading one set of masters for another?

"What's the plan, then?" he asked. "You've seen us. We've admitted to what we've done. I'm sure you've taken our measure in ways I can't even comprehend. So. What now?"

"I was sent to find you. To kill you, if I thought it necessary. *Your* spell," he pointed at Sintifi, "was felt across the realms. It shuddered through Olequan like an earthquake. To many, it was an ill-omen. To some— myself, for instance— it was a call."

"We," Oponsi said, indicating them all, "are more than willing to discuss how we can work together."

Sintifi waited, although Korudu made no objection to her including him, even though he'd only just found out about the true tower a short time before. No, what he was waiting for was Oponsi's "but." He could hear it waiting behind the other words like a jungle cat waiting to pounce on an unsuspecting deer.

Ilvisar simply gazed at her, obviously waiting for the same thing. Arrogant, yes, but no fool was the Raaleth.

"But we want assurances," she finally continued. "We want reciprocity. If we share our knowledge with you, it's only fair that it flows both ways."

"Assurances?" Ilvisar frowned. "Of what sort?"

Sintifi had to shake his head. No matter how many times he'd thought himself to be ahead of the game, Oponsi showed that she was always one step ahead of him.

"That we won't suddenly find your people lording it over us," she said. "That when the dragons are gone, and the dragonkin are either dead or turned back to what you say they used to be, that we're all equal."

Ilvisar laughed out loud. "But we are *not* all equal. My people live for thousands of years, while your light is there and gone in an instant. Even the Xarlug were said to have longer lives than yours."

"Longevity isn't everything," Oponsi sniffed. "Besides, if you've been hiding in your city for as long as you say, why are there still too few of you to challenge the dragons? It's been longer than humans have been alive, according to what you tell us. In that time, we've spread across the five realms. Why haven't you?"

Ilvisar didn't answer.

"I'll tell you why," she continued. "Because you can't. You might well live forever, but children don't come along very often, do they? You may have the years, but we have the numbers. By quite a large margin, I would imagine."

Sintifi had never been more proud of, or in awe of, Oponsi. There was no one else in the world, human, dragonkin, or otherwise, who could have recovered from the shock of meeting Ilvisar, to understanding what such a meeting might mean, to making reasonable demands more quickly than she did.

Now, it just remained to be seen what the response was going to be. He took a long swallow of his wine, fully aware that should Ilvisar desire it, it would be his last. If the Raaleth's magic wasn't enough, those swords he carried would snuff out all three of their lives in seconds.

Or he might just leave. To return to Olequan and back into hiding. To leave the humans on their own, to face the consequences of what they'd done. What *he'd* done, really.

For several moments, Ilvisar did neither of those things. He merely sat and calmly gazed at Oponsi. Then, he nodded.

"Agreed. At least as far as I can. Understand that I am not a diplomat. I have no authority to formally make such a deal. However, I have an offer to make that I hope will satisfy your concerns."

"Out with it then," Oponsi returned, but her eyes were bright with an eagerness and anticipation Sintifi didn't think he'd ever seen in them.

"I would see this other tower. The one my people built. Perhaps I can even help with any mysteries that may linger about it. Then, I will return to Olequan and take one of you to be your representative. He can speak with our queen, with the authority of your people behind him. From there, we can come to terms on how to proceed and free us all from the dragons."

"Who?" Korudu asked, but even as he did, he grinned at Sintifi.

"Sintifi, of course." Ilvisar hadn't missed the look. "Falaern will also want to know more details of this spell he cast. Do we have a deal?"

"We do," Oponsi said, not even bothering to ask Sintifi how *he* felt about it.

"Wait a minute," he said. "I don't have the authority of all the humans behind me, though."

"You have the blessings of those who matter," she said.

"I do? Who would that be?"

He should have known better than to bother to ask.

"Me," she snorted.

Part Two

ALLIES

Chapter 31- The Five Realms

The town looked strange without the tower. It was still there, but it was destroyed; broken-off to half its former height, with jagged stone jutting from the top, rather than the smooth finish it used to have.

It made the whole town seem smaller, somehow.

Hersha supposed that was because there were now several dragonkin occupying it. Not just visiting the way he and others used to. But actually staying there, all the time, watching the humans' every move. And punishing those that they felt deserved it, for any infraction, no matter how small.

He hated it. He hated what had happened to the tower and had been one of those who had driven off the blue dragonkin. At the time, his rage was incandescent, burning hotter than the fire in his gut. How dare they? How could they think to defy the edict and come to his home and destroy it?

When all was said and done, and Hersha had seen the aftermath of the ruined tower, then found Kio's body lying in the rubble, smashed almost beyond recognition... then his rage had cooled. In its place was a vast pit of remorse.

Word had come then, from Chimbod herself, telling them of things that had happened in the world. Hersha hadn't known any of it. Red dragonkin had attacked Festival, where Akofi was. Blues had retaliated, while whites had been seen at Festival, as well. The world had gone crazy, so the dragons had decided that a change was needed.

Now, there were blue, black, and white dragonkin in Droy Thus, while all those, plus reds like Hersha, were in every other realm. The edict was over. Dragonkin were being assigned to occupy towns. Or destroy them entirely.

So far, they seemed to have overlooked Hersha. There had been no demand for him to go somewhere else. He was glad of that, so he tried to just blend into the scenery in Lankari and act as if he was supposed to be there.

But he hated what the town had become. He hoped— even though it might mean that he would never see his friend again— that Akofi, Bekasi, and any others, just stayed away.

"What was that about?" he heard a harsh voice snarl.

It was a voice he recognized. That of a black dragonkin named Maezar. There were three black dragonkin in Lankari, and Maezar was the worst of them. While all of them were cruel and given to hurting humans for no reason, Maezar seemed to take inordinate pleasure in such things. To hear his voice now, in that tone, meant another poor human was about to be tortured.

Hersha turned to leave. He had been walking along one of the paths…the very path he and Akofi had been on right before Akofi learned he was going to Festival, he realized… lost in his own thoughts. Maezar's voice came from around the bend, but he— and whoever he was talking to— were still masked from sight by tall, thick plants.

"I…I… don't know," a human quailed. "I wasn't doing anything."

"You were," Maezar growled. "I caught the hand-movement. You were attempting to cast magic on me!"

"No! I couldn't! I don't know how!"

An ill-favored, then, and thus no one who could possibly be a threat to Maezar. What was more, the black probably knew that, but was taking the opportunity to inflict harm anyway.

Hersha turned back, so that he was facing toward the voices again.

"Liar," Maezar said, but Hersha could hear the barely restrained glee in his voice. There was a spitting noise, then a startled yelp from the human. "I'll give you a chance," Maezar purred. "You can jump to the left or the right. Not forward or back, only left or right. I'm going to spit in one of those directions. If you guess right, it must mean you're innocent. If not… well, you won't have to worry for too long. It will only take several minutes for my acid to eat through your skull."

"But I didn't... I..." the human was blubbering with fear.

It didn't make any difference which way the human moved. Dragonkin were much faster. Maezar would simply watch, then spit whichever way he moved, making it seem like he had done so first. The poor human was doomed.

Unless...

Before he even knew what he was doing, Hersha had rounded the corner.

"Leave him alone, Maezar."

The black dragonkin's head snaked around to stare at him. "Who are you, again? Histur or something?"

"My name is Hersha, and this man did nothing to you. He can't use magic, you idiot. He's ill-favored."

Maezar drew back at Hersha's insult. "Idiot, am I? Better watch yourself, or you'll find you bit off more than you can chew."

Hersha wasn't the largest dragonkin As a matter of fact, he spent a good amount of time not much bigger than a human. Shape-shifting was magic he excelled in, whereas most of his kind had no use for it. In his natural state, he wasn't large for a dragonkin, but still, he dwarfed the black.

Not that Maezar seemed to care. None of the much smaller black dragonkin did. They had their acid, their stings, magic of their own, and what was more, it seemed like they had the blessing of Gillbriss to do whatever they wanted, *and* Gillbriss had been given authority over all the humans by the other dragons.

"You'll leave him alone," Hersha said again, "or..."

"Or what?" Maezar laughed.

The gout of fire hit the ground right next to the black, drowning out his mocking laughter. "Or I'll burn you to a cinder," Hersha said quietly.

When he stopped, Maezar had drawn even further away. He glared with pure hatred at Hersha.

"This isn't over," he growled. "Gillbriss will be told."

"Then tell her." Hersha stalked forward. "Tell her what you've been doing, too."

Maezar laughed. "She isn't your soft-hearted Chimbod. She wouldn't care if we killed every human in the whole place."

"But Chimbod would," Hersha returned. "And *I* would. Leave. Now."

He meant for Maezar to leave Lankari entirely, but he knew that was asking too much. For the moment, it was enough that Maezar glowered at him, glanced once at the ill-favored, then launched himself into the air and away.

"Thank you," the ill-favored whispered.

He was down on his knees, his face wet with tears, but he didn't look at Hersha. It was as if he was ashamed to.

"It wasn't a problem," he said, even though it had taken more courage than he'd known he had. "Just... stay away from any of them, okay? They're not safe."

The ill-favored nodded but didn't reply.

Not safe, Hersha thought as he took to the air as well. No, the black dragonkin weren't safe to be near. Then again, seeing what the world had become, were any of them safe to be around?

Haiteng felt it. He wasn't sure when it had started, but it was like an itch at the corner of his mind. Something he had forgotten, maybe? Or overlooked.

But no, it wasn't that. This was something more... personal.

He stretched, his great body spanning the length of an Ascani city, his claws longer than a lance those ridiculous knights or whatever they were in Obristan used for sport.

Usually, he felt powerful when he did that. Even after all this time, all these years had gone by, his body still amazed him. He'd never known that anything could be so... glorious... as he was.

The others, too, he supposed, each in their own way. Chimbod and Fimbruss were closest in form, while Gillbriss took an entirely different path. He would never understand why she chose to be so much smaller than her siblings. Tophonoss... well, he could barely remember where she came from or what she really looked like.

But none of them could compare to him. His form was perfect, for the land, the air, or the ocean. Out of them all, he and his children were the only ones to take to the depths. It opened up whole vistas of the world that the others would never be privy to.

So what was it? Why did he feel... off?

He stretched again and realized what it was.

He felt weaker.

Weakness being a comparative term, of course. Compared to anything else that walked the earth, other than maybe two of his siblings, there wasn't a thing alive that was even close to his power, but Haiteng knew. He wasn't as strong today as he had been yesterday.

Nothing could cause that, though. The dragons were tied to their realms. As long as the realms endured, the dragons did as well. As long as the dragons lived, the realms persisted. That was the nature...one of the natures... of the magic. It was a perfect loop. The land protects the dragon, the dragon protects the land.

He rose to his feet, then into the air, gliding out from the massive hole that led from the surface deep down to one of his many resting places. It had nothing of value in it, so even the most desperate would-be hero would think twice before risking Haiteng's displeasure by trying to despoil it. His riches were elsewhere, everywhere, spread across all of Ascana, being used to further his vision of what his realm should be.

As he rose high, then higher, the coolness of the air helped bring clarity to his mind.

It was Gillbriss, he reasoned, and her handling of this situation with the humans and the old Raaleth magic they must have used. She was laying waste to towns in his realm, as well as to those of Obristan. Fimbruss had forbidden any of them to enter his realm, or for their children to. He claimed that he had no need of them, Usturg was well under control.

Maybe he was right, too. He'd been slowly cultivating the idea that he was worthy of worship for ages. Now that plan, which had seemed the very definition of hubris, was bearing fruit.

In the meantime, Gillbriss was tearing Haiteng's realm apart. Which was hurting the land, weakening it. Thus, he was getting weaker as well. That could not stand.

He turned toward Droy Thus. Gillbriss wanted more power. Tophonoss was indifferent to anyone's suffering, and Fimbruss had removed himself from their great plan. All that was left was Chimbod. Chimbod who was most like him in temperament and ideals.

It was time to end this. The humans had been cowed. They wouldn't dare rise up again. He and Chimbod would tell Gillbriss it was over and that it was time to reinforce the edict.

He'd work on rebuilding those towns that had been razed. Eventually, he'd even bring Festival back.

The land would heal and become stronger. Then, so would he.

"Watch them run."

Gravris leaned over the edge of the building and made a noise.

Far below, several humans had gathered into a circle, watching as two men beat a third. The crowd cheered, and money was passing from hand to hand. Gravris and her new friend had been watching for some time. The single man had done better than expected, but it was almost over now. Blood ran from several spots on his face and head, and he was holding one arm awkwardly.

The other two, bruised and slightly-less bloody, were closing in for the kill.

"Wait," Assa said. "I want to see what happens."

She peered over the edge as well. If anyone below had looked up all they would have seen were two black shapes silhouetted against the sky. They never would have been able to tell from that distance that one of the observers had jet-black scales, while the other's were fiery crimson.

"Why? It's done. Or near enough. The fun is just about over."

"Maybe not." Assa turned with a sly smile. "What if I— help— the other one. Just a little."

"Why do that? Why help any of them?"

"To make it more entertaining." Assa turned her focus back to the action below, her eyes bright. "Won't it surprise the other two?"

"More fun to make them all scramble like bugs... but you're my guest."

"Thank you," Assa almost purred.

She muttered something beneath her breath. Magic, of some sort that Gravris didn't recognize. That shouldn't have surprised her. Assa was a red dragonkin, one of Chimbod's children, and they were known for having the highest affinity for magic. Gravris had plenty herself, of course, as they all did, but those from Droy Thus...

A sudden bellow rose from the street below. Gravris pulled her attention from Assa to what was happening there.

The lone man had grown. He was quite a bit taller than he had been, and his chest, arms and legs were now all twice, maybe three times, the size they had been. Strangely, his head had not grown proportionally, which seemed be causing him some consternation.

That was funny enough, but now, the man appeared to be taking out his fear and anger on those he'd been fighting.

Moving faster than Gravris had ever seen a human move, the giant was on the first man in a flash. He grabbed him, lifted, then spun him over and slammed his head into the ground. His victim went limp and fell in a boneless heap when the first let him go.

By the time he'd turned to the second, that one was trying to run away. The crowd was holding him back, though, jeering at him and shouting that it was his turn, now.

The giant man broke bones with a savage glee, howling all the while.

It wasn't until a few moments had passed that Gravris realized that the man was still growing. He was getting bigger and bigger, his massive shoulders rising around his now seemingly tiny head. His howls and bellows became more strident, even as he finally disposed of the second of his assailants.

People began to move away, some laughing nervously, while a few— the smarter ones— took off running.

By the time the rest had decided that fleeing was the prudent thing to do, it was too late. The man finally stopped growing and… exploded. With one last anguished scream, his body was unable to contain whatever magic Assa had pumped it full of.

Onlookers were drenched with blood and gore before they were even able to turn away.

Gravris watched with unbridled glee. She had come up with inventive ways to hurt humans on several occasions, when she was bored and could be bothered. Her brothers and sisters were masters at it. She'd never seen anything like what Assa had just done, though.

"Oh, very good," she whispered as she drew back. "Now, should we scatter them?"

"A better idea," Assa preened, "is to not bother the rest at all. They'll wonder how that happened, and more… wonder if it could happen to them."

"And it could!" Gravris said. "We could do it to another, in a little while, when they think they're safe."

"Exactly!" Assa appeared as excited by the prospect as Gravris was. "I like Reclium," she proclaimed. "I wish I had come here before!"

"I wish you had, too." Gravris came close to Assa and rubbed against her side. She wasn't as large as the red, but that didn't seem to make any difference. "Teach me?"

"The magic? Why not?" Assa laughed. "But we'll have to find someone to practice on."

Gravris made a show of looking about. "That's not a problem. We *are* in Reclium, after all."

"We are," Assa agreed. "And I just might stay here. No matter what Chimbod says."

Gravris eyed her sideways. "And Gillbriss?"

"Her, too. They're so worried about the human's magic. I think…" she trailed off.

"What? What do you think?"

"I think the humans showed us the way. We are strong and there are a lot of us. Many more than five. Who says we have to listen to them?"

"Heresy," purred Gravris. "Treason."

"Well," Assa answered. "As you said, we *are* in Reclium."

Chapter 32- Once-Realm of Olequan

"Has there been any news, Arastug?"

Arastug moved closer to where Falaern sat, a book opened and face-down on a small table set beside her chair. She radiated calm majesty, as she always did, but he'd known her for a long, long time. Longer than most of his people usually lived. Yet, Arastug still felt vital. Old, certainly, but not so much that he'd slowed down too badly. His mind was still sharp, he could still travel from one end of Olequan to the other without stopping— although that wasn't nearly the feat it had once been, to be honest.

He suspected his longevity was a gift from Falaern, but he'd never asked and she'd never said. Maybe she had just lost too much and didn't want him to go, as well.

"No, your Majesty," he said, bowing low. "But that's not surprising."

She frowned, which was something he never wanted to see but did more and more these days. He supposed that after enough time, anyone would be worn down, trying to hide their whole kingdom from the dragons.

"We shouldn't have sent him," she said.

Such vulnerability was never openly displayed. Falaern allowed it now only because he was the only one present. She'd sent her aides and handmaidens away when she'd summoned him.

"We should have," he said gently. "We needed to know who threw that spell, and no one is more equipped for such a journey than Ilvisar."

"He's young and hot-headed," she said.

"He's not. Young, yes. Hot-headed, no. I wouldn't call it that anyway. What he is, is full of confidence and righteous anger over what happened to our people."

She finally looked at him, and her mouth twisted into that sad smile that he'd come to know and love.

"What else?" she asked. "I can see it all over your face. There may not be news from Ilvisar, but you have something else to say."

Now it was his turn to smile. "You know me too well, your Majesty. There is something else… although I'm not sure what it might be."

"As much as I usually enjoy them, this is no time for your mysteries, Arastug. Speak plainly."

"There was another— disturbance, I guess you could call it. Something that caught my attention, again from the human world. Like the one that ran through Olequan and—"

"No," Falaern interrupted. "Not like the first one." Her frown returned. "I felt nothing, Arastug. There was no new disturbance."

"But I—" Arastug stopped to think before he spoke any further. It was a trait he'd forced himself into as a young man which had served him well. Patience was ever a hallmark of his people, the Helgarlug, but Arastug took it to another level. He never allowed himself to speak without thinking.

His fingers combed his beard while he considered what Falaern was saying.

There *had* been something. He was sure of it. He'd been walking back to his quarters delved into the hill when he'd felt it. It hadn't lasted long, but it was as if something had shot him in the top of his head. Something that pierced his skull, then down through his brain and into his heart, before passing lower and out of his body.

"You didn't feel *anything?*" he asked, almost plaintively.

"No," she replied. "But you did. Didn't you?"

It spoke volumes about his relationship with Falaern. There was no doubt in her voice. He'd said that he'd felt something, therefore he had.

"I did, your Majesty."

"And I did not. Nor did any of my handmaids, or I would have known. They would not have kept it to themselves. That can mean only one thing."

She'd come to it before he had. In truth, he'd probably known already, but he hadn't wanted to admit it. Why would he?

What a disturbance like that portended could only mean one thing. The magic involved was powerful, but it *wasn't* Raaleth. It had to be Helgarlug magic.

The Helgarlug had their own type of spell casting, not nearly as powerful as the Raaleth. It was why the Raaleth magic used earlier had been felt by everyone. There was no disguising such things.

But Helgarlug magic wasn't as grand. It wasn't as showy and didn't have nearly as broad an effect on the world.

On the contrary, their most effective spells were very localized. The type that could be imbued into something. Like weapons. The Helgarlug had once been very, very adept at enchanting weapons of all kinds. Most of those had been destroyed by the dragons, along with those who'd wielded them.

Yet, somehow, somewhere out there in the human and dragonkin world, one had just been used.

But why now? Who owned it and how had they used it? What was the weapon?

Arastug looked at Falaern. "We may need to send someone else out."

"And who would that be, my friend? Who would know what they were looking for?"

There was really only one answer, wasn't there?

"Me." His voice sounded small even to his own ears. Ilvisar hiding himself from the dragonkin was one thing. The lad had magic that could do it. Arastug had no such magic, and his appearance wasn't exactly inconspicuous.

"I should forbid it," she said quietly.

"But you won't." He forced himself to smile at her.

"No. In fact, I would command it if you weren't already set on going. Times are apparently changing. For good or ill remains to be seen. But the time is fast approaching when we can no longer stay hidden. The war is coming again, if it ever really left. This time, we need to be more prepared."

"That's not all we'll need," he said. "If we're to have any chance, we'll need allies."

Chapter 33- Craydon, Ascana

It wasn't easy staying hidden throughout the day. Men and women came and went, carrying in sacks of grain or bales of hay and stacking them neatly. Most of the time, they worked in silence, only occasionally grunting at one another. At first, Kori was mystified by that, until he remembered that these weren't people who were doing work they'd chosen to do. They weren't the regular farmers who had picked this as their profession.

These were slaves to the dragonkin. Forced to work at whatever task they were given. Defiance did no good. Not unless one wanted to end up dead.

So when one middle-aged man happened to move a couple of bags and find their hiding hole, it came as no great surprise when he looked in at them, glanced around quickly, and then replaced the bags he'd taken away.

"What are you doing?" Kori heard another voice call.

"Rats," the man nearby replied. "I thought I saw a big one run over here. Didn't want him spoiling everything, so I thought I'd chase him off."

"Didn't even see him, though, did you?" the first voice said. "Slippery little things."

If the first man replied to that, Kori didn't hear. Even as they talked, their voices receded, until they had left the barn entirely.

"Close one," he muttered.

"What if they stack too much here?" Toni whispered. "How will we get out?"

"They won't." Not that he knew for sure, although he suspected the man who'd discovered them might try to help with that. But there was nothing to be done about it either way. For all they knew, a dragonkin was out in the fields right now, overseeing the work and making sure that no one was shirking their duties.

And if not, maybe it was far overhead, looking for whoever had—

The screams came from outside. Where there had been near silence only a moment before, now came the sound of pandemonium.

"What is it?" Toni asked.

"They found it," Kori guessed. "The one I killed."

"Oh, no." Toni's whisper was full of horror.

Kori could see it in his imagination. The dragonkin swooping low, breathing its steam or acid on any humans it came across. Picking them up and rending them limb from limb or biting their heads off. Maiming and killing with wanton abandon anyone it could reach.

He should go out and turn himself in. It was the only way to stop what he was sure was happening out there.

But then... what would happen to Toni? To Wyman, who the dragonkin must know he'd lived with? And those who came in and out of the barn that day? Would the dragonkin believe they hadn't known he was in there?

He put his head down and tried to block out the noises, but it was no use.

Thankfully, they didn't last long. Kori realized that the screaming was too short-lived to be that of people being brutally tortured and killed. It was more the sound of panic.

Then, the screaming stopped, but a voice sounded from just on the other side of the wooden wall he and Toni huddled against. The dragonkin, whichever color it was, was right there, haranguing those who worked in the area.

"The greatest sin has been committed."

The dragonkin's voice was calm and measured, the very picture of reasonableness.

"One of our own has been murdered. Such a thing has never been known to happen in the history of the world, and why would it? Dragonkin and human have always been allies— friends, even. What possible reason could one have to destroy the other?"

The dragonkin was ignoring all the death and torture Kori had personally seen them commit over the last few weeks. Everyone else had seen the same things, but who was going to tell it that it was lying?

"We need the one responsible. If they are turned over, all will be well and life can return to normal."

The dragonkin paused.

"If not, we have no choice but to assume that the murderer is being harbored. By one of you. In that case, we will have to use every power at our command to root out this evil doer and bring him to justice."

No one spoke. Kori strained to hear, but he couldn't make out so much as a whisper. Toni's hand stole into his, and he knew she was thinking of the man who'd discovered them, just as he was. He braced himself to hear that same voice speak now and say that he found fugitives hiding in that very barn.

"No one?" the dragonkin said after several silent seconds had passed. "Very well. Perhaps you are all truly innocent and have nothing to do with it. I'll move on to other fields, other sections of our fair city. Someone will know something."

There was a rustling, as of a large body beginning to move.

"Oh, but first," it said again, as if it had just thought of something. "I wish to leave you all with a reminder. Of what will happen if you defy us."

Kori heard another sound. One he recognized from the night before. When the black dragonkin had drawn back its head and spit acid, destroying the beer barrel behind Toni's bar.

"No," he whispered, but that was drowned out by the sudden, agonized scream of a woman.

It went on and on. Her cries of torment building until he thought he would go mad. After what seemed like forever, the cries quieted, until finally, they choked off into a burbling moan.

He didn't want to know. He didn't want to see it.

The dragonkin left. He could hear it flap its wings and lift into the air. It wasn't until several more seconds had passed that he heard the voices of the workers begin to speak all at once.

"Help her!" someone yelled.

"There's nothing to do," another said more quietly. "She's gone."

Another one. That was all Kori could think. Another human killed for no reason. The dragonkin hadn't believed for a second that the poor woman had anything to do with the death of the other. It was simply an excuse to be cruel again.

He realized his hand had gone to his axe. Almost unconsciously, he ran his thumb along the side of the razor-sharp edge.

That axe had killed a dragonkin with one blow. Maybe he'd just gotten lucky, but that bright flash that had occurred at the same time made him think differently.

As he was now. Maybe fleeing *wasn't* the answer.

Maybe finding the remaining two dragonkin, the other black and the blue, was the answer. Find them one at a time, alone.

Then, maybe he could do something good.

The rest of the day passed with agonizing slowness. Their little hole was cramped and felt moreso as the day wore on. It seemed that neither of them could move without disturbing the other. Even dozing off was only a brief respite. A few minutes later, they'd be back awake, scratching at flea bites or stretching to try to relieve cramped muscles.

Twice during the day, Kori changed the bandage on Antonia's arm. He'd been afraid of it getting infected, but it seemed to be healing okay. At least, it didn't stink any more than the two of them did after being crammed into their hiding place all day.

Finally, through the small cracks between the wooden wall boards, Kori could tell that daylight was fading. Soon, they'd be able to re-emerge and— hopefully— sneak across the fields and into the woods.

The dragonkin had never returned, which he was grateful for, but it also made him even more concerned. The thing had come and delivered its warnings and threats, then flown off after killing one more innocent. Kori strongly suspected it was watching, probably from overhead.

They would just have to take their chances and hope that any of the dragonkin were watching somewhere else, like in Craydon itself, closer to where the Inland Trader was. With any luck, they would believe that Kori would still be hiding there somewhere.

As the light truly started to fade, the final loads were carried into the barn and stacked. He assumed that, by now, the barn was going to be quite full.

Outside their hiding space, Kori heard the sound of a sack being thrown down.

"Ooof. Last one for the day," a voice said. "Glad to be going home now."

It was the same man as before, letting them know that it would be safe to come out.

When they heard the barn door slide shut, Kori quickly moved the bags that had blocked them from view and slowly climbed out.

The barn was— as he'd hoped and expected— empty of people. But there were a lot more of the sacks and bales than there had been the day before. Enough that there was now only a narrow aisle open to get to the doors. Kori knew next to nothing about farming or the storage of grain and seeds, or whatever was in there, but he suspected this wasn't the normal way to load a barn.

Which meant the aisle had been left there on purpose. So… it was probable that more than that one man knew they were there. And yet, not one of them had turned them in to the dragonkin.

"Wow," Toni said from behind him.

Kori looked back over his shoulder. She was staring down at the ground, at something that had been left there.

A leather bottle and something wrapped in a rag. Toni slowly squatted down next to them and unwrapped the bundle. Inside were three thick slices of crusty bread which were only a little moldy and two dried-up apples. The bottle was full of good, clean water.

"They knew," she said softly. "That we were there, I mean."

Kori nodded. "They did. There's still some good out there, I guess."

Toni gathered the items and stowed the bundle inside her shirt. She handed the bottle to Kori, who did the same, nestling it against his book.

"Want me to look at your arm once more?" he asked.

"No." Toni shook her head. "It hurts, but a normal hurt, you know? Like I had a big chunk of wood shoved into my arm. But it's going to be okay, I think. Let's not waste the bandage or the water."

"All right." Kori thought he probably should check it, but then again, they hadn't been doing anything to get the wound dirty or tax it. Once they were across the field and safely hidden among the trees, then it would be time to check on it again.

He made his way down the narrow pathway to the door, which he slowly opened, trying not to make any noise. For the most part, he succeeded. Once they were both outside, he shut it, but had no way to lock it. He would just have to hope that no one else opened it, and that it would look normal in the morning.

A few, short minutes later, they were looking across the fields at the dark shadows of the forest.

"It's not that far, right?" Toni asked.

"It's not. We can make it in just a couple of minutes," he agreed.

Sure. Just a couple of minutes, during which a dragonkin could come swooping down and crush them both. Or breathe on them. Or… well, he'd been playing the possible ways a dragonkin could kill them over and over in his mind all day. There was no sense in rehashing them now.

He looked up and wasn't sure if he should feel cursed or blessed. The moon was full and very bright, the sky perfectly clear with only a few wispy clouds lit by the moonlight.

On one hand, that was a blessing. They could see a dragonkin, even one of the black ones, silhouetted against such a sky. They could see where they were going better, less chance of tripping on a rock or carelessly discarded hoe.

On the other, of course, they'd could easily be spotted as well.

"Well?" Antonia asked. "Are we?"

"We are," Kori said. "Quickly, but not running. At least not yet."

"Why not?"

"Too easy to make a mistake. If we see or hear anything that could be a dragonkin, we drop and freeze, right? We're just part of the ground at that point."

Toni grimaced but nodded. It wasn't much of a plan, and she knew it. He did, too. It relied entirely on pure, dumb luck. The same thing that had always seemed lacking in his life.

"Got to come up for me some time, though," he muttered.

"What?"

"Nothing. Let's go."

He left the relative safety of the shadows and started across the field.

If lying in the snow, listening to the snow troll eat Slode and his men, had been the most stressful event of Kori's life so far, it now paled in comparison to crossing that field.

He'd said they'd move quickly, but they didn't. Those first steps were the hardest he'd ever taken, and given that she stayed right there with him, they were no easier for Toni. Each time he inched forward, the dirt he disturbed sounded like an avalanche to his ears. They were too exposed, too out in the open.

But moving faster was out of the question. Want to be noticed after you've done something wrong? Run. Everyone knew that the way to get away with something was to simply walk, to act as if you belonged wherever you were, that you'd done nothing wrong.

This was different, though, right? This was being out where they could be seen, where they had no business being, so anyone spotting them, acting as they were supposed to be there or not, was going to know they were sneaking away. It was only a short jump from there to knowing that they— he, really— were the ones who'd killed that dragonkin.

An owl hooted, and Kori gasped and jumped, making Toni do the same.

"We might as well be ringing a bell!" she whispered. "We have to go faster!"

Kori nodded, knowing that, of course, she was right. He reached back and groped for her hand. When she took it, he started moving more quickly. Not running, but not taking one hesitant step after another, either.

He kept his eyes roaming. Down, so that he wouldn't stumble among the hillocks and random stones which dotted the ground. Then forward, seeing how far— how *very* far— they still had to go. Over his shoulder, to make sure Toni was okay and also to look past her, to see if anyone was chasing them.

And always, always, always back to the sky. That's where they would come from. They wouldn't chase them on all fours. They'd dive from on high, giving them no chance to get away.

How was he supposed to prevent it? How was he supposed to fight that?

By the time they were halfway there, he was panting, his breath puffing out in visible clouds in the cool night air. Behind him, Antonia was doing the same, but she was staying right with him.

Then, she stopped, pulling him to a halt, as well.

"There! Oh, gods! There!"

Even though her voice sounded panicked, she remembered to keep it down, to no more than a whisper.

Kori looked to where she pointed.

A dragonkin, in the sky, just as he knew it would be. It was flying over the town, but up high, so that it had a wide range of vision. It was showing no sign of heading in their direction, so maybe it had just gotten up there.

"Down," he said, and pulled her gently to the ground next to him.

But when she was lying flat on her stomach, he moved around her, slowly, picking up handfuls of dirt and casting them across her back, her legs, her arms.

"What are you doing?" she hissed.

"Hiding you," he said. "I'll do the same to myself as soon as I'm done."

Their clothes were darker than the dried dirt around them. They'd still stand out, lying down or no, without something else. He kept tossing dirt onto her until her form was at least broken up enough that maybe the dragonkin would miss her. The whole time, he kept his eye on the one in the sky.

It was starting to circle now but had headed off to the other side of town first, which gave him a couple of minutes.

He moved away from Toni, ignoring her almost silent squeal of protest. If he was seen, he didn't want the thing to spot her, too.

He crouched and ran, several yards farther toward the forest, looking back over his shoulder. For a moment, he thought he might actually make it all the way, but then the dragonkin circled around toward him.

He tripped at the same time, sprawling into the dirt. He rolled onto his back, wriggling against the ground, then onto his front to do the same.

It wasn't perfect, but it would have to do.

He turned his head so he could at least see part of the sky. The dragonkin was there, coming closer and closer with every second. It was still flying at the same speed as when they'd first seen it, though, so it didn't have them in its sight yet.

When it was nearer, he could tell from its size and the stinger on the end of the tail that it was the other black one. Where the third, the blue one, was he didn't know, but at the moment, he'd just have to concern himself with what was there.

It passed out of his sight. He would need to roll over to spot it again and there was no way he was going to do that.

But he didn't hear it land, either. A thing that big was going to make noise coming down, no matter how slowly it lowered itself. That was one thing…

His eyes shifted back toward Toni, who was staring at him, her eyes wide with fear.

Kori began to shift, but she shook her head slightly and rapidly, telling him not to.

It was close still, then.

A snow-troll was much easier, he decided.

As he waited, though, Kori was suddenly assailed by a new feeling. He was getting tired. Not tired like needing sleep. Tired of this. Of hiding. Of running. Of always living in fear.

Why should he? He did nothing wrong. He didn't start whatever was going on with these dragonkin. It wasn't him killing people for no reason. And the dragonkin he'd killed was attacking them and would have destroyed them both if he hadn't.

What was coming over him wasn't exactly the red rage that he'd felt in The Inland Trader. It was more… blue. Cold, but calm. Like he supposed the ocean was on certain days. But it was no less powerful.

The feeling he'd had hiding in the barn returned, only stronger now, and with more certainty. He was through hiding.

Well, after this— assuming he and Toni survived— he was. It was hard to combat a dragonkin from the sky, especially when he wasn't even on his feet.

But confronting them on his own terms? Well. That was something else altogether.

Kori was done running. It was time to bring the fight to them.

Chapter 34- Lostin, Ascana

It was easy enough for Nettie to get off the ship. She was a sailor, the same as all the others. It was customary for most of the crew to disembark in a port town, leaving only a few to oversee the dockworkers as they unloaded the cargo. For the rest, it was a few short hours of shore leave. Only until the new cargo was loaded and the ship needed to be made ready to sail once again.

She'd stayed near the center of the pack of sailors who'd made their way down the gangplank and onto the dock. From there, they began to spread out. Some had been to Lostin before and knew that— even if it was a small port-city without much going for it— there were still places where amusement could be found. Amusements of varying types, including the one that Nettie had in mind.

She'd tucked the item she needed under her baggy shirt, wrapping it around her waist so that it wouldn't be seen. It might not fool a careful observer, but she was counting on the fact that no one would be looking at her that closely.

She was right, too.

Two men stood nearby, one of them obviously bored and wishing he was anywhere else. That one must be Radley; the one Captain Stanford knew.

The other glared at everyone going past, his eyes roaming over them looking for… who-knew-what? Anything he could use to try to enforce his claim that Jarmen Stanford was a thief and smuggler, she assumed. Tilford. The "dockmaster."

He wasn't really watching the sailors, though. Not beyond making sure they all looked as they should. No, he was really interested in what came out of the holds or what didn't. He'd spent a lot of time aboard, and Nettie had no doubt the man had memorized just about every crate, bag, and barrel.

She moved easily past him, giving him the same side-eyed glance of derision that the other sailors did. Tilford ignored them all as being beneath him. Which was good. Nettie didn't want him singling her face out of the others in any way.

When they'd passed the two men, Nettie followed a group across the dock and down a street, then peeled off when they were among the buildings.

"Good luck," one man muttered to her, while the rest continued on to the tavern they'd chosen.

She ducked into a narrow alley, then took the time to look up, making sure that this time there was no black dragonkin looming overhead. When she was as comfortable as she could be that she was not being watched, she pulled the garment she'd brought out of her shirt.

It was the dress she'd worn from Mrs. Cloven's to the dock in Pharax. The same one she'd swore she would never wear again and had almost thrown overboard. Now, she was glad she hadn't.

A distraction was needed to get Viktoria and Dommick past Tilford. Nettie wasn't so worried about Radley, but Tilford had it in for them— and probably anyone else he could lord it over. So, she pulled the dress over her clothes and looked down.

It wouldn't work. The dress was... revealing. But the clothes beneath it were not. She'd be the world's most bashful prostitute in a getup like that. She had to—

She looked around again. This time, not limiting herself to the rooftops on either side. It wasn't only a dragonkin she was worried about watching this time.

The dress came back off in a hurry; then, with a sigh and reddened-face even though she was alone, she took off her shirt and pants. As quickly as she could, she threw the dress back over her head and adjusted it, making sure to emphasize the attributes she would need to play her part.

Now... there was nowhere to hide her other clothes with her, so she tucked them down next to the wall and hoped they'd be there when she got back. Her shoes were another problem, so she took them off as well, leaving them with her clothes, and scurried barefoot out of the alley.

From there, it was a short, hurried walk back to the dock. Her heart was pounding in her chest. Nettie didn't think she'd ever been more… uncomfortable. Not even when leaving Mrs. Cloven's house. Then, she'd just had to walk along, letting whoever wanted to leer do so. Now, though. Well, now she to do a bit more.

The sailors who were going ashore had all left by the time she got back. Nettie would have expected others dressed as she was to be there to greet them, but they were all staying safely in their respective houses. Probably the dragonkins' presence had forced the change. All of which meant she was seen as she approached the two men. Not so much by them, but by others working the docks.

The catcalls and whistles were enough to set her cheeks burning. No self-respecting woman who did what Nettie was pretending would be embarrassed by such minor things, though, but that was all right. She could use the shame for another purpose.

It wasn't until she was only a few steps away that Radley turned and looked at her. His eyebrows went up in surprise, but before he could say anything, Nettie had stepped past him and in front of Tilford.

Tilford was a small, short man, so his eyes were at an advantageous level for Nettie to distract him. Most men, she would have thought, would have been surprised enough to gawk for a moment.

Not Tilford. "Move aside, whore! You're in my way."

Plan A wasn't going to work. He made that very obvious immediately. But Nettie had a back-up ready.

"There you are!" She forced her voice out in a rough squeak that she hoped she could keep up. "You owe me money and I wants it now!"

"What are you talking about?" Tilford stopped trying to peer around her and sneered up at her. "I owe you nothing!"

"Oooh! A thief, you are, then? Use a girl, make her promises, then cast her off!"

"Tilford?" Radley said, his voice quivering with amusement. "You?"

"Don't be stupid," Tilford sneered, but his eyes never left Nettie's. "I wouldn't touch this creature for a thousand gold."

"Oh, you did the touching all right!" Nettie shrieked. "And the getting touched. Just the way you like it, you said. Nothing too strange for you, you said!"

By this time, her loud voice— plus the fact that it was Tilford being harangued— had begun to draw a crowd. Dock workers gathered around them, muttering and snickering.

"Good for you, Tilford!" one sang out. "I kind of wondered if…" He left it hanging but others laughed anyway.

"Back to work, all of you!" Tilford snapped.

"Back to work, he says!" Nettie crowed. She was beginning to enjoy herself. "Same thing he says to me when I stopped for a drink of water. Small he may be, but lusty all the same!"

More laughter.

Nettie hoped that by now, Captain Stanford had seen what she was doing and gotten Viktoria and Dommick off the ship. It would have been so much easier to try to disguise them, but there was no way Tilford would miss their very pale skin and dark eyes. Complexions that clearly marked them as being from Reclium.

The group around her ignored Tilford's command to return to work and continued to cat-call and laugh. Radley didn't join in, but neither did he do anything to stop it. When Nettie glanced quickly at him, she saw that he was fighting to keep the grin off his face.

"I wants my money, I do!" Nettie squealed. "I earned it fair and square; I did!"

"I'm warning you," Tilford snarled. "If you don't move away from me, I'll—"

Nettie was probably less alarmed than she should have been to see his hand drop to his belt and the knife sheathed there. She hadn't looked carefully enough and didn't realize he had it. Still, she didn't think he would actually do anything with so many others around.

She put her hands on her hips, thrust her bosom out as far as she could, and drew herself up.

"You'll what? Try to stab me? Again? Only with something I might feel this time!"

With that, she thought she might have actually gone too far. The men around her erupted in laughter. All except for Radley, who looked troubled. Then, she noticed that he wasn't looking at her. Instead, his eyes were tracking something behind her. Nettie could guess what it was. Captain Stanford must be escorting Viktoria and Dommick off the ship.

Tilford, however, was still focused on Nettie, and he was not amused. His face was a deep red and his snarl had grown to almost animal proportions. Without another word, he whipped his knife from his belt.

Nettie stumbled back, only half-pretending to be scared. She fell into the arms of a man standing behind her, who grabbed her to stop her from tumbling to the ground. Nettie fought back an angry outburst as he took a liberty or two while helping her maintain her balance.

"Back away from me, whore," Tilford growled. "Another clever word and I'll cut your tongue right out of your pretty head."

Nettie wanted nothing more than to get away from him now. She had intended on distracting Tilford, one way or the other, but hadn't intended on being stabbed. And she couldn't very well fight him, or he'd know she wasn't what she was pretending to be. He'd realize something was amiss, and that could be the end of everything.

"Easy, Tilford," Radley said, quietly. "There's no reason to be—"

"You shut up, too," Tilford told him, never once taking his eyes off Nettie. "Or I'll report you to the dragonkin."

Radley frowned and seemed about to say something, but a shout from the crowd cut him off.

"Hey, why not pass her around, Tilford? It hardly seems fair you get all the perks of the job! Show some good will!"

Nettie couldn't see who had shouted, but if she could have, she would have marked him out to be visited later. It didn't matter, though. She could see the change come over Tilford like the sun setting. His rage began to ebb. The color drained from his cheeks, and a sly grin stole over his features.

"Good idea," he said. "Why should I have all the fun?"

"I don't think so! I haven't said I would—" Nettie tried to stay in character.

Someone— probably the same man from before— grabbed her from behind.

Nettie threw an elbow back and had the satisfaction of feeling it sink into something soft and heard the "oomph" of suddenly expelled air. But just as quickly, another grabbed her arm.

Now, she did fight. She didn't care anymore if they realized she wasn't what they thought. What they wanted wasn't going to happen. She looked pleadingly at Radley. "Help me!" But he only averted his eyes and began to back away.

Tilford slowly put his knife away and watched her struggles with open amusement.

There was no one who was going to stop it, and she couldn't fight them all.

"Lobelia!" A deep voice cut through the clamor. "Lobelia! What are you doing?"

A man— a huge man— pushed his way through the crowd. He was well over six-feet tall, probably closer to seven, with an enormous frame. His stomach protruded, but from the way he easily waded through the men between him and her, it wasn't all fat. His bald pate shone in the sun, but he wore a long, brown beard that covered his chest.

His dark eyes flashed as he neared.

"What are you doing?" This time, his shouted question wasn't directed at her. It was yelled at the man to her side, who still had one hand encircling her arm and the other where it most definitely did not belong. "Get off!"

The newcomer reached out and shoved the man. He was gone so quickly Nettie almost didn't see him go, but he took three other men down with him.

Just like that, the frenzy was over. Already, those at the edge of the crowd were peeling away, slinking off to pretend they had been at work this whole time. Within only a few seconds, the only ones left were the huge man, Tilford, and a scared and panting Nettie.

The man turned to Tilford. "What's the meaning of this?" he thundered. "Even for you, this was low, Tilford."

Despite the difference in their sizes, Tilford didn't seem at all intimidated by the large man.

"What difference does it make?" he said. "She'll only service most of them later on, anyway."

"At her rates and her consent," the man said. "You're lucky I don't—"

"Don't what, Librarian?" Tilford interrupted. "Be very careful what you say next."

The Librarian, whoever he was, took a step closer. He looked Tilford up and down. "Your dragonkin threats only go so far, little man. Run away, before I get mad."

To his credit, Tilford didn't run. He didn't even leave at first. He turned his gaze to Nettie, took in her disheveled clothes and hair, snorted a quick laugh, then turned and sauntered away. He didn't even bother to look back. But he only went to a small building at the edge of the dock, where he could watch the ship from its windows. He wasn't done with Captain Stanford quite yet.

"Thank you," Nettie said. Her heart was still pounding. It wasn't until she'd said it that she realized she'd used her own voice.

"Where are they?" the man asked quietly.

"Who?"

"The one I'm supposed to meet. The girl. And apparently some dolt who attached himself to her."

Nettie stared at the huge man, unsure of how to answer. He gazed back at her, before his mouth twitched into a small smile. "Mrs. Cloven. She contacted me. You're Nettie, right? Brave, what you were doing here, but a little stupid, too."

What could she say to that? He was right, on both counts. But stupid or not, it had served to get Viktoria and Dommick off the ship. The fact that she now felt that if she had just waited, this man— the Librarian— could have accomplished the same thing much easier was something she was going to choose to ignore.

"I think Captain Stanford got them off a few minutes ago," she said. "While I was trying to distract that jerk, Tilford."

"You did manage that." The Librarian sighed, then turned and scanned the area. He glanced at the ship, then nodded briefly and said, "This way."

Before Nettie could even think to ask how he knew, the giant was striding away, leaving her to hurry after. Not a single man looked at her as she went past, even though a cool breeze told her that a rip in her skirts was showing more than she was comfortable with.

"Can we stop somewhere for a moment?" she asked.

The Librarian looked down at her. "Where? Why?"

"My clothes," she explained. "My real clothes, not—" She spread her skirt between her two hands. "— this."

"Sure. As long as they're nearby."

"They are." With that, she moved faster, passing her new guide and going back to the alley where she'd changed. There was still no sign of a dragonkin overheard or anyone else around. When the Librarian turned the corner, he snorted, then stopped and turned his back on her.

"Make it quick," his voice carried to her.

She did. Quicker than when she had changed the first time. Now, back in a normal shirt and pants, her boots on her feet once again, she felt more like her old self. Her sigh must have been loud enough to alert him that she was finished.

"If you're ready, come with me," he said, and set off again.

Nettie ran out of the alleyway and fell into step next to him, although she had to take one and a half strides for each one of his.

They walked silently for a few moments, not seeing too many others about. Lostin was quiet for a port city, which probably had more to do with the dragonkin than any lack of trade. Although now that she thought about it, the harbor was less crowded than she would have thought.

"Why do they call you the Librarian?" she asked suddenly.

"I can read," he answered. "And I like books. I have several that I own." He sounded proud of that, as well he should be. Books weren't cheap, and most people either borrowed them from friends or simply didn't bother at all. "Plus," he continued, "I'll let kids read them. As long as they're careful." He shrugged, the movement like two gigantic boulders moving up and then down again. "Most are."

I would bet, Nettie thought. She couldn't imagine wanting to make this guy mad.

"What's your real name, then?"

"Halli Serksson," he answered.

"Halli? That doesn't sound Ascani."

"Nor should it. I was born in Usturg. Came here as a young man seeking adventure."

"Here?" Nettie asked incredulously. "No offense meant, but Lostin isn't exactly…"

"No," Halli agreed. "But after enough years of other grand adventure, I was ready for somewhere quieter where I could settle and read my books."

"Oh." Nettie let it go, although inside she was thinking that if that was the case, what was Halli doing mixed up with Mrs. Cloven and agreeing to help two refugees from Reclium?

"Here we are." Halli stopped in front of a business and looked up at the sign.

"Wave's Crest," Nettie read. An inn.

Somehow it didn't surprise her one bit that Dommick had ended up in a place where he could get a drink. The man had an almost uncanny ability to sniff out spirits of any kind. Then again, Viktoria seemed the type that would be decidedly uncomfortable in such a place.

And as much as she didn't want to be adversaries with the other woman, that thought somehow didn't bother her very much.

"In we go," Halli said, and Nettie followed his massive frame through the door.

Chapter 35- Greenfair, Obristan

It seemed somehow impossible, yet— right there— Greenfair gleamed in the sunlight. Shilong had taken Lamorak home in a matter of hours rather than days. The land had sped by beneath him faster than it ever had on a horse, no matter how quickly it had run. After his initial shock, then the first several moments of abject terror, Lamorak had found himself almost enjoying the flight.

And Shilong had remained relatively low, as well. Flying quickly, her head turning from side to side at the end of her sinuous neck as she searched the sky for other dragonkin.

Once, in the distance, they had seen one other. Luckily, it had appeared against the mountains of the north, otherwise even Shilong might have missed it. It was brilliantly white, so it contrasted against the dark stone. Higher in the sky, in front of a cloud... it would have been nearly impossible to see.

Shilong had gone up, then, in a steep climb which had set Lamorak's heart pounding all over again. Magic must have held him to the dragonkin's back, because there was no possible way he could have hung on.

She stayed there, above the clouds, for several minutes, before coming back down. She looked back at him and said, "I would have stayed longer. It's probably safer, but I'm not sure you humans are built for that."

Her voice reached him clearly even over the noise of the wind rushing across his ears. He suspected she would have been able to hear him, as well, but, as it stood, he couldn't answer. His jaws were clamped tightly shut as shivers racked his body. The air at the height they'd just descended from was brutally cold.

"Oh." Shilong sounded a bit surprised. "I guess I was right. Sorry about that."

They had descended by then to where the air was much warmer, so Lamorak was able to croak out a few words. "It's... f..f...fine. I'm...oo...oo...okay."

Shilong smiled, maybe taking him at face value or maybe not, then turned her attention to scanning the sky again.

But that was the only dragonkin they had seen during the entire journey. Finally, she glided to a landing on a hilltop not far from Greenfair. Lamorak found that he was able to climb down on his own, and he resisted the urge to kiss the earth. Enjoyable at times or not, he was glad to be back on the ground where he belonged.

Only then did he walk to the edge of the hill and look over his home city. He'd seen it from other angles before, in his time with the Honor Guard, when he'd been sent out to patrol. But he didn't think he'd ever seen if from that particular vantage point. No roads ran up to this hill, so most likely no one came to it.

This must be how *they* see the whole world, he thought, staring down at his city.

Greenfair was a marvel. The streets were laid out in an orderly fashion, but no mere grid. No, anyone could do that. *His* city had streets that curved, but always in ways that made sense. Follow one of them and find yourself in a neighborhood of shopkeepers and artisans. Their homes were built over the top of their shops. Nearby was a school where all children— no matter their social status— got an equal education. Take one of the roads that spoked out from that neighborhood and visit another, maybe where the bureaucrats retreated to after their days in the official government buildings— which were located in one well-kept commune, just over there— had come to an end.

And so on. From where he stood, Lamorak could almost trace the lines of society, could tell where each person belonged. Manse may have been bigger. Festival was more exciting. But there was nowhere on earth like Greenfair.

"It's a beautiful city," Shilong said, as if she could read his mind. "A real testament to what you humans can accomplish if you want to."

"And we did it ourselves," Lamorak said with some pride.

"Of course, you did," she replied. "How else would it be done?"

Lamorak glanced at her, but she didn't seem to be mocking him. Instead, she seemed more curious than anything else.

"No help from dragonkin," he said. "We don't have them. Or, actually, I guess we do have a dragon, but no one knows about her. So she had nothing to do with it."

"Oh, that. No, I suppose Tophonoss didn't have anything to do with it, but Greenfair *is* a marvel. One that truly shows the glory of the Raaleth and the other races."

Now, Lamorak frowned and turned fully to her. "What are you talking about?"

Shilong drew back. "The Raaleth. One of what you call the Evening Folk. This was their city, once. Long ago, of course. When your kind came it was mostly ruins, but the footprint was still there. All your ancestors needed to do was rebuild the buildings, really. They don't look the same, but the... flow of the place, I guess you could say. That was all Raaleth and the others."

Lamorak just stared at her. The way she said it— so easily. Casually, as if she was sharing common knowledge.

Suddenly, Lamorak felt very uneducated. Rainaldus probably knew about it already. Maybe everyone but him did. Maybe he was the only way puffing out his chest at the ingenuity of humans, when it wasn't even theirs to begin with.

"I should... I should get down there," he finally said.

"You should," Shilong agreed. The dragonkin faced him. "I wish you luck, Lamorak. With whatever it is you came to do."

The way she said it made Lamorak think that she knew what he was there for. Or at least suspected there was more to his visit than he'd told her.

"Why?" he asked.

Shilong adopted a look of pure innocence. "Why, what?"

"Why are you helping me? From what we've seen... the dragonkin are killing humans for any reason. But you... you helped me now, and you helped all of us at the border. Why?"

"Haiteng is a great lord," the dragonkin said by way of answer, which wasn't an answer to his questions at all.

"Okay, sure. I'll agree to that, I guess..." he waited for her to continue.

"Gillbriss is not." Shilong's face darkened. "There is more going on than we know. Haiteng has never kept secrets from us before, but then... at first it was simply that we were to allow other dragonkin into our home. But we could go where we wished, as well. Then, we actually had assignments. Places we needed to be, things we needed to do, and most of those were horrible. This was not Haiteng. He would never. This was more how things have been done in Reclium."

"And you don't want to do those things." She had said as much back in the clearing where he'd come around after his encounter with the road bandits.

"More than that," Shilong growled. "I will *not* do those things."

Lamorak reached out and put a hand on her shoulder, feeling the tough, yet strangely soft, blue scales beneath his palm.

"Thank you, Shilong. I wish there were more that felt the way you do."

"Goodbye, Lamorak. Say hello to Prince Calidor when you see him again."

She lifted off the ground with no apparent effort, circled the hill once, then flew off, heading back in the same direction they'd come. Lamorak watched her until she was out of sight, then turned back to Greenfair.

"Raaleth planning, huh?" He grunted softly. "Figures."

At first, Greenfair seemed the same as it always had. The streets were clean, and people went about their daily business with the same efficiency or lack thereof that they always had. Some nodded a friendly greeting as he passed, while others acted as if they didn't even see anyone else around them. In short, they acted the same as humans all over the world.

It took him a few minutes to wonder why no one was paying him any attention. No one seemed to take any real notice of him. One or two might have grimaced at his size or maybe the condition of his well-worn clothing, but that was all. Then, he remembered he wasn't wearing his armor. There was nothing that marked him as Honor Guard.

As a matter of fact...

He stopped and turned slowly, taking in the scene from every direction. People, yes. Of all sorts, doing all manner of jobs.

But nowhere did he see anyone in armor or even armed with a sword, for that matter. In fact, now that he'd noticed, there wasn't even a knife in view.

The citizens of Greenfair had apparently been disarmed.

That wasn't to say that they had always walked around armed to the teeth and ready for a brawl. But Greenfair— Obristan in general, really— had always had a bit of a martial bent to it. In addition to being the home of the Honor Guard, there was the Palace Guard. They didn't travel with the prince or other members of the royal court. Their job was to protect the building and grounds themselves. So that no matter what might occur, those royals would always have a place to return.

Local matters were handled by a city watch, much the same as the world over, Lamorak would have imagined. They kept the peace, settled disputes, and intervened when needed.

Thus, it was simply good fashion to be seen with a sword. There were the plain, heavy-duty blades like the one he carried, but those tended to be worn by men like him. Those for whom the sword was a tool of the trade. Then, there were more decorative "weapons." Those tended to have ornate hilts, jewel-encrusted blades, and scabbards made of exotic materials. They looked pretty but were next to useless in an actual fight. Which was fine, since so were most of those who strapped them to their waists.

It had become so fashionable in the last several years that no one of any means would have been caught dead without at least a shiny dagger at their belt.

Yet now, he was the only one in the street with a weapon of any sort.

Which made him distinctly uncomfortable.

He was just turning back to continue on his way to the Honor Guard compound and his suite of rooms, when three men approached him. Briefly, they reminded him of the men on the road, and his shoulder, healed or not, gave a slight twinge. But these weren't those men. These appeared to be much more foolish.

"What's your name, friend?" the one in the middle said when they'd neared. They stopped several feet away, though. Close enough to talk, but out of immediate sword's reach, which meant maybe they weren't as foolish as Lamorak had first thought.

All three wore dark pants with dark gray shirts tucked into them, as if it was some sort of uniform. Their shoes, however, must not have been included in the budget, since only one wore halfway decent boots. One of the others had on sandals that were held together with twine, while the third was actually barefoot.

"My name is my own," Lamorak returned. "Unless I have reason to give it to someone."

"You have reason," the barefoot one snarled. "Reason is we're asking."

But the middle one held up a hand. "Settle down, Declan. This man has done nothing wrong."

"Nothing wrong?" the one named Declan protested. "He's got a sword, Sebastian!"

"I don't see a sword," Sebastian said. "What I see is a man who just wandered into our city and might not be aware of certain rules. Do you see a sword, Levi?"

The third man, the one with the sandals, peered at Lamorak, then glanced at Sebastian with a confused expression.

"Well, I mean, there's one right there, isn't there? That thing on his belt? Isn't that a sword?"

"Oh, for…" Sebastian put his hand to the bridge of his nose and pinched, closing his eyes and sighing. "Of course it's a sword. What's wrong with the two of you?"

"Us?" Declan squeaked. "Us? We're the ones doing as we should! You're the one who—"

"Doesn't want trouble," Sebastian cut him off. "Don't we have enough already? Look. You two go on your way. You're right. This man has a sword, so I'll sort it out with him. You won't give me any trouble now, will you?" he said to Lamorak.

Lamorak shook his head, equal parts amused and disturbed by the scene playing out in front of him. "Nope. No trouble from me," he said aloud. "As long as you don't try to take my sword," he finished silently.

"Good. You two hear that? I think I heard of someone two streets over still selling beer. Why don't you head over there and see if you can sniff it out, huh?" Sebastian waved his hand in a generally easterly direction.

"Beer? But that's been outlawed for a week now," Levi said.

"Yeah…" But Declan was coming to the conclusion Sebastian had obviously wanted him to. "Yeah, it is. So we should go find it, Levi. If it *is* there…" he grinned at the other man… "we can confiscate it."

Levi smiled back, but Lamorak didn't think he'd caught Declan's meaning at all. With a cheery "okay," he nodded to Lamorak and Sebastian and headed off behind Declan.

Sebastian watched them until they were nearly out of sight, then turned to Lamorak. "Honor Guard?"

"If I say yes?" Lamorak replied.

"Then I'd say, welcome home." Sebastian grimaced. "It just might not be the home you remember."

"What's going on here?" Lamorak asked him. "Since when it is against the law to wear a sword in Greenfair?"

Sebastian eyed him in a manner that told Lamorak he had been dead wrong after all. This was not a foolish man. This was one who was doing what he needed to survive and possibly feed his family. But, at the same time, he was finding ways to keep his humanity.

"I think you might very well know the reason why. Come on, walk with me, and stay on my right. That will help hide the fact that you're armed."

"All right." Lamorak fell into step next to him. He noticed right away that Sebastian began walking in the direction of the Honor Guard compound.

"The dragonkin," he said quietly, after they'd gone a few steps. "They first showed up several days ago and said they were now in charge. There were questions, of course, about what had happened to Prince Calidor. Those that asked didn't last very long. Soon enough, no one dared. After that..." Sebastian shrugged. "Orders. No alcohol. No swords. No leaving the city without permission."

"And people stood for it?"

"What do you think? You see your best friend get torn limb from limb, or your father roasted alive, or your cousin boiled in his own skin... it doesn't take much more than that."

"No, of course not." Lamorak had known that, obviously, it was just that he'd been hoping against hope that Greenfair had remained free. But seeing the rest of Obristan, destroyed towns and others under dragonkin control, he should have known better.

"Where were you?" Sebastian asked him.

"Festival," Lamorak replied.

Sebastian grimaced and stayed silent for a few seconds. "Some word has gotten back," he finally said. "A little. It sounds like it was bad."

"It was. Most of us didn't get out. Only three of us who went with the prince." He knew what Sebastian wanted to know but was reluctant to tell him. He'd just met the man and wasn't sure how far he could really be trusted.

Then again, he could have made real trouble for Lamorak apparently. He hadn't said yet, but Sebastian and the other two must have been some sort of patrol, looking for rule breakers. The fact that he hadn't even tried to talk Lamorak into giving up his sword, and was actively helping to hide it, spoke volumes.

"He's alive," he said quietly. "Safe, as far as I know. He stayed back, days from here, to try to help those he could. He sent me back here to—"

"To?" Lamorak almost winced at the hope he heard in Sebastian's voice.

"To see what the situation is like. And..." He looked around and lowered his voice even further. "To see what was left of those who could fight."

To his credit, once again, Sebastian didn't react.

"I don't know much, but Honor Guard is still housed in their compound. We haven't seen them much. The Palace Guard... we believe most of them were killed when the dragonkin arrived. Some of them are staying in the palace. There's been crashing and clouds of dust, so we assumed some of them have knocked down walls to try to fit inside."

"You make it sound like there are several," Lamorak said. "Most towns we've observed have only had a few dragonkin occupying them."

"Huh," Sebastian snorted. "A few? There's more than a few. All colors, too. Blue, red, and white."

Lamorak felt his head spin. Okay, so there were more dragonkin than they would have thought. He'd have to find a way to deal with that. At least Declan hadn't said there were black dragonkin in town. From what he'd seen, those had been the cruelest.

"Here we are," Sebastian said. "I'll leave you to it, since I can't go in there. Besides, I need to find out what those two idiots are up to, now." He stuck out his hand to clasp Lamorak's. "There's those of us who will join in. I was city watch, when it still existed. Not much compared to Honor Guard, I know, but... well, I know the streets and the people in them. I'll try to pass by every so often."

Lamorak shook his hand warmly. "I hope there are more like you Sebastian. I'll get word to you. In the meantime, don't say anything about me being here, and most especially not about Prince Calidor."

Sebastian's look of horror at the mere suggestion he would do such a thing was enough for Lamorak. He wasn't going to say a word.

With a nod, he turned and strode to the barred gate in the compound wall, hoping that someone on the other side would be smart enough to let him in quickly, without too much fuss.

Chapter 36- Droy Thus Jungle

For the first time since meeting him, Akofi thought Rainaldus might have gotten in over his head.

The guardsman had plunged into the thick jungle to chase after their mysterious visitor, but within moments seemed to be completely lost. Not that they had known where they were before, of course, but he didn't appear to have any idea where the strange man might have gone.

"They're good," he heard Rainaldus mutter.

The young man stopped walking, then simply stood with his hands on his hips, his eyes roaming over the ground and any nearby plants and trees. Finally, he took a deep breath.

"I can't find any sign of their passage. Not a single one. We know he went this way, right? Yet... nothing. No tracks, no bent or broken stems, no leaves torn from plants...nothing."

Then, he looked up at Akofi and Bekasi with a smile. "Just what I would expect from one of the Evening Folk."

"That's great," Akofi replied. "But they seem to have given us the slip. So, let's head back to where we were, okay? We can work out how to get to Lankari from there."

To his surprise, it was Bekasi who protested. "Are you out of you mind? We just saw one of the Evening Folk! They're all supposed to be dead, yet here they are... or were, anyway. Where's your curiosity?"

"In direct conflict with my sense of survival," he countered. "Just because Rainaldus made a fair point about them probably not wanting to kill us, doesn't mean they'll be thrilled with us hunting them down."

"We're not 'hunting' anyone," she sneered. "That's ridiculous. We're just trying to—"

"Hello!!!"

Akofi and Bekasi both jumped. While they'd been arguing, neither of them had kept on eye on Rainaldus, who now had his hands cupped around his mouth to make his shout louder.

"Hellooooo!!!" he yelled again. "We want to talk to you!!!"

"Are you out of your mind!" Akofi's yell was almost as loud. He stalked to Rainaldus and grabbed his hands, pulling them away from his face. It didn't escape him that he was only able to do so because Rainaldus let him. The strength in his arms was so great that when Akofi first tugged, it was as if he was pulling on a stone statue.

"What's wrong?" Rainaldus asked. "They must want us to follow, or we wouldn't have seen that one. Probably never had heard any of them, either." He lifted his hands and shouted again.

Akofi turned in exasperation to Bekasi, but she only shrugged. Neither of them, unless they wanted to use magic against him, were going to stop Rainaldus from shouting.

After a minute, though, he stopped on his own. He lowered his hands, then adopted a posture of listening. Akofi strained his own ears as well, but all he could hear were the normal sounds of the jungle. The calling of birds starting up again, after they had fallen silent at the disturbance, the rustling of leaves in the breeze or from small animals, and, in the distance, the growl of something much bigger.

"Great," Akofi said. "Did you hear that? Whatever it was, it's probably coming this way."

"If anything," Bekasi told him, "it will move away from us. Most predators don't want anything to do with humans."

Akofi didn't miss the "most."

He turned back to Rainaldus, who by now had sort of sagged in disappointment. The eager smile— the first real one Akofi had seen on his face— had faded. His normal stern, upright posture wasn't quite as rigid.

"I guess they—" he said.

Which was when Bekasi gave a short scream.

Akofi and Rainaldus both whirled to her, then spun to where she was staring.

Their visitor was back. He'd come into view behind them somehow. Whether they'd passed him or he'd circled around, they had no idea. But there he was, taller and broader than Rainaldus, watching them calmly, with his hand well away from his axe.

As if by magic they didn't know— so silently did they appear— four more stepped into view on all sides of them.

"It's them," Rainaldus whispered.

"We're surrounded," Akofi groaned. "I knew it."

But the newcomers made no threatening moves. They simply stood still and gazed at the two mages and Rainaldus. Akofi noticed that all of their eyes were the same color. The pupils so dark as to be almost black, while surrounding them— the "whites" of their eyes— was a light gray hue.

"I am Rainaldus," the guardsman said to the one who had first appeared. "From Obristan."

One of the warriors— for surely that's what they were— said something in a harsh, guttural language. Whatever it was, it made two of the others laugh, while the one Rainaldus had spoken to gave a quick, fleeting grin.

"Welcome, Rainaldus of Obristan," he said, in perfect common language. The same language the dragons had taught all humans to speak, in order to make communication between the realms easier.

"You speak our language?" Rainaldus seemed stunned.

"Some of us," the warrior said. "We've learned from listening to those in the villages here speak. Not all of our people choose to, however."

Akofi wasn't sure that he liked the idea of them being close enough to the tower villages to pick up the language. How that was possible, he couldn't even begin to guess.

Then again, the thought came to him, if these Evening Folk could hide from the dragons, who they'd gone into battle against, then he supposed it wouldn't be so hard for them to hide from mere humans.

"What are you doing here?" Bekasi asked.

"We could ask you the same," the warrior replied calmly. "Your kind doesn't often come into the jungle. Not for long, anyway. Those that do seem to take some sort of bizarre amusement from it."

Akofi thought of Kio and his love for camping in the jungle, fending off the dangers with his magic. To prepare him should he ever need it, he'd always said, although what that circumstance might be was never mentioned.

"We're lost," Rainaldus said. "We had to leave the road, so we thought we'd be safer cutting through the jungle. We're trying to get to their home," he gestured toward Akofi and Bekasi, "Lankari. But now..." He spread his hands. "We don't know where we are."

"Far from Lankari," the newcomer snorted. "But why was the road unsafe for you?"

"Dragonkin," the guardsman answered. As usual, his way was to be honest and direct. Akofi wasn't sure it was the best time for that, but then again, these people might have a way of knowing if they were being lied to.

"There are always dragonkin," the warrior answered. "Why is this different?"

"Do you really not know?" Akofi's surprise led him to speak up and thus draw attention to himself. "The dragonkin have been attacked by humans and are retaliating. They've killed many, wiped out whole towns. Just a couple of days ago, we were attacked."

The gray-skinned warrior cocked his head. "Yet here you are. I would think such an attack would be the end of you."

"And normally, you'd be right," Akofi answered. "Only, this one," he pointed at Rainaldus, "and one who's no longer with us killed it."

There was muttering at this, which made Akofi aware that more of them spoke his tongue than were letting on. The leader considered, then turned back to Rainaldus.

"Is this true, Rainaldus of Obristan?"

"It is," he replied. "Although, it was more Akamah, who gave his life to accomplish it."

"Still..." The warrior regarded him, then nodded once. He stepped forward and put out one arm to clasp Rainaldus's forearm. "My name is Orgoth, of the Yegrub clan. Well met."

"Well met," Rainaldus answered, looking for all the world like a child meeting his hero for the first time.

"Are you the Evening Folk?" Bekasi asked, in her normal, blunt manner.

"Evening Folk?" Orgoth looked confused. "I'm not sure what that term means. If you are asking if we are of one of the Elder Races, then yes, we are that. We belong to one of the three that battled the dragons when they rose but, ultimately, were defeated."

"The Xarlug," Rainaldus said quietly.

"Again, with information you've known and have been holding back on?" Bekasi spat.

"No." Rainaldus shook his head but kept his eyes on Orgoth. "No. I haven't held back. I just remembered... stories my mother had told me when I was small, but that was it. She never truly spoke of them. The Xarlug, who never gave up fighting and were completely wiped out. Exterminated."

Orgoth's answering smile was grim. "And was it your mother who gave you your Raaleth blood?"

"No, my father," Rainaldus answered. "At least that's what I always thought. My mother was human."

"But well-learned. More so even than these," he indicated Akofi and Bekasi.

"They just know different things," Rainaldus said. "And the last few days have been a shock to them."

"Perhaps with more to come," Orgoth said. "Come. We'll guide you."

"To Lankari?" Akofi asked.

"No," the Xarlug answered. "To our home. From there, we will see. If you are allowed to go on, we will guide you to your town."

Akofi wanted to argue, but the memory of how easily they had negated his magic, plus the obvious, excited agreement of Rainaldus, told him that he didn't have much choice.

Still, he had never liked feeling helpless. While they walked, he'd think and plan. There had to be some way for his magic to work while around them. Some way that he could protect both himself and his friends if it came down to it.

Evening Folk or not, he was going home and no one was going to prevent that.

They had been walking for several minutes when Akofi realized that one of the Xarlug had approached and now walked next to him. He hadn't noticed earlier because their guides had taken them off any semblance of a trail, even that of a large animal pushing through.

Now, they walked through dense undergrowth, with two Xarlug in the lead, pushing the plants aside, then letting them fold back naturally when the others had passed. They took turns doing this, always two in the lead, then back to the rear of their little chain of people, taking their turn again when they reached the front.

For his part, Akofi had kept his eyes either on the ground, trying to avoid tripping over roots or fallen branches, or to the trees, scanning them for any sign of danger.

When he did finally notice the Xarlug next to him, he jumped, then tried to conceal his startled motion, which made the one walking beside him grin.

"Relax," she said, in a strangely musical voice.

Akofi's reaction wasn't merely to the fact that she'd approached him so quietly, but also because she was dressed as Orgoth was. A simple loincloth, nothing more, and this one was most decidedly female.

Yet, all those who had appeared earlier had been male, he was quite sure of that. So that meant there were others who hadn't revealed themselves, which he supposed made sense.

"I'm Shagar," she said. "And you're one of the human mages. I can feel the power in you."

Despite his discomfort, Akofi found himself pleased at her words. "Thank you."

"It was a little difficult to nullify your magic," she said cheerfully. "At least, for a human."

"Oh, that was you?" On the one hand, Akofi was a little offended by her amendment of what she'd said. On the other... "How?" he asked. "How did you do that?"

She laughed. "How does the sun rise? The rain fall? How does a mother uggana know when its whelp is in trouble?"

Akofi didn't actually know any of those things, especially the last, since he had no idea what an "uggana" might be.

"Exactly so," Shagar said, obviously pleased with herself. "Some things just are."

"Wait." This from Bekasi who walked slightly ahead of them. She turned to look at Shagar, ignoring her lack of clothing better than Akofi had. "Are you saying that it's just something you can do? Not some form of magic you learn?"

"What is magic?" Shagar returned. "For us, the Xarlug, it's merely using what is already there. The forces around us every day."

"Can all of your people do that?" Akofi asked.

Frankly, he found that thought terrifying. A whole hidden race, who had observed them for years, centuries even, but stayed unknown? And they could nullify humans' magic with a thought? Very, very disturbing.

But Shagar laughed again. "No. Of course not. Only some of us are blessed to be able to see the forces, to feel where they are, and be able to reach out and tweak them..." She held out a hand, snapped her fingers together, and then twisted them. A leaf spun violently, then tore from its branch to settle slowly to the forest floor.

"Just so!" she beamed.

While that was something of a relief, it still meant that one of the Xarlug had shut down both he and Bekasi. Unless there were more of them.

He looked around, trying to spot some sort of difference, besides gender, between Shagar and the others, but he was unable to. She wore no special jewelry, no tattoos adorned her skin, nothing.

"I am the only one," she said. "The only what your kind might call a witch. At least here. In Eral Krurmar, there are others."

"Eral Krurmar..." Akofi said it slowly, trying to work out the unfamiliar syllables. "That's..."

"Our home," she said. "At least for now. It's where we went to hide from the dragons, when the others gave up fighting. Before that though, we fought on, for many a year, but they were too powerful for us to face alone. So we finally fled, to a place that was long prepared. In your tongue, Eral Krurmar would mean 'Last Rest.'"

"Last Rest," Bekasi said. "There's something beautiful in that."

Shagar shrugged. "Perhaps. But to my people, it's a lament. It means that we will never again see the rest of the world, or the ocean that we once loved."

There was so much that Akofi was finding out, so much that he'd never known. He'd noticed before how Bekasi seemed to be much more interested in the world around her than Akofi had been. Yet now, with this, he found that he wanted to learn more. He wanted to know everything.

"How did—?" he started but was interrupted by her upraised hand.

"We're almost there," Shagar said. "Now is the time for quiet. Try to walk less like lumbering giants."

Which was funny coming from a woman who towered over Akofi by almost a full head. Then he noticed that the only sounds of their passage were from him and Bekasi. Even Rainaldus was lighter on his feet and seemed to have a better knack of avoiding twigs which snapped underfoot than they did.

Now the Xarlug slowed down and spread out, some fading into the jungle as if they had vanished. Hands went to weapons hung at waists, as Shagar closed her eyes for a moment— while still striding silently along— and then opened them again but did not speak.

Finally, Orgoth put his hand up, signaling a halt. Rainaldus had been walking next to the warrior chief, if that's what he was, but he now stopped as well, hand to the hilt of his sword.

Akofi saw no reason for their halt. There was nothing that he could see that distinguished this section of jungle from any other. Trees, vines, plants, dirt, fungi, and insects. The same thing as in every other foot of the place.

The Xarlug fell still and motionless. After several seconds, Orgoth looked to Shagar. She shrugged and said, "None around that I can tell."

It was said casually, but Akofi got the impression that Orgoth and the other Xarlug had been waiting for her approval before going on.

And she had been searching, somehow, for some unseen threat that only she could feel.

Her word, though, was enough. Hands fell away from weapons and the party suddenly took on a more relaxed air. Instead of going two by two, now one male walked forward, past a tree, and actually did vanish.

Akofi gaped. Whatever that was, it was magic that he'd never seen or felt. Magic that shouldn't even be possible. Vanishing wasn't something he'd ever mastered or known of anyone who had. The same with traveling through some sort of mystic portal, although every student coming up through a tower had dreams of making either of those things happen.

"Come on," Shagar said lightly. "It's safe now."

She strode forward without waiting for them. Akofi glanced at Bekasi, who was staring back at him.

"If we go," she said, "we might not be able to come back."

"If we don't," he answered, "we'll never know."

Which didn't sound at all like him, but... he needed to see more of these Xarlug, these Evening Folk who still lived. Legends come to life, even if it was a legend he'd never heard of.

One look at Rainaldus was enough to tell him which way the guardsman was going. He was practically straining to follow the Xarlug as one after the other they walked past the same tree and vanished.

"All right, then," Bekasi said. "But together."

She reached out for his hand. Akofi took hers and they walked toward the tree.

As they passed it, Akofi felt a cool breeze on the right side of his cheek. A huge rock protruded from the jungle floor, almost completely camouflaged by moss and plants growing on and around it. An opening yawned beneath it, with plenty of room for Akofi and Bekasi to pass through without ducking.

Not magic, then. Just a cunningly concealed entrance to...

What?

Stairs, leading down into the earth.

To Eral Krurmar, the Last Rest.

Chapter 37- Northern Ascana

"Another step and we're in uncharted territory," Visgar said.

It was just he and Gunnvid, standing on the border between Usturg and northern Ascana. He knew it was the border because there was a thin covering of snow on the ground under their boots. Less than a stride away, however, there was grass. Slightly withered and brown, maybe, but grass, without a speck of snow to be seen.

Turning his head from one way to the other, there was a distinct line that ran as far as he could see. Snow on the Usturg side, grass in Ascana.

Gunnvid grunted but didn't say anything else.

"I've never heard of the border being like this," Visgar continued. "To my understanding, it was always more of a gradual change. You know, getting warmer as one moved south, until you were in Ascana without even realizing it."

"Fimbruss has grown more powerful," Gunnvid rasped.

Visgar nodded at that, but he had his doubts that was really the reason. If it was, wouldn't that mean that Haiteng had grown weaker? While it was possible, it wasn't something he wanted to bet his life on.

And crossing the border with an army at his back, as well as all the attendant hangers-on that came with it, might be doing exactly that.

Gunnvid believed— truly believed— that it was his sacred duty, his calling, to spread the word of Fimbruss's glory to everyone. Not just everyone in Usturg, which they had barely started, but to the entire world. As far as he was concerned, they'd work their way down through Ascana, gaining converts the whole way, then into Droy Thus, then back up into the soft underbelly of Obristan. By then, with the world conquered and converted behind them, they'd have the strength to take Reclium.

Visgar had stood beside the map table while his old friend had outlined his plan, his rough voice speaking calmly and quietly. But his zeal had broken through, anyway. The fervor in Gunnvid's demeanor had first startled, then alarmed, Visgar. It was one thing to lead a rag-tag group of men around Usturg. That was sort of the way of life. One that Fimbruss encouraged.

It was quite another to believe you had a holy writ to bring the world into order.

And now… here they were.

"What about Usturg?" he asked.

Gunnvid didn't turn from his contemplation of what was in front of him. "What about it?"

"Well, we haven't finished here, have we? Narfasker was our only real conquest… if that's what we're calling it."

"Conversion," Gunnvid interrupted.

"Conversion, then." Although Visgar believed it more likely that most of those "converted" would be turning back to whatever they had believed as soon as the Children had moved on. "Still, other than a couple of minor towns…that's not a lot."

Now Gunnvid did look at him. "Funny time to bring this up."

Visgar nodded. "I've been thinking it, though. Now…" He pointed at the line between the realms. "Once we cross that, it's a whole new world. One realm has never attacked another. Not once."

"Fimbruss will protect us."

"I'm not doubting that." Even though he was. "I'm just wondering if we should—"

"Once we have Ascana seeing the glory, the rest of Usturg will fall in line. How could they not? It's the glory of their own leader, their own dragon, that they'll see celebrated."

That was a long speech for Gunnvid. By the time he finished it, his voice was little more than a hoarse whisper. He never would have made it in front of anyone but Visgar.

That— that little bit of trust, of not being too cautious to show vulnerability to Visgar— was what kept him by Gunnvid's side. Their long history together was one thing, but the relationship which had developed, that was what really counted.

"All right, then." Visgar smiled and clapped his hand on Gunnvid's wide shoulder. "Let's get them moving. We have converts to... er... convert."

Gunnvid hardly ever smiled. He didn't now, either, but his perpetual scowl grew a little less deep. "Move them out, then," he rasped.

The two men turned from the border and back to their horses. A short distance beyond them, stood rank upon rank of the Children of Fimbruss.

Northern Ascana awaited. Beyond that... the world.

"What's it called?"

No one had an answer for Visgar.

The Children had marched for several hours after crossing the border, without coming upon anything of note. A few farms scattered here and there. An inn by the road. All of those had been thoroughly searched. Although, exactly what they had been looking for, Visgar wasn't really sure. He'd ridden on, his horse next to Gunnvid's, doing his best to ignore the screams.

Converting folk, he thought to himself, would work a lot better if they were left alive. But since Gunnvid allowed it, who was he to say differently?

At one point, he'd considered excusing himself. To fall to the side and let the column pass him, until it was only those in the rear that remained. He'd fall in among them until he'd found Estrid. She'd be tired from the marching, but safe. Enough knew that she belonged to him so that he didn't have to worry about her being harassed.

But he let that thought go. For one, Gunnvid would be displeased, doubly so if he thought it was so that Visgar could visit a woman. And also, he wanted to be front and center when they finally came upon a town or city.

Now, they finally had.

It wasn't a large city, at least not by what he'd heard of being Ascani standards. For Usturg, it would be quite large, but the northern realm didn't have nearly the population of its southern neighbor. Which was a fact that maybe Gunnvid should have taken into consideration, but he didn't seem to care. He was probably right not to worry about it. Those in Usturg loved to fight and to raid other towns. It was encouraged by Fimbruss, or so he'd always heard.

Almost, Visgar mused, as if they had been being trained all these years.

Those in Ascana? Merchants, farmers, and sailors. He'd heard of Ascani soldiers as well but couldn't imagine they counted for much. Hardly a match for what was drawing up outside their town now.

"Make camp," Gunnvid rasped.

Visgar nodded, reigned his horse around to face the front ranks and bellowed the order. Immediately, men began to fall out, each moving to their assigned tasks. The baggage train, carrying tents, blankets, and most importantly food, would be catching up within an hour. Before that, there were sites to prepare.

As he watched, Visgar felt a sense of pride, which was something he never would have believed. The Children were acting more like a real army every day. Orders relayed down the line, no one carping or complaining. Everyone moving to do what was necessary.

He turned back to Gunnvid, ready to share his feelings, but his old friend wasn't paying any attention to the army behind them. He was sitting as still as a statue on his horse, his eyes fixed on the town.

More likely, Visgar realized, it wasn't really the town that had his attention. What did flew high in the sky above.

Two of them. Neither were the white of Fimbruss's, both dragonkin appeared dark, perhaps black, against the bright blue sky. Visgar looked more closely.

One was larger, with an elongated body and flying without the use of wings. Blue, then, one of Haiteng's and native to Ascana.

There was a lump on the end of the other, smaller one's tail. That one did have wings, and Visgar knew that could he see it clearly, it would still remain black. One of Gillbriss's, said to be the cruelest of them all, even before the world had turned as it had.

The two dragonkin wheeled around one another, as if in conversation. Then, they broke off the pattern and both headed directly toward the Children.

Visgar's horse shied nervously as the dragonkin approached. He couldn't blame it. The mere sight of them, coming closer with every second, was turning his own blood to ice. Gunnvid, however, showed no sign of fear, and his horse must have sensed it, because it didn't so much as snort.

"Easy," Gunnvid said quietly.

He was talking to him, Visgar thought. Gunnvid's horse hadn't moved a muscle.

With effort, he got his mount— and his own fear— under control.

Just in time for the two dragonkin to alight in front of them.

Up close, they were awe inspiring. Not as much as when Fimbruss flew overhead a few days ago, but enough. Visgar had only ever seen dragonkin at a distance. This close was a whole different story.

The blue was magnificent. Longer than if both he and Gunnvid had stood their horses nose-to-tail and a blue so vibrant it almost felt as if it had to be fake.

The black was... terrifying. Just the way it looked at them, the twitching of its tail. Visgar had the sincere impression that this one would kill them just as soon as look at them.

"Welcome," the blue began, the voice betraying her as female. "What are you doing in Ascana?"

"Spreading the word of Fimbruss," Gunnvid said without hesitation.

"We don't need it," the black snarled, his voice deeper than the blue's. "Go back north, while you can."

"No."

Visgar almost choked. No? That was all Gunnvid was going to say? He looked closer at his old friend.

Gunnvid gazed at the two dragonkin as if they were nothing more than a minor annoyance. Something unimportant that needed to be dealt with before he could get on with his real work.

The black dragonkin laughed, but it was devoid of any joy. It was a cruel, merciless laugh. That of one who was looking forward to doing something very, very unpleasant.

"No?" he snarled. "Strange word to have it be your last."

Visgar looked to the blue, but there was no help there. She was grinning as she watched her black brethren, waiting for him to act.

Gunnvid put one hand to his mouth and let loose a stunningly loud whistle that cut through the air like a knife. From behind them, a roar went up. Visgar's head snapped around, to see the Children— hundreds of them— rushing forward. Gunnvid's whistle had been some sort of prearranged signal, and those that answered it must have started preparing as soon as the dragonkin were in sight.

Visgar wasn't quite sure what it meant that he hadn't been privy to any of it.

"We're bringing Fimbruss's glory to this town," Gunnvid said calmly. "We can do it with you or over you. It's your choice."

The dragonkin watched the approaching horde of men. It bristled with enough weapons to make anyone want to run.

Any human, maybe. The dragonkin didn't seem worried at all. Instead, they simply took to the air, out of reach of swords and axes.

Where they were met with a hail of arrows before they could even climb out of range. Visgar could only look on in stunned surprise. Where had the archers come from? And— more unbelievably— arrows apparently hurt dragonkin! He wouldn't have thought it possible, but the sharp heads and sturdy shafts penetrated the scales. They weren't big enough to do any major damage, but it was enough to keep the dragonkin away.

The blue tried to come lower, her jaws open to breathe steam, but ended up with several more arrows sticking out of her. She screamed in rage and pulled up, leaving the Children unscathed.

The black, however, spit acid. He didn't need to descend to do that, and several men were left screaming as the flesh melted off their bones. But it could only do so much, and there were hundreds upon hundreds of Children left.

Then, to add to the black dragonkin's misery, it was attacked from above. A blazing streak of white fell on it from far overhead. Wings folded back, the white dragonkin of Fimbruss came down hard on him, its claws raking at the black's back and shredding his wings. They tumbled out of the sky together, until the white was able to pull away and soar free. The black, his wings now useless, slammed into the ground.

Visgar couldn't see where it had landed, but the mass of warriors who ran that way signaled that it was close. Shouts of triumph rang out as weapons rose and fell.

He tilted his head back and scanned the sky. The blue dragonkin was circling with the white, the same way it had been with the black shortly before. She didn't appear at all bothered by the fall of the black. Instead, it appeared that the two were having a conversation. Then, the blue broke off and soared away, leaving the white to rule the sky by itself.

With one last shriek, it landed, in nearly the same spot the other two had.

"Lord Gunnvid," the dragonkin said. "Fimbruss blesses your work here."

Gunnvid inclined his head. "Thank him. And thank you for the timely aid."

"The city is yours," the dragonkin answered. "Do with it what you will but bring them to see the light."

"As always," Gunnvid replied.

Without another word, the white launched itself skyward. Within moments, it was gone from sight.

Visgar had sat throughout the entire ordeal like a raw recruit who was stunned by his first sight of battle. He slowly turned to look at Gunnvid, who had gone back to calmly studying the town.

"What..." Visgar started, but he wasn't quite sure how to continue, what he should ask.

That whistle, and the Children had come running, but when had that become a thing that happened? He'd never heard of it, or seen it being put into practice. The archers? He knew they had some few among the converts, but that many? Who had given the signal to fire? And the white dragonkin... Gunnvid had reacted as if he'd known it was going to appear to help them.

"When did—?" he tried again, but Gunnvid ignored his question and pointed.

There, where the buildings started to group together more tightly, there was a bright flash. It was followed by another, then another, until Visgar realized he was looking at several men on horseback. Their armor was so shiny it reflected the sunlight like a mirror.

The town, or city, or whatever it was, wasn't walled. Visgar didn't believe many in Ascana were, since there was no reason to be. But still, they must have a contingent of Ascani soldiers housed there. The same soldiers who were now assembling to face them.

Gunnvid didn't give any orders. Behind them, the roar of the Children of Fimbruss began to die down. Visgar assumed that meant the black dragonkin was now dead and probably in so many pieces as the soldiers took what they would as trophies.

The Ascani kept coming, until finally they seemed to have reached their full complement.

There were a few dozen of them, give or take. Not much, really. Certainly not enough to stop the Children, especially without a dragonkin to provide support. Visgar had to admire their courage. Surely, they could see what they faced and had drawn the same conclusion he had.

"I'll go," he said. "I'll give them a chance to either surrender or join us."

"No," Gunnvid said. "Kill them."

"What? Why? They have no chance, and they must know it. If we show mercy to them, those in the town will—"

Gunnvid's eyes were icy as he turned them on Visgar. "Kill them, then anyone you meet on the street. Only after the city is completely subdued will we stop."

The city was subdued already, Visgar thought. What was the point?

But he could see it in Gunnvid's eyes. He wouldn't be questioned in this. For some reason, Gunnvid was testing Visgar's loyalty. Maybe that was why he hadn't been told about those signals and the archers. Gunnvid was doubting him.

"As you say," he finally said.

He looked to the city again, then stood in his stirrups and turned back to the mass of men.

"Forward!" he yelled. "No mercy!"

He didn't wait for the others. Instead, he spurred his horse forward, feeling it leap beneath him. The ground sped by, until he was close enough to see the faces of the soldiers arrayed against him.

Bravery was there, certainly. But so was fear and resignation. One or two looked ready to flee, but to Visgar's surprise they didn't. They held their ground.

He was the only one on horseback. The others came at a run, a wave that was going to overwhelm the few defenders and submerge the town in death. For a few seconds, not more than a minute or two, he'd be on his own. Which suited him just fine. Maybe a few dead Ascani soldiers would show Gunnvid that he was still as loyal as he ever was.

If not, there was the town itself, and Visgar would do whatever it was he needed to.

Only after would he finally find Estrid.

Chapter 38- Obristan Forest

"She needs a name, you know."

Calidor nodded at Yarah's words, watching the girl interact with Otto, the old man they'd recruited from the ruined farm.

"She does," he agreed. "Any suggestions?"

"I wish she would talk. Then she could tell us what her real name is. Until then… I don't know. I guess it doesn't really matter what we call her."

"It might," he said. "Names have power."

She snorted. "No, they don't. I know many names and not once has it helped me in casting a spell. That's just an old superstition, tossed about by people who know nothing of magic."

"Not like that," Calidor said with a laugh. "I don't mean magic power. I mean just… power. A name can influence many things. How someone perceives another. How that person sees themselves. Whether they have confidence or humility or feel there are things they need to live up to, which can lead to shame if they fail."

Yarah narrowed her eyes. "Are we talking about her? Or you?"

"Me? Why would we be talking about me?" Calidor broke the twig he'd been playing with and threw it aside.

"I don't know. That was just awfully deep for a casual question about a girl's name," Yarah said.

"My father's name wasn't Calidor, if that what's you're asking. It was Agras. He was a good prince, too. His people loved him, and he loved them. He taught me a lot."

"What happened to him?" she asked.

Calidor shrugged. "An accident. Hunting and they stirred up a bear. Father's Honor Guard had ridden too far out." He stopped and grimaced. "In truth, they were probably told to do so, since Father had company that day. He probably wanted to be alone."

"Not your mother?" Yarah guessed.

"No, not Mother. She was back at the castle in Greenfair, with me. She knew, though. It wasn't a very well-kept secret. Still, she did her duty and pretended it didn't bother her. But... that day, the bear came out of nowhere. Enraged, was the word I heard used when they delivered the news to my mother, although what it was so angry about I couldn't say. It... killed them both in moments, before the Honor Guard could do anything about it. Lord Campbell tried to resign his commission over it, but I was old enough to understand by then, and I refused to allow it."

Yarah remained silent.

"I suppose that's one of the reasons I never took a wife," the prince continued. "I know myself, and the things I enjoy, too well. I refuse to treat anyone who I would make a vow to the way Father treated Mother."

He watched Otto and the girl. The old man was good with her. He was showing her how to cut up some roots he'd found, telling her all the while the names of all the pots, pans, and spoons. Who knew they could be so different and have so many disparate back stories?

"She still needs a name," Yarah said.

Calidor nodded. "She does."

The meal, when it came, was better than anything they'd eaten in the last several days. It was plants only, if one considered roots and mushrooms to be plants. No meat, at least not yet. Otto knew how to hunt, or so he said, and how to make traps, but hadn't had the time yet.

Calidor thought the traps were a good idea but couldn't imagine hunting would work. The old man hadn't stopped talking since they'd brought him back. Calidor thought it was probably feeling needed again that had made the difference, but then again, it had started on the way back. Otto and the girl seemed to connect, and he'd really opened up.

For her part, the girl responded to him, too. She still didn't speak, but Calidor had seen more than one genuine smile since they'd returned from the farm. At one point, the old man had taken her hand to guide her through a rough patch of ground— although Calidor thought it more likely that she was helping him— and had continued to hold on for several minutes after.

It was good to see and gave him hope that maybe his plan would work. If they could find those that remained, those the dragonkin had left alive through oversight or some other reason, maybe they could make...

What? A community of some sort?

Not that. That would just be inviting the dragonkin to come for them.

No, they had to stay hidden and safe. So not a community so much as a... sanctuary.

Maybe.

"I'm glad you've joined us, Otto," he said. "This food is excellent. I can't believe what you've done."

"Oh, it's nothing," the old man said. "When I was younger, I was quite the wanderer. Lived off the land a time or two. It was on one of those journeys that I met Ophelia and brought her home with me..." He smiled sadly. "My wandering kind of died-off after that."

The girl reached up to touch his arm, then returned to eating.

That brief exchange wasn't lost on Calidor. "This young lady needs a name," he said. "Yarah and I were discussing it. We know she doesn't want to talk— or maybe can't. But unless she can tell us what her name is herself, we'll have to come up with something."

The girl didn't look at him, which— if he was being honest— he was starting to miss. Instead, she looked up at Otto.

"She has a name," he said. "It's Oriana."

"Oriana," Yarah smiled. "I like it. Did she tell you that?"

"Nope. I guessed it." Otto grinned. "I needed to introduce her to Potunia and the rest. The first few names I tried she didn't like, but Oriana was okay with her. So Oriana it is."

"I like it," Calidor said. "Oriana. It means 'hope,' you know."

"I did not know that," Otto said. "But it fits her."

"It does," Calidor agreed.

There was power in names, he'd told Yarah. Here, right in front of them, was the proof of that.

The nights stretched long when one was lying on the ground in the woods. Calidor had made that discovery well before now, during the several nights they'd spent in the wild after fleeing the destruction of Manse. Yet, somehow, night after night, the sheer length of that time managed to surprise him.

It had never been that way before. In Greenfair, he usually retired to bed long after dark had fallen. Sometimes on his own if he had been in a more pensive mood and had spent the evening in his library. More often, though, in the company of someone else, along with a half-finished bottle of some sort.

Then, he'd sleep until the sun was well up. He'd rise, wash the excesses of the night before off, then dress and be ready for his day. Whatever that day might hold. The sheer fun of being a prince— a man of privilege. Or perhaps the tedium that came with being the head of the whole realm. Either way, the days flowed by, then the sun would be dipping below the horizon and he'd start the whole thing over again.

Now, he lay on his back and watched the silhouetted branches against the sky. There was enough of a moon that it wasn't pitch dark, so he could see the leaves, shapeless masses for the most part, that undulated in the breeze. And the woods were noisy at night. He had made that discovery as well. They were never silent, whereas before, the most he'd heard if he awoke in the middle of the night, was the breath of whomever was lying next to him.

He could hear that now, too. The quick, shallow breathing from Oriana. The snores from Otto. Closer; the deep, regular breaths of Yarah.

That one... ah, now *that* one made him ponder. She was beautiful. Dark and mysterious, powerful and capable. At one point, he'd thought she and the other mage— Akofi— had been together, but then she'd chosen to stay with him. He still wasn't sure why.

He did not, however, think it was because of any deep carnal attraction.

For the first time in his life, Calidor found that he was fine with that. His own ambitions in that regard were muted, to say the least. There was just too much to do. Too many people to try to save.

Even if he had no idea how to really go about it. For all his searching, the only ones they'd found over these last few days had been Oriana and Otto.

Maybe he'd been wrong. Maybe the dragonkin had been too thorough, and he was too late.

No. He rejected that thought. There *were* more. He *would* find them. He would find a way to get word out so that people could find him. Although how to do that and keep that knowledge from the dragonkin would be quite the trick.

Still… he'd do it.

Tomorrow, though. Tonight, it was dark, so it was time for sleep. All he needed to do was close his eyes.

Instead, he watched the shape of the leaves and thought about how long the nights were.

"We need to do more," Calidor declared over breakfast. Otto had once again proven his worth. He'd made a sort of soup, and it was the best start to a day since Festival.

"More what?" Yarah asked.

"More to find my people. Just wandering aimlessly like we've been doing… it's going to take too long."

"What do you suggest then?" she asked.

Calidor shook his head. "That's the problem. I'm not quite sure."

"Sometimes," a voice came from behind him, "the best thing to do is to stop looking."

He spun around to see three men standing between the trees. Two of them, in front of the third, wore threadbare clothing and carried wooden staffs. Neither of them had a sword or even a knife as far as he could tell. Those staffs, though… in the hands of an expert fighter, they could be deadly.

But even with that, it was the one behind them that concerned him more. Dressed no better than the other two, the man was a giant. Bigger even than Lamorak, he stood a full head-and-shoulders above those in front, who were both about Calidor's own size. He was as broad across as both of them put together, and his face was hidden in the shadow of the trees. Calidor was pretty sure, though, that he was being observed with a much more malevolent glare than the two grinning men in front.

"Welcome," Calidor said, but not in the tone he hoped he'd use when he came across other refugees from the dragonkin.

"Well, thanks," the one on the right said. "This looks like a welcoming sort of place."

As he spoke, his eyes slid across the group gathered there. They lingered for a moment on Yarah, but then— chillingly— stayed focused on Oriana even longer.

"We have food," Calidor tried. "Enough to share a bit. Then, maybe even enough to spare to ease your journey."

"Journey?" This was the second man, who hadn't spoken yet. His voice was high-pitched, with a sinister sneer to it. "I was thinking we just might join your little band. See what else it might be that you could share."

Both of them laughed, but, so far, the giant behind them hadn't said a word or moved a muscle.

There had been a time in his life when such men never would have come anywhere close to Calidor. The Honor Guard would have stopped them well before. But there was no Honor Guard here. It was just him, Yarah, one old man, and a young girl.

Of course, these men also didn't realize who and what Yarah was.

That thought, while it brought him some comfort, also seemed to set off something else within him. He was not going to depend on Yarah for protection. What if something happened to her? What if she chose to go back to Droy Thus?

No. *He* was Prince of Obristan. *He* would protect his people.

But...those long staffs.

Lamorak and Rainaldus had shown him a lot, including how to use those. He didn't have one, of course, because he hadn't thought of it. And his sword was probably buried under rubble in Manse.

But they had done more than just that. They'd shown him how to fight.

"Ah," he said, smiling widely. "Well, we can always use more men to help out. Let me get you something to—"

He grabbed the pot that Otto had made the morning's soup in. It was still hot and he felt his palm blister as he picked it up. He could hear the men rushing forward, which was fine with him. In one smooth motion, he spun and splashed the contents into the face of the nearest man.

There wasn't much left, most of it was already in the bowls they were eating from— each with its own name, apparently. It was enough, though, to startle the first man, who screamed and clawed at his eyes.

Calidor lunged forward and slammed the pot down hard, directly into the man's face, hearing the satisfying crack of his nose breaking. Now, he yelped even louder and dropped his staff.

Calidor grabbed it and rose, just in time to parry the blow from the second man. He was off-balance, however, and the next attack caught him a solid blow in his ribs. He doubled over, but came back up just as quickly, feeling a smile stretch across his face. He'd been hit harder, much harder, in training with the two Honor Guard.

"What are you smiling—?" the man started, which was as far as he got before Calidor was on him, staff whirling. He managed to block one blow, then Calidor cracked him across the back of his right hand, causing him to cry out and drop one end of his staff. That was all the opening the prince needed. He slammed the end of his own staff into the man's mouth, hearing teeth crunch. The man's eyes rolled up into the back of his head, and he collapsed.

Calidor spun back to the first man, but he was sitting splay-legged on the ground, a dazed expression on his face. Even as Calidor looked, Otto raised the heavy skillet he'd used once already and bashed the man on the head once more. This time, he fell back with a gurgle.

Which only left the giant.

Who hadn't moved from where he stood. For that matter…neither had Yarah.

"Do something," she said, her teeth clenched tightly. "He's very strong."

Somehow, she was holding the man in place, by magic he assumed.

He walked over to the giant, staff held cross-body in front of him, ready in case he broke through her hold.

When he reached the man, he almost recoiled in surprise. For all his size, the man looked… innocent? He had an expression like that of a young child, unsure of what he had done wrong.

"Who are you?" the huge man asked. His voice trembled, as if he was afraid.

"I'm Prince Calidor, ruler of Obristan."

"Prince? Oh, no!" Tears began to leak from his eyes, and then he dropped to his knees, eliciting a quick curse from Yarah. "I'm sorry! I didn't want to do nothing! They said I had to!"

Calidor glanced back. The man Otto had hit was still unconscious, but the other was starting to stir.

"Yarah," he said quietly, "please do something with that one."

"But—" she started.

"It's okay. There's no danger here." He turned back to the giant. "What's your name?"

"My name? It's Vect, sir. Just Vect."

"Where's your family, Vect?"

"Dead, sir. All dead, when that dragon came down. It breathed fire and my mom and pop got all burned up. They were screaming something terrible, but I couldn't do anything. It was too hot." As he spoke, more tears flowed, until the huge man was racked with sobs.

Calidor stepped forward and put his hand on Vect's shoulder. "Have you hurt anyone else, Vect?"

Vect nodded, his head still bent miserably down. "They made me do it. Said if I didn't, they'd call a dragon to burn me up, too. I don't want to get burned up!"

"No, of course not." Calidor glanced back again. He should kill the two of them. Execute them for crimes against the kingdom.

He found that he just didn't want to. The dragonkin had done enough killing for them all.

"It's all right," he told Vect. "You can stay with us now, if you want. You'll be safe from the dragons. Would you like that?"

Vect looked up, his eyes bright beneath the tears. "Really? You mean it? I would serve the Prince?"

"Yes, but only if you do what I say. Does that work?"

Vect nodded violently.

"Okay, then," Calidor said. "The first thing is, I need your help with those two."

Vect glowered toward the fallen men. "I can hurt them. Like they made me hurt others."

"No. I have another idea. Just... hold on a moment, okay?"

"Okay," Vect said, but he kept staring at the other men, his huge brow furrowed.

Calidor walked over to Yarah. "Can you make them forget they saw us? Maybe give them a suggestion that they should range somewhere else? Like... I don't know, just somewhere."

"I can do better than that," she answered. "What if they both sort of had the idea they were wandering missionaries, out to spread the word of peace and love. My spell would wear off after some time... probably a few days, but they would have gotten pretty far by then."

"Perfect," he smiled. "And our new friend and I will move them some distance away before they wake up."

He called Vect to him and asked him to pick one of the men up. Vect threw one over his shoulder with no apparent effort, and when Calidor struggled with the second, he tossed that one over the other shoulder, then looked at the prince with a wide grin.

Calidor returned it. "Right. Let's go this way, then. If they get too heavy, let me know."

They returned twenty minutes later, without the men. Not once had Vect made any complaint or even acted as if he were carrying a burden. When they came back, Calidor asked him to help Otto clean up, and the giant happily set to.

"Your next recruit," Yarah commented.

Calidor nodded. "It was a good warning, though. Not to get too comfortable."

"I don't know," she said with a smile. "I saw you. Seems to me, everyone else ought to be watching out for you."

She patted his arm and walked off, leaving him with a strange feeling that he couldn't quite identify. Then he realized it was the warm glow of pride. The pride one feels when they've done something well. It was new for him, but he found he quite liked it.

Chapter 39- Orluduna, Droy Thus

Sintifi's worries about getting out of the tower without being seen by dragonkin turned out to be unnecessary. For one, as Oponsi had scoffed, what did the dragonkin care about *him*? He was just another human, free mage or otherwise, among many. She had walked to Korudu's tower without a care in the world, and none of them had bothered her in the least.

Well, he didn't quite have Oponsi's self-assurance; arrogance, he supposed some would say, but she did have a point.

Which just left Ilvisar. He didn't appear to be any more concerned than Oponsi. He simply grew still for a moment, whispered a few words, and then his features changed once more. He was now close to Sintifi's own height, with a dark skin tone, and rounded, "normal" ears. No one, even upon close inspection, would ever be able to tell that he was anything other than what he appeared.

"What about you?" Sintifi asked Korudu.

"I'll stay here. Maybe someday I'll see this other tower, but right now... I might attract attention heading off into the jungle. The dragonkin *do* know me as Master of the Tower."

"Not that they respect you as such," Oponsi said.

"No, I suppose not," Korudu replied easily. "As long as others recognize and respect it."

It wasn't a pointed barb, yet Oponsi seemed to get the gist. She grimaced, then inclined her head. "I do both, Korudu. I hope you know that."

"Thank you. Now, I would like to be kept in the loop on things. Including what I can do from here."

"I can be the messenger," Sintifi volunteered.

"How would you do that?" Oponsi's voice was exasperated. "You're going with that one to his home."

"Oh, right." He hadn't really forgotten as much as gotten caught up in what seemed to be a rare moment of mutual respect between Korudu and Oponsi. One that he would have liked to see continue.

However, he wanted to see Olequan even more. Now that he knew it existed, that some of the Evening Folk still lived... it was beyond his wildest imaginings.

"Let us go, then," Ilvisar said. "I would see this other tower, but my mission has drawn to a close. I was assigned to find who had cast the spell that caused such chaos, and I have done that. Falaern must be informed."

"Have patience," Oponsi told him. "We'll get there soon enough. Then I'm sure you have some high-and-mighty secret way to get back to your land and take Sintifi with you."

He did, actually. Sintifi had already experienced it. Relatively short hops across the realms, but far faster than walking, or even taking a Gulari would have been. He was pretty sure that if Ilvisar had wanted, they could have covered even more distance. But maybe the further he went, the greater the magic used, and the more likely to be spotted by dragonkin.

"Of course, I do," Ilvisar replied. "And if Falaern agrees, I'll be happy to teach it to you."

"Good. If we're to be allies, there will be no secrets."

With that, Oponsi stalked from the room.

Sintifi shook his head. "Sorry about her," he said to Ilvisar. "She's... well... proud, I guess."

"No need to apologize." Ilvisar turned a grin on Sintifi. "I like her. She shows a great deal of spirit. Which will be needed in the days ahead."

There was no telling with people, Sintifi realized, what would resonate with them and what wouldn't. He guessed that included an Elder Race, as well.

"Be well," he said to Korudu. "Keep your head down and out of sight of the dragonkin."

"I have my responsibilities, my friend," he replied. "But..." His eyes twinkled. "Come back soon and let me know what it was like!"

"I will," Sintifi laughed, hoping very much that it was true.

Ilvisar watched Oponsi lead the way through the town. He suspected that Sintifi could have as well, but his friend deferred to the older Oponsi, which was only proper. In truth, Ilvisar himself should have taken point, being by the far the most powerful of them all, but he had already discovered that he couldn't locate what they referred to as the "True Tower" on his own.

So he followed behind, watching as Oponsi did exactly what she had told them.

Back straight, facing resolutely forward, as if she couldn't even be bothered to notice what was going on around her, she walked with a purposeful stride. Like she belonged there, as she had said.

It seemed to work, too. No one paid any attention to them as they wound their way through the tight streets. As a matter of fact, people were paying very little attention to each other in general. They were all busy with whatever small tasks occupied their days.

Once, above the huts, he saw a dragonkin, one of the red, native to this realm, but it merely soared in the air, crossing in front of them some distance off. It flew lazily, as if it had nowhere particular to be, and its head never turned their way.

Ilvisar was pretty sure of his disguise. The magic needed to maintain it was so low level that even another Raaleth would have had a hard time picking up on it, unless they were searching for exactly that. So he wasn't too concerned with the red.

What did concern him was one of Tophonoss's children. One of those could be hidden nearby, difficult for Ilvisar to detect unless he actually tried. He didn't know how many of them were in Droy Thus, or even how many of them existed, but it wasn't a chance he was willing to take. They were sly. If he allowed it, and one was nearby, he wouldn't put it past them to merely shadow him until it had seen where he was going.

"Hold a second," he said, keeping his voice low.

Oponsi glanced over her shoulder with a scowl, but she did stop.

Ilvisar took a moment to cast out his senses and search. There were dragonkin around, although none in the immediate area. A black one, two reds, and one white. He could find no sign of one of Tophonoss's, though.

"All right, continue."

Oponsi snorted and went on her way.

Twice more, Ilvisar stopped them to do the same thing. Overly cautious, perhaps, but better to not be taken unaware.

She never asked him what it was that he was doing, although Sintifi gave him an odd look or two.

Finally, they reached a building with several people sitting at tables arranged in a low-walled court in front of it. Most had glasses of some liquid or another in front of them, some also had plates of food. From inside came the sound of music being played. To Ilvisar's ears, used to the tones of the Raaleth, it sounded harsh and discordant, but the humans seemed to be enjoying it.

Inside, a bar ran along one wall, with a large human behind it. He glanced up as they entered, then nodded toward a door on the other side of the room. Oponsi walked to it without a word.

People had noticed them, now, but none seemed to have anything to say, or even appear overly interested. They were there, they were walking across the floor, and that was it.

On a hunch, he reached out. There was magic, subtle, yet powerful, coming off of Oponsi. Ilvisar was impressed. She had thrown a spell without a whispered word or even a small hand gesture. From the feel of it, it was what was responsible for the patrons of this tavern to not take undue notice of them or where they went.

She pushed open the door and entered, moving to the side so that she could hold it for both him and Sintifi to pass through.

"Most impressive," he said quietly. "I never noticed your spell casting."

"That was the point," she answered.

For the first time in a very long while, Ilvisar was taken aback. Did Oponsi mean she had cast the spell and it was designed so that *he* never noticed the spoken word or gesture, even if she had made them? Or was she really that good that she could do it with neither?

He didn't know, but it did reinforce that, yes... he liked this Oponsi.

Sintifi kept his eyes on Ilvisar. He had an idea of what the Raaleth was doing when he'd had them stop, having done the same thing every time they'd come out of one of his magic gates. He supposed Ilvisar was most concerned about the children of Tophonoss, which made sense. Sintifi had yet to see one of those, so he had no idea what they might look like. Then again, he'd never come across a description of Tophonoss herself, either. Not even in ancient writings of the Raaleth, although the few they had managed to translate so far spoke of her in dread tones.

Out of all the dragons, it was Tophonoss most often regarded as being responsible for the final defeat of the Raaleth and those other two races. The other dragons had been fierce enemies, and no one had been able to stand against them. But Tophonoss had never let up. She was determined to see the end of them all. Based on what Ilvisar had said, it was only because the other dragons didn't believe that the Raaleth still lived, that they survived at all.

Now, it seemed as if the remaining contingent of those ancient people was about to rejoin the fray, if that was even the right word.

From what he'd been able to gather so far, the world was in shambles. Manse, the capital of Ascana, had vast sections completely destroyed, while some towns and smaller cities in both Ascana and Obristan had been totally reduced to rubble, their people killed. So far, he hadn't heard of that happening in Droy Thus.

There, it was more that the dragonkin had taken to supervising every aspect of magical education. They didn't seem to care about the day-to-day activities of the towns. Humans could work at mundane jobs all they wanted. The dragonkin were only interested in the magic.

Sintifi knew what they were doing. They had recognized the spell that he, himself, had thrown when he was hiding at Festival. They knew it to be that of their old foes, but since the Raaleth were long gone, the magic must have come from a human. The question of how that had occurred must have been eating at them ever since. Therefore, they would watch where magic was most often used.

He also had no doubt that if they knew of— or discovered— the True Tower, it would be the end of it. Sintifi didn't think a dragonkin, or even many of them joined together, possessed the power to harm that tower. But the dragons did. And if it was found, Chimbod herself would destroy it with magic and fire. He didn't think there would be a single stone left unbroken.

All of which was why he was glad Oponsi was with them. He recognized the spell she was using now, and could throw it himself, although not so easily or effectively. There was supposedly one other young girl in Orluduna with the same affinity for that branch of magic. Magic of the mind, he supposed it might be called. Oponsi had learned of her a couple of years ago and brought her to the True Tower. What had become of her since, Sintifi had no idea. He'd never actually met her, had only heard the stories.

Still, it was with a sigh of relief when Oponsi closed the door behind him.

The room was mostly bare, except for a few wooden crates containing bottles that were waiting to be sold and a couple of barrels of honey-wine yet to be tapped.

Oponsi gestured to one of those. "Move it."

Sintifi complied, grunting as he pushed it out of the way to reveal a trap door, which he then opened. A wooden ladder led down to a hidden room, stacked high with boxes and more crates.

Ilvisar looked down at the room below, then turned to Sintifi with a quizzical expression.

"Contraband," Sintifi explained. "Nothing serious. Books with unsavory passages that the masters of the towers don't like. Some food items that are illegal to import from Ascana for some reason I don't understand. Some stuff from Reclium, even."

"For what purpose?" Ilvisar asked.

"Deception," Oponsi said shortly as she pushed past. "Keep moving."

She descended the ladder without waiting for them. Ilvisar followed, then Sintifi, who closed the trap door. At the bottom, Ilvisar waited for him. "What about the barrel that hid the entrance?"

Before Sintifi could answer, they heard the door to the room open. A moment later, the barrel was shoved back into place and the door was shut again.

"The barman knows," Sintifi answered. "Not everything, just that there's another way out down here. Whenever one of us comes, he gives us a few minutes, then comes into the room and moves the barrel."

"And if he is questioned by a dragonkin?" Ilvisar asked.

"He can't say much," Sintifi shrugged. "He doesn't know more than that a few low-level smugglers use the room. He makes a little extra money every month from it."

"Plus, he'd die," Oponsi added. "If he were questioned too closely, an implanted spell would activate. His brain would be destroyed so thoroughly that no amount of magic could bring him back."

She said this while moving along the narrow room toward the end farthest from the ladder.

That was news to Sintifi.

"Um. Does he know about that?" he asked.

Oponsi didn't answer, or even bother to look back at him, which was all the answer he really needed.

He glanced at Ilvisar, but the idea that a person had some sort of death-spell in their brain, ready to destroy them at a moment's notice, didn't seem to bother him. Instead, he had already turned and was following Oponsi.

"This seems like a lot every time you wish to go to or from the tower," Ilvisar said.

"There are other ways," Oponsi answered without turning around.

"Such as?" But even as the words left Ilvisar's mouth, Oponsi muttered a sound and vanished.

Ilvisar stopped in his tracks, which almost made Sintifi laugh. "She activated a sort of door like in the towers. If she hadn't, we would have just kept going until we came out in the jungle."

The room appeared to continue, becoming more narrow as it went. What Ilvisar hadn't noticed was a band of dark metal, less than an inch wide, that was set into the walls, the floor, and the ceiling. It was this that Oponsi had used to move from one space to another, much like the area on the stairs in Korudu's tower.

Moving through thin air, especially without having some sort of anchor point on the other end, was impossible as far as Sintifi had known. Yet, it was something Ilvisar did without effort. Now, he was shocked by the poor-man's version of that magic?

"It's not the presence of the gate," Ilvisar said. "I can see that. It's the magic behind it." He turned to face Sintifi. "Who created this spell? Was it you? Or was it her?"

"Her? Maybe?" Sintifi shrugged. "I don't know really. It's not that uncommon."

"But it is," Ilvisar insisted. "That other one I used to find you was like magic one of our children could do as they clumsily learned. This... this leads to a hidden place. A place hidden by *my* people. The only way for it to work is to use that same magic."

"Raaleth magic?" Sintifi frowned. "I mean, Oponsi is powerful, but... I didn't know she could do that." Then, another thought occurred to him. "Wait. If the dragons— and your people— could feel it when I used that spell to call a dragonkin, then why weren't you aware of this one before now?"

"Because unlike the one you so blindly used, this one is not pure Raaleth magic. It's been changed, somehow. I would say tainted, but it doesn't appear to work any less effectively. There is human magic woven within it."

That was... well, that was something else entirely, Sintifi thought. He wasn't even aware that it was a thing. So was this something Oponsi had done and just never spoke about? Or had it been there from the beginning?

He was starting to realize that he knew a lot less about both Oponsi and how they had come to the True Tower than he'd thought.

It was one thing to know that Komea had discovered it, but how—
exactly— had that come about? Just by trying and trying until he
could read an ancient book? Sintifi had never questioned that before,
but now, maybe there *was* more to that story. And how did Oponsi
become the current master?

"Are you two coming or not?" Oponsi had returned, or at least
her upper half had, leaning out of thin air as if she had no substance
below the waist. The look might have been comical if it was anyone
else, but Sintifi wasn't about to laugh at her expense.

"Yes," he said. "Right away."

He hurried forward, passing through the momentary coldness of
the gate.

Then, he waited on the other side for Ilvisar to step through. He
had to wonder. Would the Raaleth find it strange? Or would it feel
like going home?

More so, how was *he* going to feel when the situation was reversed,
and he accompanied Ilvisar to Olequan. The butterflies in his
stomach that started to flutter around whenever he thought about it
returned. For all that, though, he could hardly wait.

Chapter 40- Heldum, Reclium

As long as he kept moving, kept his purpose in the forefront of his mind, he was able to keep the pain at bay. The burning in his limbs, in his chest, and in his head, stayed with him, but he could keep it tamped down to a smolder. As long as he was moving forward in his quest for that book, it didn't roar into an inferno threatening to utterly consume him.

He was finding now that whatever magic the two dragonkin— Sormat and that other red one— had used, it allowed him to feel joy in what he was doing. Reyson discovered that for the first time as he began to make his way up through Darkbreath Tower.

The door at the bottom was almost jammed shut by debris strewn about by those who had taken over the lower levels. Reyson sneered at that, since it meant that no one was coming down there on a regular basis to clear the rabble away. It had been a weekly task that he'd assigned to the other life-takers, just in case such an entrance or exit was needed.

The truth was, however, that it was very rarely used these days. Supplies came in by being winched up the side of the tower, the muscle power being supplied by several beefy individuals with more muscle than brains. The type who would perform mindless labor for hours on end for meals, drinks, and the occasional chance to entertain themselves. The variety of those entertainments sometimes provided voyeuristic opportunities for Lord Maganti and his guests as well.

As for those guests? They gained access the same way, via a luxurious basket complete with padded benches, windscreens to block the weather, and an array of wines to enjoy during the ascent.

Then, of course, there were the more secret ways in and out of the tower. Those that only Lord Mitrik Maganti and a few others knew of. Reyson was one of those select few, but it seemed that Maganti's son, Dommick, had not been.

Reyson could have taken one of those routes, once through the door, but he chose not to. Instead, he strode across the filth-encrusted floor and listened to the human cockroaches scuttle fearfully away. It just showed the depths to which these "people"— if they could even be considered as such— had sunk. Reyson wore no sword, his had been destroyed in the same fire that had burned him to ashes. His clothes were ill-fitting and ill-made, stolen from the line of a poor family in one of the hollows that dotted the hinterlands of Reclium. After he'd killed the peasant who'd chased him to take them back, the rest of his family had faded away, staring after him with resentment as he'd walked off.

"Good time?"

The voice was soft— weak, actually— although he supposed she thought it was a tantalizing invitation. Perhaps to those who scraped out some sort of life there, it would have been. For him, it was beneath contempt. When he saw the age of the girl, and the man standing back in the shadows watching carefully, he understood even more.

The pain and fire only had the chance to spike for a moment when he deviated from his course to crush the man's throat with one quick blow. And that momentary discomfort was offset by the pleasure he experienced when he felt the cartilage flex, then break, under the side of his hand.

Someone else would take the girl, he knew. It was a temporary freedom, at best, that he'd given her. But it was one less parasite infecting what was once a mighty and proud edifice.

He wanted to clear them all out. Send them running before him. Work his way from floor to floor, up the tower, until he came to the locked and guarded metal door that led to what was now the realm of the Magantis. But that would have taken too long, and the spell that forced him on— ever on— would never allow it.

Instead, Reyson made do with what came to him.

A hand reached out to grab his sleeve, whether in supplication or threat he didn't know and didn't care. The snap of finger bones breaking were drowned out by the sudden howl of pain. Reyson smiled and walked on.

"Money, mister? Please? Just enough to feed my—"

A broken jaw and shattered eye socket sent the woman reeling. When she fell, she didn't make a sound, nor did the three small children behind her who stared from him to her. Reyson smiled and walked on.

Upstairs, across the expanse of the tower. At each new level, he was approached. Some begged, some threatened, some tried subterfuge. The result was always the same. Reyson continued to smile and walk on.

He kept to his course, never deviating beyond that one quick instance on the first floor. As long as he did that, he kept the pain away and his wits clear.

Now, he finally arrived at the top level the clan had abandoned years before. There was the door— heavy iron— with no way of opening it from this side. A guard would be posted beyond, or at least they should be, able to see anyone approaching through a narrow eye-slit. Sometimes, the guard gave a warning to anyone who neared too closely. More often, the offender was met with a crossbow bolt, smeared with a deadly yet slow-acting poison. Much money was gambled on how long it would take someone struck with such a bolt to die.

Those that lived on this floor had mostly learned to stay far from the door, out of line of sight. That crossbow bolt often found its way into a stomach that hadn't been anywhere near the door. Such was the entertainment of those on the other side.

Reyson hadn't expected to be recognized when he approached. His clothing was far from the rich garments he usually draped his body in. His hair had been completely burned away, including his eyebrows, leaving him bald. He hadn't eaten in days, and didn't seem to feel hunger any longer, but it had made him even leaner than he had been. He was sure his cheekbones were starker, his eyes more deeply sunken.

So it was with no surprise that the crossbow bolt shot from the door and punctured his side. It passed in and out, tearing open a gaping wound on the way.

Reyson shook his head. Whoever was behind that door was a horrible shot.

Or… he reconsidered. Perhaps they had done exactly as they had intended. The wound he suffered would have caused agony in anyone else. Enough to put them on their knees, where they could be used as target practice for other, more skillful, shots.

In Reyson, it accomplished nothing other than tearing the shirt he had stolen. The wound didn't even bleed. There was the quick flare of red flames, accompanied by white-hot agony, then nothing. The rip in his flesh might as well have been torn in a loaf of bread. It was there, nothing more.

From behind the door, he heard a brief exclamation of surprise. Then, he was at it.

He raised his fist and banged on it.

"Open!"

His voice was the same as it had always been. It seemed that having his throat and vocal cords burned to ashes, then brought back, made no difference. Now, as long as the guard behind the portal wasn't new, they should recognize him.

"Reyson?" The voice came thinly through the thick metal. "Er…I mean… Lord Reyson? Is that you?"

"Yes, now open!"

"But we're not supposed to—" the voice started.

By now, he'd been standing still for too long. The pain was building, but slowly. As if the magic somehow recognized that he'd reached an impassable obstacle but didn't really care. It would give him a little leeway, but not much.

"If you don't open it, I'll take the basket, come back here and bury all of those crossbow bolts in you, one at a time!"

The sound of bolts being thrown and locks turned was immediate. It took almost a full minute before the last one was complete, and the door finally swung open, forcing Reyson to step back.

The man inside had moved several paces from the door, his crossbow held at the ready. Arranged on a small table beside him were several knives and a heavy iron-bound club. Even in his new state, Reyson approved. This one knew what he was about.

Not that he going to say so, of course. He crossed into the small room and waited.

The guard swallowed at the sight of him, then cautiously crept forward, reached around him, and pulled the door shut. None of those on the other side even attempted to come close.

Reyson swallowed the urge to break the guard's arm, to do exactly as he had said he would. It would serve no purpose other than to sate his hunger for violence, though, so he ignored the guard and moved to the next door, pausing only long enough to pick up two knives from the table.

"Key." He reached back without looking.

The guard gave him the heavy iron key, which Reyson fitted to the lock and turned. Anyone not knowing the exact order of turns, clockwise and back, would be met with a spray of lethal gas. Darkbreath Clan was nothing if not wary of intruders from other clans.

The door opened and Reyson walked through without removing the key or looking back.

Behind him, the door quietly closed and he heard the key turning again. The guard was no doubt breathing a sigh or relief and rightfully so. He had no idea how lucky he had been.

The journey through the lower levels of the clan-occupied floors of Darkbreath Tower was uneventful. Reyson encountered a few servants, who squeezed against the wall and lowered their heads as he passed. Even if they didn't recognize him, they knew he wasn't one of them, thus he was to be avoided. He met no one of consequence until he came to the level Maganti's library was on. The same level where that woman, Victoria Autumn, had caused him so much trouble.

Even the thought of her sent a burning through his mind. This one, however, had nothing to do with the dragonkins' spell. This one was his own. A rage so intense it made him stop for a moment, ignoring that other pain, to gain control of his emotions.

It was her fault. If she hadn't tried to steal that book for Sormat. If she had just had the good grace to die when she should have. If she hadn't somehow seduced that idiot Dommick to her cause…

If none of that, Reyson would still be in his position, enjoying the fruits of his years of labor.

"Can I help you?"

The voice came out in a high-pitched sneer that sent knives scraping down his spine. If he hadn't already controlled his anger, the speaker might have met a sudden, bloody end.

Instead, he turned to her with a grin, which was as close to a polite smile as he could work up at the moment.

"Hello, Celest," he rasped.

"Reyson?" Her perfectly thinned eyebrows rose at the sight of him.

Dark eyes roamed over his body, while he did the same to her. As if in defiance of the clan name, Celest was clothed head to toe in blinding white. Her shirt was too tight and short for her torso, forcing her breasts up and out, while leaving her stomach bare. Beneath that, she wore a long skirt, slit up to her left hip, which left little to nothing to the imagination when she moved.

Her hair was dark, like that of her father and brother. Her mother could have been any of a number of women Lord Maganti kept. If Celest knew who it was, she had never said. Her skin was as pale as any of those who lived in the ever-night of Reclium. Overall, she was an attractive woman; if one liked the spoiled, sadistic type.

"Where's your father?" he asked.

Celest shrugged and flowed past him, heading for the same sideboard full of wine and other bottles that Dommick had usually been found near. "Who knows? Tormenting someone? Watching some horrible perversion?"

"Then why aren't you there?" Her act wasn't fooling him. Celest was every bit as deranged as her father.

"Bored." She filled a glass with something more than wine, then slowly turned and looked him over again, her eyes lingering on the rip in his shirt and the hole in his skin beneath it. "You look different. Rough day?"

The pain was starting to flare up again, causing him to grimace. The expression wasn't lost on her. She smirked and said, "Guess so."

"Where is your father?" he asked again, forcing the words out through clenched teeth.

Her trilling laugh set whatever nerves he had left on edge. "I told you; I don't know. Nor do I—"

Her words were cut off with a squawk. Reyson's right hand was around her throat, squeezing hard enough to cut off her air. He might not have to breath anymore, if he chose not to, but she certainly did. The glass dropped to the floor and shattered as she beat at him.

Reyson had helped train her. Celest was deadly. She could fight as well as any man and knew the places to hit that did the most damage.

Now, she might as well have been trying to fight the tide. Nothing she did made any difference.

He shoved his face close to hers, glaring into her eyes.

"Where?"

She tried to jerk away, but he held her firmly. Finally, she pointed up. The only things above were the roof, storerooms, and the private bedrooms of the Magantis.

Reyson snarled and let her go. She tumbled to the floor, coughing and retching. A shard of glass cut into one knee, but she didn't appear to notice the crimson stain on her pristine white skirt, as she gasped for air.

He was there, in his bedroom, but he was alone for once. Face down and snoring on his bed, apparently exhausted from whatever he had been doing, he hadn't even removed his boots.

Lord Mitrik Maganti, head of the largest and most dangerous clan in all Reclium. Not just in Heldum, their influence spread all over the realm, and into the others besides. At one time, Reyson had taken great pride in being so highly placed in such a clan. Now, it meant nothing to him.

"Get up." He was vaguely aware that he was mimicking the same words Maganti had used with him the last time they'd seen each other.

There was no response from the man on the bed, however. The pain and burning was starting to rise, so Reyson had no time to be as patient as Maganti had been with him. He grabbed the man's ankles and pulled him off the bed in one sudden movement. Lord Maganti slid from the bed and onto the floor, his face smashing into the polished wood.

He yelped loudly, then cursed, and rolled, coming to his feet remarkably quickly, his nose streaming blood. As he'd insisted his children be trained to defend themselves, Mitrik was not a man to be toyed with, either. He'd spent long hours dueling and learning, when he wasn't engaged elsewhere. To anyone else, his sudden surge and blazing eyes would have set off alarm bells.

To Reyson, it was just an opportunity to hit him, something he'd longed to do many times in the past.

His fist caught Maganti under the ribs, doubling him over and sending him reeling back onto the bed.

"Where did it come from?" Reyson growled.

Lord Maganti coughed harshly, breathed in a stuttering, wet breath, then looked up blearily. "Reyson? What do you think you're doing?"

"What I have to. Now."

"What the hell is that supposed to mean?" Mitrik's head seemed to be clearing. He grabbed a corner of the blanket and dabbed at his nose. "What are you doing here? Did you get it back?"

"No. Where did *you* get it?"

"That's none of your business!" Maganti started to stand, but Reyson put out a hand and shoved him back down.

"Tell me now. I have no time for your games."

"You're treading on thin ice, Torneau. I'll have your skin peeled off—"

Reyson drew one of the knives he'd taken from the guard room and drove it into Maganti's thin thigh. He ignored Maganti's scream as he leaned on the blade.

"Where did you get it?"

"I don't know! It was stolen!"

Reyson didn't believe him. He twisted the knife in the wound.

"Ahh! Fine! Fine! Just get off!"

He knew all the ways of pain. How best to cause it and how much a man could take before he broke. He knew how much would cause someone to reveal secrets and when to back off to allow them the faculty to speak. He took the pressure off the knife, but kept it buried in Maganti's leg.

"It came from a private collection. Someone in Ascana who specialized in relics of the Evening Folk. Parts of old weapons, armor, things like that." Maganti reached down and clasped his leg around the blade. "Gods, that hurts! Take it out!"

"More," Reyson told him.

"I don't care about the other stuff. Who cares about stuff a bunch of dead people had? But I like books, okay? So I wanted it. I tried to buy it, but when that didn't work, I sent a few men in after it. A couple of weeks later, I had it."

"What is it?"

Maganti grimaced, then spoke again through gritted teeth. "No idea. That's the truth! It's written in some language I presume is theirs. Those Evening Folk! It was good to display, just to show the others that I could take whatever I wanted. So they'd better mind their manners."

All of which sounded exactly like something Maganti would do. Reyson had no doubt that whoever had been in possession of that book was no longer alive. Or that they hadn't died easily.

"Why would Sormat want it, then?"

"Sormat? Who's that? No, no wait! Wait!" He'd seen Reyson tense to twist the blade again. "She's that dragonkin, right? I don't know why she'd want it."

Reyson considered. That was probably true, as well. The dragonkin wouldn't have bothered telling Maganti she wanted it. Not when she'd sent Autumn in there to take it. Which meant... Sormat didn't want anyone else, dragonkin or otherwise, to know about it.

"Who could read it?" he asked.

"No one? Who can read that gibberish they spoke in?"

Reyson snarled and pushed on the knife, causing Maganti to scream again. "Stop! Stop! All right. I guess a dragonkin could maybe read it. Beyond that..." He was sweating and panting now, obviously wracking his brain to think. "Droy Thus! Those wizards who live there. Maybe them? Other than that, I don't know. I swear, I don't."

Maganti threw his head back and started to weep. Funny how this didn't seem to appeal to him as much as when he made others do it.

Droy Thus? That was on the other end of the world. How could Viktoria Autumn possibly...?

A ship. The whore had gotten her out of Pharax before he'd even shown up. He had to hand it to her. Chaol hadn't fooled him for a second, but Severina Cloven... Maybe she hadn't fooled him so much as bested him. After that, he hadn't been thinking as clearly as he should have been.

The woman had taken a ship all the way to Droy Thus. If not there, then surely to Ascana, where she would make her way south.

The book was there, which meant he was going there as well.

He yanked the knife free, causing Mitrik to yelp again. For a moment, he considered killing the man, or maybe just disfiguring him. But he couldn't be bothered.

Instead, he left the bedroom, intending to leave Darkbreath Tower and never return. And if Mitrik Maganti was stupid enough to try to stop him, he wouldn't leave a soul in the tower alive.

Chapter 41- Craydon, Ascana

When Toni nodded, telling him that the sky was clear, Kori sprang to his feet and wheeled around. There was no sign of the dragonkin in the night sky. Wherever it had gone, it had either climbed higher than his eyes could follow, or it had gone to ground somewhere.

While he was scanning the sky, Antonia made it to his side.

"That was close," she said. "Let's get moving again. If we hurry, we can make it into the woods before it comes back."

"No," Kori said.

Toni's eyes were wild as she stared at him. "No? What's that supposed to mean? No?"

"It means no, I'm not running into the woods to hide. You should, though." He turned to her and took her by the shoulders. "You're an amazing woman, Toni. I don't think I could have made it through these last days if I hadn't met you. But you should go. Get out of here while you can and make a life for yourself somewhere without dragonkin."

"What are you talking about?" she asked. "There is no place without dragonkin. Not anymore. And why aren't you coming with me?"

"I'm going back. I'm going to—" Now that he began to say it out loud, he realized how silly it sounded.

"You're going to what?" she demanded.

He couldn't meet her eyes and the ridicule that he knew was going to spring up in them. He'd never worried too much about such things before, but he didn't want to see it in her. Not in Toni.

"I'm going to kill them," he said quietly, almost flinching at the anticipated explosion of laughter.

"You can't," she whispered. "Are you crazy? How would you even—?" Even as she asked the question, though, her eyes fell to the axe at his hip. "Your uncle's axe. You think that will allow you to just *kill* them?"

"No." Kori shook his head. "Not easily. But… it will even up the odds. I just need to find them alone and surprise them. That's all."

Her laugh, when it finally came, wasn't one of ridicule or even humor. It was simple disbelief.

"Kori, they'll never let down their guard. Not now that one of them has been killed. They'll be watching for it, and they'll probably call in more. And if you do manage to kill another one of them? The remaining one will destroy all of Craydon and kill everyone in it!"

He hadn't thought of that. Toni was right, of course. He let go of her shoulders and stepped back. "Then I'll have to think of a way to get them both, one right after the other. That's the only way to save everyone."

Toni shook her head. "I can't stop you, can I?"

"No. I'm sorry, but… I feel like I have to do this."

"Then you'll have to do it without me." She raised her wounded arm partway, grimacing at even that much. "I'm already wounded, and I was an innkeeper, not a fighter. I wouldn't be of any use to you."

"You're more than that," he said quietly with a small smile. "And I don't want you to come back with me. I want you to run. If I fail… I don't want you anywhere near."

They gazed at each other for a moment, before she stepped forward and kissed him hard. His arms went around her and they stayed that way for a few minutes, reluctant to let go and make it real.

But finally, it was time. Toni stepped back, wiped a hand across her eyes and turned to the forest. Kori simply watched her walk, then jog, away, before he turned back to Craydon.

He didn't try to hide. If a dragonkin spotted him, then it might miss her. Besides, he could always claim he had gotten lost hunting or something and was just now getting back to the town. Maybe they'd believe that before they bit off his head.

Besides, he needed time to think. Toni had been exactly right. If he killed one dragonkin, the other was going to know something was happening wreak havoc on the town. He was actually surprised they hadn't done it already, now that he thought of it.

Maybe if he made some sort of trap... something to lure one down and keep it pinned while he went after the other. Only, what could possibly do such a thing? It would have to be strong, and hidden, and tempting. How it could be both tempting and hidden, he wasn't sure, but maybe if...

A noise behind him made him glance back just in time to see Toni catch up to him and take a place at his side.

"What are you doing?" he demanded. "You need to go!"

"I decided not to," she answered. "You need my help."

"You already said you weren't a fighter."

"And I'm not. But I'm a thinker. And I think I may love you, Kori, and you're a good man. But a thinker, you aren't."

He drew back at that, a retort on his lips. Or at least the start of a retort. He couldn't get anything other than, "I am too!" to come to mind, though.

Which made him think that maybe she had a point.

"I don't want you hurt," he said.

"That makes two of us. So I'd better be clever. And you'd better be fast."

Kori fell silent, trying to think of something that would show her she was better off leaving. But all the way back, he couldn't come up with anything. By the time they'd reentered the town, he was already finding that he was glad she'd stayed with him.

"Where are we going to go?" Toni's whisper was soft, but since it was only the early hours of morning, shortly past midnight, neither of them wanted to chance speaking loudly. Craydon slept around them, and the dragonkin were sure to investigate anyone they found wandering around.

"I'm not sure," Kori whispered back. "The barn again? We can wait until tomorrow night and—"

"And what? Try to run across the fields again? What are we doing, Kori?"

"I told you! I'm going to kill the dragonkin. Then we can—"

"Get both of you killed," a new voice cut in.

Kori felt his cheeks flush as he realized that both he and Toni had begun to speak louder as they went back and forth. Whoever this was, they had come upon them without Kori even being aware they were nearby.

He turned slowly, hands out to show that he wasn't going to pull his axe from his belt. What he saw only deepened his shame.

There wasn't one man behind him, there were five. One was facing them with an easy smile— which seemed like it might be a good thing— while the others were all alert and looking in different directions, including scanning the sky.

"What are you doing back here?" the man asked. "We left you food and some water. Why are you still here?"

"I came back," Kori said. "Toni decided to join me. I can't... I couldn't just leave this place with the way I left it."

"What's that supposed to mean?" The man spoke with an air of authority, as if he was used to asking questions and having them answered. He still didn't show any signs of anger or aggressiveness, however.

"I heard yesterday, what happened outside the barn, when the dragonkin came."

"And?"

"He did it," Toni said, stepping forward. Kori flinched at her bluntness, but he didn't deny what she was saying. "He was the one who killed that other dragonkin. With one blow."

The new man looked from Toni back to Kori, obvious disbelief on his face. "One blow. Sure you did."

"He did!" Toni spat. "I was there! He did it to save me!"

Her insistence must have triggered something in the other man. He gazed at her, back to Kori again, then nodded. "All right, then. Come with us. We need to get off the street, and that barn isn't going to be safe."

Kori was going to protest, until it occurred to him that only a few minutes prior he'd been arguing with Toni about where they should go and what they should do. This man seemed to have a place in mind, and Kori didn't have a better alternative, nor was he interested in fighting all five of them.

Still...

"My name is Kori." He thrust out a hand. He could tell a lot about a person from their handshake. "Kori Hordsson. From Usturg."

"I got the Usturg bit right away," the man chuckled. He took Kori's hand in a firm, sure grip. "Elsdon Drace. Commander of the Ascani Knights. Or at least what's left of them."

The Ascani Knights? Kori had never heard of them, but he was pretty sure knights were those guys who rode around in all that heavy armor, wielding long, sharp poles. These guys were dressed in ordinary worker garb, although each of them did have a well-taken-care-of sword in hand. Except for Elsdon, who hadn't drawn his from the sheath he wore on a belt around his waist.

"Let's go," Elsdon said, and started past Kori and Toni. Two others formed up so they'd be walking behind them, while the other two slipped away between the buildings.

"It doesn't seem we have much choice," Toni said.

"Oh, you do," Elsdon said over his shoulder. "You'd just be stupid to make the wrong one."

Kori thought he meant because Elsdon and his men— the Ascani Knights— were their best chance of staying alive, but he supposed Elsdon could have meant it differently. Either way, he agreed. Their best choice was to go with them.

"Ideas, remember? Maybe this is a good one." He took her hand, and they followed Elsdon down the street.

"It's not much," Elsdon said as he opened the door, "but it's home."

The building he'd led them to was apparently unused. At one time, it had been a school, with several rooms where classes of children learned to read and write, to add numbers together and subtract them again. Even Kori knew that Ascana was big on that. Math was vital in the pursuit of running businesses.

The thought of all those kids sitting at desks, which had now been shoved to the sides of the rooms, with their little heads bent over books, brought back a flood of nostalgia. He could see himself doing the same thing, only not in a nice building full of other kids like this one had been. He had been on his own, with his mother nearby, helping him sound out words as he'd struggled through the pages. Those were some of his most cherished childhood memories, and he tried not to let the image of his father slamming the door open and bringing violence and chaos into the house ruin them.

He reached to his shirt and pressed, feeling the soft, leather cover of the book that he carried press into his skin. It was still there. Good. He would hate to have to tell Elsdon— and Toni, for that matter— that he needed to go back to the field to find it. But if it had fallen out, he would have.

"There's spare bedding," Elsdon went on. "We've been finding what abandoned things we could on our little night journeys" He stopped and smiled at them. "Hadn't expected to find an abandoned dragonkin slayer, though."

"I'm not a killer," Kori said. "I mean. I have been, I guess. But I don't like it."

"Good. That's a good thing to hear. A man who grows to like it is someone I don't really care to be around. But I have a feeling about you, Kori. I think we're going to get along just fine."

He waved them on and led them into a small kitchen. The room had been another classroom at some point, but the Knights had set it up differently, including an old wood-burning stove where an urn simmered on top.

The room was empty except for a couple of scarred tables and rickety chairs. Elsdon poured coffee from the urn into three cups, then brought them over to one of the tables. He kicked out a chair and indicated they should take two others.

"I'd like to hear your story," he told Kori. "From there, maybe we can work out a way to help each other."

Kori sipped at the coffee. It was too bitter and too hot, and it tasted wonderful. He realized it had been quite some time since he'd had any.

"I killed a dragonkin," he said simply.

"That much I gathered," Elsdon said. He glanced down at Kori's hip. "I'm guessing that axe had something to do with it, am I right?"

"How did you know that?" Toni asked.

"I didn't. It's just that you've touched it about a hundred times since I've seen you. It's important to you, as well as whatever it is you have in your shirt. Since I don't think whatever *that* is killed the dragonkin, I'm guessing it's that axe. Which is a very nice-looking weapon, by the way."

"It was my uncle's," Kori said. "But that's not really important."

"It could be," Elsdon said, "if it's what I think it might be. Let's leave that for now, though. Tell me what happened."

"All right." Kori took another sip from his cup, then started telling Elsdon everything he could remember, from his time running from Slode to now.

A good hour had passed by the time Kori finished his tale. He realized that even with the time they'd spent together, there were several things that Toni would have been hearing for the first time as well. Like exactly why he had left Usturg in the first place. He was almost afraid to look at her when he finished, sure that her return gaze would hold nothing but disgust.

But when he did summon the courage to look her way, there was nothing but compassion in her eyes. He let out a slow, silent breath that he hadn't even realized he'd been holding.

"Wow," Elsdon said. "That's quite the story. You've lived a lot in a short time. One might almost be inclined to say you're making a bunch of it up. Except that I believe you."

"You do? All of it?" As he'd spoken, Kori had been aware of Elsdon's considering stare and had also been slightly mystified by the few questions the man had asked.

"All of it. Mostly because I was there, too. In Manse, during Festival. I had just returned from bringing an escort out to accompany Prince Calidor from Obristan, and his retinue, into the city. I had another night of duty, then I was looking forward to a couple of days off. I was going to show one of the Honor Guard I'd met around Festival, since we'd both discovered a desire to see the world."

"But you never got there," Toni said.

"Not once dragonkin started falling out of the sky. I gathered what men I could, and we went into the city, to try to save anyone we could. I like to think we did some good, but... it got to be too much. We had no choice but to retreat. Soon after, we got word from a friend that the Knights weren't being thought too highly of any longer. Staying anywhere near Manse was a bad idea, so it was time to go. We went. The first town we ended up in was attacked by one white and one red dragonkin. They laid waste to it, and I lost three of my men in trying to save others. We barely got out alive and left our armor and a lot weapons behind."

Elsdon stopped with a sigh. "It doesn't matter from there. We moved on, then again, then again, until we reached here. Where— to my surprise— we found our friend from Manse. The one who'd warned us to get out. Since then, we've stayed here, working by day and doing... other things... by night."

"When do you sleep?" Kori asked.

"In shifts," Elsdon laughed. "Some of us sleep during the day, then we rotate."

"But don't the dragonkin catch on to that?"

"Not yet," Elsdon shrugged. "But we have help there, too." He turned to Kori. "But enough of that. This axe of yours. May I see it?"

Normally, Kori didn't really like handing his axe over to anyone. But he supposed in Elsdon's case, it would be all right. The man had been nothing but honest with them, so far. He reached down, slid it free, then carefully handed it across the table.

"It's a beauty," Elsdon said, looking down at it and turning it back and forth so that it glinted in the lantern light. He held it up before him and studied the blade carefully. Finally, he grimaced and slowly handed it back to Kori.

"What did you see?" Toni asked him. "You said something about it, earlier."

"I did," he nodded. "I suspect— strongly— that your axe is something I'd read about. I thought if I ever saw one there'd be some way of recognizing it. But... there isn't. I suppose they were too smart for that."

"Who was?" Kori was looking at the axe blade now, trying to see if there was anything he'd missed all the countless other times he'd examined it.

Elsdon leaned back in his chair. "The Evening Folk," he said quietly. "I have the feeling that axe was forged by them."

Kori glanced at Toni, but she was frowning at the knight. "Why would you even think that?"

"Because of what you've told me. There are stories— not so much in fashion any longer, I suppose— about the horrible weapons the Evening Folk had and how they used them to slaughter innocent dragonkin. It was one of the reasons they all went to war, so long ago. Now, though..." He spread his hands. "Maybe the weapons weren't the cause of the war but were forged because of it."

"That's an awful long time for a weapon to survive," Kori mused.

"It is," Elsdon agreed. "If it was something easily done, there would still be a bunch of them around. I suspect that if a dragonkin saw this one, and you didn't kill it, it would recognize the axe for what it was."

Kori thought it over. What Elsdon was saying did make sense. He was also sure that his uncle had no idea what he'd had. All of which made Kori wonder even more where he had gotten it from.

Elsdon climbed to his feet. "Now, though, it's time to sleep. Tomorrow is my turn in the fields again, then we'll need to figure out what we're going to do. Killing the black dragonkin seems like a great place to start, so we'll get a plan together tomorrow. In the meantime, don't fret. You're safe here."

"That's nice to say," Toni told him. "But how do you know that?"

Elsdon grinned. "The same way we rotate our days and nights. We have help."

"That's at least the third time you've said that," she replied. "Who is this help?"

"Haven't you figured it out yet? The same one who told us to get out of Manse, remember. There are three— excuse me— two, dragonkin in Craydon. And one of them is a friend. The blue one is named Lijing, and she's been working with us since we got here."

Chapter 42- Greenfair, Obristan

The best news that Lamorak had received in longer than he could remember was finding out that Bodwyn yet lived. His old friend was in the Honor Guard compound when Lamorak entered, sitting on a bench and looking over the now empty training yard. He hadn't even noticed Lamorak's return, which was something to be concerned about, but that could also be dealt with later.

"Sleeping on duty?" Lamorak asked when he neared.

Bodwyn's head swung around, but slowly, as if he was coming out of a daze. He stared at Lamorak, blinked, then his eyes opened wide, and he leapt to his feet.

"Lamorak!" he shouted. "You're alive!"

He swept Lamorak up in a fierce hug, squeezing so hard he could feel his ribs creak.

"I am!" Lamorak laughed. "But not for long if you don't ease up."

Bodwyn let him go and stepped back, a sheepish grin on his face. "Sorry about that. Got a little carried away, I guess."

Lamorak studied his friend, noting the differences since he'd left to escort Prince Calidor to Festival. More gray in Bodwyn's hair and beard, but that was to be expected given the state of the world. Lamorak was sure his own had more salt than pepper these days. Beyond that, Bodwyn wasn't wearing his armor. Instead, he wore a loose tunic and rough pants, along with good, sturdy boots.

He also carried more weight than he had. Always a big man, larger than Lamorak and maybe even Rainaldus, Bodwyn had never been what anyone would have considered fat. But now, his arms seemed a bit pudgy, and Lamorak had felt a protruding belly under that loose shirt.

"Why is no one training?" Lamorak asked, letting his eyes move from his friend's smiling face to the empty training ground.

"Not allowed," Bodwyn said. "Like most things."

"The dragonkin?" Even though he knew the answer, Lamorak felt the need to actually hear it.

"Who else? No fighting, not even to train. No weapons. No armor. No drinking, either. I guess we're fortunate they haven't outlawed food... yet."

"So... the Honor Guard?"

"Might as well be done with," Bodwyn shrugged. "They didn't make us leave. To be honest, they don't seem to care where we live. But some left, anyway. There are still a fair number here: me, Cadwent, Keridoc, Bolles... some others. But it's mostly because we have nowhere else to go."

Lamorak was stuck on the fact that the Honor Guard wasn't even together anymore. It was going to make his mission that much harder... Then he stopped and frowned. Something Bodwyn had just said. He looked back at his oldest friend, ice forming in his veins.

"Wait. You said you all had nowhere to go? But _you_ do. Right?"

Bodwyn half-shrugged, but his eyes glinted wetly in the sunlight.

"Where's Elanor?" Lamorak asked. "What happened?"

Bodwyn tried to wave it away. "It doesn't matter. It's done, now."

"It does matter," Lamorak replied firmly. "Tell me."

Bodwyn looked away. "She was crossing the street. A dragonkin was angry about something, apparently, and just... breathed. Down the entire thing. Came out of nowhere from what I've heard and... well, it was a red one. The stones are still melted lumps."

Bodwyn didn't cry. He had probably played the scene over and over in his mind until it had lost just about all meaning. But for Lamorak... Bodwyn's wife was one of those people who made life a great joy. She could hold her own with any of the Honor Guard when it came to ribald humor, and she kept Bodwyn in line when he needed it. She cooked Lamorak more meals than he could count and was always on the lookout for who he should consider settling down with.

Or... she had, anyway.

Lamorak sank onto the bench Bodwyn had just vacated. He'd seen a lot of death since leaving Greenfair. He'd even helped kill a dragonkin. But nothing had hit him quite as hard as the news of

Elanor's death. Maybe it was because he'd thought of Greenfair as a safe place. It was his home. And seeing it from the air, sparkling like a diamond, had made it seem untouched by the troubles of the rest of the world.

Even walking down the street and seeing dragonkin and people without swords, all that had seemed minor compared to what he'd witnessed in the last few weeks.

But now... now he knew that Greenfair was no different.

"Glad you're back," Bodwyn said quietly. "And the prince?"

Lamorak shook his head, then drew in a deep breath. He'd have to mourn later on. Much later, he supposed, if ever. When the dragonkin were gone and the world was back to normal. Or, more likely, a safe, new normal.

"Not with me. We didn't think it was smart for him to come back here."

"Ah, so he *is* alive. That's good, anyway. And young Rainaldus?"

Lamorak let out a short, sharp laugh. "You're not going to believe this."

They talked for the next couple of hours, sitting on the bench in the sun. For a brief moment, it almost felt like old times, before or after training. Only neither of them were bleeding from the cuts they'd given and received, and the clash of weapons from others still going at it was missing. He filled Bodwyn in on all that had occurred since they'd left, and listened to Bodwyn's tale, as well.

Finally, their talk ran down, and reality crowded in on them again.

"You going to stay here?" Bodwyn asked.

"I thought to," Lamorak replied. "My old room still available?"

"Pfft," Bodwyn scoffed. "Like we'd let anyone else take it."

"All right, then." Lamorak stood, then looked down. "You coming?"

"Nah. Think I'll sit here a bit longer. You settle in. See you at dinner. It's Keridoc's turn to cook. He's actually not half-bad, so you're in luck."

Lamorak shook his head. The Honor Guard cooking for themselves. He supposed they were doing their own laundry and housekeeping, as well. Then again, they were alive, which was more than he'd feared on many nights that he might find.

"See you, then," he told Bodwyn and turned away.

"See you, then," his friend returned, then. "Oh. Lamorak. You should leave that sword hidden in your room. I can't believe you made it here without anyone noticing."

"I didn't. I'll tell you about it over dinner."

With that, he made his way into the main building of the Honor Guard compound.

He ran into a few members that he knew as he walked the corridors leading to his quarters. Every time, he was greeted warmly, asked about Prince Calidor, and then warned about carrying his sword. It was a strange feeling to see them all without armor or weapons. Not that the Honor Guard wore their armor at all times, but there was always someone heading out to a duty station somewhere.

It wasn't until he'd answered the same question and heard the same warning three times that something occurred to him. Not once had anyone asked him about Lord Campbell. Either they all already knew that he had met his end, or they were simply afraid of what it meant that Lamorak had shown up alone, without their commander with him. He supposed there had been time for the news to reach Greenfair before the world had gone mad, so maybe that explained it.

When he reached the door to his rooms, he hesitated before opening it, a sudden reluctance to do so creeping over him. Once he went inside, it would be like none of it had happened, right? He was going to be home again, relaxing in his own quarters while Prince Calidor, Yarah, and the little girl were still out there, living in the woods. And by this time, anything could have happened. Maybe Calidor had collected more of his people, or maybe he was lying dead already, cast aside and buried under fallen leaves.

He had no way of knowing, and even less of doing anything about it. So deciding to live out the rest of his life standing in front of his own door wasn't going to do anyone any good.

Finally, he turned the knob, went inside, then shut the door firmly before turning to look at the room.

It was just as he had left it. Even the large windows were still intact. After all the ruin and desolation he'd seen the last couple of weeks, it seemed surreal that the glass was still in one piece. Near his favorite chair was a table which held the book he'd been reading, the cloth bookmark still in place. He had to pick it up and look at the cover to even remember what it was.

Ah. A treatise on the best methods for fighting from horseback. The author had covered hunting— and defending oneself— from large beasts, as well as the best tactics to use during a pitched battle. He paged through until the end, but what he now knew *really* should have been included, wasn't. There wasn't one word that he could see about fighting a dragonkin.

He set the book down with a snort, unable to imagine that he'd ever want to pick it up again. Not that he needed it. He remembered very well what was required. An inhumanly strong young Guardsman and few Droy Thus wizards. Give him those couple of things, and Lamorak would kill as many dragonkin as anyone could wish.

On his own, though… well, that would be a different story.

He walked through his quarters, almost afraid to sit down. He seemed to have forgotten how comfortable… how lavish… everything was. Stuffed chairs and a long couch. Tables to put drinks or books on. A bed large enough for three to sleep soundly. And that mirror he had been so proud of.

He didn't even glance into it. He knew that his reflection would be different from the Lamorak he saw in his mind's eye. Thinner, older, more haggard. None of it mattered. It wasn't about how he looked. It was about what he needed to do.

He opened his wardrobe door to find several full suits of clothes, from everyday wear to formal dress appropriate for the highest level of function. Shoes of all types as well.

He looked down at himself and realized for the first time just how truly filthy he was. His clothes were dirty, stained, and ripped. His fingernails were split and ragged, with dirt caked in the creases of his hands. When he reached up, he could feel how much longer his hair had grown and how greasy it was.

He grimaced, then proceeded to make room behind all of those clothes to hide his sword. If a dragonkin came this far, it wouldn't really matter how well hidden it was, anyway.

His next stop was his bathing chamber. Greenfair was a wonder of the world when it came to modern conveniences, and the Honor Guard compound shared in those. Lamorak twisted a handle and listened to air and water gurgle through metal pipes. A moment later, water splashed out of a spigot and into the large, marble tub. He put his hand underneath and marveled as the water slowly turned hot all on its own.

It had something to do with tanks and boilers somewhere beneath the compound, he knew. Beyond that, the appearance of hot water from a pipe in the wall could have been the work of the wizards of Droy Thus.

As the water in the tub grew deeper, his desire to become clean became a burning need. Within moments, he'd stripped off his worn and filthy travel clothes and thrown them to the floor. He'd get rid of them later.

With a sigh, he sank down into the water, while letting it run until it was up to his chin when he lay back against the far end of the tub. There was a part of him that still felt guilty about Calidor and Yarah, but the hot water did as much to wash that away as it did the filth encrusting his body.

He scrubbed hard with soap, feeling the scars that covered his arms and torso. When that was done, he did it again, then a third time, draining the water in between each one and refilling the tub. After the last scrubbing, the water appeared to be fairly clean still, so he leaned back and closed his eyes.

Just for a moment.

The pounding at his door woke him. He jerked up with a gasp, then almost laughed at his own foolishness.

"Lucky I didn't drown myself," he muttered. Then he raised his voice to yell, "One minute!" in the direction of the door.

He climbed from the tub and wrapped a rough towel around his midsection.

"What?" he snarled as he opened the door.

Bodwyn— because who else would it have been?— stood on the other side, his hand raised in preparation to knock again.

"Grumpy when you're woken up from your nap, aren't you?" his friend said.

Bodwyn didn't wait for an invitation. He simply moved forward, almost as if daring Lamorak to try and stop his larger frame from moving where it wished. Not that he had any intention of doing so.

Lamorak had slept deeper than he ever thought he would have, but still, his dreams were full of fire and screams, and he was glad to see his smiling friend. He was even more glad to see the dark glass bottle Bodwyn had in his left hand.

"Thought that stuff was off-limits?"

Bodwyn shrugged. "I won't tell if you don't. Glasses?"

"Same place as always. I'll be right back."

He left Bodwyn to dig the glasses out while he went to his wardrobe and pulled out a shirt, underclothes, and a pair of pants. Once he was dressed, he rejoined the other Guard in the sitting room.

"Here's to your return!" Bodwyn handed Lamorak a glass and raised his own.

Lamorak copied that gesture as well as the one that followed. Only, when he raised the glass to his lips and took a deep swig, he almost spit it out. Fire ran down his throat, threatening to close it completely and bringing tears to his eyes.

"Good gods! What is—" But fell silent at Bodwyn's raised hand.

His friend wasn't smiling. Instead, he stared solemnly at Lamorak, waiting for him to finish.

Well, if Bodwyn could down the stuff, so could he. Knowing what to expect made finishing the amount in his glass easier, if not more pleasurable.

Without asking, Bodwyn refilled their glasses and raised his again. Lamorak did the same.

"To those who are gone," the larger man said, his voice catching a bit. "And to those we await. For Prince Calidor's safety."

That was a lot to drink to with one glass, so Lamorak made sure to down it in one go. When he finished, Bodwyn was lowering his own glass, before sinking into one of the chairs.

"What is this stuff?" Lamorak finally got to ask.

Bodwyn peered down at the bottle. "Not sure, to tell you the truth. I found it in one of the cellars. I'd never really been down there, since the wine steward always served us. This one was tucked away, along with a few others. I think old Brentley either had his own private stash, or he was running a side business. This one might be from Reclium, though."

Reclium. No wonder it tasted like poison. It very well might be, but neither he nor Bodwyn seemed to be suffering from it. Other than a slight light-headedness that could have been because he hadn't had a proper drink in so long.

"What happened to Brentley, anyway?" Lamorak asked.

"Gone. With the rest of the servants. None of them stayed on, which I thought was short-sighted. The dragonkin mostly leave us alone in here. They might have been better off staying put."

"Why would they leave, then?"

"Who knows?" Bodwyn splashed a little more of the clear liquid into each of their glasses. "The dragonkin promised that everyone would be equal now, so maybe they thought they could do better somewhere else. Maybe they were right."

Given what Lamorak had seen of dragonkin and their promises, he had little hope for that.

"Anyway," Bodwyn said. "I came to collect you for dinner. I know you know the way but thought we could share a toast first. We've done that, so let's go eat." He pushed himself to his feet and set his glass and the bottle on the table next to him.

"Not bringing that?" Lamorak asked.

"Nah. You keep it. There's more down there if we want it."

He turned and left the room, only weaving slightly. Lamorak was sure he was walking much more steadily as he followed.

Twelve. Counting himself and Bodwyn. That's how many Honor Guard were still present.

They ate in the main dining hall, where most meals were taken. The last time Lamorak had been there, the tables had been mostly full, with servants bearing platters of meat, vegetables, and bread, as well as flagons of beer and wine and urns of water.

Now, they all sat at one table, after getting their own plates from the meal Keridoc had set out at the far end. When more was wanted, they rose and retrieved it themselves.

"This is it?" Lamorak had been unable to conceal his surprise when he'd been told that no one else would be joining them.

"This is all of us left here," Cadwent told him. "There are others in the city, but we don't see them much. I guess they thought there wasn't much sense being Honor Guard, when there was nothing left to guard."

Lamorak could understand that, actually. Lord Campbell gone, he, himself, only now arrived home, and— most importantly— the Prince was missing. Alive or dead, those who had remained had no idea, and the dragonkin had made it clear that Greenfair, all of Obristan for that matter, was no longer ruled by Prince Calidor, anyway. Now it was overseen by the dragons of the other realms.

"There is, though," he told them. "Something to guard, I mean."

One by one, they put down their forks and turned their attention to him.

Of those left, three of them were senior Guardsmen. The three Bodwyn had mentioned earlier in the training yard. Cadwent, Keridoc, and Bolles. The others were all junior members, with few scars and less experience. It was from these that Lamorak needed to build his army of resistance.

He sighed. Where to start?

At the beginning he supposed.

"Most of the trip to Festival went well," he began. "Until it didn't..."

When he'd finished talking, a heavy silence hung over the dining hall. No one resumed picking at the end of their meals or raised a cup to their lips. Some of them gazed at him— silently judging, Lamorak assumed— while others simply stared down at the table.

"So you left him?" This from Bolles.

Bolles was lean to the point of being thin, but Lamorak knew that not only was he strong, he was fast, as well. Aside from Rainaldus, Bolles might have been the quickest Honor Guard of them all. He was also known for his perpetual frown. If Lamorak had seen the man crack a smile three times, it would have surprised him. For all that, though, Bolles's strongest trait was loyalty, to both the prince and to the Honor Guard and its traditions. He was older than Lamorak but had never voiced a single complaint when he hadn't been chosen as part of the escort to Festival.

"I did," Lamorak answered. "With his express orders."

He'd left out the part he was about to tell them, wanting to tell the story of how he had arrived there alone before he told them all exactly what his mission and— hopefully theirs— was now .

From the look on Bolles's face, he was thinking that he wouldn't have left Calidor alone no matter what he had been told to do.

"He sent me back here," Lamorak went on, "to find you. All of you. And more than that; he wants me to gather the Palace Guard and the City Watch, too."

"Gather them?" Bodwyn asked. "For what purpose?"

"To free Greenfair and then the rest of Obristan." He stopped and chuckled. "With what I've learned of our prince these last few weeks, I would think he means us to go on and take the rest of the world, as well."

Now there was muttering, especially among the younger Guard.

"How are we supposed to do that?" one of them asked. "There are only twelve of us!"

"Twelve of us here, now," Lamorak corrected. "There are others we can locate. Besides, in the towns I've passed through, there were only a few dragonkin. That's all they needed. How many could there be here?"

He caught Bodwyn's sideways glance to Cadwent. Then, his oldest friend cleared his throat.

"Lamorak," he said. "Even if there were 'only three,' as you say, that would still be enough. Dragonkin can't be killed by—"

"They can," Lamorak cut in. "Didn't you hear what I told you? I helped kill one. They're mortal just as we are. So, enough of us with swords, bows, axes, whatever. A little surprise and luck, to say nothing of planning… and we'll have them."

"There are more than a dozen here," Cadwent said quietly.

Lamorak heard him, but it didn't register. Not really. A dozen? More than a dozen? That would be… there just weren't that many…

"Blue, red, and white," Cadwent went on. "No black ones that we've seen."

"There are others," Bolles growled.

"Not this again." Keridoc scowled and shook his head.

Lamorak was still trying to process the news. "A dozen. More. Okay… that just means we need to plan *really* well. And we'll need everyone we can get."

"It won't be enough," Bolles said. "Not unless we have a way to see the others."

"What others?" Lamorak had no idea what the man was talking about.

"The ones you can't see. They're here, too. I've felt them. Almost seen them."

Lamorak could see on the men's faces that they thought Bolles was speaking nonsense. But something in his demeanor, added to the fact that this was Bolles, famous for not having a sense of humor or an imagination made Lamorak take notice.

And… he remembered Yarah telling them about Tophonoss… and not even knowing if she had dragonkin of her own.

"Tell me about them," he said sitting forward. "I want to know everything."

Chapter 43- Lostin, Ascana

Nettie followed Halli into the Waves Crest Inn, expecting to find Dommick with a drink in his hand, laughing loudly, while a dour Viktoria glared at him.

She was totally wrong, but she never would have guessed she was going to see what met her eyes.

Dommick *did* have a drink in hand, but he wasn't laughing loudly. Nor was anyone else in the room, of which— thankfully— there weren't that many. No more than twenty souls sat or stood, each silently staring at Dommick, who was on his feet and—

Singing. Dommick was singing and holding the attention of everyone, including the barkeep.

Nettie scanned the room until she located Viktoria, in a chair at the back corner, facing the doorway. Another man sat at the same table, thin and with a slightly rat-faced appearance, but he didn't appear to be talking to her. Instead, he was watching Dommick along with everyone else.

At first, Nettie felt as if she was about to scream in frustration. After all she'd just gone through to get them off the ship safely and without being seen, this... this... complete and utter idiot... was making himself the center of attention!

Then, she heard the song itself.

Reclium was known as a realm of misery. It was common knowledge that Gillbriss and her brood were cruel and delighted in tormenting the humans who lived there. It was well known that those humans also enjoyed hurting each other, as well. Frankly, nothing good came from Reclium, although ships still went there and brought back some cargo. Mostly things with nefarious purposes of some sort, like poison to eradicate vermin... or people.

So how it was that Dommick not only knew, but could sing, such a beautiful song was beyond her.

His voice was deep and rich, and he sang with a confidence that Nettie never could have matched. The song was one of longing and heartbreak. For someone who had gone away, maybe to find the sun, but more likely to disappear forever into the night. Dommick sang it beautifully— and Nettie felt a tear well up in her eye before she brushed it away angrily.

She wasn't alone. Several people openly sniffled as Dommick's song concluded.

When he finished, it was as if the spell was broken. Silence reigned for a few moments, then was shattered by clapping and cheering that could have come from a much larger crowd. Dommick smiled, bowed, and said loudly, "Thank you, my friends! Thank you for making two refugees feel so welcome!"

Now Nettie *did* feel as if she could strangle him. Refugees! He might as well have shouted to those dragonkin out there that they were there! They were the ones they had been looking for!

She started forward, but the Librarian put a huge hand on her shoulder and gently held her back.

"Steady, there," he said quietly. "Let's see how this plays out."

How it played out was that Dommick had a row of markers built up on the bar from people clamoring to buy him a drink.

"Beautiful," one woman almost sobbed. "I haven't heard that one in so long…"

She grabbed his hand and kissed it, before backing away, almost genuflecting.

It wasn't until she was nearer that Nettie noticed the pale, pale skin and dark, almost black eyes of the woman. She was old enough for her hair to be silver, but Nettie would have bet it had once been jet-black.

She frowned and looked around more closely. Almost everyone in the Waves Crest— and yes, that included the barkeep— had that same pale skin, those dark, dark eyes, and the black hair that said they were from Reclium.

While she was still trying to process that, Halli carefully guided her to the table in the back. The thin man saw them coming, got to his feet, and scurried past, nodding to the Librarian, who nodded back.

Nettie sat where he indicated, staring around the room, unable to believe what it was she was seeing.

"I'll be back," Halli said. "Your friend can't possibly use all those tokens himself."

"Hmmf," Viktoria snorted. "You don't know him."

Halli actually laughed at that and walked across the room, his huge frame moving surprisingly lightly. When he was gone, Nettie turned to Viktoria.

Viktoria gazed back at her, before her lips twitched into what passed for a smile from her.

"Apparently, we're not the first refugees from Reclium to turn up here. There's a sizable population of them in this town. How did you not know that?"

Nettie shook her head. "I've never been here. It wasn't a stop on any of the voyages I'd been on, and— wait! How did you get here? And how did the Librarian know where you were?"

"If you mean that big guy, you'll have to ask him. As for us, we snuck off the ship when Captain Stanford told us to. I… I saw what you were doing. Thank you. For that. And for… well, for all of it. You didn't have to do it."

Nettie found herself strangely touched by Viktoria's words. "It was…" She was going to say it was her pleasure, but that was stretching things to the point of breaking. "I'm glad it worked. All of it."

Viktoria nodded, as if she realized what Nettie had been about to say. "That thin guy who just scurried out. He met us and led us here. He said we were expected, which I didn't like at all. But then he said that *she* had arranged it. I asked him who he meant, intending to stab him if I didn't like the answer."

"Mrs. Cloven?" Nettie said. "She arranged this?"

"And a lot more," Halli growled from nearby.

Nettie jumped. How a man that size moved so quietly was something she wouldn't have believed if it hadn't just happened.

Dommick grinned at his side, but whether that was at Nettie's reaction or simply his normal expression, she couldn't tell.

"Here." Halli pushed a mug of beer across the table to Viktoria, while Dommick handed one to Nettie and then took the chair beside her. "We've got a lot to talk about," the Librarian said.

Viktoria hadn't been lying when she'd told Nettie that she would have stabbed the thin little man who'd just scurried off. She had a knife, short, but sharp, hidden under her shirt in her waistband. It wasn't the long knives that she preferred. Those had been lost back in Reclium, and as much as she missed having them, they weren't worth dying to go back for.

That didn't mean she didn't know how to use the one she had now, though. It was only the man telling her shakily that he'd been instructed to say that "Mrs. Cloven had sent me," that had saved him.

After that, she'd allowed him to lead them there, where they'd found— to their great surprise— people from Reclium. People who understood what it was like to free the night realm and had been more than happy to bustle them deeper inside and act like they had always been there.

Then, Dommick— of course— came up with what he thought of as a brilliant plan to thank everyone for their help.

If his voice had been any less amazing, Viktoria would have punched him in the mouth to shut him up. As it was, however, his song had done more to bring them goodwill than any amount of simply being a fellow refugee ever could have.

Now, this huge man, who she'd seen earlier with the thin one, was back. Along with Nettie in tow.

Viktoria had breathed a huge sigh of relief when she'd seen Nettie enter the Waves Crest. Whatever she had been playing at with those men, it looked like it was going to get her into trouble. The type that any woman alone with a crowd of men would fear the most.

She looked okay, though, and was dressed back in sensible clothes, so whatever had occurred, she'd escaped any harm.

The girl seemed to have a knack for that, she supposed.

"How do you know Mrs. Cloven?" Nettie asked the man, snapping Viktoria from her thoughts.

"Oh, me and her go way back." The Librarian settled his huge arms on the table, playing with his mug of beer between his hands. "We have... let's say, common interests."

"But she told you we were coming here," Nettie pressed. "We were on the ship, so how did word reach *you* before we got here?"

That was a good question and one Viktoria had been wondering herself.

"Birds," Dommick quipped, then burped.

Viktoria glared at him. "Birds? What's that supposed to mean? Are you drunk already?"

"No! At least not much. Well, maybe a bit, but that's only because I used two of those free drinks before our friend here dragged me away and insisted I share them." He grinned and slapped the man on the shoulder. "Oh. Plus the barkeep gave me one himself."

So the answer was yes. Viktoria shook her head. She should have left him in the tower. Why did she ever—?

"He's correct," the large man said. He reached out across the table to Viktoria to shake her hand. "My name is Halli Serksson. Some folks call me the Librarian. Long story."

"Not really," Nettie said. "He likes to read and lets kids borrow his books sometimes."

Halli grinned. "Not so long, then."

Viktoria grunted, suddenly unhappy. She didn't like being kept in the dark, and now, it seemed that, not only did Nettie know more about their tablemate than she did, but Dommick— Dommick!— of all people, knew something she didn't about birds?

"Birds," Dommick repeated happily, continuing from where he'd left off. "You can train them, you know? Strap a message around their leg and send them off to whoever you're trying to communicate with. Easy. My family used them a lot to send orders around Reclium." He drank, then shrugged. "Beyond, too, I would imagine."

"And that's the same way Severina and I communicate at times," Halli agreed. "Although there are other methods. Some slower and more reliable. One—a quite a bit faster, but only used in dire circumstances."

He didn't elaborate on that any further but did go on.

"Severina told me that you were heading this way and hiding from the dragonkin, especially the black ones. When I got her message, I sort of wondered at that, since who in their right mind *wouldn't* hide from a black dragonkin? But also, we're in Ascana. The armpit of the realm, maybe, without much going for it, but Ascana nevertheless. Then, a day later, what shows up in town? Not just one black dragonkin, but two, along with a truly immense blue who, thankfully spends most of its time in the water. Now, Lostin has never been big or important enough for even one full-time dragonkin in residence, and now we suddenly have three? And two of those being Gillbriss's children? Something wasn't right. So I sent out some messages to others I know. Guess what I heard?"

"Those dragonkin are after me?" Viktoria guessed. It wasn't hard, really. Sormat must have had all of them on alert.

"No, actually. No mention of you at all, except in the initial message from Severina. We'll get to that in a moment, by the way. What I learned is that Lostin isn't special. Dragonkin of all four colors are appearing in towns in Ascana, Droy Thus, and Obristan. Reclium, too. So far, it appears that only Usturg has been unaffected."

"That doesn't make any sense, though!" Nettie protested. "Why would Haiteng allow such a thing?"

Halli held up one huge finger. "My question exactly. It's because of what happened at Festival, from what I understand."

Nettie and Viktoria looked at one another. Viktoria wasn't even quite sure what this "Festival" was. And she couldn't imagine how anything that had happened there could cause dragonkin to defy the dragons' edict about staying in their own realms.

Halli looked from one to the other, amusement on his face. "Ah. You've been gone awhile. I almost forgot. Let me grab another of our friend's free beers, and I'll fill you in."

He rose from the table, pinched three of Dommick's tokens between his fingers, and took them to the bar.

Viktoria didn't want another drink. She wanted answers. More than that, she wanted to be out of this bar, where others were watching her and listening to their conversation. Any of them could be working with the dragonkin. Any one of them could leave at any moment and turn them all in.

"Hey," Nettie said quietly. "We're safe. He wouldn't have brought us here if we weren't."

"So... you trust him?" she challenged.

"I do. He knows Mrs. Cloven. Plus, he saved me from…"

Viktoria had almost forgotten that Halli knew Mrs. Cloven. That did say a lot, assuming he wasn't lying. Plus, he'd known they were coming and had helped them get off the dock, then had gone back for Nettie…

She crossed her arms and scowled. "Fine. But if he turns out to be a traitor, I'll gut him."

Nettie raised her eyebrows and glanced over at the immense frame of the Librarian. She picked up her mug and grinned. "Good luck with that," she said, right before she took a drink.

"So," Halli said when he returned to the table. He kept one mug, gave another to Nettie, then pushed the final one to Viktoria.

"Hey," Dommick said. "Where's mine?"

"In your gut already," Halli told him. "I don't mind you drinking your fair share and more, but I need you able to walk out of here on your own. Make that one last."

He took a drink of his own and then began to speak. He told them about what had been occurring, as near as he could tell, in the five realms. Halli seemed to have a great deal of knowledge about what was happening not just beyond Lostin, but outside the borders of Ascana, as well. When he got to the part of magic being used against the dragonkin, Nettie started.

"That was why!" she exclaimed.

Halli stopped and looked at her. As a matter of fact, all three of them were staring at her, Dommick with his almost-empty mug halfway to his mouth.

"Sorry," she said. "It's just... I couldn't figure out why Panyan, the dragonkin who'd rescued me after the raider attack, would do what he did. Why bother saving me if all he was going to do was try to drown me?"

Halli was nodding. "My understanding is that the wizards of Droy Thus, who are responsible for this whole mess, tried a few different things at first. I wasn't sure what they were, but that certainly sounds like something they would have done."

In a strange way, Nettie felt better about the whole episode. It had troubled her that the dragonkin would have tried to kill her in such an odd fashion, rather than the almost countless ways it had of doing so that would have been quicker. She'd thought maybe Panyan had just enjoyed the cruelty of it for some reason, but now she saw that wasn't the case. He'd been compelled to—

Drown himself? Surely not. No human could force a dragonkin to do anything, not even with magic.

"Anyway," Halli went on. "After the red dragonkin was pulled to Festival, everything went crazy. Dragonkin attacking one another, and humans getting caught in the middle. Then, the dragons pulled it together. No more battles between dragonkin, but they're making sure something like that doesn't happen again. And they appear to have let their children indulge in their darker natures. Human life isn't worth a hill of mush. Not if they anger a dragonkin."

With that, Halli stopped to finish his beer. Nettie picked up her own mug and took a long drink.

She was having a hard time processing what she'd just heard. Ascana was supposed to be safe. Yet, whole towns had been destroyed, their populations wiped out. Outlying farms were burned for amusement. Manse itself had huge tracts that were little more than piles of rubble. And it was everywhere. The whole world had become a place where humans were simply... playthings...dispensable.

"I don't understand," Viktoria said. "What does all that have to do with me?"

For a moment, Nettie wanted to berate her. What did it have to do with her? Nothing! Why would it?

Then, she remembered that Viktoria *did* have something that at least one dragonkin wanted. They really *were* after her.

"May I see it?" As if reading Nettie's thoughts, the Librarian held out his huge hand, palm up, toward Viktoria. Viktoria stared at it, then up at his face, then with a scowl, and a quick look around to make sure no one was paying them undue attention, she reached into her shirt and pulled out the book with the black leather-looking cover. She handed it to him silently.

"Hmm." Halli opened it carefully and peered at a page. He grunted, turned to another, then grunted again.

"What does it say?" Viktoria asked him.

"I have no idea," he answered. "But Severina was right, it's written in the language of the Raaleth."

"The Evening Folk?" Nettie asked. "How could that be?"

"They wrote," Hallie laughed. "More and better than we do. It was just a long time ago, so not much is left."

"Then how do you know that's what it is?" she asked.

"Not much doesn't mean none. Besides," his face split in a grin, "I *am* the Librarian, you know."

He handed the book back to Viktoria, who turned it over, studying it again. "Then, it doesn't do anyone any good. Why should I keep it? I could burn it, or throw it in the ocean, or—"

"*I* can't read it," Halli said. "But there are a few who can. I think that's where you need to go."

Nettie was confused. He was sending Viktoria away? She'd thought that once they reached Ascana, they'd all be safe. She had planned on seeing if Dommick— well, both of them, of course— wanted to go inland with her. Maybe see where her parents lived and set up a new life there.

Now, they were supposed to go somewhere else?

"Where?" Viktoria asked, but Nettie could tell by the tone of her voice that she already had an idea.

"Where it all started," Halli said. "We need to get you to Droy Thus."

"Not me," Nettie heard herself say. "I'm going home."

As soon as she'd said it, she felt a twisting in her gut. She would abandon this woman and Dommick? She would just go home and forget about them and the danger they were in? Droy Thus was a long way from where they sat. They didn't know Ascana or how things worked, at all. They could barely even stand to be in the sunlight!

"That's fine," Halli said. "No one is expecting—"

"No," she cut him off. "That was stupid. I'm just... scared, I guess. I'm going, too."

"You don't have to—" Viktoria started to say.

"I said, I'm going, so just shut up about it!" Nettie snapped.

To her surprise, Viktoria did just that.

"Well good!" Dommick said. "You know what they say. Three's a crowd! Wait... does that work? Well, it doesn't matter. Three of us it is. Let's have one for the road, shall we?"

The Librarian clamped a hand on his shoulder before Dommick could rise however. "Four," he said. "At least for a bit. Let's get out of here and back to my house. I have some arrangements to make."

Chapter 44- Arastug

He hated it. He hated, hated, hated being in the outside world. Arastug hadn't even realized how much he'd loved being in Olequan. Even with the shrunken borders and with the relatively few Helgarlug like him remaining. Even with the lack of new experiences, Olequan was wonderful! Olequan was the best place in the whole world!

Olequan was safe, was what he really meant.

But it was going to take a Helgarlug to find who had used a Helgarlug weapon. Not that a Raaleth couldn't. And not that there weren't others of his kind who he could have sent. But a Raaleth would have to stop constantly and openly search for the magic of the weapon. And Arastug wasn't the type to send someone else to do something dangerous that he wouldn't do himself.

So now, there he was. Hiding behind a tree, trying to blend into the bark, while one of Tophonoss's children sniffed around nearby.

It had been a close thing. Falaern had given him an amulet that would alert him by heating up whenever one of the dragonkin— no matter whose they were— was nearby. As long as he wore it against his skin, he'd have plenty of warning. *If* he was paying attention, that was.

He hadn't been, and by the time the warmth he'd felt registered in his mind, it was almost too late.

He could see the dragonkin, which was an ability his people had that the Raaleth did not. There wasn't much that could hide from a Helgarlug when they were actively seeking it. Doors that would remain unseen by anyone else would stand out from their surroundings as if they had been built in plain sight. A treasure was stashed somewhere secret? Not if one of Arastug's people were around. Might as well leave it laying in the middle of the floor.

Still, with all that, the dragonkin was hazy and indistinct. It was small, smaller even than those of Reclium. The one searching the area right now might be very young, he supposed, or it could be that they were just a small variety of dragonkin to begin with. This one was only the size of a horse, but that was the end of the resemblance.

In shape, it was much like the others. Four thick legs which ended in sharp talons. Wings, currently folded back against a long, sinuous body. A wedge-shaped head, with spikes starting between the triangular ears and running down the spine, along the tail, to end in one large sharp prong, standing up at the end.

The color... changed. One moment, it was the brown of a tree trunk, the next the dark green of a bush it'd passed in front of. Occasionally, it took on no color at all, seeming to become transparent.

"Where are you?" The dragonkin's voice, like its appearance, was deceiving. It didn't sound as if it came from the thing's throat. It seemed instead to come from somewhere right next to Arastug. It also changed, like the dragonkin's skin color, in mid-sentence, going from a deeper, male sounding voice, to a higher pitched, more feminine one.

Arastug remained completely still, hoping it would pass him by, but knowing that it probably wouldn't.

He reached down, moving so slowly that someone watching might not even notice the motion. His axe was at his belt.

He hadn't worn the thing in ages, not since they'd moved Olequan. But he hadn't been about to leave the Hidden Realm without it.

"I can feel you," the dragonkin hissed. "I can taste you in the air."

Arastug doubted that, or it would have been on him already.

"Human?" it mused. "You don't taste like human." It lifted its head and sniffed. "Nor smell like one. No...what is it? Something I knew once... long ago."

Which meant it wasn't a young dragonkin. If it truly did recognize the scent of a Helgarlug, it was older than a lot of its kin. And, it was on the right track, which made Arastug very uncomfortable. It also changed how this encounter needed to end. He'd been hoping the thing would just go away, but now...

Now, it needed to die. If it figured out what it was smelling, or tasting, or whatever it was doing, that would be the end of it. It would flee immediately, and not because it would be afraid of Arastug. No, it would flee to tell Tophonoss, and Arastug wasn't nearly far enough from Olequan to allow that to happen.

"Near... you're close," the dragonkin hissed.

In truth, Arastug *was* much closer to it now, but only because the dragonkin had weaved its way that much nearer.

He carefully, silently, pulled his axe from his belt.

It felt good in his hands, he had to admit. When he had put it away, he'd never wanted to touch it again. Never wanted to feel how easily it sliced into flesh, or the sudden, jarring stop when it had hit thick bone. It didn't matter if it was dragonkin flesh and bone he'd been hewing through or not. It all made him feel sick.

Yet now? He had no choice.

"Here," he said quietly, knowing that any sound he made, no matter how low, was enough for it to pick up on.

"There..." The dragonkin let out a long, slow breath, as if enjoying its discovery. Arastug pressed against the tree and listened as it approached. It wasn't trying to be careful. If it had been, it never would have made a sound. Certainly not the cracking of dead twigs and shuffling of fallen leaves.

He tightened his grip on his axe and stepped out of hiding.

"There!" it said again, its voice rising to a high-pitched squeal.

Without a moment's hesitation, it charged at him. The speed almost caught Arastug off-guard, but he remembered. He remembered the battles and how quickly the dragonkin could move. How suddenly the man next to you— a friend of many, many long years, perhaps— could suddenly be gone. How devastatingly fast a home could be smashed to bits, along with everything and everybody in it.

So he was ready. As it neared, he planted his feet and swung his axe, looping it around and overhead, as if he was about to split a log for firewood.

But he was old, and he hadn't done it for far too long. And his hands were slick with sweat, which made the haft slippery.

He could make up all the excuses he wanted. The fact remained that he missed.

He'd aimed for the thing's head, hoping to open it wide with one blow, ending the fight before it ever really began. But, again, the dragonkin was fast. It skidded to a stop and jerked its head back, the blade of the axe narrowly missing as it sank into the forest floor.

"You can see?" it hissed. "What are you that—? Oh. I *remember*!"

Arastug wasn't the only one who could remember the bad old days apparently. The dragonkin shimmered and changed colors rapidly, so much so that it blurred in Arastug's sight.

"Won't she be happy?" it chirped, sounding almost like a bird now. "Won't she be pleased? Won't she—?"

Which was as far as it got before Arastug had charged it. It was about the size of a horse, he had thought, which was a big animal. Bigger than any Helgarlug, Raaleth, Xarlug, or human. But Helgarlug were stronger than they appeared. He bowled into the dragonkin, knocking it back several lurching steps.

When he did, he pried his axe loose from the dirt with one hand, bringing it around just in time to intercept the back foot of the dragonkin as it clawed for his stomach.

The blade, designed and forged by Helgarlug smiths long ago, made for just that purpose, flashed brilliantly as it sheared through the claws.

The dragonkin screamed, a high screech that changed midway to the roar of a jungle predator as it fell back. Blood, as red as any other creatures, dripped smoking to the ground.

But this dragonkin had the same abilities all the others did. It spat, or blew, or breathed, or whatever those of Tophonoss did and a flash of its own light shot from its mouth. The crackling bolt hit Arastug in the chest, knocking him off his feet this time. He felt his hair rise all over his body.

The dragonkin stumbled to the side when it tried to put weight on its wounded foot. It snarled and whined, paying more attention to the damage than it was to Arastug...

... who slowly climbed to his feet. Shaken, but unharmed. In addition to his axe and Falaern's amulet, he had donned another of his old possessions. Armor, though not forged by Helgarlug. Weapons were their specialty. The armor he wore came from elsewhere, gifted to him for services rendered, for friendships formed.

The dragonkin's head snapped back toward him and it snarled.

"Helgarlug!" it spat. "Tophonoss will eat you. Eat your kind. Eat your—"

This time, Arastug's blow was better aimed. It took the creature in the shoulder, shearing through with another brilliant flash. His armor was again put to the test as the dragonkin's tail lashed around, the spike on the end hammering into his side. When he reeled, his axe blade twisted, opening the wound in the dragonkin's shoulder even wider.

The dragonkin went berserk. It rushed Arastug, blood spewing from shoulder and foot, claws lashing out, tail coiling around. It breathed again, more lightning hit him, knocking him back.

Arastug dodged, let his armor take the blows he couldn't avoid, and tried to strike back. In its frenzy, the dragonkin was changing color, shrieking, laughing, trying to fly or jump. It was all he could do to even know where it was coming from. Twice more, he felt the blade hit, saw the bright flash, and felt the flesh part.

Then, the dragonkin was on him. Somehow, it had gotten past his defenses. When it hit, it was with all its weight, plowing into him as he had done to it. As strong as he was, he was no match for its bulk when it was ready for him.

It pushed him back, until his heel hit a root and he tumbled over. The dragonkin went with him, screaming victory as its jaws snapped at his face.

Then, it began to cough. Arastug barely turned his face in time to avoid the blood it suddenly spat out, except for a few stinging drops which hit his cheek.

He closed his eyes and waited for the end, silently apologizing to Falaern for failing in his mission, for revealing where Olequan was.

The dragonkin didn't move.

After a few more moments, Arastug opened his eyes. The dragonkin was lying half on and half off him. Its eyes were open and fixed on his face, but there was no life in them.

His axe was buried in its neck, right where it joined with the thicker body. Blood still pumped sluggishly from the wound. Somehow, even as he'd fallen, he'd managed to land the fatal blow.

With a groan, he struggled out from underneath it, then stood swaying and staring down at it. Finally, he half-heartedly kicked it, then turned away.

He didn't go far. He'd have to bury it or hide it somehow. It wouldn't do for it to be found so near to Olequan. Not with those wounds. It would be a sure sign to Tophonoss that an old foe had emerged from hiding and killed one of her children.

In a minute or two, though. First, he needed to sit and rest. Just for a few.

He retrieved the pack he'd set down when he first saw the dragonkin and got a flask of water, which he drank in one long series of swallows. Then, he sank down against a tree and studied the dragonkin.

In death, it was clearly visible, colored a mottled gray and black, with shades of brown and dark green mixed in. It was ugly. Uglier than anything he'd ever seen.

He sighed heavily. He really missed Olequan.

Chapter 45- Eral Krurmar

For the first several minutes, walking down the steps and into the earth felt just as Akofi would have thought. Dark, damp, and claustrophobic. He had never been afraid of tight spaces or the dark, but then, he'd never been below several tons of earth looming above his head either. If the roof decided this was the time to collapse— as it surely would someday— all the magic in the world wouldn't help them. They'd be crushed like bugs.

Bugs like the ones he was sure were crawling everywhere, even though he couldn't actually see any. Yet, they had to be there. Bugs lived in the dirt, some tunneling very deep. So they must be there... somewhere.

While he walked along and fretted about such things, Bekasi seemed to be perfectly content. He'd never felt her stiffen in sudden fear or show the slightest bit of hesitation.

And Rainaldus? Well, it was ridiculous to even think about that when it came to him. He was in his glory. Akofi could hear him, several steps ahead, talking with Orgoth and getting more excited by the moment.

Shagar, the female Xarlug, walked just in front of them. Once or twice, she'd looked back and smiled, which made her tusks curl inward. That, in turn, made Akofi wonder how the Xarlug did things like eating, drinking, or... kissing? Did they even know about that? Such thoughts occupied his mind for a few seconds, before it swiftly went back to worrying about where he was.

And where they were all headed.

"This is amazing," Bekasi said quietly.

"Huh? What is?" Akofi asked absently.

"Open your eyes! Look around you!"

He could hear the exasperation in her voice, although he wasn't sure what she was referring to. He *did* have his eyes open! He *was* looking around!

He saw the stone walls and the graceful arches that they became overhead. The steps with the inlaid pattern on either side that was only revealed when he looked down several of them at one time...

Wait. The walls weren't stone nor was the ceiling. It was all dirt, with roots sticking out, and—

No. Clearly stone.

When had that happened?

"How did you do all this?" Bekasi asked, addressing Shagar.

"Do all what?" the Xarlug asked.

"This. All of this." Bekasi waved her arms, indicating everything around them. The steps, the patterns, the stones that Akofi just now noticed were set into the walls and glowing to provide light. "Everything here."

"We've been here a long time," Shagar answered. "Long before you humans built your towers. Before the Raaleth even knew we had left."

Akofi frowned. The way she said it was like it should be common knowledge. Yet, not only had he never heard of these... Xarlug, as they called themselves, but he had no idea what she was talking about when she said they had left.

So, in what he knew some found to be an off-putting manner, he blurted, "I don't understand. You left *where*? And why? And how long ago? Were *you* there? Personally?"

Shagar's shoulders shook at her silent laughter. "When you finally decide to speak up, you really go all out, huh? Well, just keep on walking. All your questions— or some of them, anyway— will be answered soon enough."

Which wasn't very satisfactory, but Akofi could tell it was also all the answer he was going to get at the moment. He tried to stifle his curiosity and spend the time actually noticing the things around him. Now that he was walking along a stone lined tunnel, he felt better than he had when it was dirt. It seemed much more permanent.

Besides, from the way Shagar had spoken, this tunnel had been there for… centuries, at least.

His eyes fell on the glowing stones embedded every so often in the walls, first on his right, then on his left, and so on. How they glowed was the mystery, so he reached out with his senses. He suspected some sort of fire-type magic, and he was very curious to see how it worked.

Only, it wasn't fire magic or any other kind. At least not that he could tell. The stones simply glowed.

"What are those?" he asked, unable to help himself. "Why do they glow like that?"

"Because we ask them to," Shagar replied. "Now, time to stay quiet. We're nearing our destination."

Even Rainaldus's voice had gone silent, Akofi realized.

The stairs were coming to an end. Orgoth, Rainaldus, and the four other Xarlug were waiting for them in a large chamber with no easily discernible way forward. Moments later, Akofi, Bekasi, and Shagar joined them.

Orgoth looked over the three humans, smiling at the sheen of sweat on both Akofi's and Bekasi's faces. Heading down or not, it had been many, many steps. Rainaldus, of course, looked as if he could run back up them and do it all again.

"What you are about to see, none but the Xarlug of Eral Krurmar have laid eyes on. Are you prepared?"

Akofi glanced at his companions, quickly realizing that he was the only one who *didn't* appear excited.

"Yes," he said, eager to show them that he was as ready for the unknown as they were. "We're prepared."

"Excellent," Orgoth smiled.

He motioned to one of the warriors who had moved to the end of the chamber. Akofi noticed that the Xarlug was standing next to a rock, with what appeared to be a narrow, deep channel carved into it. The warrior took a heavy metal pole, about three feet long, from where it had been strapped to his back. He pushed one end into the slot, wiggled it around a bit, then pushed it forward, so that it rotated down through the channel, until it made a loud clicking sound.

"A lever?" was all Akofi had time to think, before the room started to move.

With a suddenness that made his stomach lurch, the floor seemed to drop from beneath him. He didn't actually leave the ground, although for a moment, he thought he might have. Nor could he help the involuntary yelp of surprise that escaped his lips. When he heard the same from Bekasi, he didn't feel so bad.

Orgoth, Shagar, and the warriors all seemed to take their rapid descent in stride, as if this was something they did every day. And perhaps they did.

After his initial shock, Akofi began to relax. He couldn't say he enjoyed it— not like Rainaldus appeared to be doing— but he was no longer quite so anxious.

Their plummet slowed, until the walls that had been sliding upward past them opened up on one side to reveal…

A city. An actual city, deep under the ground.

That was the only way Akofi could think to describe what he was seeing.

The ground sloped away from their platform, until it reached what appeared to be a cliff edge. Below that, spread out farther than he could see were buildings which appeared to be carved from solid rock. Light glinted from windows and from tall poles, making it easy to see the hundreds… maybe more… Xarlug who inhabited the place.

For once, even Rainaldus seemed awestruck.

"They tried to kill us all," Orgoth said quietly, almost as if it were part of a ritual. "They drove us from the land. They took the seas away from us. But we survived. We rebuilt. And when the time has come, we'll have our revenge."

"Revenge will be ours," the other four warriors and Shagar intoned.

Then, Orgoth turned to the humans, smiling once more. "It's with those words that we always come home. Welcome to Eral Krurmar, the Last Rest."

The descent to the city was achieved without incident or fanfare. There were no gates to pass through, no walls designed to keep intruders at bay. As a matter of fact, there was no sort of formal boundary at all.

They took a set of stairs that switch-backed down the cliff to the floor of the massive cavern in which the city was located. From the bottom, it was a short walk until they were among the buildings.

Now that they were closer, Akofi thought that the Xarlug city had much in common with the villages of Droy Thus. The buildings were all low, mostly one-story, with the occasional two-story structure dotted among them. Constructed from stone, and in some cases seemingly carved from one solid piece, they were open and airy, with large doors and windows that could be closed with wooden doors or shutters. For a moment Akofi wondered where the wood had come from, since they were deep underground, but then realized that for these Xarlug, ascending to the surface jungle far above was no great hardship.

Which would also account for the fruit he saw on a table, as they passed what appeared to be a tavern.

The city didn't have the stale, close feeling he might have thought would be the case with anything underground. Nor was it cold or clammy. It was a pleasant temperature, maybe just a little cool for his preference, but there seemed to be plenty of airflow moving through the streets. He wondered at that but didn't bother to ask.

He was so busy looking around that he never even noticed when the four warriors who had accompanied them had disappeared. It seemed that one moment they were there, the next it was just him, Bekasi, and Rainaldus, walking in the company of Shagar and Orgoth.

It was then that Akofi noticed that the Xarlug of the city dressed quite differently from their new friends. While they all— including Shagar— wore nothing more than loincloths, the Xarlug of Eral Krurmar wore much more. Full shirts, in many different colors, pants of leather or other softer fabrics. Boots, sandals, and moccasins were worn on feet. The variety of colors and styles was more than he'd ever seen, even during his short time at Festival.

And while he was noticing that, the people of Eral Krurmar were taking equal notice of the newcomers.

As they passed, conversation stilled and heads turned in their direction. Some gaped openly at the sight of outsiders, others frowned, and a few pointed and laughed quietly. Orgoth strode along as if he never even noticed.

Shagar, however, began to fume. Her shoulders hunched, and her eyebrows drew together. She started to mutter, then stopped suddenly and tuned on two men who had been following behind them.

"Do I need to turn you both into tunnel worms?" she exploded, taking a step toward them. "Get gone, before I lose my temper!"

The Xarlug, both of whom seemed fairly young to Akofi, paled at her tirade and scuttled off down a side street.

Shagar turned in a slow circle. "That includes anyone else with something to say! These are our guests! Have you all forgotten what that is!"

Akofi thought they probably had. Unless there was even more going on than he'd ever thought, the Xarlug hadn't had much— if any— contact with those who lived on the surface. Of course the ones who lived here, especially if they never went above ground, would stare at those who looked so differently from themselves.

"Easy, Shagar," Orgoth said. "They're just curious. They mean no harm."

Meaning no harm or not, however, Akofi was glad they were being accompanied by the huge warrior.

"Come on," Orgoth said. "Not too much further, now."

Orgoth's "not too much further," must have meant something different from Akofi's understanding of the words. They walked for several more minutes, then more beyond that.

The city looked much the same everywhere they went, with streets that curved, then ran straight, then curved again. Other lanes crossed the streets, with more, and narrower, passageways connecting those. Orgoth mostly stayed to wider, main roads, but it wasn't long before

Akofi was completely lost. The only way he had to get any sort of bearings was to search for the cliff face they'd come down. He could still see it, but which way would have led to it was beyond him.

Finally, though, they came to their destination.

By far the biggest building they'd seen yet, this one was three stories tall, with a few balconies that opened to the square in front of it. That square was several yards across on each side, as if it had been designed to hold large numbers of people at one time. The buildings along the edges were also larger than most others, with the air of official business about them, although what that might be, Akofi couldn't tell.

"We're here," Orgoth said. "And it's here that my leadership ends."

"What do you mean?" Bekasi asked.

"I'm a simple party leader," the Xarlug said. "I take patrols up top. To gather wood, fruit, meat. And, apparently, the odd stranger who insists on calling for us." He smiled at Rainaldus as he said that. "But that's all. Down here, I'm back to being a soldier. Shagar will take you the rest of the way. You're in good hands." He turned to Rainaldus again and clasped arms with him. "I hope to see you again, child of the Raaleth."

"I hope so, too," Rainaldus told him.

With a wave, Orgoth strode off, leaving them there with Shagar.

She turned to them and said, "Inside now. The Gerent will want to see you."

"Gerent?" Rainaldus considered. "That's not a title I'm familiar with."

"Nor would you be," she said, then shrugged. "But he's ours. For better or ill."

With those cryptic words, she turned her back on them and entered the large building.

Akofi hadn't been sure what to expect when Shagar had told them they were to meet "the Gerent." He did know, however, that what they were greeted with wasn't it.

Shagar had led them inside the building, then up a wide flight of stairs. At the end of a long corridor, they'd come to a set of tall, carved-stone double-doors. Akofi would have liked time to discern what those carvings were of, but he was ushered inside too quickly to really examine them.

Several Xarlug, each dressed more elaborately than the next, milled about the room. Many held glasses in their hands, although hardly any seemed to be actively drinking. The low hum of many muted conversations hung in the air, all of which died down as Shagar stamped through the middle of the crowd with the two humans in tow.

"Gerent!" she called, as she neared what appeared to be an ornate chair placed on a slightly raised dais. There, a male Xarlug sat at his leisure, one long leg over the arm of the chair. Beside him was a female in a tight dress, smiling as she refilled his glass, which was bigger than anyone else's.

He glanced around at her shout.

"What? Who would… oh, it's you. Welcome, Shagar." He didn't sit up, but he did look her over and sigh. "I've told you; you need to dress to come to my throne room."

"Not a throne room," she replied, in the tone of someone who'd said the same thing time and again. "Just the administrative center. You're not a king or even a regent. You're the Gerent."

"Same thing," he sniffed. "At least, it's grown to be." He smirked at her and seemed about to say more, but then he noticed Akofi, Bekasi, and Rainaldus standing behind her. At that, his eyes opened fully, and he slowly swung around until he was facing them.

"What's this?" His voice was little more than a whisper. "Humans? Here in Eral Krurmar? But that's… not allowed."

"No," Shagar agreed. "It isn't. Not normally. But *this* one," she pointed at Akofi, "has power to rival the Raaleth. And *this* one," now at Rainaldus. "Well, he *is* Raaleth."

The Gerent stared at them for a moment, then he threw his head back and laughed loudly. Around them, others did the same, as if they had just been waiting for their cue.

"Oh, Shagar," the Gerent said when he'd finished. "You really do make me smile. It's no wonder I forgive your appalling lack of protocol."

During his outburst, Shagar had just shaken her head and waited for him to finish.

"All right," she said. "I'll show you." She turned to Akofi. "See that fireplace over there? Light a fire in it, from here."

There were actually several fireplaces spaced around the room, all fashioned from dark gray stone. But there was no wood in any of them, almost as if they were only meant to be decorative.

Akofi frowned. "It won't last, there's nothing for it to feed on."

"That doesn't matter. Just pick one and light it up. Not until I say so, though." Then, she turned back to face the chair, but didn't address the Gerent. Instead, she spoke to the woman who stood nearby. "All right, Glasha. You're somewhat competent. Block his magic."

The woman laughed. "You rise above yourself, Shagar. You do not order me to—"

"Do it," the Gerent said. He was staring at Shagar. "I want to see this."

She frowned and sighed, then nodded to Shagar, who turned to Akofi.

"Go ahead. Do it."

Akofi did. The fireplaces were big, so he kindled a large blaze, hot as he could make it, in the closest one. It burst into being suddenly, making those Xarlug who stood nearby scramble out of the way. But it was only there for a moment before it was snuffed out as quickly as it had started.

"Happy?" Glasha asked Shagar.

"Do it again," Shagar told Akofi. Then, more quietly. "Only this time, don't hold back. Use all of the fireplaces if you want to. All at once."

That was a tall order. He did a quick count and there were six, three along each wall. To do that...

No. He was Akofi. Top marks in all Lankari. Strong enough to have blown a hole in the wall of the Border House. And fire was his specialty. He'd handled six fires at once many times in the past. He was just nervous because of where he was.

He closed his eyes, reached out for his magic, felt it, and pulled it to him. He concentrated on it, seeing in his mind what he wanted, then, with a shout he opened his eyes, threw wide his arms, and fire blazed high in all six fireplaces.

But... one of them began to go out. Something that felt like it was sliding between him and his magic started to push in. A second fireplace dimmed, then a third. Akofi pushed back. Whatever was getting in his way, he'd find a way to push through it, or...

Around it. Yes. That was better. He reshaped his magic and let it move around the obstacle, and the fires grew brighter.

It wasn't easy, though. Normally, he could control six fires like that with hardly a thought. Now, he had to keep them going, keep feeding them, and find ways to do it that allowed him to get around whatever force Glasha was using.

Finally, he heard a gasp. The interference went away, and his magic flowed steadily once more.

After a few more moments, he let the fires go out.

"Even better than I'd hoped," Shagar said quietly. "You see, Gerent?" she then said more loudly. "Powerful."

Glasha was slumped against the back of his chair, her chest heaving in and out. She didn't so much look at Akofi or Shagar. Almost absently, the Gerent handed his glass to her, but he kept his focus on them.

"You were right." Then he grinned. "And that one?" He pointed at Rainaldus. "Is he powerful, too?"

"I...well, I guess I don't know." Shagar shrugged. "Orgoth picked right up on his Raaleth blood, though."

"Well, if *Orgoth* says so..." the Gerent laughed. He quieted, then slowly stood. There was something about him that was different, and it took Akofi a moment to realize what it was.

The Gerent was the first Xarlug he'd seen since entering Eral Krurmar, who was armed. A naked sword, appearing as if it was made from stone, hung from a leather loop at his hip. The Gerent moved his hand to it and grinned.

"I think it might be time to find out if Orgoth was right," he said.

Chapter 46- Northern Ascana

The town, Herenstel, was subjugated. Gunnvid would have said they were converted and brought into the fold. The Ascani Knights who had met their charge had been obliterated, cut down to a man. That, and the driving away of the dragonkin, had destroyed any thoughts of resistance that the other inhabitants might have harbored.

Although, Visgar thought to himself, the people seemed more confused than anything else. There were signs that the dragonkin hadn't treated the residents kindly. As he'd led the way through the town, he'd noticed a few corpses that looked as if they had been left to rot where they lay. The only reason for such a thing would be that their loved ones weren't allowed to gather up the remains of those who had been killed.

In addition, several buildings had been destroyed.

So the good people of Herenstel probably saw the Children as saviors when they first appeared. The dragonkin had attacked. One had been killed, the other flew away, and now— surely— life would be better again.

And then, that very same army had destroyed the knights who had been sent out to greet them. It was possible, he supposed, that those knights had been sent to stop them, but in hindsight... if that were the case, why would they have chosen to meet such a large group head-on?

No, he was pretty sure they had been sent to welcome new friends.

But that's not what the Children of Fimbruss were. Not to anyone.

Estrid must have sensed his unease. She'd been sleeping, or at least breathing steadily, with her back to him. Now, she turned toward him and reached out to put one hand on his chest.

"What's wrong?"

He glanced at her with a small smile. "Nothing. Why would there be?"

"Because you keep sighing," she answered. "Sigh. Then you think. Then you sigh again."

She was half-teasing him. But there was also truth to what she said. He *had* been doing that.

"You can tell me," she said, moving closer. "Maybe I can help."

"I doubt it. Not unless you know a lot more about the world than I do."

"Not so much the world, maybe. I know people, though."

He almost scoffed at that. He knew what Estrid used to do for a living, before he'd met her. Now, he supposed she did the same for him, although... he didn't like to think of it that way. Yes, there was comfort in her arms, but he also found that... strange as it seemed to him... he liked talking to her.

And if he took the stigma away from it, what she used to do just might have made her a pretty good judge of character, at that.

"He didn't tell me," he finally said.

"Gunnvid? Didn't tell you what?" She sat up, pulling the cover with her.

"Any of it. He wasn't surprised by the dragonkin. Not the ones who were here and not the white one who came."

"Maybe he got word just before the attack," she tried.

Visgar shook his head. "No. He knew. See, I know *him*. He wasn't at all surprised. He was waiting for it. And, I didn't know about the archers, either. Where did they all come from?"

Estrid frowned. "Well, that could be..." But she wound down before she could come up with anything.

Estrid was nobody's fool. She knew that Visgar was Gunnvid's right hand. The two of them had started the whole thing and were as tight as brothers. There was no reason for him *not* to have told Visgar about *anything*.

"What does that mean, then?" Her voice had grown much quieter.

"I'm not sure," he replied. "It feels like..." He didn't want to say it, because saying it made it real. "Almost like he doesn't trust me anymore."

"No." Estrid laughed, but it was strained. "That can't be. There's no reason for him not to."

But there was. Visgar wasn't going to say it to her, but she, Estrid herself, was very possibly the cause. Gunnvid was no fool, either. He knew that Visgar had always had the appetites of a normal man, even though he, himself, seemed not to. He'd never cared when Visgar found pleasure during his off-hours.

Never before, though, had Visgar *kept* someone. Never had he expressed any sort of desire to leave Gunnvid's side to go to someone else's.

In Gunnvid's eyes, Visgar had become distracted. What was more, he might be sharing secrets with his new love. Secrets that should remain only between them, something like a dragonkin ready to step in and help them when they reached Ascana. And since that information was only for them, Gunnvid had simply kept it to himself.

That all made sense, which, in a way, should have made Visgar feel better. Now that he'd figured it out, he could talk to his friend, make him see that Visgar was still completely loyal to him and his cause.

Yes, he'd...

His blood suddenly ran cold.

He'd nothing. Gunnvid wasn't going to give him a choice. Always a bit on the zealous side, Visgar had to admit that his friend had become a fanatic over the last several months. There was no guile in what he preached. He truly, honestly believed that Fimbruss was a divine being who watched over them all. As such, his loyalties were to Fimbruss and no one else. And if he thought Visgar was a threat to that...

"We need to go," he said, swinging his legs out of the bed.

"Go? Where?"

"Anywhere. Out of here. Right now. Come on. Get dressed. Now."

He grabbed the blanket and tore it from the bed, eliciting a squawk from her. But she did as he insisted. She jumped from the bed, pulled on a simple shift and tugged pants up under that. She had her boots on before he did.

Visgar had to admire her. She hadn't asked anything more than that first startled question. And she hadn't tried to put on one of the frilly, voluminous gowns or high-heeled shoes. She understood his sense of urgency, and she made ready in a manner that befitted that.

"Where are we going?" she repeated, as Visgar buckled on his sword.

"Out of here. We need to leave Herenstel. Gunnvid will—"

He'd taken a room at an inn and paid fairly for it, since he'd seen no reason to provoke further animosity from the townsfolk. There had been the normal sounds associate with such a place filtering up from the first floor.

Now, those noises suddenly changed. In the place of song, laughter, and chatter, came the sounds of harsh language spoken in anger, along with a scream.

Gunnvid's men had arrived already.

Visgar ran to the window and looked out. Two stories below, several men milled in the street, blocking the entrance to the inn. Some were facing the building, waiting for him to be dragged out, while others were facing out, swords in hands, daring anyone to interfere.

There was no getting out that way, even if he had been willing to chance the jump from the window.

The shouts from downstairs were growing louder. Visgar strongly suspected that if the shouter would just shut up, the innkeeper would gladly tell him what room Visgar was in. Why would he not? He owed him nothing.

Downstairs was out of the question, then, just like the window. Even if there were only a couple of Gunnvid's men in the common room, they'd quickly call-in reinforcements. And while he might be beaten unconscious and taken to Gunnvid, he doubted that courtesy would extend to Estrid.

He grabbed her hand and ran from the room, sprinting across the hall. He didn't bother to knock or call out; he just raised a boot and smashed in the door. It flew back into the wall behind, the noise canceled out by a woman's scream and a man's startled curse.

"Sorry, folks," he said, rushing past the bed, where the two lay in a tangled heap. "Carry on."

He glanced out that window first, before swinging it open. There were men down below the back of the building, as well, but not nearly so many. Five, from what he could tell, which was enough. Maybe too many, if he were being honest, but it was better than the odds out front.

"Give me a couple of seconds, then follow," he said to Estrid. "Unless you hear them coming up the stairs, then do your best to get out quickly."

With that, he backed up a few steps, then rushed forward, and— before he could think better of it— jumped out the window feet first.

A brief rush of air, then a jarring stop which sent shock waves up his legs and into his spine. He went down heavily, but— his aim had been good. One of the men had been staring off down an alley, lighting a smoke, and not paying the attention he should have. Visgar had aimed for him and, from the startled squawk, abruptly cut-off, he'd hit what he'd aimed at.

But that left four of them. Visgar rolled with the impact, feeling his teeth clash together, tasting the hot, coppery flow of blood, and knowing his tongue had been between them. He was going to pay for that move later on, but it was better than trying to fight his way out the front.

When he came up, one of the Children was on him already. Visgar scrambled back, but his heel caught the arm of the man he'd jumped onto. Going over backward was the only thing that saved him from the vicious blow that would have disemboweled him. As it was, he used it, rolling again, like a little kid showing their mother a new trick.

He was ready when he gained his feet this time, but his opponent wasn't. He hadn't expected Visgar to recover so quickly. His look of surprise as Visgar's sword slid across his neck was proof of that.

Then, there were three.

Visgar moved forward, feeling his knee threaten to give out. Maybe he'd done more damage than he'd realized.

No time for that now, though.

The three who were left were experienced. They didn't rush at him, as he'd hoped they would. When that happened, they tended to get in one another's way.

"Go get Grimolf," one of them growled at another.

"Get him yourself," that one replied. "I'm not letting you get all the glory."

The third one remained silent, and neither of the others spoke to him, which concerned Visgar a bit. Usually, when that was the case, there was a reason. That one, the silent one, could be one of those who lost all sense of reason in battle. Best to stay quiet and away from one of those.

Not that he was showing any sign of that now. He just stared at Visgar, with eyes that were so pale they could have been made of ice. He wasn't hurrying, he didn't even appear eager. Just… watchful.

Yes. That was the one to worry about.

Not that doing so made the swords the other two carried any less sharp, of course.

"Well, come on then," he said, trying to goad them. "Who wants to make their mother weep first? Assuming you have mothers and not just some four-legged, back-alley—"

The one who'd first spoken came at him, an angry cry ringing out. That answered that, Visgar thought. He was the one to goad, though the other was right behind.

Visgar parried the first blow, avoided the second, then took a cut to the arm as he got his sword around. He hacked both hand and weapon away from the second man, who screamed and fell back, clutching the stump of his arm while blood spurted into the air.

His friend had made the mistake of glancing away at the commotion, and Visgar took advantage of that, too. He lunged, caught the soldier just under the armpit, and pushed as hard as he could. It was enough. The man could hardly make a sound as steel punctured lungs, and he reeled away.

Taking Visgar's sword with him.

As quick as it was, the fight was chaotic enough that he'd lost sight of the third man. On a hunch, he dove forward, feeling the air just above his head part. He spun back, only to find Ice-eyes lunging at him. The man was fast, and good. His thrust was perfect, aimed right for Visgar's chest.

It missed, skinning along Visgar's ribs and opening a gash, but only because something had hit the man in the face. With a clang, a heavy, metal pot of some sort slammed into him. The sudden stench told Visgar what kind of pot it had been, too.

He spun back to the inn, but Estrid wasn't wasting time in celebrating her own good aim. Instead, she was dangling from the arm of the man whose room they had barged into. He lowered her as far as he could, then she let go and fell the last few feet, landing much more gracefully than Visgar had.

The man whose hand he'd cut off was down on his knees, wailing to the heavens. Between that and the noise of the fight, they only had moments. Visgar headed toward the man, but he had stopped his cries when Estrid passed him. She bent slightly, hardly looking, but when she straightened, she had a bloody knife in her hand. The man on his knees took in a deep breath, or at least tried to, then he silently keeled over onto his face.

"Come on," she told him. "We have to move, right?"

Visgar could only nod, stunned at her ingenuity in saving him, as well as her cold callousness in killing the crying man.

Speaking of which, Ice-eyes was beginning to stir. He shook his head, attempting to clear his vision. Visgar put his sword to the man's throat, then— shaking his head at his own foolishness— reversed his grip and slammed the pommel down on top of his head, instead. The pale eyes rolled up into the man's skull, and he fell limply to the side.

"Horse," Visgar rasped.

"This way," Estrid said, although how she was so sure was beyond Visgar.

He started after her but had only gone a few paces when he realized how bad his leg really was. Adrenaline and fear had covered it, but now that the immediate danger had passed, the pain was there. Bad enough he could barely walk.

Then, Estrid was back at his side, throwing his arm over her much smaller shoulders.

"Walk," she said calmly. "That's all we need to do."

They'd barely turned a corner when a shout from the window behind them made them quicken their pace. With every step, Visgar thought he could feel the bones of his knee scraping against each other. The pain was excruciating.

Estrid kept him walking, kept them moving down side-streets and alleys, hid them once when a few of the Children passed by too closely. He didn't know how she did it, but— somehow— she got them to the stables.

He watched, trying not to let the pain get into his head, as she put the blanket and saddle on his horse. Next, she helped him stand and, shaking with the effort, supported him while he awkwardly mounted.

With his weight off his leg, he felt a little relief. Enough that he could reach down and help pull her up behind him.

Then, they were off. Thundering through the streets.

All they needed to do was get out of Herenstel. They couldn't go back to Usturg, though. The bulk of the army had encamped on that side of the town.

So it was deeper into Ascana they'd go.

Where, hopefully, Gunnvid would have a harder time following them.

Chapter 47- Obristan Forest

Vect, it was turning out, was good for more than just muscle. Oh, he was excellent for that, as Calidor had learned over the last couple of days. He was able to chop huge logs into suitable sizes for the cook fire or the fire at night at a remarkable speed. They'd found an axe in an abandoned cabin, and Vect kept it with him like it was a favorite pet.

In those huge hands, the axe looked like a small— yet still formidable— weapon.

Vect, himself, however, had a gentleness to him that made such a thing almost unthinkable.

In the beginning, he seemed in awe of Calidor, although he suspected it was his title, "prince," that was really responsible for the giant's reverence. When Calidor spoke to him, he listened intently, repeated the instructions slowly and carefully back, then proceeded to do *exactly* as he'd been asked. Which made Calidor cautious in how he phrased things.

Of Yarah, Vect seemed both enamored and frightened. He often watched her, but if she turned her gaze toward him, he flushed and looked away. Calidor didn't think he'd found the courage to say two words to the Droy Thus mage so far.

Otto and Oriana though... well, they were a different story.

Otto spoke to Vect like a child, and the huge man responded. He hung on Otto's words, called all the pots and pans by whatever nonsense names the old man had bestowed on them, and could be found nearby and eager to help when he wasn't busy elsewhere.

As for Oriana? For that relationship alone, Calidor would have fought off a dozen of the bandits Vect had arrived with.

Vect seemed to know what Oriana wanted without a word being spoken. The little girl followed him like he followed Otto. At night, she curled up on his lap and fell into a sound sleep, as if all the nightmares she'd witnessed were blown away like so much dust. Vect, too, slept the sleep of the innocent.

"If *they* can heal," Calidor told Yarah, watching them together, "then maybe there's hope for the rest of us."

Yarah looked at him for a moment, and Calidor couldn't tell what she was thinking. Maybe he was being silly. Too… romantic, for lack of a better word. Or just blindly naive.

"Maybe there is," she finally said, but the way she said it made him think there was more behind her words. He just couldn't imagine what it was.

On the third day after depositing the two bandits several miles away, Calidor finally got ready to leave the campsite.

"We'll be fine here," Otto told him. He pointed to where he had carefully hung a pot in a nearby tree. "Shimmer is on watch." He pointed to another tree, adorned with a long metal spoon. "Scoopy is watching that way. If anyone comes, we'll hide."

Calidor would have felt more comfortable leaving Vect or Yarah with them, but he needed them by his side. He just had to hope that the two would be okay until they'd returned.

So, with those misgivings front and center, the three left the campsite and made for the road.

"Do you have any idea where we're going?" Yarah asked him.

Calidor nodded. "Mostly. We're along the Conqueror's Road. That's really all that matters. Obristan is a huge realm. The biggest except for Usturg. For all that, though, we're not as well-populated as Ascana, or even Droy Thus. I think Reclium might have us beat for numbers, too, but who can really tell with them?"

"Thanks for the lesson," Yarah replied dryly. "But it doesn't answer my question."

Calidor laughed, which made Vect chuckle quietly, although Calidor doubted he knew at what.

"Let me finish, if you would. Most of the people live along this road, or one of two others. So, no matter which way we go, we *will* find a town."

"Which the dragonkin know as well," she said.

Calidor nodded in agreement. "Sure. And that's what we're counting on, remember? We're looking for people that need help because of the dragonkin."

Yarah was quiet for a few moments, then, "But you don't know how far any of these towns are."

"No, but I'm not worried. I like to walk. And if you get too tired," he grinned, "Vect here can carry you. Isn't that right, big fellow?"

Vect stared at Calidor wide-eyed, then glanced at Yarah and blushed. He stammered, but Calidor laughed and patted his arm. "Don't worry. She's in good shape. She'll walk."

Yarah muttered something under her breath, but when Calidor asked her to repeat it, she refused.

Calidor laughed again, then quickened the pace.

"It's still standing," Yarah said quietly.

"It is." Calidor watched the village but didn't see any movement. If the dragonkin had come and slaughtered everyone, they had left the buildings intact, which would have been the first time he'd seen such a thing. "Can you tell if there are any dragonkin around?"

Yarah muttered some words and moved her hands, keeping her gestures under control.

They stood just off the side of the road, under the boughs of the trees. Calidor had told Vect to stay back a bit, showing him where to stand behind a wide trunk, but instructing him to peek out every few seconds to make sure everything was okay. It was disconcerting to look back and see the huge man's head appear every four seconds like clockwork, a look of pure concentration mixed with worry plastered all over it.

"There are," Yarah said after a minute. "Two of them from what I can tell."

"And people?" he asked.

"Those, too. Not too many, though. Not enough for all those buildings."

It was what he had feared. Either the dragonkin had killed many of the people or they had been driven away.

"Do we pass it?" Yarah asked. "Try to find another place that's been knocked flat?"

It would be the smart thing to do. Trying to help those right under the noses of the dragonkin was just going to lead to them being killed themselves. Besides, there were others to worry about. Vect, for all his size, wasn't a fighter. Oh, he could do a lot of damage, but it would be accidental.

And Otto and Oriana waited back at the campsite, guarded over by nothing more than cookware.

No. Stupid was stupid. Calidor had started taking in those in need and there was no sense in—

A scream came from town. It built suddenly, then died down into a warble of pain, mixed in with babbled speech, begging for mercy.

Without a second thought, Calidor was running down the road toward the village, unsure of how his sword had even found its way into his hand.

For all his haste, the prince slowed as he reached the town and plunged in among the buildings. There was no doubting which way to go. Screams had split the air twice more while he ran. They came from near the center of the village, where most Obristani towns had squares. Designed as places people could meet, markets could be set up, and entertainment offered, it was really the only place where large numbers could comfortably gather.

Yarah had said there weren't that many humans left in the place. Those that were all seemed to be gathered in the town square.

He reached the edge of the small crowd, who stood with their backs to him. Whatever was going on was happening in front of them, still hidden from his sight.

Calidor forced himself to be calm, even as another cry rang out. This one was weaker, though, as if whoever was voicing it was running out of strength.

He put his sword away but kept it loose in the scabbard, ready to be drawn again at a moment's notice. Then, he began to work his way into the crowd.

After he pushed gently past the first two men, the others stepped aside, without even looking to see who they had made room for. Calidor glanced back to see Yarah, her brows drawn down in concentration. She was clearing his path, while beside her, Vect stood rigidly. His greater height let him see over almost everyone else. Whatever he was looking at, he didn't like it.

When Calidor reached the edge of the crowd, he could see why, although he could hardly believe his own eyes.

He'd been right about the screams dying down, but not about who had made them. It wasn't one person, it was two, both on their knees and trying to hold on to one another.

Neither of them was old. As a matter of fact, they were quite young, maybe Calidor's own age. The woman had long brown hair, while the man's was short and blond. Both wore the simple, sturdy clothing of the working class, although what they actually did was beyond him to tell.

Neither of them was unscathed.

The man shirt was open, his chest a mass of blood. Some of it had come from a large wound that left his skin hanging open, exposing the red meat of muscle and a glint of white bone beneath. More of the blood had come from his mouth. He held one shaking hand up, then leaned forward and spat several teeth onto the street in front of him.

The woman was no better off. One hand had been completely severed. It lay on the street nearby. Her hair had been ripped out of her head in bunches, leaving angry, bloody patches where it once had been. Her clothes were still mostly intact, but the blood that pooled beneath her indicated that she was wounded somewhere beneath it.

"Do I need to ask again?"

Calidor tore his gaze away from the two on the ground and toward the speaker.

He was a measly little fellow, with a sharp mustache and dark eyes. His hair was too long and almost as dark as someone from Reclium.

He wore the fancy clothes he had donned as if they were a uniform of some sort. But more disturbingly, he also wore a lazy smile, as if torturing a man and woman was no more than a day of merriment.

There were two others as well. Good-sized fellows, although not nearly Vect's size, one bore a long-handled hammer, its head stained red, while the other wielded a nasty-looking butcher's knife. That one grinned at the woman, then lifted the blade to his lips and kissed it.

"We didn't…" The man panted, trying to force words out through his shattered mouth. "We did nothing… wrong…we…"

The small man didn't bother listening. He made a quick motion and the one with the hammer stepped forward and swung it, cracking into the man's lower leg as he knelt on the ground.

His scream was almost drowned out by the woman's. But that was quickly cut off when the knife-wielder stuck his blade under her left eye and pushed slightly. Blood flowed in a thin stream down her cheek. He leered at her and made a shushing sound. The woman choked off her cry, while the man continued to writhe on the ground and scream.

Calidor had had enough. More than.

He'd thought to see what was going on and to look for the dragonkin, but he refused to let this atrocity continue.

He stepped into the square, free of the ring of people, and yelled. "Stop this! Immediately!"

The small man's eyebrows rose in surprise. The other two men turned to him.

"Who the hell are you?" the leader asked.

"Prince Calidor," he answered. "Your rightful ruler. Drop those weapons." He spoke over the men to those in the crowd. "Someone get a healer, if there's any left in the village. Bandages, at least. Someone else bring chains for these." He waved his hand at the torturers.

No one moved. Not until the small man and the other two began laughing.

"Oh, the prince, are you?" the small one jeered. "Traveling the land in your golden carriage?" He made a show of looking around.

"Where's your Honor Guard? Not that it matters. Our friends are much more powerful than yours."

His laughter was enough. Not only did he enjoy what he had been doing, he felt confident that no one was going to challenge him.

Calidor did. He strode forward, almost without thinking, drew his sword, and plunged it into the man's chest, aiming dead center, just as Lamorak and Rainaldus had taught him. If he was being honest, he would rather have cut the man up some, made him feel a bit of the pain he'd had inflicted on these others, but there was no time for that.

"Behind you!" The voice came from the far side of the crowd, so it wasn't Yarah or Vect who yelled.

Calidor spun, but the man with the hammer was right there, too close to avoid or get his sword up in time to block the blow.

Only, he didn't have to. The man froze, hammer overhead, quivering, but his eyes were wide with fear.

Calidor dispatched him the same way he had the small man. The hammer-bearer finally moved, but only to slide from Calidor's sword to land bonelessly in the street.

But the third man hadn't rushed toward Calidor or anyone else. He was crouched behind the woman, the knife pressing into her throat.

Calidor noticed for the first time that silence had fallen. The husband was no longer screaming. His throat had been cut, and now the one who had done the deed threatened to do the same to the woman.

"There's no way out of this," Calidor told him. "You're going to die for your crimes. The only question is how. Let her go, drop the knife, and it will be quick. Otherwise…"

"Otherwise, what?" The man's voice was raspy.

"Otherwise," Calidor said. "I'll give you to them."

He nodded to the crowd behind and around the man, who glanced quickly to where Calidor indicated and then swallowed hard.

"How do I know you won't do that anyway?"

"You don't." Calidor began walking toward him. "But you're not going to stall until those dragonkin arrive."

The knife-wielder's face drained of blood. "They'll kill you," he half-whispered. "Just like the rest of—"

That was as far as he got before he froze like the hammer bearer. Calidor glanced over at Yarah.

"Go on," she said. "He doesn't deserve to live."

"No," he agreed. "I suppose he doesn't."

He reached the two, bent to remove the knife from the man's hand and the woman's throat, then gently took her hand and helped her to her feet. He led her to the crowd and gave her into the keeping of an older woman who was weeping with equal parts relief and grief.

Then he turned back to the still-frozen man.

From overhead, came the roar of a dragonkin.

Calidor scrambled backward, just as what seemed to be a piece of the night itself landed in front of him. The black dragonkin came down on top of the knife-wielder, its claws digging into him. He didn't even have time to squeal before he was crushed underfoot.

The dragonkin hissed laughter, its bright yellow eyes locked on Calidor.

"We've been looking for you, *Prince* Calidor," it said.

Calidor thought to lie, to say that he had no idea who the dragonkin was talking about. Then, he looked past the beast in front of him. He saw the hope, however faint, on some of the faces surrounding them. More wore expressions of defeat, however, believing that there was nothing that could be done, no way for them to escape what Obristan had become.

If he was being honest with himself, Calidor didn't see a way out, either. He was no match for a competent swordsman, not even in the same league as Lamorak. There was no way he could defeat a dragonkin, let alone two... wherever the second one was.

"You've found me," he said, and was strangely proud that his voice remained steady. "What do you want?"

"Me? Be glad I can't have what *I* want. Otherwise, I'd open you from top to bottom and watch you run around trailing your guts behind. But Gillbriss has sent word. *She* wants you."

"Gillbriss has no place in Obristan," Calidor replied. "Nor do you. Go on your way. Before it's too late."

Pure bravado. And an attempt to buy time, to try to think of...
something.

Because the mention of Gillbriss had made his blood run even
colder than the appearance of the dragonkin had. Gillbriss's cruelty
was legendary. If he found himself in front of her, there would be no
coming back from it.

The dragonkin knew very well that his threats were empty. It
laughed again, a hissing, sibilant stutter. Then, it drew its head back,
preparing to spit.

Acid. The black dragonkin spit acid. It had said that it couldn't kill
Calidor, but that didn't mean it couldn't hurt him.

But when it tried to do as much, it couldn't. It made a strange,
coughing sound, and jerked, as if it was fighting something.

Yarah emerged from the crowd behind it, her hands clenched
tightly at her side. Vect was right there with her, his axe looking
ridiculously small in his enormous fist.

"Do it!" Yarah growled through clenched teeth.

It was the hardest movement Calidor had ever made in his life.
He might as well have been frozen solid in a block of ice or stood
neck-deep in a pit full of mud. The air itself seemed to hold him back,
but he went anyway.

He reached the dragonkin in two steps and then lunged. His
sword sunk between the scales at the base of the neck. When the
blood spurted out, it covered his hand. Immediately, he heard a hiss,
and his skin began to burn as if he'd stuck it into a fire.

But the strike wasn't enough. The sword wasn't long enough to
reach anything truly vital.

"Stupid," he berated himself. "Rainaldus would have moved to
the side, to a shorter path to the heart. He would have avoided the
blood..."

The dragonkin moved, breaking Yarah's hold. It screamed pain
and fury at the sky, then lashed toward Calidor. It tried with an open
mouth, but the prince moved quickly, taking only a glancing blow,
which was still enough to spin him around and send him crashing to
the ground.

"At least I got one hit in," he thought, tensed as he waited for the claws, the teeth, or the acid to take him.

Instead, he heard what sounded like a startled yelp. Calidor took advantage of the moment and rolled, coming to his feet as he did.

Vect had chopped into the dragonkin's tail with his axe. It wasn't a war weapon; it was a woodcutter's tool. But it was sharp, and Vect was immensely strong. Even as Calidor watched, the huge man swung again and again. By the fourth blow, he'd severed the dragonkin's stinger completely.

The dragonkin reeled around, screeching, and drew back to spit again.

When a rock hit it in the eye.

It spun that way, only to have a young man rush forward on the other side, a knife, no bigger than the one used by the torturer, in his hand. It was a puny weapon, but enough to open a shallow gash in the dragonkin's side.

Vect hit it again, this time in the joint where its wing met its body.

No matter which way the dragonkin whirled, it was met with some sort of attack from the opposite side. It tried to fly, but the blow Vect had dealt it made its one wing useless. Instead of lifting off, it stumbled, and Calidor rushed forward. His sword was gone, so he picked up the hammer the other man had used. Without thinking, he jumped and drove it as hard as he could into the dragonkin's eye.

The scream was terrible, but a dragonkin was still a dragonkin.

A woman leapt forward, only to be met with claws the size of knives. They opened her the way the dragonkin had threatened to open Calidor. Another man was bitten nearly in half, while yet another was crushed. The dragonkin finally spit, and two people died screaming as their flesh seemed to melt off their bones.

But no one ran. No one gave up. And as much as they all hurt it, no one did as much damage as Vect. He hit the dragonkin again and again, always seeming to know just where to attack. It moved slower, then even slower still, as Yarah recovered enough to hinder it.

Finally, it collapsed, with one last wavering scream of hatred.

The dragonkin was dead. Calidor was panting, while around him others laughed, cried, shouted, or simply stared in disbelief. In all, seven of the villagers lay dead. Yarah looked exhausted, and Vect seemed about ready to burst into tears.

There was another, though. Yarah had said there were two dragonkin in the village.

"Look!" a boy shouted.

Calidor barely registered the yell. His hand was bright red and throbbing with pain. He thought he might pass out from that and exhaustion.

But it did sink in, and he turned to where the boy was pointing. There was another dragonkin. Larger than the black, it was hard to tell what color it was. It had wings, so not a blue, but whether it was white or red, Calidor couldn't have said. Not silhouetted against the bright sky like it was.

Not that it mattered. What did was that it was flying away. Whether it didn't care to fight the villagers or was scared or had just become bored, he would never know. Calidor was just glad that it was going.

Then, he looked around again. They couldn't stay there. Even if the dragonkin who'd left didn't care, others would. They'd come for revenge.

He'd set out to find a few people that he could help, that he could bring to safety.

Now, it seemed that he had nearly a whole village to do that for.

Chapter 48- Orluduna, Droy Thus

The True Tower. Every time he saw it, every time he returned home, it took Sintifi's breath away.

It wasn't so much how it looked, although that was impressive. It seemed to be carved of one piece of dark stone, with no joints or fittings that could be seen anywhere. If that was truly the case, it was surely the largest stone to ever have been carved. The tower rose high, like the human-built ones, but was somehow more graceful. And it was sturdier, he was sure.

A dragonkin wouldn't be able to knock this tower down, not even a piece of it.

One of the five true dragons, though? Sintifi was pretty sure that nothing made by man or Raaleth could withstand one of them.

Which is why it stayed hidden. Why they had never revealed its existence outside of the relatively few mages who knew about it. Word could not reach the dragons— any of them, not even Chimbod— of its existence.

He paused and soaked it in. Again, not so much the looks of the thing, or its remarkable construction, but the way it made him feel.

When he was there, he felt a strange mixture of awe, pride, and hope. Awe at the might of those who'd come before, who'd had the power to create something like this. Pride because *they* were using it, finding more secrets of the builders and the dragons themselves every day. And hope, because— especially now— there was nowhere in the world that represented resistance to the dragons the way this tower did.

"Well," Ilvisar said. "It is Raaleth. Well done."

He dropped his eyes and followed Oponsi, who was walking toward the entrance without so much as glancing up.

Sintifi frowned. He would have expected more from Ilvisar. What, exactly, he wasn't sure, but certainly more than a casual, "well done."

"That's it?" he said, catching up to the Raaleth. "Well done?"

Ilvisar glanced at him with a grin. "What else would you have me say? Someone stumbled upon an empty tower and started to live in it."

"No! I mean… yes, I guess that's kind of what happened, but there's been more since then. A lot more!"

Ilvisar nodded. "There has. Like children playing with fire, you started a blaze you can't put out. Forgive me if I'm not enamored by the fact that one of your kind found this place. Had they not, maybe none of what's happening right now would be."

Sintifi frowned even harder. "Fine. Maybe we weren't as careful as we should have been. I suppose we could have just fled. Maybe hidden ourselves away somewhere and let the world go on without us."

His words weren't lost on Ilvisar. The Raaleth stopped walking and looked up again. When he lowered his gaze back to Sintifi, he was no longer smiling.

"Your point is well taken, Sintifi. Forgive me. In truth, I'm bothered by this tower. Not that it still stands, but that it has been revealing secrets to your kind. And more than that, I am bothered by the thought that you— humans— have learned to use magic that once belonged solely to the Raaleth. Not even the dragonkin ever managed that."

"They don't need to," Sintifi shrugged. "They have their own."

"As do you," Ilvisar reminded him. "Yet… here we are."

"We're not as complacent as the dragonkin," Sintifi replied. "The oppressed never are as satisfied as those doing the oppressing."

"Well spoken!" Ilvisar cried. "Remember that when you meet Falaern and the others. Perhaps they will agree with you. For what it's worth… I do."

"Are you coming or not?" Oponsi was already at the door, glaring back at the two of them.

Sintifi and Ilvisar walked toward her, but she refused to go in until they'd reached her. Then, she put out one bony finger and poked the tall Raaleth in the chest.

"Let's get one thing straight. This tower is mine. I am the master of it. Is that understood?"

"Understood," Ilvisar said easily. "I have no designs on it. Although, if my people truly choose to leave Olequan, others may have different feelings."

"Well, disabuse them of those when you go home," she said. "We didn't build it, but it was abandoned when we found it. We didn't steal it from anyone. If something is cast off, it's the right of whoever comes behind to take it."

Her jaw was firmly set, as if she expected an argument.

Instead, Ilvisar laughed. "This is a day for well-spoken and passionate speeches! Oponsi, Sintifi, my friend, I have no desire to take your home from you or to see it destroyed by the dragons. For me, this place is like a ruin. A chance to see the former glory of my people. I wish to look upon it, before returning home. Understand, Olequan still exists, but it is diminished. There is nothing like this in the realm, although at one time…"

"Understood," Oponsi said. Sintifi couldn't be totally sure, but her voice might have grown softer.

She nodded, then turned to the door and spoke quietly. Sintifi didn't need to hear her, since he knew the words of opening, too. He wondered if Ilvisar did. Now that it had come to it, he realized he never asked if the magic to enter was something Oponsi or her predecessor had come up with, or if it was some simple Raaleth spell they'd learned from within the tower itself.

Regardless, the door swung soundlessly open. Inside, it seemed completely dark, until they crossed the threshold.

The chamber they were now in glittered like a million stars. From the outside, the stone of the tower was dark, almost black, and featureless. In here, it was still black, but flecked with gold, silver, white, and yellow. There was no apparent light source, yet the chamber was lit enough to set those flecks sparkling.

Ilvisar took a deep breath and turned in a slow circle.

"Remarkable," he whispered. "I can feel them. Those who came before. Those who did this."

The Raaleth closed his eyes and stood still for a moment. When he opened them, he seemed much more solemn than he had outside.

"This way," Oponsi said, but her voice, also, had grown quieter.

Sintifi didn't say a word. Ilvisar's reaction had surprised him. Ever since they'd met, the Raaleth had displayed a slightly arrogant manner. Like he knew he was better than any human. Now, he seemed cowed by the very first chamber they'd come to.

"Most of the tower is empty," Oponsi said. "Or at least it was when we'd found it. Since then, we've moved in, so to speak. Some chambers— we don't know what they were originally used for— we took for bed chambers. Others for study rooms and even a kitchen and dining area. There aren't many of us here. Only about twenty know this place even exists. And most of them aren't here at any given time."

As she spoke, she made her way to a spiral staircase near the far wall. It wound up through the ceiling of the room and beyond. Sintifi knew what was up there and wasn't looking forward to the walk.

He didn't know how it was Oponsi did it at her advanced age. Tough or not, climbing stairs was hard enough when one was young…

She stepped on the bottom tread and spoke shortly. The stair began to turn, appearing to come out of the floor as it rotated, carrying her upward. Ilvisar laughed softly and stepped aboard, followed by a still-gaping Sintifi. This was, he realized, the first time he'd ever entered the tower with Oponsi.

All this time, he'd trudged up every one of those stairs, when there was a better, easier way…

He opened his mouth to say something, but Oponsi's voice floated down to him, cutting him off.

"The library," she said, mostly to Ilvisar. "The only room that had seemed untouched when we got here."

Ilvisar knew that Sintifi was disappointed in his reaction to seeing what they referred to as the "True Tower." In truth, he'd been shielding his emotions for quite some time now, almost since meeting Sintifi.

When Arastug had selected him to leave Olequan and seek out the humans who had used Raaleth magic, Ilvisar had been well-aware of why *he'd* been the one chosen to go. He was strong, fast, and smart. He was a match one-on-one for any dragonkin, no matter whose it may be. And he was intelligent enough to avoid detection when he needed to.

But he had never expected to find what he had. For one, Arastug had been right. Humans were quite simply everywhere. There were far more of them than there had ever been Raaleth, Xarlug, and Helgarlug combined. They had spread to every corner of the five realms, in vast numbers.

That was worrisome enough, since Ilvisar suspected that the ultimate goal of sending him was to see if the world was ready for them to reappear. If it was, the Raaleth and Helgarlug would emerge from Olequan and take their rightful places in the world again. Only… would there be room for them?

More than that, though, it was *what* the humans were doing… without even realizing it, as far as Ilvisar could tell.

The humans had used Raaleth magic. They'd known that ever since the effects of that spell had been felt in Olequan itself. But what they hadn't realized, and the humans didn't seem to either, was that they were now using magic that was all their *own*.

Long ago, before Ilvisar was even born or the dragons had risen, the Raaleth had magic. The Helgarlug had their own, and so, too, did the Xarlug. All those were similar, yet with their differences. Then, there were the dragons, with yet another kind of magic.

Raaleth couldn't use dragon magic, just as dragon could not use Xarlug, and so on. They were all separate.

Then, the dragons rose and took their places atop their kin, demoting the others to mere dragonkin. The magic of those lesser dragons didn't diminish. It was still powerful enough, just not nearly as much as that of their new overlords.

And humans? They had been around for the last few centuries before the dragons rose. But they had been primitive and brutish. Warlike, they probably would have wiped themselves out, had it not been for the dragons. They'd taught the humans, introduced civilization to them, and watched them grow, each in their own realm and in their own manner.

For one dragon, Chimbod, that hadn't been quite enough. She'd had her children teach the humans magic. How she knew they'd be able to use it, when none of the other races had been able to, was something Falaern could never figure out. But use it they had, until they had taken to it as easily as any dragonkin ever did. Soon enough, at least in the eyes of the Raaleth, the humans in the realm called Droy Thus were more often able to use dragonkin magic than not.

Chimbod wasn't stupid, though. She'd controlled what they were taught and what was kept from them. Her children were always stronger, the humans never really a threat.

Then, they had somehow stumbled onto an abandoned Raaleth tower, one overlooked by the dragons when they'd destroyed every other vestige of their foe. From there, they had learned a Raaleth spell and used it.

Only... it wasn't just *that* spell. Since coming to Orluduna, Ilvisar had seen evidence of more Raaleth magic, even in the magic portal in the tower in which he'd met Oponsi. They didn't even know that they had done it.

The humans had taken dragonkin magic and merged it with Raaleth, changing both in the process to become something...more.

They had no idea what they had done or how truly powerful it could make them.

And Ilvisar had no intention of telling them.

Not that it mattered. Not when he saw what was before him now. Oponsi had said that most of those who knew of this "True Tower" were not present. But four of them were. They were all here, in this vast room that was clearly too big to fit inside the confines of the tower he'd seen from outside. All bent over a tome on a table in front of them, laboriously figuring out what it said.

Ilvisar could have told them. It would probably be demanded of him, not that he would obey.

All the books, every single one he could see, were written by Raaleth. From where he stood just off the moving stairs, he could see titles that indicated histories, fables and stories, sciences, and most of all… magic. Books of spells and conjurations. So many books must contain magic that even he didn't know about. Perhaps no one but Falaern herself did, now.

The humans would learn it, though. Given enough time, they'd learn it all.

Suddenly, Ilvisar felt a chill in his bones and a very great need to return to Olequan. But he couldn't do it while allowing this to continue.

The library had always been Sintifi's favorite room in the True Tower, as he was sure it was for Oponsi and most of the other mages who called it home. It was here that he'd deciphered the spell that could draw a dragonkin. It had been gone over by Oponsi and others, until they were sure it could be done. And since he was the one who had found it, he was the one who'd had the "honor" of casting it.

It had exhausted him, and— worse— set off a battle between the dragonkin that had resulted in the mess the world was in right now.

On one hand, he felt guilty about that. On the other… not as much. The world needed to change, and it wasn't going to unless it was dragged into it, kicking and screaming.

So it was with mixed emotions that he edged past Ilvisar and studied the room himself. Nothing much had changed, other than the faces of those studying intently. Sintifi wasn't even sure he knew the names of these mages. They all came and went so frequently that there wasn't much time to make friends.

He turned back to Ilvisar with a broad smile, ready to share the wonders of the library with the Raaleth, but the look on Ilvisar's face stopped him.

Far from wonder, distress was etched all over the Raaleth. Sintifi had suspected that Ilvisar had downplayed his reaction to seeing the tower, but that was based on how he— a human— would feel, so he wasn't really sure.

Now though, he couldn't understand why the golden-skinned man was reacting as he was.

"What's wrong?" Sintifi asked him, with a nervous laugh. "You look like you've seen a ghost. Assuming your kind have those, of course."

He'd meant it as a joke, to try to break Ilvisar out of whatever fugue he'd fallen into. But the Raaleth paid no attention to him. Instead, he spun to Oponsi.

"You must leave. Now. Immediately. This library will be sealed until Falaern herself decrees it can be opened."

Sintifi drew back, but Oponsi merely studied the Raaleth calmly.

"I knew it," she finally said. "You just couldn't help yourself, could you? It was all right when it was just a stack of stones and some empty rooms. But now that you see something of real value, you want it for yourself. Well, I'm sorry, Mr. Raaleth, but it's not going to work that way."

Her voice was calm, but Sintifi could hear the anger boiling just beneath the surface. He'd been on the receiving end of Oponsi's displeasure before. He had no desire to be anywhere near the brunt of her anger now.

"I am sorry," Ilvisar said, although he sounded anything but. "But I must be firm on this. These books are not for you. Not yet. Now. I insist that all vacate this room."

Oponsi scoffed. "No. My mind is firm on this, too."

She was building her power. Sintifi could feel it. He didn't know if Ilvisar could, but it was there, coming off Oponsi like almost visible waves of force. She wasn't a fool. Ilvisar was a Raaleth. His magic was greater than hers, so she needed to—

When she let loose, it was like a tree had fallen on Sintifi. He staggered to the side, sure that his nose had just spurted blood all down the front of his robes. He didn't even know what spell that was, or how she had done it without speaking or gesturing. Some ability she'd been honing, he supposed.

The spell was meant to incapacitate. If he'd been the target, Sintifi would have been flat on the floor, unable to move from the weight of it.

Ilvisar, who was the intended target, was faring better.

He lurched when Oponsi hit him with her magic, but he did not fall. Instead, he put one hand up next to his face, crossed the other in front of him, and spoke in that liquid language he'd first spoken with Sintifi.

The force on him lessened. Sintifi could almost see as it began to double back, folding over so that it was twice as thick, to descend upon Oponsi.

With a curse, she snarled a few syllables and the force winked out of existence.

She might have tried to conjure up something else, but Ilvisar was too fast. He threw out the hand that had been crossed in front of his body, and Oponsi folded as if she'd been struck in the stomach. Ilvisar twitched, and Oponsi's head snapped back, her teeth smashing together with an audible click. She collapsed in a heap.

All of which had happened in only a few seconds. The other mages were just starting to gain their feet when Ilvisar turned to them. He chanted quickly, moved his hands in a sweeping gesture in front of him, and all four fell just as Oponsi had, although with less violence.

Which only left Sintifi.

Ilvisar turned to him.

He was strong. Almost as strong as Oponsi, he'd always believed. Although after seeing what he just had, he was no longer so sure.

"Ilvisar," he tried. "This isn't right. We can—"

"No, my friend. We can't." To his credit, Ilvisar did sound sad. And his eyes were kind as he said something.

Just like that, Sintifi couldn't move. Well, he could, but so slowly and with so much effort that it made it seem silly to even try. The same with thinking, really. What had just happened? It was there...

somewhere... in his mind, but it felt like really hard work to try to find it. And there were better things to do.

Like walk down the stairs behind Ilvisar. Were they walking? Maybe the stairs were moving? He wasn't sure.

When he realized he was outside, he thought how nice the evening was. There was someone with him, saying something that he didn't understand, and then a very bright light.

The person told him to follow and stepped into that light. How did he do that?

Sintifi didn't really have time to worry about it. He took a step forward, just as he'd been told, and the light swallowed him up.

Chapter 49- Craydon, Ascana

"Where *are* they?"

Kori turned away from the window he'd been peering out of. The light was beginning to fade and there was still no sign of Elsdon and his men returning from working in the fields. He was sure that something had happened to them. The black dragonkin had found out that they were plotting against it. Or their "friend," the blue— whatever its name was— had decided that siding with its own kind was better than being in league with humans. Or—

"Stop," Toni said. "Just come away from the window and relax. They'll be back soon."

"Too tired to do what we'd planned tonight, too," Kori muttered.

"They'll sleep for a few hours, then," she countered calmly. "We weren't going after the black until early in the morning anyway."

Which was what *really* had Kori on edge. When he'd been lying in the field, watching the dragonkin circle, knowing that it was hunting them, it was easy to get hyped-up. He'd been scared. More than he could ever remember being, even when he'd been playing dead while a snow-troll had eaten Slode and his men only feet away. Kori didn't like being afraid, which made him angry. So... fear into anger. Easy.

But this! This interminable waiting. With nothing to do but pace the floor and stare at the walls. Toni had tried to get him interested in other things, but he was just too distracted. Which was something else that was eating at him; what kind of man turned down an invitation like that?

He plopped down, then jumped back up again almost immediately. He strode to the window and glanced out.

Movement!

He peered harder, but it was only some kid, hurrying past and hunched over something that he was carrying. It looked like a loaf of bread, but the way the kid was holding it made it seem like it was the most precious treasure in the world. With the state of things in Craydon, maybe it was. Maybe he had a mother and a little sister at home, and he had been out risking his life to get even that much. Maybe even now that sister was sick in bed, with sweat making her hair damp and her lips all cracked and—

He sighed heavily and closed his eyes. What was he doing? It wasn't bad enough that he was waiting to instigate a fight with a dragonkin, now he was inventing sob stories just to keep his mind occupied.

He returned to the chair and sat.

"About time," Toni said to him. "Just try to stay put. You're driving me crazy."

"How can you be so calm?" he asked her.

"Maybe because I'm not the one with the magic axe? My role is pretty much to stay hidden, in case one of you needs to be pulled away."

Kori could hear the bitterness in her voice. She viewed her role in the whole thing as "less than."

"You know that's important," he said. "If Elsdon and the others know that anyone who gets hurt will have help to reach safety, it saves a lot of worry."

"I know." Toni's voice was still hard, but then she stopped and took a breath. "I know," she said again more softly. "It doesn't mean I have to like it, though." She held up a hand to stop anything else he might have been about to say. "Your life was fighting, I get it. And these Ascani Knights trained hard for it. My role was serving alcohol to those who mostly didn't need it. It didn't exactly prepare me to battle a dragonkin."

Kori really had no answer for that. The thing was, she was right. Everyone's lives took different paths. To him, spending his drawing ale and pouring wine instead didn't sound so bad.

But he'd never really had that choice. Even the barkeeps in Usturg kept weapons close at hand. Business didn't matter. Being brave, being a fighter, did. In Ascana, Haiteng had made it all about business. The more successful the business, the better for the whole realm.

Fimbruss had taken a different tack. Fight, be brave, be tough. When the time comes, you'll be needed.

It had escaped most that "the time" never came. For generations, those of Usturg had raided each other's villages, engaged in vicious duels to the death, and competed in limb-breaking games when times were relatively peaceful. But the call to arms for the good of the realm had never come.

He supposed it might have by now. And he wondered how many that he had known were on the march, coming down into Ascana from the north or into Reclium from the west.

Or not. He hadn't been home in weeks now. Well before all the troubles. Maybe Usturg was just staying out of it all, and Fimbruss was still encouraging his countrymen to fight each other. Who knew?

He was still stewing when the door finally opened, and Elsdon and his men— dirty and tired— lumbered into the house.

Toni had a hot drink ready for them all, as well as a hearty, if meager, meal already prepared.

"This is nice," Elsdon said, taking a cup and bowl from her. "Thank you!"

She shrugged. "We had all day to do nothing. I thought it was the least I could do. But... I used a lot of the food that was here. I'll have to get more tomorrow."

Elsdon smiled and moved off to take a seat at the table. "Don't worry about tomorrow. We'll have to see how tonight goes first."

Kori didn't join the meal. He greeted the men but stayed put in his chair. It wouldn't do to get up and start pacing again. Not when they had been the ones out laboring in the fields all day.

One by one the men finished and stumbled off to the two rooms they used to bunk down in. There were eight of them, in addition to Elsdon. Kori made an even ten. But he wasn't sure if even that amount was going to be enough against a dragonkin.

Finally, Elsdon finished. "Soon," he said to Kori. "Get some sleep yourself, if you can. Axe or not, this isn't going to be easy."

With that, he made his way to the room he'd taken as his own. Minutes later, the house was silent except for the rumbles of exhausted snores from the sleeping rooms.

Kori got up, went to the window, and peered out again. Just a few more hours, he thought.

The streets of Craydon were deserted, as Kori would have expected for that time of night. He had to give Elsdon and his men credit, though. They'd only slept for a few hours, yet he never would have known to watch them, now.

They moved in a disciplined fashion, always with men keeping an eye out overhead, while others roamed ahead and to the sides. And they were quiet. There was no unnecessary talking, no clanking of weapons.

"We'll be there in a minute," Elsdon told him, keeping his voice low.

"How does this friend of yours know to be there?" Kori asked him.

"We got a message to her during the day. We have ways, so don't worry about that. And Lijing is good. She'll have found a way to get Margam to be elsewhere."

"Margam?" Antonia asked. "Who's that?"

"The black one. Brother to the one you guys killed. He's been in a rage ever since, as you can imagine. Lijing has been the only thing stopping him from destroying the entire town, but she's not sure how much longer that will last. If Margam starts thinking clearly, he'll fly off, probably back to Gillbriss. Then it won't matter. Craydon will be done for."

Kori grimaced. He'd done what he'd felt he needed to back in the Inland Trader. If he hadn't, Toni would certainly be dead, and he probably would have been, too. But he'd never meant to put the whole village at risk. How could he have when he'd never expected to be able to kill the thing?

"So, we need to kill this Margam," he said.

Elsdon nodded. "Wasn't ever really the plan before this. But then again, we didn't even know a dragonkin *could* be killed."

"They've been ruling with fear forever," Toni said. "Even here in Ascana. They weren't exactly cruel, not like in Reclium, but no one ever thought to question Haiteng or his children. Doing so would have been suicidal."

"Right," Elsdon agreed. "But we should have listened to the old stories. If the Evening Folk could do it, even if they were more powerful than us, then why couldn't we?"

"They had better weapons, apparently," Kori said.

"That's one thing," Elsdon agreed. "But I think it's more. I think they weren't as afraid as we've been. But enough for now, we're here."

"Here" turned out to be an intersection of three streets. They came together in such a manner that the roads widened at that point, a natural place to find a well, and indeed, there was one there. At one time, this would have been a gathering place for those who lived in the area. Somewhere that greetings would have been given, gossip spread, and acquaintances made. Since the dragonkin came, though, it would have been left empty, since no one wanted to gather in groups unless they had to.

"She's here," one of Elsdon's men said, nodding toward the sky.

Kori looked up just in time to see something huge descending. Without wings, the dragonkin flew in a sinuous path, its great body winding from side to side. But it landed in the street without a sound and even somehow avoided destroying the small roof over the well.

"Elsdon," Lijing said in a light, musical voice.

"Lijing," Elsdon replied as easily. "Thanks for coming."

"I didn't have much choice," the dragonkin answered. "Your message said it was urgent."

"And it is. The situation has changed. I think its time that we took matters up a notch or two."

Lijing frowned and a bit of steam escaped her nostrils. "Meaning?"

"Meaning it's time for Margam to die."

Kori was surprised to hear Elsdon putting it so bluntly, but Lijing appeared less bothered.

"We've been through this," the dragonkin said. "You can't kill him. You don't have the power, not even all of you together. And I can't be seen to have helped in that. If I attack him, and Gillbriss or Haiteng examine his body, it will be evident. Then, my life won't be worth anything."

"As I said, though," Elsdon replied. "The situation has changed. Kori?"

Kori cleared his throat, suddenly uncomfortable being called attention to. But he had agreed to do whatever was needed. Actually, it had really been his idea when he'd decided to return to Craydon.

"This is the one who killed Grambar," Elsdon said.

Lijing swung her great head around to study Kori. "A human? That can't be."

"But you knew it was," Elsdon said. "Both you and Margam knew it. You just didn't know how it was done. Go ahead, Kori. Show her."

It was with even more reluctance that Kori pulled his axe free and held it out toward the dragonkin.

Her reaction was immediate. She drew back, almost stumbling. Her tail lashed once and demolished the stones of the well.

"Get it away!"

Kori lowered it, watching the dragonkin as he slid it back into the loop on his belt.

"Where? How did you get that?" Lijing asked. Her voice had taken on a tremble. If Kori hadn't known better, he would have said she was afraid.

"My uncle," he told her. "It was his axe. He gave it to me several years ago, now. I don't know where he got it."

Elsdon was nodding. "Now you know how he killed Grambar. He has the weapon of an Evening Folk."

"It's a Helgarlug weapon," the dragonkin almost spat. "Made for nothing but killing my kind!"

"Exactly," Elsdon said. "Now all we need is a way to get Margam close enough for Kori to bury it in his skull. And that's where you come in, my friend."

Lijing still looked skeptical, and she kept her distance from Kori, who made no attempt to get closer to her. But she listened.

It came faster than he had thought it would. Kori had assumed that Elsdon would lay out his plan to Lijing. Then they'd have another long, monotonous day to wait, until night fell again. They would wait until then to make sure that the chance of some innocent bystander getting caught in the battle was diminished.

But that's not what happened.

"We'll do it now," Lijing said. "Margam is getting suspicious. Even of me. He says he's beginning to think that I know who killed his sister. He's ready to either tear the town apart or go get help if I don't agree to let him."

"Now it is, then," Elsdon agreed. He looked toward Kori. "Are you ready?"

That was the million-gold-piece question, wasn't it? Kori *had* been ready. When his fear had turned to anger, just a step away from that red-rage. But this way? This methodical plan that gave him time to think? This was different.

"I'm ready," he answered. Whether he truly was or not, it didn't matter.

"Some of you get out of sight, then," Lijing said, lifting off effortlessly from the ground. "I'll be back in a few moments."

"Stick to the plan," Elsdon said to everyone in general.

Then, there was nothing to do but watch the blue dragonkin fly off. When she'd left, the night seemed to grow even darker.

Five of Elsdon's men ran off, taking cover where they could and making sure they were invisible to the dragonkin flying overhead. Three more of them gathered at one side of the opening, while Elsdon, Kori, and Toni took the other.

"Go back," Kori said to Toni. "This is dangerous."

"What happened to me pulling anyone wounded to safety?" she asked.

Kori shook his head. "I don't care. I don't want you hurt. That's all I care about."

Her face had been set in grim determination, but it softened at his words. She reached out to touch his cheek. "I don't want you hurt, either."

"And I don't want *anyone* hurt, except for Margam," Elsdon interrupted. "Kori's right, though. At least pull back. Hide for now, then come out when you hear the fighting. Margam will be too busy to even notice you then."

Toni looked ready to argue but then relented. With one last glance at Kori, she moved down one of the streets and was quickly out of sight as she stepped into a doorway.

"Now we wait," Elsdon said quietly.

They didn't have to wait for long.

The two dragonkin came in swiftly and without a sound. One moment, Kori was looking at the men across the street, the next, there were two dragonkin filling the space between. One was the larger blue, while the other was much smaller, but so black he seemed like a hole in the night.

"Which one?" Margam growled. "Who was it?"

"How should I know?" Lijing answered, as if the question was the most idiotic she'd ever heard. "Ask them yourself."

Margam snaked his head around, then back again, taking in Kori, Elsdon, and his men.

"All out at night? All armed? What is this, Lijing?"

"Your doom," she laughed.

With that, she was up and gone. How far, Kori didn't know, because he wouldn't take his eyes off the black dragonkin.

Margam cursed when Lijing flew off, but he didn't panic. "I knew it," Kori heard him growl. "Traitor. She'll be next."

He didn't bother talking to the humans. Lijing might have told him that the one who had killed his sister was there, but it didn't seem like Margam really cared which it was. He simply pulled his head back swiftly, shot it forward, and spit.

Elsdon's men had been waiting for it. As soon as Margam moved, so did they, scattering, but the dragonkin was faster. One of them didn't make it. The gob of acid caught him squarely in the side. His screams started almost immediately as the acid ate through his clothes and into his flesh.

Which was when Elsdon dashed forward, with Kori right on his heels.

The plan was simple. They'd attack from all sides, harrying the dragonkin while delivering what wounds they could. If they were fast, and lucky, they'd stay unmarred while they wore Margam down.

But the dragonkin wasn't having any part of it. He spoke a word that seemed to hurt Kori's ears, and another of Elsdon's men suddenly froze in place. His face twisted in horror before blood began running from his mouth as he collapsed soundlessly to the street.

Two down already and the battle had hardly begun. Elsdon's friend— the blue dragonkin— was being no help.

Which meant it was going to be up to Kori.

He sprang forward and swung his axe in a horizontal arc, slamming the blade into the dragonkin's rear leg. The light flashed, and he felt the weapon sink deep. Margam's roar of pain was almost enough to deafen them all.

"Again," Elsdon yelled, and Kori swung again.

Only, Margam avoided it. With a rush of wind, he launched himself into the air, so that Kori's blow missed him entirely.

He was going to leave. To find Gillbriss and tell her who and what had killed his sister.

Suddenly, he slammed back to the street, his legs splaying beneath him, and his jaws slamming shut.

"No, no," Lijing laughed cruelly. "You stay down there."

Magic, Kori supposed. The blue had thrown some sort of spell which had caused Margam to fall back to the ground.

The Ascani Knights were on him, then, hacking with their swords. Margam shook them off, bleeding from several cuts, and spoke again. Another knight went down, his bones seemingly dissolving inside his skin.

Kori had never really seen a dragonkin use magic like that. He'd thought that only the red ones were proficient with it, but if that was so, he never wanted to run into one of them. This was horrible enough, and unless he put a stop to it, Margam would destroy them all without even having to resort to his teeth or claws.

The dragonkin opened his mouth again, and Kori jumped forward. Whatever Margam had been about to say was lost as Kori's axe clove into his lower jaw with another flash of light. The sound of something heavy and wet hitting the ground was drowned out by Margam's next scream of pain.

Kori was vaguely aware of Elsdon and the others screaming. He thought he heard one voice urging him on, to attack again. There might have been another warning him of some danger, but what it was, Kori didn't know.

Margam was weaving. Kori didn't know if he could spit or not, but without half his jaw, at least he wouldn't be speaking another spell.

Do it just like the other one, he thought. He raised his axe overhead, preparing to bring it down right between the dragonkin's eyes. That would end the whole thing.

There was a sharp, intense pain in his stomach. It bloomed like a poison flower, freezing him where he stood.

He looked down, confused by what he saw.

It was thick, and black, with scales, and seemed to be coming out of his stomach, which made no sense because his back hurt, too. His legs felt funny, and he thought that whatever the thing was, it was all that was holding him up.

Someone grabbed something from him. From his hands, which fell empty to his sides.

He supposed he should try to pull the thing from his stomach, but his whole body was getting cold. The night was growing darker, too. Maybe the moon was going behind clouds.

Then, there was a bright flash which made everything stand out clearly. Whatever was stuck in him thrashed, lifting Kori and sending him flying through the air. It pulled itself out of his body, which was nice— he guessed— but it was hard to even feel much of anything.

Not even the ground when he hit it. But the dark that came next seemed like a good thing.

Chapter 50- Somewhere in Ascana

Arastug stumbled. The weapon had been used again. Not just once, but at least three times, in fairly rapid succession. The only reason he would have noticed it was if it had been used against a dragonkin. Which meant that whoever now wielded it knew what it could do. Maybe not that it was a Helgarlug weapon forged long ago, but certainly that it could hurt dragonkin.

It was one of the last weapons created, too. It had to have been, to be that powerful. Powerful enough to call to him through all the intervening miles. His people had gotten better and better at imbuing the weapons with magic as the war had raged on. Unfortunately, true proficiency had come too late, and there were too few of them made to be of any consequence in the end.

He was still in the realm of Obristan, but the weapon had been used somewhere in Ascana. He could tell that much. He still had a long way to go. For that matter, he was still a day's journey from the human city of Greenfair, not that he had any intention of going there. But it was a good reference point. He'd be able to follow the old road, that which the humans called the Conqueror's Road, for some strange reason. As far as he was aware, humans had never conquered anything.

Still, the road ran true all the way into Ascana. He'd shadow it during the day, staying in the woods when he could, then utilize it at night. His hearing would allow him to get off of it before anyone came along close enough to see him.

Not that he was too worried about that. From what he'd witnessed so far, human travel had been severely curtailed. He'd only had to avoid a couple here and there, regardless of whether he'd traveled day or night.

And he was far enough from Olequan now to not have to worry that his presence would give away the location. He'd seen another of Tophonoss's children once but had avoided it easily enough. More worrisome had been the one time he'd felt *her*, but she was far away and hadn't noticed him. Even coming that close, though, was enough to set him shaking and hiding for hours after she'd passed.

Arastug was no fool. Falaern might have a chance— albeit a slight one— against Tophonoss. However, the dragon could chew Arastug up and spit him out without even making an effort. He had no desire to draw her attention.

So he traveled, on foot and alone, as only one of his people could. The Raaleth could cover great distances with magic, using portals that allowed them to step from one area and emerge into another miles away. The Xarlug were more like Arastug's people. They had their own magic but using it in the manner of the Raaleth wasn't in them. They'd walk or run, as he was, for miles at a time.

But no one, not Raaleth, Xarlug, dragon, or human, could journey as the Helgarlug. Discounting the time spent hiding from Tophonoss, Arastug had rested for a mere few hours since leaving Olequan. He had no need to now, either. Helgarlug legs could march for days on end without stopping, even while the Helgarlug mind drifted off into a sort of waking sleep. Aware enough of their surroundings to warn of danger, but blissfully unaware of the passing hours and miles.

All in all, it wouldn't be long before he homed in on the weapon's location. If it wasn't used again, he'd go directly to where it had been. From there, he'd sniff it out, or— if it was again wielded— adjust his course.

One way or the other, though, he'd find the one who had made use of it. If they could determine where the weapon had come from, they might find more of them. Tales were told, but not often believed, of a secret stash of such weapons. The most powerful ever forged and then enchanted. Legend had it that they were hidden away when the dragons destroyed the last bastions of the Raaleth.

Where was a matter of debate, as was the very existence of such weapons. Arastug, himself, has always scoffed at the tales.

But the one that had just been used…

The first time, he'd thought it had felt powerful. Now that it had been used again, and used more than once at that, he was much more certain.

He'd never seen a weapon of such power. It was wasted in the hands of a human, of course. But if they could be persuaded, one way or the other, to turn it over to him… well, he might be able to track where it came from. Such weapons left trails, even after all these years. Didn't they? Or was that just another legend?

Arastug sighed and continued on, his path paralleling the road. It didn't matter. What did was finding it. Everything that came after would be determined then.

And it wouldn't do to get too excited. It was one weapon. How much damage could it really have done?

No, it wouldn't do to get excited.

But that weapon…

Chapter 51- Lostin, Ascana

The Librarian's home was exactly what Viktoria would have expected. Small, she supposed some would use the word "cozy," although she didn't really know what was meant by that, and full of books. They were everywhere. On shelves, stacked on tables, on all but one chair, and even on the floor itself.

For the first time since meeting the huge man, he seemed a little flustered.

"Sorry," he growled, when they entered. "I don't usually have guests. Guess I kind of forgot how the place can look."

"Sorry for what?" Dommick smiled. "I think it's charming. Remarkable, really. Even Father doesn't have this many books, and he considers himself a great collector."

"Have you really read all these?" Nettie asked, her voice full of awe.

Viktoria honestly couldn't have cared less if he had or not. What she did care about was that she'd found the place to ditch the book she carried. She didn't have to go all the way to Droy Thus, wherever that actually was. With all the books here, she could just slide it between a couple, and Reyson and Sormat herself could look until the world ended, and they still might not find it.

But when she put her hand inside her shirt and touched the leather-like binding, she knew it wasn't going to work.

Oh, sure, she could hide the book, but what good would it do? Other than get Halli killed, of course, when Reyson came knocking. Besides, at this point, she didn't think Reyson was tracking the *book*... he was tracking the person who carried it. Her. Leaving the book here would just make him even angrier when he found out he'd wasted his time with her.

She withdrew her hand and tried not to sigh. She glanced quickly at Nettie, but she was busy looking at book after book, her eyes alight as if she'd found some great treasure. Halli had muttered something about having to do something and disappeared into another room. And Dommick was scanning the shelves, maybe looking for a book, but more likely searching for a hidden bottle.

"Are we really taking him with us?" She stepped next to Nettie so she could keep her voice down.

"I think he's taking us," she replied, equally as quietly. "Besides, I think he can help us."

"With what? We'll have to stop every hour for something to eat. Look at the size of him!"

Nettie actually grinned at that. "He seems pretty self-sufficient. Besides, do you really want to try to get all the way to Droy Thus on our own?"

"This is *your* land," Viktoria returned. "You can guide us."

Now Nettie did actually laugh out loud. "Sorry," she said when she finished. "It's just that… well, not very long ago, you wouldn't have trusted me to guide you across a street. Now you want me to take you all the way to Droy Thus?"

Viktoria scowled, but she really had nothing to say to that. The fact was, Nettie was right. She hadn't trusted her.

But that had changed, hadn't it? When Nettie had gone off the ship first, when she'd put herself in harm's way so that Viktoria and Dommick could escape notice, and when she'd agreed to go all the way to Droy Thus with them. Especially when it was so obvious that all Nettie really wanted to do was go home and forget about her time in Reclium…

"I'm sorry," Viktoria found herself saying. She couldn't meet Nettie's surprised expression. "I'm not used to… I'm… I'm just not good at trusting people."

"Comes from living where we do," Dommick said cheerfully.

Viktoria muttered a curse. She hadn't even noticed that he'd made a circuit of the room and was now right behind them.

"You come from Reclium, too," Nettie said. "Yet you don't seem to mind people."

"Oh, I love people," Dommick beamed. "But Viktoria and I come from different places. I was raised in luxury… isn't that right?" He didn't wait for Viktoria to comment. "While she came from the mean streets. Where life was even crueler than my family and…" He stopped and his face grew serious. "No. That's silly. And nothing to make light of. Reclium *is* a cruel place. If I hadn't been who I was, I never would have survived. The fact that she did is… well, it's remarkable. She's a remarkable woman."

His face reddened, and he coughed and turned back to the shelves as if continuing his search.

Viktoria could only stare at him. What was all that about?

"You are, you know," Nettie said. "What he said. Now if I could just get you to lighten up a bit."

She smiled, then went to join Dommick, leaving Viktoria alone with thoughts she'd rather not have. Not one, but two people who seemed to care about her? And worse, that she cared about in return? No. Bad enough when it was just Chaol.

She was using them, that's all. Them and Halli, as well. Just using them to get to Droy Thus, to get rid of the stupid book, and to find help against Reyson. She already had that part planned out. Both Mrs. Cloven and this Librarian were spellbound by a book they couldn't even read. Those who could? They'd be manic to get their hands on it.

Which meant Viktoria could sell it to them. The cost would be to rid her of Reyson, and maybe even Sormat. They were wizards, right? Sorcerers who could perform miracles?

They'd perform that one, all right. Or Victoria would burn the book right in front of them.

"Are you really planning on going all the way with us?"

Dommick asked the question but didn't look at Nettie. Instead, he continued to peruse the stacks and stacks of books that were everywhere.

"I guess so," she shrugged. "It sort of seems like I should."

"Why?" Now Dommick did look at her. "This isn't really your fight, is it? Not anymore. You're home, you can go wherever you want."

Only she couldn't. Not really. Not with the way things had changed in Ascana and in the rest of the world. The dragonkin would want to know why she was roaming the land. Of course, the same thing was going to happen when it was four of them, but she had the feeling that Halli had something in mind for that.

"I'll go home after we get Viktoria safely to Droy Thus," she finally answered. "How about you? What will you do then?"

"Huh. You know? I don't know." Dommick put his back to a shelf and leaned against it. He stuck his hands in his pockets and looked down at the floor. "At first, when I met her in my father's tower, I just thought she was some thief. Which she was, but I really didn't care what she wanted. Take it and go. But then when Reyson showed up and started beating her..." He stopped and shook his head. "I don't know. It was like something inside my head just... clicked. It wasn't right. So I hit him in the head. The next thing I know, I'm trying to help her out of the tower and then... poof... I'm here."

Nettie *didn't* quite get it. There had to be more.

"Still," she said. "You did come along. You could have left at any time. So, why not now? Now that you're out of Reclium. You could probably stay right here, among those others who've escaped."

Dommick smiled and looked up. "What? And miss all the fun? No, I'll go along, too."

Nettie nodded. That part, at least, she understood. It was like... well, something that had started, even if she hadn't started it, and she wasn't going to stop until she saw it through. Which meant getting that book where it needed to go, which meant helping Viktoria. After that? Home. No stopping, no other sidetracks. Just home.

"All right," Halli boomed as he came back into the room. He had a huge sack thrown over one shoulder but carried it as if weighed almost nothing. "We'll head out now. We have one stop to make before leaving Lostin, then it's on the road. Or near it, anyway."

"What's that supposed to mean?" Viktoria asked him.

"I'm not sure the road is completely safe, so we might use some other routes I know about. We'll see how it goes."

"What's in the bag?" Nettie asked.

"Supplies," Halli answered. "Things we might need. Now, are we done asking questions or should we just hang out here and wait for a dragonkin to stick his nose through the door?"

The question was obviously rhetorical, since the Librarian didn't wait for any sort of answer. He strode to the door, opened it, then stepped aside waiting.

Viktoria could certainly take a hint. She was out and looking left, right, and up before Nettie took two steps. But she went as well, copying the other woman, while behind her Dommick strolled casually onto the street.

Nettie turned in time to see Halli linger for a moment, looking back into the room filled with his precious books, before he shut the door firmly and turned away.

"Where do we need to stop?" Dommick asked, falling into step beside the huge man.

"A friend's," Halli answered.

Which was all the answer he'd give. But they didn't have long to wait to find out who he meant.

Halli led them down several streets, then turned into a narrow alley. He stopped before a ratty-looking door, raised his great fist, and knocked softly.

Footsteps sounded, then the door cracked open just a bit. A bright, green eye peered out at them, skimming over Nettie, Viktoria, and Dommick, before taking in the Librarian. Whoever it was grunted, then opened the door further to allow them all inside.

The room was dark, made even more so by drapery hung so that anyone who might have peeked through the gap when the man had opened the door wouldn't see anything beyond. Now, Nettie could barely make out their host before he disappeared behind that same curtain.

"Well?" his voice floated back. "Don't just stand there. Why would I let you in to have you just stand there?"

Halli pushed carefully through the curtain, letting the rest follow him.

When she reached the other side, Nettie didn't know which to look at first: the room or the owner.

He was about Dommick's size, so taller than either Nettie or Viktoria, but not nearly the height of the Librarian. However, he was hunched over with his shoulders rising up around his neck. He was thin, but with a thick head of white hair and the most startling green eyes Nettie had ever seen.

He glanced at them, then continued to the far side of the room, where a huge fireplace stood. No fire was lit, but the ashes confirmed that one had been recently.

The rest of the room was like the Librarian's house, only it wasn't books that crowded every surface nor was there any normal furniture. Instead, the room was crowded with several large workbenches, stacked high with… things. More things than Nettie had ever seen in one place.

Pots, pans, and utensils. Writing implements, shoes, and hats. Jars, bottles, mugs, and vials of every conceivable shape.

Whatever it was this man did, whoever he was, it was clear that he never threw anything away.

"What is it, Halli?" he asked. His voice betrayed his age, but it was still firm enough to not waver.

"Passage," the Librarian said. "And a few swords."

"Passage I can do. The swords… that I'm not so sure of."

Halli snorted. "Of course you are. You have them, you just don't want to give them up. Come on now. This was part of the deal."

The man's mouth twisted in displeasure. "That deal was made a long time ago. There's no cause—"

"And it's never been called in," Halli interrupted him. "Until now. This is a small price to pay."

The man shook his head and breathed out heavily. "Fine. This way."

With the massive jumble of stuff in the room, Nettie hadn't even noticed the doorway to her right. The man led them in that direction, then down a short hallway, until they came to another. He looked back as if counting how many of them there were.

"Three," he said. "That's all. One for each, and none of them will fit your massive hands, Halli. So three and three only."

"Fine, Ashby. That's all we'll need. But they choose which ones. And you come clean about them, too. Understood?"

"Yes, yes. Let's just get this over with."

Ashby opened the door and stepped aside.

Nettie crossed into the room and felt her jaw drop.

All Viktoria could think as she looked around was that everyone in Lostin, maybe all of Ascana for all she knew, was a hoarder of some type. Halli with his massive collection of more books than anyone could ever hope to read. This new guy— Ashby or whatever his name was— with his piles of junk.

And now… weapons.

Except that in this room, things appeared to be more in order. Axes with axes, spears with spears, swords with swords. All arranged by thickness, length, or some other method.

She could see just about every type of instrument she could imagine that was designed to let blood out of a body.

"Three," the man said again. "And don't paw through them all. You tell me what you want, I'll find it for you. I have a system, and I don't want you all messing with it."

"A sword, I suppose," Dommick said. "Not one of those great big ones that get too heavy two minutes after you pick it up, though. Something lighter."

Ashby snorted in what was clearly contempt but made no other comment. Instead, he walked to a rack where several blades were hanging point down, from the crosspieces of their hilt. He began looking through them, and Viktoria saw him pass over what appeared to be several fine blades with jeweled hilts before pulling one free.

He turned and held it out to Dommick. "This one."

It was as plain as a sword could be. No etching on the blade, which was shiny, but still duller than most of the others. There was no ornamentation on the hilt or pommel, just gray metal wrapped in rough leather to provide a gripping surface. In short, it was the type of sword given to any random soldier just starting out.

"No," Halli said. "He chooses, not you. That was part of the deal."

"I actually like this one," Dommick said. He held it up and studied it. "Good edge on it."

Dommick moved off several paces until he was well away from the others, then gave the sword a few swings and lunges.

Viktoria scowled. She'd almost forgotten their quick sparring on the ship. Dommick was good. Very good. He would have been a match for any life-taker Viktoria knew of, other than Reyson, of course.

The old man, Ashby, seemed to think so, too. He strode forward, interfering with Dommick's next thrust, and took the sword from him with a grunt. He put it back where it had been— exactly where it had been, Viktoria noticed— then went to a different rack and selected a new sword.

Still plain, still unadorned, but somehow this one seemed… better.

Dommick lifted it and his eyebrows almost simultaneously. "Well, this is… something else. I'll take it."

"It's an excellent weapon," Ashby said. "If I have to give it up, it should go to an excellent swordsman."

"Where is it from?" Dommick asked, peering down at it.

"Its provenance is lost," Ashby responded. "It's old. One of the oldest I have. Don't get too excited, though. It's human forged. Even I don't have any of those others here. The ones made by the Evening Folk. Keep your eyes out on your travels, though. If you find one of those, I'd be interested in it."

Viktoria had no idea what the old man was talking about, but he didn't bother to elaborate. Instead, he turned to Nettie.

"And you, girl? What does a pretty thing like you need a weapon for? Can't you just bat your lashes and wiggle your hips to get out of any trouble?"

"I'll take a sailor's saber," she said, ignoring his other comments. "I lost mine when my ship was attacked."

Ashby studied her and then nodded. "A sailor. Merchant, navy, or raider, then?"

That question seemed to raise Nettie's hackles, although Viktoria thought it was a perfectly reasonable one.

"Navy," she growled.

"All right. Don't twist your undergarments so. I'll find you something."

While he did that, Viktoria began looking around on her own. She could use a sword, but it wasn't her preferred weapon. Knives were better suited for her. Not as heavy and they could be hidden, even thrown if they needed to be, although that worked best with smaller, purposely-balanced-for-the-act ones.

Then... she couldn't believe what she was seeing. They weren't black, like hers had been, but they were a dark gray, which was close enough. Almost identical, the pair of knives were as long as those she'd lost and just about the same width. She picked them up, one in each hand, and it was as if she had been walking around with no clothes on and was suddenly swaddled in a cloak that could protect her from all harm.

"I want these," she said, even before Ashby finished giving Nettie the sword he'd found for her. The old man turned toward her with a frown.

"I said one each," he snapped. Then, at a low growl from the Librarian, he softened. "But I suppose they *are* a set. Fine."

"Sheathes," Halli said. "You know that's part of it, Ashby."

The old man shot Halli a dirty look, then stalked off to the side of the room. He rummaged around a cabinet and then a drawer, then finally returned with four dark leather scabbards.

Viktoria had expected him to bring them the most beat-up, worn-out sheaths he could find. Instead, they were all made of fine leather, stitched with heavy twine, and thick enough to protect both blade and bearer.

"Here," he said. "If you're really taking my things, at least keep them safe. And I want them back! Both the weapons and the sheaths."

They took the offered scabbards and strapped them on, Nettie and Dommick hanging their swords from their belts, while Viktoria slipped on a back harness that fit as if had been made for her. Ashby even helped adjust it the small amount it needed.

"Now, you've got what you came for," he said to the Librarian. "It's time to be off."

"It is," the Librarian agreed. "So, open the way."

"Can't you just take the road?" the old man said.

"No. It's too dangerous and conspicuous. We need to be inland fast, then south."

Ashby sighed, then shook his head. "It's dangerous, you know. Don't blame me if—"

"We won't," Halli told him. "None of us will. You're doing the work you agreed to, as you have been all these years. Let us through, then you've never seen us. You have no idea where we went."

"Nor do I," Ashby said. "All right, then. Come."

With that, he led them back out of the room by the same door they'd entered through. Back along the short corridor, until he stopped in front of another door. But he didn't open it. Instead, he reached out and twisted the knob, back and forth, in a rapid pattern Viktoria couldn't follow.

There was a click, almost like when Captain Sanford had reached into his desk on the ship.

"Pull it up," Ashby said, indicating what looked like one of several small rugs ranged along the floor of the hallway.

Dommick did it. He grabbed the rug Ashby indicated and pulled. Or at least he tried to. The rug didn't move.

"Not to the side," Ashby said. "Up."

Dommick frowned, put his hands to either side of the rug and pulled.

The whole thing came up as if it had been hinged to the floor on one side. The rug was rigid, and Viktoria could see that it was affixed to what appeared to be a trap door.

From the opening it revealed came a cold draft of air. Whatever was down there was hard to know, since it was pitch black. Even eyes born and raised in Reclium couldn't see well.

"No." Nettie's voice was firm. "I'm not going down there."

Viktoria looked at her. "Of course we are. It's just dark. So what?"

Nettie shook her head. "You don't understand. I... I just can't."

The woman wasn't even looking at her. She was staring at the dark hole, sweat beading on her forehead even as the chill air came from it.

Viktoria moved close to her. "Just a bit at a time, remember? The same way you got me to see in the sunlight. This is like that. I'll go first, then you stay close behind me. Dommick will be right behind you."

Nettie swallowed hard. She glanced once at Viktoria, then nodded rapidly. "All right. I'll try." Her voice was shaking, though.

"Good." Viktoria turned to the Librarian. "Are we going or not?"

"We are," Halli said. "Lower yourself carefully. There're steps, but they don't start for a few feet."

Viktoria could already see that far. Hard, stone steps, beginning with a type of landing that was almost her own height beneath the floor.

"Let's get this over with, then," she said, and jumped down into the darkness.

Chapter 52- Somewhere in Reclium

Two days of walking and climbing through the mountains of Reclium had taken their toll on Reyson. His body had gone through multiple traumas, and while it had healed itself well enough, every injury had come with fresh agony, to say nothing of the torturous healing process itself.

In addition, that burning sensation, the one that would end up flaring through his entire body, had become a constant companion. A somewhat low-level reminder that he was doing Sormat's work. Hers and her red dragonkin friend, whatever its name had been. The magic may have been content to leave him alone as long as he was making progress, but it had no patience for his now forcibly slow pace.

He realized he'd almost come to think of the spell Sormat, and that other had cast as something alive. Like it was some sort of sentient being that tracked his every move and judged his intent. He supposed viewing it as a sort of unwelcome companion wasn't entirely inaccurate.

But for now, that companion was going to have to remain unhappy.

He crested the hill he'd been climbing and groaned, which wasn't a sound that often escaped his lips, either prior to or after his transformation.

Before him spread a deep valley, with steep walls. On the other side appeared nothing but more mountains.

Somehow, Reyson had gone astray. He'd been attempting to follow the primitive roads and tracks which crisscrossed Reclium, taking a short cut when he knew one. One of those must have gone awry and now...

Now he was stuck, with the heat building just that little bit more. There was no way to climb out of that valley once he went into it. There was nothing there that would draw any sort of living creature to the place. Rocks and dirt, that was it. No stream running through it, no water of any kind that he could see.

Which meant he needed to go back. He was being forced to turn around and retrace his steps, to find where he'd gone off the path and rejoin it.

The anger that boiled up in him had nothing to do with the fire that was soon going to feel like it was consuming his body. It had to do with *him*. He had *never* gone off-track before, not once in all his years of tracking down those Maganti wanted dead. Some of them had stayed in Heldum, others had fled to distant towns, while a few had braved the wilds. None of them had escaped him.

Yet this woman, this Viktoria Autumn, had somehow done what no others had managed. She'd escaped him.

And now? Now he'd made an error that he'd never made before.

It must be the magic. Whatever was animating his body and allowing him to think and pretend he was still alive was affecting him. He wasn't analyzing the situation as sharply as he once had. That was the only explanation.

Even in his initial choice after leaving Darkbreath Tower the latest time. He should have simply returned to Pharax. It was the only legitimate port in all of Reclium. Instead, he'd decided to cut to the coast nearest Heldum and work his way down, watching for smugglers' coves. There were whole sordid, little villages set up to receive illicit goods. Not just for the Magantis but for some of the other clans as well. Reyson was fairly certain that Gillbriss and her children knew of them, but their existence only added to the chaos of Reclium, so why would they care?

But Viktoria hadn't gone to one of those. She'd been in Pharax, with the old whore, that much he knew. She'd taken a ship from there, not from some rundown shanty of a dock in the middle of nowhere.

So why…?

It was useless. He couldn't have said why he made such a decision anymore than he knew when he'd become lost.

It didn't matter. What did was what was coming next. The heat was going to be with him until he turned toward the coast again. If he had to walk for half a day or more to find the path, it would burn him with every step.

But standing there was only going to make it come on even quicker and probably more intensely. So there was no sense in delaying it.

"Damn you!"

The surge of fire almost made him stagger to his knees as soon as he turned.

"I'm going!" he rasped. "I'll get there quicker if you ease off!"

But the fire— the magic— didn't listen. Whether sentient or not, it didn't care.

His luck this time was better than it had been over the last several days. He found the path where he'd left it, only a few agonizing hours away. The fire died down, but to a slightly higher level than it had been before, as soon as he stepped foot on it and began walking again.

Pharax lay along it, a good three days of walking, less if he could find a cart to take. But over the two days since he'd left Heldum, carts had been few and far between. If he didn't know better, he would have said that word of his moving through the area had gone out.

He needed something, though. Something that would let him travel much more quickly than he was doing now.

And not just through Reclium, he realized. Even if he got lucky again and found the exact ship that had taken Viktoria back in port, it would be days of sailing to reach wherever she'd gone to. And finding that ship was extremely unlikely.

Severina Cloven, then?

He didn't relish the thought of going back there. Well, that wasn't entirely true. A part of him wanted to do *exactly* that. Wanted to do it almost as badly as he'd wanted to hit Maganti. But he very much doubted she'd be taken unawares. If she was even still in Pharax. For all his disdain of her and her profession, she was a crafty, old fox.

But her time would come. Just as Chaol's finally had.

No, what he needed was some way to quickly cover ground in any realm.

He just wasn't sure what that was going to be.

Until he looked up, to a nearby hill, and saw the dragonkin sitting on it, watching him go by. He turned off the path and began walking toward it. The dragonkin remained unmoving and watched him come.

It was even smaller than most of Gillbriss's children, yet still far larger than he was. If it had been a horse, he would have had no doubt that it could carry him. But Reyson wasn't sure it worked the same way for something that flew. Would the dragonkin's wings support them both? Or maybe it was some sort of magic that would provide enough lift.

"I need passage, quickly," he said to it, as soon as they were face to face. "You're going to carry me."

The dragonkin drew its head up on its long neck and peered down at him. There may have been amusement in its face, but who could really tell with these things?

"I am?" it rumbled, its deeper voice revealing itself as a male. "Strange. No one has told me. I'm glad you've come along to set me straight."

"I don't have time for games," Reyson growled. "I'm on a mission for Sormat. I'm sure you know her, right? She won't be happy if you don't help me."

"Sormat," the male sneered derisively. He spit, and the wet, wad of acid sizzled against a nearby rock.

It might have been meant as a warning to Reyson, before the dragonkin did the same thing to him, but he honestly didn't care.

"Sormat can go sit on sharp rock," the dragonkin continued. "What do I care what she wants?"

"All right, then," Reyson said. He drew the sword he'd taken from Darkbreath Tower before he left. "If you don't carry me, you don't fly ever again."

The dragonkin didn't laugh or sneer or even respond. He just spit again, moving faster than Reyson would have been able to counter. The acid caught him on the left arm, almost instantly burning through his clothes and into his flesh. Although it hurt, it was nothing compared to what he'd been through.

"Have it your way, then," he snarled and closed with the dragonkin.

Despite what he'd said, he had no interest in severing the dragonkin's wings. He needed the dragonkin intact enough to carry him wherever he needed to go. So, instead, he went after the tail.

Reyson had always been strong and fast, but the magic that had reanimated him had made him even more so. He was past the dragonkin's head and down along his body in a flash. His sword slashed down, black blood sprang out, spattering Reyson's face with a hiss, and the dragonkin screamed.

Before he could pull his tail away, Reyson swung again, cutting deeper this time, then again, severing the stinger in three quick blows. Each one sent acidic blood spurting onto him, burning his flesh and even his right eye, but he kept at it.

He sprang away, just as the dragonkin whirled on him, claws outstretched. He caught Reyson a solid blow, tearing through his shirt and into his back, opening his flesh and tearing into his spine.

Reyson grunted and fell, his legs no longer usable. Almost immediately, though, the fire coursed through him, quicker this time than ever before. He heard snaps and pops as broken bones reknit and an icy numbness as his back healed. He came back to his feet and leapt forward; sword point angled toward the dragonkin's throat.

At the last minute, he changed course, lifted the point of his sword, and sent it scraping along the dragonkin's cheek, straight for his eye. He stopped with the tip a hairsbreadth from the orb.

"What are you?" the dragonkin whispered.

"Your death," Reyson said. "Unless you agree to carry me."

"What's stopping me from flying away?" the dragonkin asked.

That was actually a good question. He supposed the dragonkin could do exactly that. Or take him high in the air and simply dump him off his back, sending Reyson plummeting. He might come back from such a fall. But it wouldn't be easy and certainly not painless.

"Nothing," he admitted, pulling his sword back and stepping away.

The battle had been fierce, but very short. And— unlike the dragonkin— any damage Reyson had taken had been burned away.

"I should kill you," the dragonkin said. He had pulled his tail around and was sniffing at the wound, studying the ragged stump where his stinger had been.

"You can't," Reyson said. "You must see that by now. And if you try, I really will take your wings away. Then I'll kill you."

The dragonkin growled deep in its throat.

"We can fight again," Reyson told him. "Or you can leave. I suppose I won't try to stop you at that. But I have an offer to make you."

"What's that?"

His words had piqued the dragonkin's interest, as Reyson had known they would. The dragonkin of Reclium were many things. Cruel and capricious, sly and devious. But above all else, they were greedy and jealous. What one had, the rest wanted. They were almost as bad as the humans who lived in the night realm.

"Take me where I need to go. I really am working for Sormat, whether I want to or not. Let me get my hands on what she's after. Then, together, we can take it to her."

"Why would I want to do that?" the dragonkin asked.

"Because," Reyson replied. "Maybe we can figure out what it does. And then we can use it against her."

"So? Let's say I kill Sormat? So what? Dragonkin fight all the time. What does that do for me?"

"Really? You don't see it?" Reyson needed to keep playing on this one's greed, his need to be more that what he was at the moment. "You don't think that something she wants, something that she desires enough to do this to me, would be valuable? After you kill her, and you have this thing, you can probably be the most powerful dragonkin in all of Reclium. Second only to Gillbriss herself."

The dragonkin seemed to consider. "This item— whatever it is— is it dangerous to dragonkin?"

Reyson shrugged. "I don't know. But given how she's acted; I believe it might be." Although he didn't understand how a book could be that, he wasn't going to elaborate now.

"How about a 'true dragon?'" The words were spoken with so much bitterness that Reyson had no illusions about who he was referring to.

"I believe so. Whatever it is, it's powerful and dangerous. With something like that in your claws…"

The dragonkin nodded. Then he glanced back at his tail again. Without warning, he spit again, catching Reyson full in the face.

Reyson screamed and fell, clawing at his skin as he felt it dissolve. It was like being in the fire all over again. He couldn't see because his eyes burst, his screams choked off as his tongue slid down his throat.

Everything went black, then he started to regain his sight. The world was blurry, and his face still seared as if someone was holding a burning torch to it. He just didn't know if it was still the dragonkin's acid at work, or the healing from Sormat's magic.

Finally, it began to abate. He was panting and whimpering, writhing on the ground, but he managed to pull his hands away. He forced himself to steady, then slowly climbed to his feet.

The dragonkin was still there, curled up several feet away. Reyson's sword was on the ground, so he picked it up and slammed it into the sheath at his belt.

"That was for my tail," the dragonkin said simply. "And to watch you squirm. Now, tell me where we're going."

Reyson nodded. He'd won— sort of. He had his way of finding Viktoria and the book much more quickly.

But the dragonkin was never going to be an ally. Reyson was no fool. He'd watch for the right time to end their partnership.

And he had no doubt that the dragonkin was going to be doing the exact same thing.

Chapter 53- Greenfair, Obristan

"There," Bolles rasped.

He and Lamorak were out among the people in Greenfair, dressed in normal, everyday clothing. They'd left both armor and weapons back in their rooms at the Honor Guard compound.

"I don't see anything," Lamorak muttered. He glanced again to where Bolles had indicated, but he couldn't identify anything out of the ordinary.

"Maybe not," Bolles grunted. "But it's there. I can make out a form, like one of these damn dragonkin, but smaller."

Lamorak shook his head and chuckled. Not at Bolles, but in a predetermined manner. They needed to appear to be two men walking down the street, carrying on a normal conversation.

This was the third time they'd gone out together, searching for those other dragonkin that Bolles claimed were around. The ones that no one but him seemed to be able to see. Those that just might belong to the secret dragon which ruled over Obristan, at least if what Yarah had told him was correct. Each of those other times, however, Bolles hadn't spotted one. Even so, their walks had given Lamorak the opportunity to study Greenfair and what it had become.

What he found… surprised him.

When he'd ridden across Ascana and then back into Obristan, they'd found towns devastated by the dragonkin. Those not outright destroyed had been occupied, the people forced into labor of all types. With the way things had been going when they'd escaped, Lamorak assumed that Manse— the largest city in the realms— had since been destroyed as well.

But now, seeing Greenfair, the capital of Obristan, he wasn't so sure of that.

Greenfair hadn't been destroyed. There were signs of dragonkin occupation here and there. But for the most part, the buildings were intact, with not even a hint of damage, other than to the palace itself where some dragonkin had blasted out entrances big enough for themselves to fit through. The people mostly went about their days as if nothing at all had changed. Most businesses, other than taverns, were still open and plying their trades.

If anyone had noticed that the former daily flow of traffic into and out of Greenfair had mostly stopped, they weren't mentioning it. They simply carried on.

Fooling themselves, Lamorak thought. Then again, who could blame them? The fear they all must have felt when dragonkin showed up in a city in Obristan had faded, leaving behind an uneasy normalcy, as people tried to pretend it was all just as it should be.

But now, finally, Bolles had caught sight of one of these mysterious dragonkin. The problem was, even when Bolles quietly told him exactly where it was, Lamorak couldn't see it at all.

He believed the older guardsman, though. Bolles was no liar and was far from being prone to flights of fancy. If he wasn't absolutely certain he'd seen something, he never would have mentioned it.

"What's it doing?" he asked.

Bolles shrugged. "I can't tell. It's just there. Watching, I guess."

Even as he said this, a mild stir went through the crowd. A dragonkin, red and much larger than any human, soared by overhead, its head hanging low on its long neck, yellow eyes surveying the ground below. What it was looking for, Lamorak couldn't have said, but it passed without issue, not even pausing when it flew above the area where Bolles said the other dragonkin was lurking.

"I don't think they can see them either," Bolles said quietly. "I've seen that before. Whenever the other ones pass, no matter what color they are, they eyeball each other. Like a challenge. I keep waiting for them all to just start fighting. Hoping for it, really. Maybe they'll solve our problem for us."

"I wouldn't count on that," Lamorak replied. "The big dragons have too tight control."

"Maybe so," Bolles agreed. "But they still don't look at those mostly invisible ones like that."

They turned a corner, away from where Bolles said the strange dragonkin was. Two more random turnings, just in case, then they'd head back to the Honor Guard compound.

"You believe me, right?"

The fact that Bolles even asked such a thing showed more than anything else he'd encountered so far the changes in Greenfair. In the past, it wouldn't have been a question, and, even if it was, Bolles never would have asked.

"I believe you," Lamorak told him. "The question now is, what are we going to do with it? It's bad enough Prince Calidor wants me to liberate Greenfair from the dragonkin, but now we have to worry about invisible ones, too?"

"Maybe we always did," Bolles said after a few seconds of thought. "Maybe we just never knew it."

Bolles words stayed with Lamorak all the way back to the compound. Maybe the older man was right, and they always should have been worried about the dragonkin, invisible or not. But they hadn't been.

Greenfair was an old city, with even older bones, according to Shilong. Well, maybe not bones, but…something.

What had she said? Greenfair was built on the runes of an Evening Folk city? Or above it? Something like that

Not for the first time, he found himself wishing that Rainaldus was with him. With his love for anything Evening Folk, combined with the knowledge he had gotten from who-knew-where, Shilong's words might have some sort of value to them.

But for Lamorak, they were just that… words. And he couldn't kill a dragonkin with words.

He could with a sword, though. Or a lance. Probably even with enough arrows, pumped into the right spot. Normal, human weapons. They didn't need the magic of Droy Thus wizards to tip the battle for them. They were Honor Guard and they could do it themselves!

If he just kept telling himself that, maybe he'd even start to believe it.

"Another one," Bolles muttered. "Or maybe the same one."

"Where," Lamorak asked.

"Near the compound. It's moving, though, going up the street slowly."

"Is it watching us?"

"Can't tell with this one, either," Bolles said.

"All right, then." Lamorak sighed. "Let's take another lap around the block. We don't want it noticing us going in there."

When they came back, the invisible dragonkin was gone. Lamorak and Bolles made it safely through the gate and back to the main building. As they came inside, Bolles grunted and rubbed his eyes with the heels of both hands.

"What's wrong?" Lamorak asked him.

"I don't know. My eyes are itchy. Probably just dust."

"Maybe." Lamorak didn't say anything else, but if it was dust, then why did his own eyes feel just fine?

They were halfway through another bottle of wine from the cellars. It had become a nightly ritual, ever since Lamorak had returned a few days ago. Bodwyn made the journey to the cellars, found a suitable bottle— or at least one near to hand— and brought it to Lamorak's room, where the two of them took their time finishing it off.

"So, you knew all this," Lamorak said accusingly.

"I guess so?" Bodwyn's shrug and tone turned it into a question. "I guess I don't know that I *knew* anything. But it's not new to me, if that's what you mean."

"Why didn't I know about it, then?"

"I have no idea," Bodwyn told him. "Maybe some of us had other interests besides just bashing each other with swords all the time."

"I have other interests!"

"Sure," the larger man chuckled. "But most of them are too busy sighing and swooning to teach you much history. Come on, Lamorak. How often did you actually pick up a book and read it?"

Lamorak frowned and took a larger swig of the wine than he had intended. It went down hard, and he spewed a bit onto his chin when he coughed harshly.

"Come on, man," Bodwyn chided him. "Let's not waste it. When the cellar's empty, we won't be able to get more."

"Sorry," he muttered, wiping at his chin with a hand.

But he wasn't really thinking about the wine. He was thinking about what Bodwyn had just told him. That, along with what Shilong had said... there was something there.

"How do they know?" he finally asked. "The people who wrote those books? How do they know that Greenfair is built over an old Evening Folk city?"

"How should I know?" Bodwyn asked. "I'm no historian. I just thought it was interesting." He paused and took a smaller sip than Lamorak had. "Although..." he mused. "I do seem to remember something about finding ruins when they built the palace. It must have been ages ago, because I don't even know when that happened. But maybe they're still there. You know, like some grand thing only Prince Calidor and his cronies can look at."

Lamorak didn't think so. If that had been so, Calidor would have said something about it. Maybe not before Festival and what had happened since, but certainly after. When they'd been trying to figure out what to do.

"No," he said. "If they are there, Calidor didn't know. But... do you think there are others?"

"Other what?" Bodwyn asked. "Ruins? Probably. Since you say the dragonkin told you Greenfair was built over it, I would say you'd have to go down." He pointed one meaty finger at the floor.

"Yeah." Lamorak agreed that was probably the case, but that didn't mean they had any way of doing so. To do something like that would be beyond—

Then, his gaze fell on the bottle Bodwyn had just picked up again to refill their glasses.

"I'm telling you, Lamorak," Bodwyn said. "There's nothing down here. Other than wine, of course."

"The Honor Guard compound is old, too, right?" Lamorak replied. "Not as old as the palace, but still...it's old."

"And?"

"And maybe there's some sign of the old Evening Folk city down here, too."

Bodwyn shook his head. "And that means what, exactly? There are better ways to spend an evening than crawling around an old cellar. Like drinking some of these bottles."

Bodwyn's earlier caution about them running out of wine seemed unnecessary as Lamorak looked around now. At one point, the compound had been the home to a great many Honor Guard. And they'd hosted banquets at times, including those having the prince and his retinue in attendance.

From the looks of things, the wine cellar was capable of providing for its earlier function for many, many years. Lamorak didn't think he and Bodwyn could drink it dry if that was all they did for the rest of their lives.

"I had no idea the cellars were this expansive," he said. "How did old Brentley ever keep it all straight?"

"Maybe he had notes. Or... well, he was doing this for a long time. That guy was *really* old. Maybe he had just memorized where everything was over time."

It was possible, Lamorak supposed, but unlikely.

From where he stood, Lamorak could see hundreds and hundreds of bottles of wine, all neatly slotted onto racks so that they lay on their sides. The cellars had low ceilings and seemed to be separated into several different rooms, divided by stone arches, which must have held the weight of the building above. The nearest rooms were lit by flickering torches, although how they stayed lit was something he didn't know. The light was already present when they'd come down the stairs, and Bodwyn said he had never had to light them.

Lamorak moved forward a few paces so that he could peer into one of the rooms farther off. It was hard to tell, but he thought he could pick out another dark arch on the far side, leading into yet another chamber.

"This is crazy," he said. "If this continues, it goes way beyond the footprint of the building."

"Only one way to find out," Bodwyn said. "If, that is, you're going to insist on us actually exploring it all."

"I guess that depends on how big it really is. Grab that torch." Lamorak took one as well. "Let's go see what we see."

The cellars were indeed bigger than he ever would have guessed, and storing wine was only one use to which it was put. Walking from chamber to chamber, they soon passed the last of the wine racks, yet the rooms stretched out in front of them, as well as to each side.

"Does this place go under all of Greenfair?" Lamorak said.

"I don't know. But why would it?" Bodwyn had stopped complaining when he saw how vast the place was. Now, he was as fully engaged in the discovery as Lamorak was.

"These *are* cellars, right?" Lamorak looked up. "I mean, this wasn't once the first floor of a building or even several buildings."

"Who can tell?" Bodwyn joined him in studying the ceiling. "I think if stone gets old enough, it would be impossible for us to tell which are older and which younger."

"Which means we have no idea if all of this... including the ceilings... was built at the same time."

For a few moments, they did no more than look around, silently awed by what they were seeing.

"Did Brentley know about this?" Bodwyn finally asked. "And just... not say anything to anyone?"

"Maybe he wasn't as happy about being a servant as we'd thought," Lamorak answered.

They began walking again, staying on a straight path to avoid getting lost. Chamber after chamber went by, all mostly identical, all completely empty, and all refusing to give any sort of clue as to their purpose.

After a bit, they stopped again.

"This is getting us nowhere," Lamorak sighed. "Not only do we have no idea what these rooms are for, there's nothing to help us with the dragonkin."

"Not to mention that we don't know who built them," Bodwyn added. "The stonework looks the same as that above in the city. We don't know that this was made by the Evening Folk."

Lamorak frowned. He'd been so sure! Even more so when they'd seen that there was more to it than just wine storage. But Bodwyn was right. There was no telling who built the place and nothing that would help them.

"Let's head back," he sighed. "We're going to have to try to think of something else."

"Not so fast," Bodwyn said. "I agree we haven't found anything, but we've only been going in a straight line. There're all those other rooms to the sides."

"You want to start taking those?" Lamorak grimaced. "I don't relish the thought of getting lost down here."

"Me, neither. So, we'll leave markers to guide us back."

"Markers? What kind of markers?"

"Wine bottles. Let's go get a bunch and we'll leave one in the middle of each arch we pass through."

"Good idea," Lamorak agreed. "And we can move it to the side when we come back so that we'll know we've already checked that way. Actually, now that I think of it, we can even come back tomorrow night if we have to."

"Right." But then Bodwyn frowned.

"What's wrong?" Lamorak asked him.

"Brentley is not going to be happy that we messed with his system."

"Forget him," Lamorak grinned. "He shouldn't have tried to keep all this for himself, then."

They didn't need to return the next night. Whether through dumb luck or some hidden sixth sense of Bodwyn's, they found the door after only a short time.

It was the first time they'd come upon anything other than empty chambers with arches leading to even more of them.

The door was made of stone, like the walls around it, but from one solid slab, rather than masonry blocks fitted together. It was carved with scenes and figures that were intertwined around one another.

Lamorak felt that if he could stay there and study it, eventually it would tell a story, but for the moment, it was a jumble of chaotic imagery.

"Should we open it?" Bodwyn asked.

"We should," Lamorak said, but neither of them stepped forward to be the one to do it.

"I'd feel better in armor and with my sword," the big man said.

"Me, too," Lamorak agreed. "Maybe we should go get ours."

Neither of them moved in that direction, either.

"Looks heavy," Lamorak said.

"Too heavy for *you* to move," Bodwyn said.

Lamorak drew back and scowled. "You're crazy. *I* could open it. *You* would probably need help."

"Maybe," Bodwyn said. "But I'm getting old. You? You're just… well… I don't want to say it."

Lamorak didn't really look at him. He kept studying the door. Was that a dragonkin being ridden by a human? No. Not a human, too wide for that. And overhead, it was almost like scales… the belly of one of the dragons? Fimbruss, maybe, or Chimbod? Who could really say?

He sighed, stepped forward, took a deep breath, and grabbed the handle. It twisted easily in his hand and the door—

Swung open without a sound, as if it had been used every day instead of sitting abandoned for years upon years.

"Had to have been built by them," Bodwyn muttered.

Lamorak nodded.

Beyond the door was a set of stairs, heading down into the earth. They only went a short distance before making a sharp turn to the right.

A cold draft came from below, raising gooseflesh on Lamorak's arm.

"We're going down there, aren't we?" Bodwyn said.

Lamorak nodded and stepped through the door. The stairs went down, but there were no lit torches below. It was as dark as any other cave would be.

"Not just us," he decided. "Go back and get the others. Tell them to bring swords, but no armor. It's too noisy and we might have to run."

"What are you going to do?" Bodwyn asked suspiciously.

"Nothing. Just watch this hole and make sure nothing comes out of it."

"You don't have a weapon," Bodwyn pointed out.

"I'll hit it with a wine bottle. Go on."

Bodwyn grimaced but went, leaving Lamorak alone at the top of the stairs. When the larger man was out of sight, Lamorak lifted his torch closer to the carvings on the door. If he didn't know better, he would have said it depicted the dragonkin and others all living in harmony. At least near the top. When he lowered his eyes to look toward the bottom though, the carvings changed.

Bodies lay under the claws of dragonkin, which according to what he'd always heard of the war between them and the Evening Folk was to be expected.

But there were dead dragonkin, too.

The dragonkin didn't make this door. They wouldn't have celebrated defeats like that.

What was more, the door was made *after* the war. After the Evening Folk had been utterly destroyed.

But if that was the case... then who had carved it?

His gaze slid to the stairs again. Whoever it was, they had fled *that* way.

Maybe…just maybe… they had left something down there that would help *them*. Something they could use.

For the first time, Lamorak began to feel that maybe Calidor's plan wasn't so impossible, after all.

Chapter 54- Eral Krurmar

Akofi knew what was coming, but he had no way of stopping it. Not with physical force, certainly, and not with magic, either. He may have impressed these Xarlug, but if he tried to interfere, he was sure they'd slap him down quickly. There was nothing to do but stand back, watch, and hope the young guardsman was as good with his sword as he was confident.

"Are you ready?" the Gerent asked, a big smile creasing his face as he drew his stone blade.

"I have no wish to fight you," Rainaldus said.

It could have come across as a wheedling attempt to get out of a fight he had no stomach for, but the tone of Rainaldus's voice told a different story. There was a bit of sorrow in it, some resignation, and even a little bit of arrogance. There wasn't a trace of fear.

"Oh, it'll be fine," the Gerent replied, obviously not hearing the same thing Akofi had. "To first blood. That's all. And I promise not to make it a deep cut. Just a little scratch."

Akofi almost found himself smiling at the Gerent's conditions. From what Rainaldus had said, that was exactly how the Honor Guard of Obristan trained on a daily basis, only they didn't stop at first blood. They kept going until one was unable to continue or gave up. Rainaldus already had a few scars on him from such exercises.

"If you insist," Rainaldus said. He drew his sword in a fluid motion that caused a few of the Xarlug gathered in the throne room to mutter.

The Gerent raised his eyebrows and grinned wider. "You know how to draw your weapon, anyway. But anyone can master that."

He dropped into a guard position and motioned to Rainaldus. "Let's have it, then."

Rainaldus didn't hesitate. He moved so quickly that he was on the Gerent before the Xarlug was ready for him. Rainaldus batted his sword to the side and lunged, the point of his blade aiming for the Gerent's side, who grunted, twisted, and sprang away, avoiding so much as a scratch.

"You're quick," the Gerent laughed. "I'll give you that. But... I don't think you're quick enough."

Through the whole brief attack, the smile on the Xarlug's face had never slipped. Even twisting away from the sudden attack hadn't changed it.

Rainaldus, however, was not grinning. He wasn't smiling, but he wasn't frowning either. His face was completely neutral, as if what he was engaged in was nothing to even be concerned about. A task to finish before he could move on to something else, perhaps.

"He's taking this too lightly," Bekasi whispered to Akofi.

"No," he whispered back. "I don't think so. I don't think he does things like that."

"Well, he'd better get his act together," Shagar said in a normal volume. "The Gerent doesn't like to lose."

If the Xarlug in question had heard her, he gave no sign of it. Instead, his eyes were focused on Rainaldus, watching for any move. But the guardsman kept circling, sword at the ready, his steps light. And though he never smiled, his gaze was every bit as steady as the Gerent's was.

"Are we fighting or dancing?" the Gerent finally asked with a laugh.

Rainaldus still didn't reply, and for the first time, his silence seemed to annoy the Xarlug. His smile slipped just a bit.

"Fine," Akofi heard him mutter, almost under his breath.

Then, he leaped to the attack. Faster than Rainaldus was, he sprang forward, sword swinging for the young man's head. Rainaldus raised his blade, but the Gerent whipped his stone blade around in a loop, going for a slash across Rainaldus's mid-section. The Xarlug present laughed and hooted, sure that their ruler had just won the game, but quickly fell into mutters.

Rainaldus had simply stepped back. Raising his sword to block had been a ruse of his own, as if he'd known exactly what the Gerent was going to do. He'd slid backwards, letting the Xarlug's sword pass harmlessly a hair's breadth from his stomach.

His own sword whipped down, smashing into the back side of the Gerent's with a tremendous crash. The added momentum took the Gerent's swing much too wide, and Rainaldus stepped inside the arc of the blow—

And punched the Gerent in the nose with the hand holding his sword.

There was an audible "crack," the Gerent gave a startled squawk of pain and surprise, and dropped his sword, which went spinning across the floor, forcing several Xarlug to scramble out of the way.

"Does that count?" Rainaldus asked quietly.

The Gerent stared at him, then slowly pulled his hands away from his nose. He glanced down at them and then opened his eyes wide.

Akofi braced himself, reaching out to his magic, but knowing that if Shagar and that other, Glasha, wanted to stop him, they could. But he didn't know the rules of the duel he'd just witnessed. Was what Rainaldus had done considered cheating? Was the Gerent the type of ruler where it didn't matter? Or, he had been embarrassed, so it was "off with their heads?"

Then, the Gerent threw back his head and laughed loudly. He raised his hands and turned them, making sure everyone could see the blood on them.

"First blood!" he cried.

Far from angry, the Gerent sounded... pleased? Happy, even. More than.

The Gerent laughed again, lowered his hands, approached Rainaldus, and enfolded him in a fierce hug, pounding him on the back and leaving bloody handprints.

"First blood!" he said again, stepping back and holding Rainaldus at arm's length. "How long has it been since that's happened?" He threw the question over his shoulder, but no one answered it for him. "I'd adopt this human if I could," the Gerent beamed.

He gazed with fondness at the guardsman, then yanked his hand up into the air.

"Winner!"

As if on cue, the other Xarlug began to laugh and surged forward, in a way they hadn't when Akofi had demonstrated his magical prowess. They surrounded Rainaldus, clamoring for his attention and congratulating him, while the Gerent, still chuckling, returned to his chair.

"Enough, enough!" he cried, and allowed a few moments for the hue to die down. "A feast is called for. Shagar, bring our guests to appropriate quarters, where they can clean up and refresh themselves. Tonight, we feast!"

"I don't understand what just happened," Bekasi said slowly.

"Your man got lucky," Shagar answered. "The Gerent hasn't been beaten in years."

Which could have been the truth. But looking at Rainaldus, who had barely even begun to breathe heavily, he wasn't so sure. He thought that perhaps it was the Gerent who'd gotten lucky.

Word of Rainaldus's victory over the Gerent must have spread quickly. When Shagar led them out of the large building that served as the Gerent's headquarters, they were met with smiles and well-wishes by most of the Xarlug they passed.

It didn't escape Akofi, though, that there were plenty of those who narrowed their eyes when they looked at Rainaldus, as if trying to gauge their own chances of success against him, or possibly even in anger that a "mere human" had bested their ruler.

Whatever the case, they didn't remain on the streets for long. Nearby was another building, much smaller than the one they'd just left, but with an ornate facade. It was only one-story, but Akofi could see that it was actually quite a long building.

"This is our guest house," Shagar said. Then she stopped and chuckled. "Okay, it wasn't that originally. It was supposed to be for those like me and— I suppose— Glasha. The Gerent had an idea that those of us who could see the aura of the world around us— what your dragon taught you was magic, from what I understand— would benefit from all living together." Her laughter was replaced by a snort. "That didn't work out. So now, the building is mostly empty, but I think you'll find it comfortable enough."

Inside, they found several rooms with various purposes. Bed chambers, sitting rooms, workspaces, and even a kitchen. All with comfortable furnishings, but no people present.

Shagar put her hands on her hips and looked around. "Like I said, it should be comfortable enough. You've certainly got room to spread out. There might be some food in the kitchen, I'm not sure who stayed here last. Whatever is there is all yours. Don't fill up too much, though. The Gerent called for a feast, and he'll expect everyone who comes to bring an appetite."

"Thank you," Akofi told her. "This will do perfectly. But we can't be here for long. We'll need to return to the surface and back to our world. There are important things happening."

Shagar nodded, but her expression wasn't as sure. "I hope you can. The Gerent might want your company for a bit, though."

"But we—" Bekasi began.

"I don't think you all understand," Shagar interrupted. "Don't let his pleasant demeanor fool you. He was surprised by being beaten. Even more so by how easily it was done. But I meant what I said back there. The Gerent doesn't like to lose. The fact that he took it so well means he wants something. And until he says you can leave…"

She left it unfinished, but it didn't need to be said. Until the word was given, they were trapped in this underground city.

For a moment, Akofi wanted to choke Rainaldus. If he hadn't been so insistent on following the Xarlug when they'd first appeared, none of this would be happening. But then he realized that he was being unfair. When Orgoth had shown himself, it was already too late. Whether Rainaldus had taken the bait or not, they were most likely going to be forced to visit Eral Krurmar.

"Why us?" he asked Shagar.

She seemed to know what he was referring to without being told.

"There are things happening," she shrugged. "Dragonkin attacking humans, which has never happened like recently. Dragonkin attacking each other, and more…" Her eyes shifted to Rainaldus. "Humans killing dragonkin."

"How do you know all that?" Bekasi asked her.

"We watch. We see. Once, we were considered the lesser of the races. Our Raaleth and Helgarlug brothers and sisters looked down on us, pitied us at times. Never realizing that we were their equals, with other gifts. The Helgarlug, especially, were proud that nothing could be hidden from them. And nothing could. Unless we wished it to be. We could blind their sight the same way we can take your ability to access the world's aura away."

Shagar grinned then. "Except you humans are growing stronger. You just proved that, didn't you? Poor Glasha won't get over that one for a while."

Akofi was finding it hard to work up the same joy that Shagar obviously had.

"Anyway," the Xarlug said. "Get some rest. Clean up. I'd say there were clothes, but I doubt they would fit you two. Maybe some would fit on the big guy, there, but even then, they'd probably be loose. Still, do what you can. I'll be back to get you for the feast." She made to move off, then stopped and turned back. "Oh. Stay in the building. Outside might not be safe."

Before Akofi could ask her what she meant by that, she was gone, leaving the three of them alone.

"Well," Akofi said, meaning to say more but finding that he didn't know what. "Well."

"I hope so," Bekasi muttered.

They didn't have long to relax. They found clean water that came from a pump in the kitchen, as well as in several what appeared to be washing-up rooms. The water was clean and cold, but not so much that it was freezing. Rainaldus seemed to take actually take pleasure in it, but for Akofi, he much preferred his water heated.

Shagar had been right about the clothing, although with enough time, Bekasi thought she could work out a spell that would shrink them down enough to fit comfortably. But since none of them relished the idea of walking around with nothing on while she worked that out, they stayed in their travel-worn garb.

Then they heard the door open, and Orgoth entered.

"Hello, again," he grinned. "I thought I would come escort you to the feast."

He looked drastically different from when they'd last seen him. Instead of the loincloth he'd had on then, Orgoth was now clothed in black pants, with shiny black boots below. His shirt was a dark gray, but he wore it halfway open, showcasing his broad chest and slightly paler gray skin.

He still had the same pleasant demeanor he'd shown from the beginning, though. Which was easy to do, Akofi thought, when you had the upper hand.

"I heard about your duel," the Xarlug grinned at Rainaldus. "I had a feeling there was something about you. What you did… it's no easy feat. The Gerent has been defeated before, but not in quite a while. Those that do beat him… well, they're not usually held in very high favor after that."

"Shagar said something similar," Akofi told him. "But he seemed to take his defeat at Rainaldus's hands well."

"He would. He had an audience. And maybe he really did, since it was such a novelty. Although, I guarantee you that he'll make a point of mentioning that this young man isn't truly human. He has Raaleth blood, after all. All to the good, though. If not, he'd have you doing tasks that *he* thinks are horrible."

"Like patrolling above ground?" Bekasi asked.

Orgoth smiled at her. "Something like that. Now, who's hungry?"

Akofi had been afraid that the diet of the Xarlug would consist of things he wouldn't be able to stomach. Being underground, his mind had conjured up visions of slimy mushrooms, dry fungus, and crunchy insects. Things that would be readily available in a cave.

Instead, they found a vast array of meat, vegetables, and fruit, many of which were familiar to them, and all expertly prepared. In addition, there was wine and beer, as well as cold, clear water to drink.

"This is amazing," Akofi said to the Xarlug seated next to him.

"Our hunting and foraging parties are very good," the Xarlug told him.

"And the drink?" Akofi held up his mug full of beer.

The Xarlug laughed. "You don't think you humans invented wine and beer, do you?"

"No," Akofi smiled back. "I suppose not. But I am glad the recipes survived."

He toasted his dinner companion, then turned his attention to his surroundings.

They were eating in the same room where they had met the Gerent and Rainaldus had dueled him. Only now, the fireplaces were all lit, and any furniture had been replaced by several long tables.

He and Bekasi were seated at the same one as the Gerent, two seats away from him on the left. In between was Glasha, the female Xarlug who had tried so hard to shut down his magic. Rainaldus was seated to the immediate right of the Gerent, talking and laughing with the ruler while devouring huge quantities of food.

It didn't escape Akofi, however, that the young guardsman was much more careful with the drink. As far as Akofi could tell, he was still only halfway through his first cup of wine.

Which made him think that perhaps he should slow down himself. He was on his third— or maybe his fourth— mug of beer, and his head was starting to get that warm, pleasant fuzziness that he found so comforting. Much more, though, and that pleasantness was going to be replaced by a splitting headache come morning.

Shagar, Orgoth, and others he recognized from the surface party shared another table, and suddenly Akofi wished he was sitting with them. He still had several questions, and Shagar— as brusque as she could be— seemed the most likely to answer.

Finally, the feast began to die down. Xarlug rose from their places and began to circulate, forming small groups to talk casually, while others still ate. Akofi glanced at the Gerent, who was still deep in conversation with Rainaldus, although it now seemed to have turned serious. He was still nibbling at his food, so there obviously was no protocol for everyone to stay seated until he was done.

Akofi rose and walked around the room a bit, exchanging pleasantries and looking the place over. It was nice enough, although he found the decorations to be a bit severe and monochromatic for his liking. He supposed that in time, he would get used to them, though, and—

With a start he realized that he was looking at his surroundings as if they were going to be permanent or at least long term. When had he started thinking that? It was the beer, he decided, and the amount of food he'd eaten.

He scowled and returned to the table where Bekasi sat. "Nice dinner," she said when he sat down, "but I think we need to get over there."

She tilted her head to where the Gerent and Rainaldus were talking.

"I agree," Akofi said. "But how?"

Bekasi shrugged. "There doesn't seem to be anyone stopping anyone else from going where they want to. Let's just switch chairs."

Akofi wasn't so sure about that. Moving about the room was one thing, but openly sitting next to the Gerent without invitation? He could see them being dragged forcibly away, thrown to the floor, where the Xarlug would laugh themselves silly. As long as the Gerent didn't have them thrown in whatever passed for a dungeon here. Dungeons were a thing, right? In Droy Thus, they had jails, but he was pretty sure places made of stone had dungeons.

"Come on." Bekasi broke in on his thoughts.

Akofi followed her lead as she got up, made her way around the table, and then confidently pulled out a chair directly across from Rainaldus, leaving Akofi with one opposite the Gerent.

He swallowed hard and sat down, firming his resolve that they have some say in what was going to happen to them. They would *not* be held prisoner in this underground city. Not when they had done nothing wrong. Not if—

"Ah, I was just about to wave you over," the Gerent said. "We've been talking, Rainaldus and I. He's convinced me. It's time."

"Time for what?" Bekasi asked.

"Time for the Xarlug to take back what's ours," the Gerent said. "And with your help, I think we can do just that. Of course..." he mused, "it seems as if you could use *our* help as well."

"We certainly wouldn't turn it down," Akofi said, almost unable to believe what he was hearing.

"Good. Now, my understanding is that this town of yours... what was it? Oh, yes. Orluduna. Strange name, but you humans have your own ways... is the place we need to go. Orgoth over there knows of it."

"We can go there?" Bekasi asked.

"More than that," the Gerent continued. "Orgoth and his group will take you there, and then he'll bring some of your people back here. What's more, we might even show you something you've never even dreamed was possible."

"What's that?" Akofi asked suspiciously. Usually, things that seemed too good to be true seemed that way for a reason.

"I think it's high time a few others woke up as well." The Gerent sat back, picked up his mug of beer and took a good swig from it. He was grinning when he set it back down and looked from one to the other. "Tell me. Have any of you ever heard of the realm of Olequan?"

Chapter 55- Five Dragons

Fimbruss

It was… glorious! There was no other word that he could use to describe it.

His siblings were all so sure of themselves— and of him.

For instance, Gillbriss thought she had it all figured out. Extend the same cruel methods she'd always used to control her humans into all the realms. Foolishness, but one that the others allowed in their sudden fear of their own humans.

And for what? Because one of Haiteng's had been drowned and one of Chimbod's drawn where it didn't want to go?

And?

What of it?

Dragonkin had been killed before. By the Raaleth, by the Helgarlug, even by humans, although that was covered up as quickly as it had happened. Dragonkin weren't immortal. They weren't impervious. They were, to put it bluntly, expendable.

Just as everything else in the world was. Everything except for the five of them, of course.

But now that things were proceeding, he was beginning to wonder.

Did the world really need *five* dragons? Would four not work just as well? Or— dare he say— even fewer?

Fimbruss had never expected to feel that way. In the beginning, when the others were arranging their realms to suit themselves, he had done the same. He'd fostered a warrior mentality on his humans, not because they had any true enemies, but because it was fun. It was like a game, to set his toy soldiers against one another and see which ones came out on top.

Over time, he decided to see what would happen if he gave them higher stakes. But not all at once. That wouldn't do.

So, he'd allowed a certain amount of worship, for lack of a better word, to foster. When it grew, he'd found that he quite liked it. Soon, it had spread far enough that he wasn't sure he could have stopped it had he wished to. Even destroying those like Gunnvid would have just made his divinity all the more apparent. A believer struck down, probably for heresy, or some such nonsense.

For a good amount of time, Fimbruss had been happy with that. But then... the chaos. The dragonkin dying, the new violation of the edict, and so on.

So... why not see if he could spread his name a little further? The question was, in which direction?

South, obviously. Reclium was too... rigid. Steep. Dark. Whatever. It was just horrible.

But Haiteng's realm? Now *there* was something.

It wasn't easy. It wasn't as if Gunnvid's army made those of Ascana into true believers, although there were a few. Plus, it didn't really matter. When the Children had taken the northern village, there was a little... twinge. A surge of energy that went through Fimbruss.

He flew high, higher than Haiteng could, higher than any but Chimbod was able to, and surveyed the land below.

Snow and ice, creeping further south than it ever had before. With every inch, *he* felt more alive, more powerful, than he ever had. It was almost like when they had all first risen.

Fimbruss laughed and did circles in the air, enjoying the euphoria.

Below him, the Children were stalled, staying put in an ever-larger camp, making sure they were ready to move on.

Which they would do soon.

Farther south. Taking more territory. Making Fimbruss stronger yet.

Tophonoss

The rest thought her mad. She knew that but didn't care. It wasn't as if she had ever been close to them.

Tophonoss wasn't close to anyone, not those who called themselves her siblings, nor her own dragonkin, whom she had reshaped after the death of Sillaneth.

That, however, was a memory she cherished, even as the others knew nothing of it. Nothing of how she had helped the Raaleth king destroy one of the five, how she had added her strength to his, and been in place to take what should have been hers from the beginning. Her sister— her true sister— had no right to usurp her place, to rise when Tophonoss should have been the one.

So, Tophonoss had done what was needed. She'd taken back what always should have been hers but made it so that no one would be able to do the same to her. How could they, when most couldn't even find her if she wished to remain unseen?

Except...

That little, nagging feeling. That kernel of doubt that always seemed to be with her.

She had helped the Raaleth king, but what of his queen? What of the one they never found? Was she still alive, even after all this time?

There was no reason to think not. Tophonoss was still alive, after all, as were the others. And if Tophonoss could hide, why not Falaern? Why not more of the Raaleth and those others?

Her new siblings were all so sure the other elder races were dead and gone. The only ones left were the dragons and their children, and the humans, who were safely under control.

Except, they suddenly weren't, and there was only one explanation for that. The elder races still lived and had emerged from wherever they had been cowering in fear of her and the others. They had secretly aided the humans, fomenting war, probably hoping that when it was over, the dragons and the humans would have killed one another, leaving the world to them.

Humans were foolish if they had taken the Raaleth as allies. The Raaleth cared for no one but themselves, which was why they had to die. They had refused to accept the new order when they should have.

If it had been meant that they should not be subservient, it would have been the Raaleth who rose instead of the dragons.

Just as Sillaneth would have survived if it had truly been meant to be.

But it wasn't. It was Tophonoss who had the power. She meant to keep it.

Let the others continue with their silly games of conquest and control. The humans weren't the threat.

The real threat was hiding, but she would find them. And if they tried to emerge…

Well, then… they'd find her waiting.

Gillbriss

Gillbriss growled deep in her throat, even though no one was there to hear it. High atop Cholgad Peak, her own personal refuge, she was alone except for the howling winds and the sleet. Even the great ice eagles of the far north flew wide of Cholgad.

It was infuriating. Dragonkin had been killed. Were *continuing* to be killed. Not a lot, that much was true, but even one was too many.

One meant that someone, several someones in all likelihood, were not sufficiently cowed. They still believed themselves free. They thought they were at war when really, they were simply meat on the hoof, ready to be slaughtered whenever she wished it.

Not in her realm, though. Her land had been in full submission from the beginning. When the humans had been brought there and given the cities with the tall towers and the ever-present night, they had learned quickly who was in charge. Dragonkin were to be obeyed without question. Humans were there for amusement, nothing more.

But in those other four realms, that had never been the case. Haiteng and Chimbod mollycoddled their humans, made them feel as if they were allies. Fimbruss encouraged his to make war, which was at least amusing, just not as personal as her methods. And Tophonoss had simply ignored hers to the point that the humans in her realm didn't even know she existed.

It was no wonder that they resisted. They had never been properly taught.

Reclium had been hers for a long time. For as long as the realm had existed. In the beginning, she had taken more of a claws-on approach.

Perhaps it was time to do the same for the others.

Only, the edict had been repealed for the time being, allowing dragonkin to cross realms. The same did not apply to the dragons, themselves, however. Haiteng did not cross into Obristan. Chimbod did not go to Usturg.

For her to take a more direct role in teaching the humans the errors of their ways, she could only act in Reclium, which was useless. Reclium wasn't the problem. It wasn't where dragonkin had died.

She needed to make a choice. Four realms to choose from.

When she did, a city, or a village, or a tower, would be erased. She'd make it seem like it had never existed, leaving only a blank space on any map to serve as a warning. One such visit should be enough.

It was one thing to kill a dragonkin. It was something else entirely to even try to harm one of the five.

Yes, she decided. That was the answer.

Now, it was just up to her to decide whose realm was going to suffer her wrath.

Chimbod

At one time, Chimbod had loved nothing more than to visit the towers her humans had built. She was proud of them. No one else, in all the realms, had done such a thing. Oh, there were tall buildings in Reclium, some that equaled the height of the mage towers of Droy Thus. But those were different. Those had been formed when Gillbriss took over her realm, ready to be occupied by the humans who had been sent there.

For *her* humans, there had been nothing but primitive villages, with straw huts as likely to fall down in a stiff breeze as to provide any sort of real shelter. She had wanted to see how they would adapt, how they would improve their lot in life, if they did at all.

To that end, she and her children taught them simple spells. If their weak flesh was too cold at night, here was a small piece of magic that would warm them. Nothing that the youngest dragonkin couldn't do from the time it emerged from an egg. Too warm? Let them figure it out for themselves… it should be easy once they knew the first piece.

To her surprise and delight, the humans did figure it out, and quickly, too. More than that, they'd built on it. If they could cool themselves with magic, why not water? Why not raise the temperature of a stick until it burst into flame?

Humans— *her* humans— took to magic like they had been born to it, and soon, they were. Magic ability became innate in most of them in a remarkably short amount of time, followed by innovation in ways to use it that Chimbod had never thought possible. It was only a matter of time before their whole society revolved around it, including finding uses for those they called the Ill-favored. Those born without magic.

Now, though. Now she wasn't so sure.

Either her humans had discovered magic powerful enough to rival the long-dead Raaleth, or they had recreated that exact same magic, which should have been impossible. Worse, they had used it to destroy one of her children. And push the whole world into chaos.

And so, now they had to be restricted. No more open exploration of what was possible and what wasn't. No more classes taught in tall towers that her children weren't privy to. Everything was done under the watchful gaze of dragonkin.

Not just her children, either. But those of Haiteng, whom she trusted, those of Fimbruss, whom she tolerated, and those of Gillbriss, whom she despised. As for Tophonoss? Her children may or may not be preset, although their enigmatic sister had promised to pass along any information they might turn up.

She flew low over the jungle, not paying much attention to where she was going or even what she was seeing. She was busy thinking back, wondering why it was she had agreed to allow Gillbriss a more open hand in crushing the rebellion— as she'd seen it.

Because the truth was, Chimbod didn't see it that way. Forbidden magic had been used for a nefarious purpose. But by who? How many? And why?

She didn't think it was a lot. A few rogue mages, perhaps. Surely not enough to warrant what was happening now.

Perhaps she should return to the cavern and summon Haiteng. The two of them had always been close, their alliance allowing them to get their own way.

Only… Haiteng didn't seem himself. He seemed… old? Tired, maybe?

Maybe, Chimbod mused, it was time for a different ally. One who had already told Gillbriss that his realm was off-limits. She'd always looked down on Fimbruss, but their brother had shown remarkable foresight.

He was just so… vain.

If Chimbod had her choice, she would prefer to continue to work closely with Haiteng. But she needed to be realistic. She needed to pair her strength with one of equal power. Tophonoss was out. Chimbod couldn't stand her and her arrogance. The same for Gillbriss, who was taking advantage of the situation.

Haiteng had grown weak, unfortunately.

Leaving only one.

Chimbod flew in a lazy circle, heading toward her entrance to the cavern. Perhaps it was time she and her northern brother had a true talk.

Haiteng

Before he rose, Haiteng had been just one of many. The dragonkin were all the same, with wings and four legs, multiple colors, sometimes on the same set of scales. Then… they rose. The five of them, although if memory served— and he admitted it was fuzzy— there had been another before Tophonoss. Green of scale, with breath that turned anything it touched to stone?

What had happened to that one and her children?

Or maybe she had never even existed.

Haiteng was tired, and his dreams were recently troubled. In them, the five rose, only to be diminished again, becoming as they once had been. When he woke, the feeling stayed with him. It was becoming difficult to tell what had once been real and what had only been in his sleeping mind.

He shook himself, trying to fight off the malaise. What was wrong with him?

Nothing that flying wouldn't fix. Maybe a deep, deep dive into the ocean, down to where the light never penetrated and fish almost as large as he swam placidly, secure in their size that no predator could harm them. Haiteng smiled at *that* thought.

He lifted off the ground and took to the skies.

The cold air high above woke him a little more. His head felt clearer, although he still didn't know the reason for his cloudiness.

The ocean did even more good, as did the hot, fresh blood of his kill. The fish had sent out a distress call answered by others far off, yet none of them had come to try to help. All of them were aware of Haiteng by now, and knew that when he was among them, death was there for one.

He laughed as he broke the surface and soared free of the water. He and his children, the only ones to brave the deeps!

No wonder he felt so good now.

Farther north, gaining speed and watching the green and brown land unfurl beneath him. Ascana, as it was meant to be. A perfect realm of efficiency and profit. A mental exercise that he enjoyed.

One now marred by the sight of destroyed towns. Of whole sections of Manse, the most beautiful city in all the realms, left as shattered ruins.

This had to stop. Haiteng didn't understand Chimbod's reluctance, but he would speak to her again, privately this time. He would rekindle their— affection?— for each other, and together they would tell Gillbriss it was over. It was time to reinforce the edict and for all the other dragonkin to leave his realm.

But then... snow?

The land, which should have been green with crops was white. It wasn't deep, but snow didn't exist in Ascana unless it was winter, which it was surely not.

So why was there snow?

With a start, Haiteng realized where his meandering— high-speed though it was— had taken him. He was close to the border with Usturg, yet still several miles south of it, squarely within Ascana.

Why was there snow?

Fimbruss. His brother had done something. Something they all swore they would never do.

The heat that was building in Haiteng's stomach was greater than ever. It was far more than what was needed to turn water to steam. He briefly wondered if this was how Chimbod felt all the time, with her inferno always just below the surface, but that thought was quickly replaced.

Fimbruss.

Something had to be done, he just didn't know what.

Then, Haiteng slowed and smiled.

The humans had a saying he'd never understood. Fight fire with fire, which to him sounded like a ridiculous notion.

Now, though, as he surveyed the land beneath him, he thought he understood exactly what it was they meant.

Afterword

Writing the Dragon Realms books have been a labor of love. They're the most complex things I've ever written, including the Travels of Solomon. However, it's also been the story that I've been able to see the clearest as I'm writing it. I'm really looking forward to seeing what happens with Kori, Viktoria, Lamorak, and the rest. And since you've made it this far, I hope you'll stick around to find out along with me.

No book gets completed by one person, and Dragon Realms has been no exception. Thanks to Marty Roberts, for his input, and to Joyce Maxstadt, for hers. These two have read every book I've written, and I can't even begin to say how much I appreciate it.

And of course, to my wife, Barb. She not only reads these things; her editing is invaluable. Every time she hands me back a section, I marvel at the amount of work she's put into it. Without her... well, let's just say you wouldn't even want to read them.

Onward to book three! Thanks again for reading, check out my website at www.jamesmaxstadt.com, or find me on FB at fb.com/GreewealdPublishing.

And if you have a moment, please leave a review on one of the many platforms where my books are sold.

Happy Reading!